STOOD UP, FOR THE LAST TIME

For a moment Lauren believed that if only Russell would call and apologize, all her fantasies about him would come true. After all, everything was supposed to be possible with a Harvard degree. Lauren lay on the bed, but still the phone didn't ring. Around midnight Lauren heard the key turning in the lock. Irrationally frightened, she went to the door to reassure herself that it was only her roommate, Carol. Carol came in flustered. She said, "Lauren—"

"He stood me up," said Lauren.

"I know," said Carol confusedly. "We just got the story at the *Crimson.*"

"What? Are you serious? A story about me and Russell, about me getting stood up? That's crazy. What are you talking about?"

"No," said Carol, "you don't understand. Let me finish. I'm trying to tell you that Russell Bernard was murdered last night."

Death of a Harvard Freshman

Victoria Silver

BANTAM BOOKS
TORONTO · NEW YORK · LONDON · SYDNEY

DEATH OF A HARVARD FRESHMAN
A Bantam Book / April 1984

ISBN 0-553-24046-3

Published simultaneously in the United States and Canada

PRINTED IN THE UNITED STATES OF AMERICA

H   0 9 8 7 6 5 4 3 2 1

For the giant C.
Thank you for making Helsinki so special.

1. The death of Rasputin

Melissa Wu was just finishing her presentation on Rasputin. From across the seminar table Lauren could see that the talk was being recited from pages so evenly and perfectly lettered as to do credit to even the most fastidious medieval monk. Lauren was always dazzled by such unnaturally neat handwriting, even if other people tended to be more impressed by Melissa's famous feet. Some anonymous wit had once summed her up as the girl with the smallest feet in the Harvard freshman class.

In Professor Tatiana Baranova's freshman seminar on the Russian Revolution each of the eleven freshmen was required to make a twenty-minute presentation, and this week it was Melissa's turn—although no one quite understood why she had chosen to report on Rasputin.

It was a bizarre presentation, Lauren thought. The other students seemed equally mesmerized by the spectacle of perfect Melissa Wu relating the corruption and depravity of Rasputin. Melissa did not come right out and say that she thought Rasputin was wicked, but her sincere shock and disapproval were evident from her tone. She had, of course, done her research thoroughly (as Lauren could have predicted), and the account of Rasputin's unscrupulous influence on the Tsarina Alexandra was detailed and vivid.

But the strangest part of Melissa's talk was the conclusion, in which quickly (she had exceeded her twenty minutes) she described the murder of Rasputin. Melissa was so far in spirit from anything violent, let alone violent death, that her account of the murder was almost comical. Melissa was fervent, even righteous, in her belief that Rasputin had

1

deserved his end... and yet Lauren was sure that if Melissa were to bump into Rasputin in Harvard Square that very evening she would not even know how to be impolite.

It was a Wednesday in November, very late in the afternoon. Outside it was almost dark as Melissa concluded. "And so five young aristocrats decided to kill Rasputin because of his corrupting influence on the Empress and on the Russian government. The conspirators invited Rasputin to one of their houses in Leningrad and offered him poisoned cakes and poisoned wine. But the poison had no effect on him." Melissa's voice expressed the bewilderment of the conspirators. "So they shot him over and over, and even that didn't kill him. At last they put his body in the river under the ice, and he drowned."

Melissa had finished. The room was absolutely silent. It was a terrifying story, Lauren thought, terrifying from both perspectives: from that of the victim Rasputin and his supernatural but hopeless struggle to live, surviving each bullet only to receive the next one; and also from the perspective of the murderers, forced as in a nightmare to murder over and over again. Despite herself, Melissa had told the story well, or perhaps the darkness outside had been particularly conducive or the group inside particularly receptive. Professor Baranova broke the silence and said in her formal, Russian-accented English, "Thank you, Melissa."

Lauren wondered if Professor Baranova had also fallen under the spell of Melissa's narration. Probably she had. If there had been one completely untouched scoffer in the room, surely those moments of genuine tension would not have been possible. But now Professor Baranova regained her grand sense of irony. "The report was very comprehensive, Melissa, and very affecting, but I think we might also glance at the larger implications of the Rasputin question." Poor Melissa, for all her preparation, usually missed the larger implications. Lauren suspected that Professor Baranova was well aware of Melissa's intellectual weaknesses, perhaps even her comic possibilities. Russell Bernard, on Lauren's right, had scribbled on a piece of paper for her benefit, "Quite a performance!" and Lauren caught his eye in agreement, pleased by his attention to her.

Professor Baranova was initiating the serious discussion. "I think it was Kerensky who once said that without Rasputin there could have been no Lenin. What exactly do you think he meant by that? What is Rasputin's significance for the Russian Revolution?"

Sandy Grayson adjusted her big, round tortoiseshell glasses and spoke up briskly. "I think that to say there could be no Lenin without Rasputin may attribute too great an importance to Rasputin and too little to Lenin. According to Trotsky..." Sandy went on, and Lauren stopped listening. She did not really like Sandy Grayson, six months out of the prep school where she had learned to be both a snob and a bore. She especially disliked Sandy today for having done the assigned reading—the first two-hundred pages of Trotsky's *History of the Russian Revolution.*

Lauren had only managed to begin the reading. She would happily have tuned out of the discussion altogether, but she was aware that an expression of attentive interest would help to protect her from being called on to speak. Lauren weighed the two alternatives, blissful inattention versus feigned interest, and just as she was about to opt for the former something happened to weight the scales in the opposite direction. The intolerable Sandy Grayson stopped her ostentatiously priggish discourse about the assigned pages in Trotsky and Russell Bernard spoke up.

"I think you might be taking Kerensky too literally," said Russell to Sandy, and Lauren's heart leaped joyfully at the sullen expression with which Sandy received this academic point of criticism. He's gorgeous, thought Lauren, and she didn't mean Kerensky. Russell continued, "It seems to me that when Kerensky says that without Rasputin there could have been no Lenin, he means more generally that if the Tsarist regime had not been so extremely and obviously corrupt, there would have been no revolution."

Professor Baranova nodded and said, "Good." Russell's class comments were frequently judged "good," while that word of praise was rarely bestowed upon Sandy Grayson. It pleased Lauren to imagine that she and Professor Baranova shared a distaste for Sandy. And an admiration for Russell. One of the best things about Russell's speaking in class was that it provided a perfectly legitimate pretext to stare at him, a pleasure which Lauren, sitting at his elbow, would otherwise have had to forego. And he really was gorgeous.

Sandy said nothing. She had fallen into a nearly expressionless, well-bred preppie sulk, and Lauren guessed that while the girl was certainly sensitive to any sort of criticism, no matter how tediously academic, she was particularly unhappy to receive criticism from Russell. Tracy Nicolson, on the other hand, was not intimidated by Russell or Sandy or the professor. She did not hesitate to speak up in her hoarse, sexy voice which always became hoarser and sexier when she was disagreeing with somebody. Waving her cigarette she said, "If Kerensky just meant that the Revolution wouldn't have happened if the Tsar's government hadn't been corrupt, then Kerensky wasn't saying very much, was he? I mean, that's a pretty general sort of thing to say."

"Maybe you're right," conceded Russell, giving her a magnificent smile of beautiful white teeth.

"Maybe I am," said Tracy, matching his smile with a rather formidable one of her own. Everyone in the room was conscious of the meeting of those two smiles, and Lauren did not doubt that their academic sparring was not merely academic. This was genuinely interesting, but then Parker Hamilton Kendall IV began to speak, and Lauren was quickly bored. At least Parker was good-natured and handsome, but he and Sandy Grayson seemed to have studied the art of being-boring-in-class from the same master at Phillips Exeter Academy. Now Lauren really did tune out of the discussion, encouraged by the sight of blond Bert Rosen sitting across from her apparently on the verge of taking a nap.

Lately Lauren was finding that she had a very short attention span for academics. She had yet to encounter at Harvard the lecturer whose brilliance could keep her from looking wistfully at the clock after fifteen minutes. She had yet to read a work of non-fiction so compelling as to make her lose consciousness of how many pages remained to be read. It had been perfectly reasonable to be bored in high school; her high school in New Jersey, after all, was entirely without intellectual content. But Lauren had imagined that at Harvard, the intellectual capital of America, academics would be thrilling—and now she didn't know whether to be disappointed in Harvard or in herself. During her first month at college Lauren had even wondered whether Harvard was the right place for someone so lacking in intellectual concentration. But now it was November, and she was ready to accept that there was more to college than just lectures and reading assignments. If, for the time being, she was not feeling receptive to the academic side of Harvard life, she was prepared to concentrate on other things. And even as Lauren was allowing herself to ignore the discussion of the Russian Revolution, you couldn't exactly say that she wasn't concentrating on the class. She was, in fact, thinking about that subject which she found most interesting in this particular seminar: comparing and reevaluating the relative attractiveness of her classmates.

They sat around a long wooden table beneath portraits of dead Harvard alumni of the last four centuries. Outside the light was now gone; inside it was dim. How had they gotten here, these eleven students? They had been chosen, twice chosen. First they had been among those whose high school records, college board scores, extracurricular activities, and personal essays had won them a place in Harvard's freshman class. And then these eleven had been selected again by Professor Tatiana Baranova to make up her freshman seminar on the Russian Revolution. She had interviewed over a hundred freshmen students and chosen eleven, supposedly on the basis of the quality of their interest in the Russian Revolution. Yet in the course of putting together an interesting discussion group, she had also, consciously or unconsciously (Lauren wondered which), managed to select a remarkably physically attractive class. And, as if in acceptance of the Harvard ideal of the diverse student body, Professor Baranova had not betrayed a weakness for any single physical type. Those eleven students were all attractive in different ways.

Lauren could not remember at what age she had acquired the habit of ranking her own beauty immediately upon entering any room. And with all due objectivity and attention to her own shortcomings (the tiny bump on her nose, an occasional pimple on her forehead), she frequently found that she was the fairest. She was fairest, of course, only in the most general Snow White sense of the word, for Lauren was far from being fair. She was a Jewish-American beauty with long, wavy, dark hair. Her eyes were brownish-green or greenish-brown, depending on the light. She had long legs and a full figure which, thanks to constant vigilance, was rarely more than a few pounds overweight. And yet, from the first day that she had walked into Professor Baranova's Wednesday afternoon freshman seminar on the Russian Revolution, Lauren had known that the prize could never be indisputably hers.

First of all there was Professor Baranova herself. She was a stunning fifty-year-old woman who had been born in Paris, the daughter of a Russian socialist—a Menshevik—driven into exile by the triumphant Bolsheviks. "So you see," she had said at the first meeting of the seminar, "I have a special interest in the Russian Revolution. Without it I would not know Paris as I do." This last line was spoken with glacial irony.

She wore her hair, blond and gray, pulled back from her face in a perfect chignon, revealing a bone structure that would have done credit to any movie star. And she had star presence too. As the professor she would have been the center of attention in the seminar regardless of her appearance and manner, but Tatiana Baranova had an additional magnetism that acted as a sort of spotlight, drawing all eyes to her. She dressed very expensively and, Lauren thought, with great care for effect. She wore wool skirts and mohair sweaters in shades of silver and beige and always the same pair of diamond earrings. Although she was the daughter of a Russian socialist, she managed to have something of the air of an aristocrat in prerevolutionary Saint Petersburg.

Tatiana Baranova was the only tenured woman in Harvard's history department. Her articles and books on Russian cultural history, particularly on the political context of nineteenth-century Russian art and music, were so highly regarded that not even the most sexist Harvard men dared to suggest that she owed her position to her husband, who was also tenured in the history department. Max Kohler was Harvard's professor of European diplomatic history. He was on leave in Washington that semester, giving advice to the State Department, so Lauren had never seen him in person. She had, however, seen a picture of him in the newspaper—and there was no doubt about it: He was a toad. Lauren could not believe that Tatiana Baranova did not have love affairs, and she would dearly have liked to know with whom.

Lauren turned her attention to the attractions of her fellow students. The most technically beautiful of the women was, oddly enough, Melissa Wu. She was anyone's vision of an oriental princess, from her long straight, shiny, black hair down to her miniature shoes. Lauren consoled herself with the certainty that Melissa had no sex appeal, probably didn't know what it was, and wouldn't want it if she knew.

Tracy Nicolson was just the opposite—harsh features and heavy makeup. She had a throaty voice and enough sexual energy to sink a ship. Looking at her Chicago high school graduation picture in the Harvard Freshman Register, someone had remarked that Tracy looked like a woman involved in her third divorce. That line had also become generally accepted: Tracy's divorces, like Melissa's feet, were already legendary among the freshman class. Lauren, who liked geographical clichés, could see Tracy as a Chicago gangster's woman: mean men, hard liquor, and two packs of cigarettes a day. As Lauren watched Tracy she became aware that under the seminar table Tracy's thigh might or might not be pressed up against the thigh of Bert Rosen, surfer boy. That would bear looking into.

Then there was Sandy Grayson. Although Lauren disliked her, she had to concede that Sandy really made a case for chinos, Shetland sweaters, and tortoiseshell glasses. Sandy was as good-looking as any woman could be within the fashion limits of the less adventurous circles of Phillips Exeter Academy. Lauren noticed that Sandy had overcome her sullenness now and was saying something boring about the assigned reading. According to Trotsky—Sandy was droning on—the crucial causes of the Revolution were to be found not in the depravity of Rasputin but in the tensions between the socioeconomic classes in prerevolutionary Russia.

Scott Duchaine responded in his gentle southern drawl, "Trotsky was a Marxist." This last word was invested with a suggestion of distaste. "So naturally Trotsky thought those economic classes were the most important thing."

Russell agreed with Scott. "Trotsky's analysis is pretty much determined from the beginning by his political ideology. He's not exactly what you'd call an open-minded historian."

Katherine Butler spoke up fiercely. She was proudly Marxist and was always defending that point of view and the Russian Revolution in general against the other students whose politics were far more moderate. Now she directed her scorn at Russell. "I suppose you think that because Trotsky was a Marxist everything he wrote was dangerous propaganda and insidious lies. And so you can be very smug and just say 'Oh he's a Marxist' and not even think about what he wrote. If you thought about it seriously you'd have to admit that the economic oppression of millions was a much more serious thing than Rasputin hypnotizing the silly Empress." Katherine was vehement and gave every impression of despising Russell. Lauren supposed that as a politically concerned Marxist, Katherine was ideologically bound to be immune to Russell's attractions.

Besides, everyone at Harvard knew one thing about Katherine Butler. She was married to a black guerrilla leader in South Africa. She had grown up in South Africa, the daughter of liberal, white American missionaries, and had gone far beyond her parents, who only hesitantly approved of her marriage and extremist political commitment. Perhaps they hoped that Harvard would have a moderating effect on their daughter, but Katherine planned to spend her summer vacations, as she had spent the past summer, taking part in the struggle in South Africa. In four years—after graduation—she intended to return to Africa for good and donate her Harvard skills in economics and political science to the revolution.

In a sense, Katherine was ideal for the freshman seminar on the Russian Revolution, since her interest in revolutions was more than theoretical. She might also have been chosen to represent the Marxist point of view, which she did very dogmatically. Lauren, however, suspected that Professor Baranova had also taken into consideration physical type: Katherine's rich brown hair, loosely woven into a single braid down her back, her handsome features, and proud carriage. Katherine, more than anyone Lauren had ever seen, could illustrate the cliché of standing or sitting "straight as an arrow." Lauren respected her, though she herself could not imagine devoting her life to the South African revolution.

So much for the women. Lauren took an equal, if somewhat different, interest in the attractiveness of the men. They too were an exceptionally good-looking collection, but here she had no trouble awarding first prize. Lauren allowed herself a furtive glance at Russell Bernard, sitting alongside her. Russell possessed a magnetism as powerful as Professor Baranova's. She, of course, had the advantage of being the professor, but Russell was also gorgeous. And black.

Russell Bernard managed to be a sort of celebrity among Harvard freshmen. According to the university myth, every Harvard student had been accepted on the strength of something special about his or her record. This was emphatically true of Russell Bernard. First of all, as a high school student in Atlanta he had helped to organize a national black students' league to lobby for civil rights. Russell had gone to Washington, D.C., and made a very good impression on a number of congressmen, one of whom, a Harvard alumnus, had followed up with a college recommendation.

And there was more. As a senior in high school, Russell had written a short story that was accepted for publication by *The New Yorker*. And he played the violin. And he was a high school soccer star. And he was gorgeous. Lauren glanced at him again. He was very black, with short hair and a closely cropped beard and moustache. He had large eyes and, resting on the seminar table, enormous hands. Every week Lauren found herself more and more attracted to him. He seemed to like her too but so far he had made no real overtures, and Lauren was behaving with uncharacteristic shyness, intimidated by both his charisma and his achievements.

She was sure that she was not the only woman in the room under his spell. Katherine Butler had her own black husband in South Africa, so presumably she found Russell less exotic. Melissa Wu probably had nothing with which to respond to sexual magic like Russell's. But what about Tracy Nicolson? Lauren suspected that something might have happened between Tracy and Russell. Tracy would certainly not have been shy. And even stiff Sandy Grayson stole secret yearning glances at Russell, unless Lauren was very much mistaken. And Professor Baranova? She had interviewed Russell and chosen him for the seminar. Lauren would have liked to have seen that interview. There must have been enough charismatic exchange to win an Academy Award.

Lauren supposed that she really ought to be able to be similarly preoccupied with Scott Duchaine. Scott was also unlike anyone Lauren had ever known. He was from one of the oldest families in Richmond, Virginia. He was handsome, adult, and, best of all, he spoke with a southern accent. And he was on the point of becoming Lauren's own beau. Last week he had very formally asked her out on a date. Saturday night they had gone to see *Casablanca* at the Brattle Theatre. Scott had treated her with a sort of gentlemanly politeness that Lauren had never before encountered. He had opened every door, insisted on paying for everything, and barely kissed her good night. Lauren would probably be even more attracted to him if he seemed somewhat less tame. Still, they were going out again this Saturday, and, on the whole Lauren was quite pleased.

Then there was Bert Rosen. He was the epitome of the Los Angeles beachboy blond, except that his last name was Rosen. Lauren was profoundly impressed by the thoroughness with which Jews turned into southern Californians. She knew enough about genetics and heredity to know that lots of California sun would not inevitably produce blond hair, blue eyes, and a straight nose. Bert added to these physical characteristics all the right touches: He kept a surfboard in his Harvard dormitory room, drove a convertible around

Cambridge, and somehow contrived to preserve a suntan in Massachusetts in November. Lauren guessed that a sun lamp was at the root of all this. Was Bert's hand resting on Tracy Nicolson's knee under the seminar table?

Brian O'Donnell was something altogether different. Why on earth was Brian in this seminar? He was the son of a Boston police chief with big political connections. Brian himself talked of one day becoming mayor of Boston. Unfortunately, Brian was obviously and hopelessly dumb. Even as Lauren watched him, he was saying that it sounded to him like Lenin and Rasputin were both troublemakers so probably there was some connection between them. Brian was a football player, which might explain his admission to Harvard—but it didn't explain why Tatiana Baranova wanted him for her seminar. Was it just to obtain a different physical type? Brian had red hair and freckles and was even nice-looking if you liked very large men. At six-and-a-half feet tall he must have weighed over two hundred pounds. Or did Professor Baranova simply want him to represent the stupid point of view, to provide comic relief? Lauren herself found him very funny though she didn't want him in larger doses, which was becoming a possibility. Brian had gotten to know Lauren's roommate Carol; Brian and Carol were both slaving for the daily newspaper, the *Harvard Crimson*, hoping to be elected to the editorial staff. Brian, of course, was working on the sports page. It was Carol who had found out that Brian's teammates called him "Beef," an item of information that Lauren treasured. Carol, however, thought that "Beef" was a very manly nickname.

Beef's contributions to the seminar were always precious. "They were both trouble, this guy Rasputin and the other one, Lenin—no respect for law and order," he was saying. Brian never failed to pronounce "Lenin" as "lemon." His tongue was easily twisted.

"Can you not see any difference between them?" inquired Professor Baranova. She was never irritated by Brian, only drily amused.

"Sure," said Brian. "Lemon was a Commie, and Rasputin was a homophiliac." This elicited a round of suppressed giggles.

Tracy Nicolson brashly pronounced the class verdict. "Good work, Sport." Brian accepted this compliment with a contented nod, and Lauren thought to herself, Good work, Beef.

Melissa Wu did not quite get the joke and, happy to see her way clear to contributing to the discussion, corrected Brian's misunderstanding. "It wasn't Rasputin who was the hemophiliac. It was the Tsarevitch Alexei. Rasputin was able to stop the bleeding by hypnotizing the little boy."

"Yeah, sure," said Brian agreeably.

Melissa was not the only one incapable of taking Brian as lightly as he deserved. Now Katherine Butler reproached him forcefully. "Lenin was not a 'Commie.' He was a Communist, a very great Communist." Katherine obviously felt bound not to let pass any slur on Lenin's name. Brian, of course, did not take her point. Most of the other students were a little embarrassed by Katherine's zeal. Lauren noticed that poor Andrew Stein, sitting next to Katherine—chewing on his knuckles—was actually quivering at the sharpness of her tone.

Andrew quivered frequently in class—in fact, whenever anyone spoke with any sort of strong feeling. His great fear, no doubt, was that someone would speak to him—in which case, Lauren was sure, he would begin to scream and tear his hair out. Andrew Stein was a gaunt boy with hawklike features, feverish eyes, and, according to rumor, a psychiatric record longer and more turbulent than any Russian novel. He was supposed to be one of the true psychotics on a Harvard campus full of would-be neurotics. His almost frightening photograph in the Freshman Register had caused someone to name him "Dr. Strangelove," and this soon spread among the freshman class. Its appropriateness was not belied by an acquaintance with Andrew in person.

Finally Lauren turned her attention to Parker Hamilton Kendall IV. Parker, like Sandy Grayson, was from Exeter. Physically he was a chiseled Robert Redford type, and Lauren saw him much as she saw Melissa Wu: exotic, beautiful, but lacking in sex appeal. The resemblance to Robert Redford was that of a weak copy.

Lauren had reviewed in her mind all of the students in the seminar and now she was ready to rank them according to their attractiveness. Each week she ranked them anew, changing the order accordingly as her acquaintance and appreciation developed. First the six women. Professor Baranova was first. (Back in October Lauren had hesitated to yield this position to a fifty-year-old woman, but now the professor's magic triumphed indisputably.) Second came Lauren herself (very modest, room for improvement). Third was Tracy Nicolson, fourth Melissa Wu. (This was a ranking of attractiveness, not mere beauty—Melissa and Tracy had recently switched places.) Katherine Butler was fifth, and Lauren took pleasure in putting Sandy Grayson last. (Sandy was by no means plain, but Lauren thought the ranking justified by Sandy's ugly personality.)

Next the six men. Russell was easily number one. Then Bert Rosen (whose appeal was undeniable even if it did not quite sweep Lauren herself off her feet). Third was Scott Duchaine, displacing Parker Hamilton Kendall IV. Parker was down to fourth (to match his numeral—the more he spoke up, the duller he seemed, the less he looked like Robert Redford). Andrew Stein was fifth (psychotic but not without interesting features—he might one day pass Parker). And Brian "Beef" O'Donnell was last, too emphatically not Lauren's type.

"Lauren," said Professor Baranova, "what do you have to say about this?"

Lauren was startled from her reflections, but caught herself before she said, "About what?" Instead she tried to answer very generally with something she thought she had heard Sandy Grayson saying earlier. "I think that it is possible to exaggerate Rasputin's importance."

"What exactly are you thinking of?" Professor Baranova pressed further. Did she suspect that Lauren had not been following the discussion? Harvard's freshman seminars were designed so that even lowly freshmen would have the opportunity to work closely with the most distinguished Harvard professors. Lauren liked the idea in principle but there were moments when she longed for the anonymity of an enormous lecture hall.

She was trying to think of something quickly, when Russell Bernard spoke up to say, "I agree. The way I see it, Rasputin was only one symptom of the corruption of the Russian ancien régime. Perhaps he was the most dramatic symptom, even a sort of symbol of the government's weakness, but that's not the same as saying he was a major cause of the Revolution."

Professor Baranova turned her attention to Russell and

away from Lauren. Russell had gallantly come to Lauren's rescue.

The two-hour seminar was over at six and the students went out into the darkness of Harvard Yard. Lauren tried to catch Russell on the way out but she herself was caught by Brian O'Donnell, who good-naturedly inquired after her roommate. Russell was walking with Sandy Grayson ten feet ahead of Lauren and Brian. Lauren was watching Russell and Sandy, trying to overhear their conversation. She saw Russell touch Sandy lightly on the shoulder in the course of talking, and at the same moment that Lauren felt a pang of jealousy she heard Brian growl alongside her. He said, "Where I come from we put a knife in them when they touch white women." Brian was from South Boston, and Lauren had read enough about racial tensions between blacks and Boston Irish to know that Brian was not exaggerating.

That did not stop her from being furious. She said viciously, "I'd rather have him than you any day." Then, throwing shyness to the winds, she ran up to Russell, put an arm around his neck, and kissed him on the cheek. She said, "You're an angel. You saved my life this afternoon in that seminar." Lauren took double pleasure in the knowledge that both Brian and Sandy were watching the performance.

Russell smiled and said, "Don't mention it. Maybe you'll save my life next time."

And Lauren said, "It would be my pleasure."

Sandy Grayson suddenly blurted out, "Please excuse me," and walked off in another direction.

Lauren and Russell stopped and watched her go. Now they were alone together in the center of Harvard Yard, surrounded by dormitories with lit windows. "Not very friendly of her," Russell commented.

"No," said Lauren. "Perhaps she doesn't like me too much." Lauren knew that it was better to present herself as disliked and therefore wronged than to admit to disliking Sandy and thus risk appearing jealous.

"Or perhaps she likes me too much," said Russell. Lauren said nothing, knowing that prying would also seem in bad taste. Russell confessed no further. Instead he asked, "What were you daydreaming about when you were so rudely interrupted by Professor Baranova?"

Lauren decided that this was the moment to be disarmingly frank. "I was comparing the attractiveness of the students in the seminar."

Russell laughed and asked, "How did I do?"

"You did okay." Lauren was delighted. Her friendship with Russell Bernard had made great strides in the last two minutes. She pushed ahead boldly. "Are you going to eat at the Union?"

"Yes," said Russell, "but at a dinner meeting for my National Black Students' Lobby. You've heard of it? I'd rather have dinner with you, but I don't think I can. How about coffee tomorrow night?"

"I'd love to." Coffee in Cambridge represented a much more intimate date than dinner in the Freshman Union. Lauren suggested the Cafe Pamplona.

"Sure," said Russell. "Eight-thirty?" Suddenly he looked disturbed.

"What's the matter?" Lauren asked.

"Nothing really," he said. "Just that the last time I went to Pamplona I went with Dora Carpenter."

Lauren, like everyone else at Harvard, knew who Dora Carpenter was. The *Crimson* had covered the story in great detail. Dora Carpenter was a black woman who had dropped out of Harvard and was living in Cambridge. Three weeks ago she had died from using contaminated cocaine. Instead of snorting it, she had injected it into her bloodstream. The contamination was a freakish thing, an unlucky chance, but it had been bad enough to kill her. The *Crimson* story had included a warning to Harvard students to beware of potentially contaminated cocaine. Dora Carpenter had been twenty-two. Russell said, "Dora was involved in the Lobby, so I knew her even before I came to Harvard. She was wonderful. I can't believe she's dead."

Lauren put an arm around him and asked very softly, "Were you in love with her?"

"Maybe," said Russell. "I honestly don't know. I'm not sure I know what it means to be in love with someone. I don't know if I've ever really been in love." And at that moment Lauren fell in love with him.

2. A date at Pamplona

Lauren Adler had been born in New York City. When she was nine, her parents, Dr. and Mrs. Adler, had moved to the New Jersey suburbs so that Lauren could benefit from a supposedly model school system. Lauren had hated New Jersey, hated the suburbs, and hated the school system. Starting in first grade, she had begun hiding a book in her lap and secretly reading during classes. Whenever she was caught by a teacher and reprimanded for inattention, she would begin to read again as soon as the teacher turned away. She resented having to pay attention when nothing of interest was being taught, and to her teachers' dismay this attitude didn't seem to affect her grades. It was this academic environment that had helped to develop in Lauren a not unjustified sense of intellectual arrogance.

Public school lasts for twelve years, seven hours a day. Lauren had a lot of time to read. In fact, by the time she graduated from high school she was ferociously well-read: lots of classics and lots of trash.

The suburbs of New York City are crammed full of smart Jewish girls and boys. That Lauren was manifestly smarter than this vast herd of dutifully high-scoring children was recognized by Harvard, Princeton, and Yale, which had accepted Lauren while rejecting all the other applicants from her model high school. Lauren had decided to go to Harvard partly because of the magically prestigious name and partly because, of the big three, Harvard was farthest from New Jersey. Actually Lauren was never quite sure whether she was attending Harvard or Radcliffe, as the two schools existed in a legally very confused state of union. Whichever it was, Harvard or Radcliffe, Lauren liked it a lot.

Lauren was awakened early Thursday morning, as every other morning, by the bells of Memorial Church outside her window. It was the price she payed for living in the center of Harvard Yard in Thayer Hall. So far, the bells had prevented her from succumbing to the temptation to sleep through her morning classes. Carol had probably already been awake for an hour, back from running (one of her little California habits in spite of which she managed to be rather more overweight than lazy Lauren). When Lauren emerged from her room she saw that Carol had already begun her daily letter to her boyfriend back home in Los Angeles. Carol was a wonder.

Lauren and Carol shared what was called a two-room double. In past decades, when Harvard was a plusher, more aristocratic institution, this would have been a bedroom and living room for one person. Now Carol lived in the living room, and halfway through the year she would trade with Lauren for the more private bedroom. "I don't need it now anyway," she said. "My Baby Doll is in Los Angeles." It was agreed that Carol could have the bedroom if Baby Doll should be able to manage a visit. On Carol's wall was a life-size poster, blown up from a photograph, of Baby Doll—also known as Bobby—in his red bikini bathing suit.

In the spirit of Harvard's much vaunted emphasis on diversity, Lauren had requested a roommate "not from the New York area." And so Harvard had given her a Jew from Los Angeles. Carol, unlike Bert Rosen, had not managed to acquire blue eyes, but she was sufficiently southern Californian to seem quite foreign to Lauren. What could you say about a culture which did not distinguish between Rod McKuen and T. S. Eliot, between Hallmark greeting cards and French Impressionism? And yet Carol and Lauren turned out to be a successful rooming combination.

First of all, they had ascertained on the very first day of college that on a dormitory floor of exceptionally innocent girls, the two of them shared the distinction of being the nonvirgins. This was an instant bond, cemented by much giggling at the expense of the other girls. In fact, Lauren and Carol had both lost their respective virginities in the same month before leaving for college: Carol with Baby Doll, accompanied by many vows of eternal love, and Lauren, more casually, with a boy she had been dating from the local community college.

"Good morning, roommate," said Lauren.

"Morning, roommate," said Carol, looking up from her letter to Baby Doll. The best thing and the worst thing about Carol was her infallibly good nature: the permanent smile and the endless squeals of delight. It could be a great comfort at times, but at other times it could drive you crazy. On the whole, though, Lauren loved Carol dearly.

"Have you been to breakfast?"

"Yes," said Carol. "It's waffles with syrup. Delicious." Carol's Los Angeles gourmet palate recognized exactly two qualities: sweet and crunchy. Waffles with syrup fell into the former category. "But you can't have any," Carol warned. "You have a big date tonight. If you're careful, you can lose two pounds by eight-thirty."

Lauren had told Carol the night before about her date with Russell. Carol had been vicariously delighted for Lauren until Lauren produced the Freshman Register with Russell's picture.

"But he's a Negro!" Carol had exclaimed, shocked.

"No kidding?"

"Oh Lauren, do you think you should?"

"He's absolutely perfect," Lauren had said proudly.

"Lauren," Carol had said in a hushed tone, "you're not going to sleep with him, are you?"

"We'll see."

Carol had gasped, but this morning she seemed fully reconciled to Lauren's date. Carol was like that. Her sunny nature always won out in the end. Lauren thought happily of Russell Bernard and decided to forego the waffles.

It was odd, thought Lauren, the mysterious sense of community which for no obvious reason seemed to bind the members of Tatiana Baranova's seminar on the Russian Revolution. Lauren felt that each of the other ten students was somehow a character in her life. During the course of that Thursday, she ran into just about all of them.

Her Tuesday and Thursday morning class was Chinese civilization with Professor Moorhead. Lauren greatly admired Professor Moorhead as a teacher because he did not indulge in showy condescending tricks to win over his audience. His lecturing style was quiet and spare and completely commanding. Sometimes Lauren could concentrate through nearly an entire lecture. Still, she always sat in the back of the hall just in case she should start dozing. She would not want to offend Professor

Moorhead. Anyway, if he lost Lauren's attention from time to time, he could at least be certain of holding the undivided attention of Melissa Wu, who sat in the front row absorbing her cultural heritage. She filled pages and pages of paper with the world's neatest notes, while Professor Moorhead could, if he cared to, gaze down upon the smallest feet in the freshman class.

Parker Hamilton Kendall IV was also at that class. He was only auditing but he took more comprehensive notes than Lauren. Lauren was impressed by the self-discipline of the regular auditor. She herself was always resolving to audit one class or another—a political science course taught by one of John F. Kennedy's advisers, an introductory biology course given by a notoriously theatrical Nobel Prize winner—but somehow she never managed to make it to any of these courses more than once. Parker, on the other hand, never missed a lecture of Chinese Civilization. Lauren considered a new approach. Perhaps instead of deciding to audit classes with famous professors, she should consider auditing all the classes that Russell Bernard was taking. Then there would be an additional incentive to go to the lectures.

Lauren left Chinese Civilization with Parker, and Melissa joined them outside. When Lauren told Parker how much she admired his self-discipline, he said that making himself go to extra classes was no harder than making himself go running every day.

"Oh, where do you run?" asked Lauren, thinking that it would be funny to see Parker in his running gear. She could barely imagine him not wearing a sweater and blazer. Carol went running every morning in a pair of Baby Doll's gym shorts, worn for sentiment's sake.

"I run in the evenings down by the river," said Parker.

"Oh!" Melissa exclaimed. "You shouldn't do that. It's dangerous. You could be murdered."

Parker blushed and said he really didn't think it was as dangerous as all that, but perhaps he ought to consider it again. He was so polite that Lauren couldn't resist teasing Melissa. "Parker doesn't have anything to worry about down at the river. For all we know, he might be one of those characters you and I have to worry about when we go out alone at night. You've heard of him. Top of the Most Wanted list. Picture in every post office: Parker Hamilton Kendall IV, notorious cutthroat and sex criminal."

Parker blushed again and began to laugh, but he politely

cut his laughter short when he saw that Melissa was not going to join in. She looked very earnest, and said without anger, "We shouldn't make jokes about things like that."

Lauren walked into the Freshman Union for lunch, and the first thing she saw was Katherine Butler sitting in the lobby behind a table of leaflets that she was urging on the passing lunchers. Lauren said hello and took one of the leaflets to be friendly. In the lunch line she idly read through Katherine's handout, which announced a rally to be held in Boston on behalf of the South African revolution. It concluded with two sentences in large print: "Even as you read this, our comrades are being murdered in South Africa. They must be avenged."

"Joining the revolution?" said a hoarse voice, and Lauren turned around to see Tracy Nicolson waiting in line with Bert Rosen. His hand was on the back pocket of her jeans, or perhaps her pocket was in his hand. At any rate, it was a mutual gesture. Something was definitely going on between them. "Just joking," said Tracy. "See, I've got one too." She waved her copy of the leaflet. Bert and Tracy were both smiling contentedly, so Lauren smiled too. Then Bert saw a friend from Los Angeles and went over to say hello. Bert's expensive-looking running clothes, maroon sweats with shoes to match, looked perfectly natural—just the thing to wear to lunch. Those Californians!

Tracy moved closer to Lauren and said, "I understand you're going out with Russell Bernard tonight." Her voice was suggestive but not at all hostile: one woman of the world addressing another.

"Yes, but how do you know?" Lauren asked.

"You know gossip," said Tracy. "But be careful about Russell," she warned. "He's a foxy guy. . . . I know. But maybe a little too good-looking. A guy like that can be a real killer, do you know what I mean?"

In the afternoon Lauren went to the weekly discussion section for her course on Nietzsche. They were discussing *The Genealogy of Morals*, which Lauren had liked a lot for the first fifty pages, before she became impatient. Nietzsche, she thought, was really too much. He got so carried away with himself but failed to carry Lauren along with him. During the discussion she doodled in her notebook and was rather pleased with herself for coming up with the slogan "Nietzsche is peachy!" Regretfully she concluded that it would probably be better not to share her rhyme with the class.

Andrew Stein was there too—Dr. Strangelove. Lauren wondered whether Nietzsche, if one had known him personally, would have seemed no more mentally disturbed than Andrew. Andrew gave the impression of having been awake all night rereading Nietzsche, and Lauren noticed that his copy of the text was covered with marginal scribbling. He was, however, unable to express any of his thoughts on the subject. Every time he prepared to speak, he was overcome by trembling and eventually subsided into terrified silence. The graduate student who was leading the discussion did not call on Andrew for fear of provoking a fit. Lauren and everyone else had realized that Andrew's academic psychoses were genuine when he had sat through the first Nietzsche hourly exam without writing a word. He couldn't write anything, he later explained, because he knew he wouldn't be able to say it right. The kindly professor, instead of giving Andrew an "E" (Harvard's eccentric equivalent of an "F"), had recommended that Andrew talk to someone about his problems. How could he know that Andrew was already in analysis five days a week?

After class Andrew walked with Lauren toward the library. They were both expected to write a paper on Nietzsche over the next two weeks. Andrew said that he didn't think he could. "The more Nietzsche I read," said Andrew, "the more I think that I should kill myself." Lauren suggested that he try reading *Fear of Flying* instead, but Andrew was in a hurry to get back to his room to reread *The Genealogy of Morals*.

Lauren walked into Lamont Library and passed Brian "Beef" O'Donnell, who was on his way out. Remembering what he had said about white women and black men she refused to smile at him or say hello. He gave her, in return, a freckled scowl. Lauren decided that when her romance with Russell Bernard really got going she would make a special point of kissing him in public in front of Brian O'Donnell.

Lauren took out a collection of assigned essays on Chinese culture from the library's reserved readings. Avoiding the big wooden desk tables, she found a red armchair, which turned out to be less comfortable than it looked. She tried to read an essay on the construction of the Great Wall, but before long she put it aside and took out of her shoulder bag her copy of *Fear of Flying* with its vaguely erotic cover.

Fortunately, the cover was out of sight when a voice over Lauren's shoulder said, "Well, well, well. Studying hard, I see." The southern drawl was unmistakable.

"Hello, Scott," said Lauren, without even turning around. "How's life on the plantation?" Lauren thought to herself that if she was going to have a black boyfriend she really had better start cutting out the plantation jokes.

"Real fine," said Scott. Lauren was crazy about the accent.

Scott wanted to talk to her about their date for Saturday night. They had not decided definitely what they would do, and now he suggested that they go see *Psycho* in the Dunster House dining hall. "If the lady won't mind a few real scary murders," said Scott, almost parodying his own courtliness.

"The lady won't mind at all," said Lauren, "especially if the gentleman will be kind enough to walk her home after the movie." Lauren was flirting happily. On the whole she thought Russell was more exciting than Scott, but for a moment she toyed with the fantasy of having two southern boyfriends at the same time: the black man from Atlanta and the Richmond aristocrat.

On the other side of the library hall, Sandy Grayson was walking by with two other girls who, if they hadn't gone to Exeter, surely had gone to Andover or someplace with a similar dress code. Then Sandy caught sight of Lauren and Scott across the room. Sandy froze for a split second before regaining her composure and walking on. But in that second she gave Lauren a look whose meaning was perfectly clear, even from thirty feet away. Lauren thought to herself, "If looks could kill. . . ."

Lauren dressed for her date with great care, though in the end, informally. After all, it was only a Thursday night date for coffee; Levi's would be fine. After trying on a number of blouses, she chose a dark green Indian cotton which brought out the green in her eyes. After a little posing in front of the mirror she decided not to wear a bra. She let her hair fall freely over her shoulders.

Carol was not pleased with Lauren's outfit. Carol believed in dressing up for a date, and dressing up required brightly colored artificial fabrics. Carol's own wardrobe included a great deal of pink and orange (neither of which suited her), and some of her party clothes were covered with sequins. These might have been the height of fashion at Hollywood High School dances, but they were decidedly out of place at Harvard. Lauren had tried gently to steer Carol into more acceptable clothing, but Carol continued to believe in the importance of dressing up. Now, as on other occasions, Lauren found herself resisting Carol's helpful suggestions and declined an offer of Carol's special strawberry perfume.

Lauren, as a matter of principle, preferred to arrive twenty minutes late for social engagements. She believed that it was better to be awaited than to wait. When she realized that she had arrived at the Cafe Pamplona only ten minutes late, she knew that it was a sign: She was definitely interested in Russell Bernard—maybe too interested. And Russell was not yet there.

The Cafe Pamplona consisted of a dozen small tables in a grotto of a room just below street level. Pamplona (the name, of course, was supposed to put you in mind of Hemingway and the running of the bulls) tended to be embarrassingly literary. On any given night there you could find at least one young poet struggling with free verse, but most people, Lauren included, did not take Pamplona's pretensions too seriously. To the average Harvard student it was a cozy place where you could get a good cappuccino. There were also rather handsome waiters, though most of them were obviously gay. Lauren ordered a cappuccino from her favorite waiter (the short one with the curly black hair and the European accent) and wondered when Russell would appear.

A man sitting in a dim corner across the room from Lauren looked up from his coffee. For a moment she thought it was Robert Redford, but of course it was only Parker Hamilton Kendall IV. The woman with Parker had her back to Lauren, but Lauren was suddenly sure it was Sandy Grayson. Parker and Sandy were clearly talking seriously, too seriously for either of them to notice Lauren. Parker seemed untypically agitated, but Sandy remained completely collected. Of course Parker and Sandy had gone to Exeter together, but was there anything else between them? Try as she might, Lauren could not overhear a word of their conversation, which was drowned out by a discussion of modern poetry at a nearer table. Lauren resolved that when Russell arrived she would greet him loudly enough to attract Sandy's attention.

When another fifteen minutes passed and Russell had still not appeared, Lauren began to feel uneasy. True, it was no later than she herself might sometimes choose to arrive for a date, but she was not pleased to think that Russell might be treating her with her own brand of casualness, calculated or uncalculated. Lauren knew the value of being or at least seeming the less interested partner in any romantic entanglement. Scott Duchaine, for instance, had been clearly cast as the aspiring beau, and it was easy for Lauren to remain the nonchalant belle because she was only charmed by, not really smitten with, Scott.

But Russell was different. Was she in love with him? What exactly did that mean? Lauren couldn't answer any more definitely than Russell could. She did know that she had been thinking about him all day, that her whole day had been somehow focused on this evening. And what was to happen in the evening? Lauren supposed that they would talk, become better friends over coffee. And then? Lauren's attraction to Russell became stronger with every passing minute that he failed to appear.

Why had she fallen for him like this? In part it was simply overwhelming sexual attraction: the eyes, the skin, the beard, the hands. Then there was also a powerful romantic fantasy, as Lauren had realized the night before when Russell had spoken of Dora Carpenter; there was a sensitive and gentle side to Russell. And there were Russell's accomplishments: his story in *The New Yorker*; his national political lobby. And he did play the violin, not to mention soccer. Lauren was not above being bowled over by the same qualifications that had convinced the Harvard admissions committee.

A few weeks ago, Lauren had searched out the old issue of *The New Yorker* and read Russell's story. It was about a black adolescent and his best friend, a white adolescent, who both fall in love with the same older, white woman. She thinks of them as just boys, does not consider them as romantic possibilities—and so the story dealt largely with the relationship of the two adolescent boys and the tension created by the unconsummated sexual triangle. After having read the story Lauren found Russell more fascinating than ever.

Finally, Lauren was under the spell of Russell's magical charisma, the same magic that made Russell so unquestionably a presence in the seminar room. Lauren knew that the moment Russell entered the Cafe Pamplona the little room would begin to gravitate around him. The waiters would look sharp, the poets would find inspiration. Russell commanded infatuation, and Lauren too had responded.

The question then was to what extent Russell's powers enabled him to discern, even to assume, Lauren's infatuation. And to what extent would he react by treating her carelessly? Enough to arrive a half hour late? Enough to stand her up altogether? Perhaps then Russell was not really a very nice person, and it would be just as well not to get involved with him. Yet, even as Lauren suspected this she also knew that Russell's lateness made him all the more attractive to her.

Across the room, Parker and Sandy split their bill and rose to leave. Lauren, regretting Russell's absence, smiled at the two of them. They were both evidently startled to see her. Parker smiled and said hello, but Sandy walked out of the café without saying a word. Could she have known who Lauren was waiting for?

At nine-thirty Lauren paid for her cappuccino and left. If Russell arrived more than an hour late, she did not want to be there waiting for him. She really should have left a half hour ago, and waiting the extra half hour was in itself a discouraging sign of Lauren's state of mind. She was furious at Russell, but she was still crazy about him.

Lauren climbed up to the street. It was dark and cold, and Lauren was suddenly frightened as she walked along beneath the high wall that bounded Harvard Yard. A panhandler appeared out of nowhere to plead for a quarter, and Lauren, momentarily terrified, walked faster. Harvard Yard itself was virtually empty. At last Lauren reached her dormitory and her room. She carefully locked the door behind her and turned on the lights. She was alone.

Lauren knew where Carol was. Carol was trying to get onto the editorial staff of the *Harvard Crimson*, and she spent her evenings at the office helping to prepare the next day's newspaper. She frequently didn't get home till midnight, and Brian O'Donnell would escort her back to the dorm. Thinking of the walk back from Pamplona, Lauren could almost envy Carol Brian's hulking protection. Still, Lauren did hope that Carol would continue to remain faithful to Baby Doll. If Carol took up with Brian he would always be hanging around the room, and Lauren wanted to see as little of Brian as possible after his remark about Russell.

Lauren was waiting for the phone to ring. If Russell called to apologize, to offer some excuse, she could still forgive him without ruining her pride. For a split second she hated Russell, wished he were dead. The feeling passed. Lauren tried to read Nietzsche. She tried to read *Fear of Flying*. She thought about going upstairs to seek consolation from her very best friend, but she didn't want to leave the room for fear of missing Russell's call.

As she waited, she lay on her bed on the Indian print madras bedspread and fantasized. Russell would become a very important man. He would be a senator in Washington, a national black leader, a celebrity of international stature whose support was valued by the American president, whose good will was sought by foreign ambassadors. His name would be a household word for millions of black Americans who would even accept his marriage to a white Jewish girl from the New Jersey suburbs and their beautiful children. In fact, Lauren would act as a sort of liaison between her husband and the white liberal public. Perhaps Lauren would be a senator herself, and she and Russell would work together on the Senate floor by day and discuss political strategy at night in each other's arms. She and Russell would occasionally deign to include at their dinner parties Tatiana Baranova and her toadlike husband, Max Kohler, who would sometimes advise them on foreign policy.

For a moment Lauren believed that if only Russell would call and apologize, all this might be possible. After all, everything was supposed to be possible with a Harvard degree. Lauren lay on the bed, but still the phone did not ring. Around midnight Lauren heard a key turning in the lock. Irrationally frightened, she went to the door to reassure herself that it was only Carol. Carol came in flustered. She said, "Lauren—"

"He stood me up," said Lauren.

"I know," said Carol confusedly. "We just got the story at the *Crimson*."

"What?" Lauren said. "Are you serious? A story about me and Russell, about me getting stood up? That's crazy. What are you talking about?"

"No," said Carol, "you don't understand. Let me finish. I'm trying to tell you that Russell Bernard was murdered last night."

3. Michael makes tea

Michael Hunt was Lauren's best friend at Harvard, and it was naturally to Michael that she now turned. On Friday night he brewed Earl Grey tea for Lauren in his British china teapot with the pattern of delicate roses, altogether inappropriate for college dormitory life. Lauren had spent the last twenty-four hours breaking into tears, trying to fall asleep, and then sleeping only to be jolted awake by nightmares. She was still horribly shaken by the murder, but the Earl Grey tea was helping her focus more clearly on the one wild notion that was becoming an obsession—that was transforming her crush on Russell into a much more serious resolution.

Lauren and Michael sat on his baby blue silk comforter, Michael reclining, Lauren more upright with her back against the wall. She sat beneath Michael's favorite Beardsley print—Salome with the head of John the Baptist. Michael disdained the several dozen French Impressionist paintings which appeared again and again on Harvard dormitory walls.

Lauren and Michael had been destined to become best friends. The Harvard Housing Office had given them no alternatives. There was really no one else in Thayer Hall for either of them. Michael's floor—right above Lauren's—consisted entirely of athletes and engineering majors, all of whom would have considered Van Gogh's sunflowers too rarefied an artistic taste. Michael's roommate lived in the living room part of the double in complete squalor surrounded by four walls, all decorated with the same motif: autographed pictures of the Boston Red Sox. Michael shuddered just walking through to his own little pre-Raphaelite sanctuary.

Michael was of a prominent Boston family. He had gone to

prep school at Exeter, where, he constantly assured Lauren, one could get a much better education than at Harvard. Michael was also terribly vain, and not entirely without cause, about his delicate blond good looks. He resented ugliness and crudeness in others and, in particular, in those among whom he had to live—the boys on his floor. These Thayer Hall boys were forever yelling obscenities out the windows at the boys of Holworthy Hall, who yelled back and sometimes threw water balloons. Michael was beginning to develop a permanent grimace.

Lauren too was out of sympathy with the dull girls on her floor. She liked Carol best, and they were united in not being virgins, but Carol's sophistication stopped right there. Lauren had known from the moment she wandered into Michael's room during the first week of school that they would be friends. She had also gathered almost immediately, despite her own lack of sophistication in such matters, that Michael was not interested in sleeping with women, and that their friendship would be different from any that Lauren had ever had with a man. Now Lauren and Michael drank tea from cups and saucers that matched the china pattern of the teapot, and Lauren told Michael everything she had been thinking about since hearing the night before about the murder of Russell Bernard.

The *Crimson* had provided the horrible details. Russell's body had been discovered in the Charles River on Thursday, and according to police estimates he had been killed some time Wednesday night alongside the river. The murder had been peculiarly brutal. Russell had received a blow on the head, possibly fatal, with a heavy object. He had been stabbed in the back three times. He had been shot through the heart once. And he had been left facedown in the river.

The river was a notoriously dangerous place at night. Every Harvard freshman was warned against it at some time or another. Across the road from the famous Harvard "River" Houses one was likely to encounter the criminal elements of Boston and Cambridge, even the more mentally disturbed criminal elements. Their presence had been proven in the past by armed robberies, rapes, and murders.

And yet the river exerted a certain fascination on the Harvard community. Just as great cities are inseparable from their great rivers—New Orleans and the Mississippi, Leningrad and the Neva, Vienna and the Danube—so Harvard too looked to its own river, the Charles. For all its comparative safety, the swimming pool in the Indoor Athletic Building was not sufficiently grand to serve as the reigning body of water. Even the status considerations of the Harvard housing system seemed to be dictated by the river. Nine out of ten freshmen, after their freshman year in Harvard Yard, hoped to move on to one of the Harvard River Houses rather than be consigned to the supposedly too distant Radcliffe Quad.

Just the day before, Parker Hamilton Kendall IV had indicated to Lauren that he went running along the riverbank every evening. Last Saturday night Lauren herself had walked by the river with Scott Duchaine—a romantic stroll. Michael, too, despite his overly ostentatious fear of assault, had occasionally promenaded by the water with some much admired young man. And Andrew Stein had once confided in Lauren, when they were leaving their Nietzsche class, that he often went down to the river alone in the middle of the night to think about philosophy. Surely most of the freshman class, with the certain exception of Melissa Wu, had at one time or another walked along the Charles in the dark. But Russell Bernard had been murdered.

According to the *Crimson*, the police were optimistic about apprehending the killer. While some river rats might hang around the banks for months, mugging one victim after another, a man who had committed murder would probably not stay put. The odd nature of the murder, the different weapons used in succession, indicated either an unstable mind or the cooperative work of more than one murderer. Either possibility would increase the likelihood of an indiscretion that might shed some light. The police also hoped that Russell's wallet and watch, both removed from the body, might turn up eventually. In the meantime, Harvard students were warned to stay away from the river at night.

"But the police are wrong," Lauren said to Michael fiercely. "I'm sure of it. Russell wasn't killed by some Boston bum who wanted his wallet. Russell was killed by another Harvard student."

"Now really, Lauren darling," said Michael, full of concern. "Are you sure you're not being the tiniest bit hysterical? If you like, I could put some of this nice Jamaican rum into the tea."

But Lauren didn't want rum. She wanted Michael to listen to what she had to say, and eventually he was subdued by her

evident seriousness. Everyone agreed that the peculiar thing
about the murder was its thoroughness: the blow on the
head, the knife in the back, the bullet in the heart, the body
in the river. It was more than thoroughness; it was irrational
overkill in the most literal sense of the word. Whoever
murdered Russell Bernard Wednesday night had wanted to
make certain beyond any doubt that Russell was dead, and
rather than running after delivering the first blow, had lingered
insanely to take further unnecessary measures. Lauren was as
certain as she had ever been of anything that whoever
murdered Russell Bernard on Wednesday night had been
present in Tatiana Baranova's freshman seminar on Wednesday afternoon to hear Melissa Wu's bizarre presentation of
the terrifying murder of Rasputin. Conscious of Rasputin and
of the poison and bullets which had miraculously failed to kill
him, the murderer of Russell Bernard had panicked at the
crucial moment and murdered over and over again, lest the
victim rise from the dead. Lauren was as sure of this as if she
had been there, because she knew that she, too, had she
committed murder Wednesday night for whatever reason,
would have been haunted by the fear that her victim just
wouldn't die.

Michael almost believed her. At any rate he was taking her
story seriously. He asked, "Have you told all this to the
police?"

That was the most frustrating part. Of course Lauren had
gone straight to the police that same morning, and she had
explained everything to the officer in charge of the case, who
had listened with an expression of apparent interest. When
Lauren finished, however, he had asked earnestly whether
this character Rasputin had known the black guy who was
murdered. So Lauren had had to tell her whole story to
another police officer, and this one understood exactly what
she was saying, only to make it clear that he thought she was
overexcited, if not entirely loony. So much for the police.
They were looking for a low-life vagrant with Russell's wallet.
That was the logical solution to the problem. And besides,
Lauren supposed, the police would probably need a damn
good reason to start investigating the Harvard community.
Harvard would not take it kindly.

"And of course all I've really got is this hunch," Lauren
said to Michael despairingly. "But it's a good hunch. Don't

you think so? The murder only makes sense if you think about Rasputin."

"Lauren darling," said Michael, "I have an uncomfortable feeling that you are not going to be a good girl and forget all about this."

"Exactly," said Lauren. "I'm going to be a very bad girl, and I'm going to find out who murdered Russell Bernard." It was becoming an obsession.

"You know," said Michael, "if one of the people in that seminar is really a murderer—"

"One of them is," said Lauren. "I'm sure of it."

"Well, he or she is not going to be too happy about you asking everyone a lot of innocuous questions like whether they have alibis and own guns. That murderer is going to figure out what's going on and invite you for a walk along the river."

"I can take care of myself," said Lauren.

"Oh, good," said Michael. "Do you think you could take care of me too?"

"What?"

"I'm going to help, darling. Let's make a list of suspects."

The solution to the mystery would clearly hinge on the question of motive. Why would a Harvard freshman want to murder Russell Bernard? Certainly not to obtain his wallet and watch. Those would have been removed from the body simply to mislead the police. To mislead them from what? Lauren and Michael came up with two basic categories of motive. The male members of the seminar might have killed Russell out of some combination of racial hatred and sexual outrage. The female suspects would have murdered Russell for spurning them.

Lauren, as soon as she had heard about the murder, had immediately remembered Brian O'Donnell's warning: "Where I come from, we put a knife in them when they touch white women." Could Brian be dumb enough to go out and murder Russell Bernard right after announcing to Lauren that he wanted to? Perhaps. There was no point in underestimating Brian's stupidity. Besides, it had not been a particularly intelligent murder. Lauren showed Michael Brian's picture in the Freshman Register.

"He looks like such a good-natured Beef," said Michael.

"I wouldn't have thought he'd murder anyone. He's not even particularly hideous compared to some Harvard football players who live on this floor."

"Enough of that," said Lauren. "I really don't think he'd go for your type."

"You never can tell," said Michael petulantly. "I have succeeded in charming the most unlikely people. Did I ever tell you about the professional hockey player—"

"At least twelve times," said Lauren, "and I still don't believe you. Do you know who is Brian's type? I think he's interested in Carol."

"Baby Doll, beware," said Michael. And then after a moment's consideration, "My mother has an Irish cleaning lady who knows everything about every Irishman in Boston. She's sure to know something about O'Donnell's father, the police chief. I shall inquire casually. Wouldn't that be a good way to start our investigation?"

Brian was the first suspect to come to mind because of what he had said, but Brian's motive could be stretched to fit the other men in the seminar. It was over Lauren's objections that Michael insisted on making a case against Scott Duchaine. Scott was a white aristocrat from Richmond, Virginia. He surely took a negative view of blacks in general, never mind of black men who might sleep with white women. Scott's breeding might prevent him from making the same sort of crude racist remarks as Brian O'Donnell, but his feelings might be no less emphatic.

Michael, as Lauren's confidant, knew all about her date with Scott last Saturday night. "You see," Michael said, "we don't know how much Scott really likes you. It's true he wasn't wildly aggressive last Saturday, just that very modest good-night kiss (which I thought was sweet)—but with a well-bred Richmond boy that could simply indicate how much he liked you. The more he cared, the less he'd push. But, don't you see, if he's in love with you, if from the summit of Richmond society he has fallen ever so inappropriately in love with a beautiful Yankee-Jewess..."

"Go on," said Lauren.

"Well, he might have wanted to protect his romance from a certain black intruder. You realize, don't you, that Russell Bernard was killed soon after he arranged a date with you. It's possible that someone specifically wanted to prevent you from meeting Russell Bernard Thursday night at Pamplona. Did anyone know about that date?"

"Why would anyone know about it?" said Lauren. "Russell and I agreed on it alone in Harvard Yard after the seminar."

"Perhaps someone from the seminar was hanging about behind a tree," Michael suggested helpfully.

"Perhaps," said Lauren, and then she suddenly remembered what Tracy Nicolson had said at lunch on Thursday. Tracy had known! And when Lauren had asked how, Tracy had just said, "You know gossip." Certainly Lauren did know gossip—who better—but in this case she would have to know more precisely. Michael and Lauren agreed that they would have to find out how Tracy knew, who had told her, when she had heard, and how many other people she had told. Did she find out Wednesday between the time the date was set by Lauren and Russell, around six, and the time Russell was killed later that night? If so, then anyone could have known about the date, and it might reveal a motive for murder. For instance, was it just coincidence that Parker and Sandy were at Pamplona Thursday night at eight-thirty? Under this theory, Scott Duchaine was the number one suspect, but, as Michael pointed out, you never could tell who was in love with you. Lauren could have had other secret admirers in the seminar.

Bert Rosen? Michael and Lauren found his picture in the Register, big handsome smile, lots of white teeth. "I can't believe his name is really Rosen," said Michael. "But I suppose he could hardly have chosen it as a glamorous stage name. Isn't he the one who's supposed to keep a surfboard in his room? I don't suppose Bert was surfing down at the Charles Wednesday night and ended up clobbering Russell Bernard with a surfboard?"

Lauren told Michael about seeing Bert and Tracy together at the Union. And she told him what Tracy had said about Russell: "He's a foxy guy. I know." What did she mean by that "I know"? Lauren would have been willing to bet that there had been something between Russell and Tracy. Could Bert have murdered Russell out of jealousy?

And what about Andrew Stein? In a way, he was the most likely murderer in the group. He was, after all, evidently unbalanced. Lauren knew that he took long walks by the river. She knew that he had been reading Nietzsche's *Genealogy of Morals*. Perhaps some combination of psychosis and

German philosophy had driven Andrew to the insane act. As for motive, he could easily have killed out of envy of Russell's brilliant sanity. Or perhaps Andrew was more conventionally jealous. Could that crazy boy be in love with Lauren? The thought made Lauren's skin crawl, but she couldn't rule out the possibility.

Michael's favorite suspects were Parker Hamilton Kendall IV and Sandy Grayson, since he had gone to school with them at Exeter. Through Exeter circles Michael would undertake to investigate them both. He already knew that Parker and Sandy had been close friends there, but he didn't know if there had been anything more between them. "Perhaps something twisted," Michael reflected, "though I think it's more likely that they were just confidants, like us. Yet I suppose that even that could be twisted if the two of them are individually twisted."

"Are they?"

"Who knows."

"Are we?" Lauren joked.

"Who knows." They both giggled.

Michael was not surprised to hear that Lauren had seen Parker and Sandy together at Pamplona, but he was interested to hear that Parker had been agitated. Perhaps Parker had been confessing the crime to Sandy. Or perhaps she had just confessed to him. Or perhaps they had done the deed together, and she, like Lady Macbeth, was steeling her coconspirator against pangs of guilt. Michael and Lauren thought that, on the whole, Parker seemed too proper and chiseled to commit murder. "Besides, he's from a very aristocratic Boston family," said Michael, adding irrelevantly, "though not as good as mine."

"But how could Parker hope to compete with a Hapsburg in the direct line?" said Lauren sarcastically. "You don't think he killed Russell?"

They agreed that it was not out of the question. After all, Parker did go running by the river at night. It was also possible that he was jealous of Russell's effect on Sandy. And then, of course, he might be in it together with Sandy. High school friendships, twisted or not, could be terribly close.

Sandy was the most obvious person to have murdered Russell on account of love rejected. Lauren did not doubt that Sandy was nasty enough and capable enough for any job. Russell had as much as admitted that Sandy was in love with him when he said, "Perhaps she likes me too much." That would also seem to suggest that her affections were inadequately reciprocated. Sandy's apparent hatred of Lauren could only have been caused by sexual jealousy.

Michael recalled that Sandy had never had a boyfriend at Exeter, "unless we count Parker, and I don't think we do." She had, however, been a perfect student. "And suddenly she falls head over heels for this black man from Atlanta!" exclaimed Michael. "I feel this is somehow a lesson on the perils of repression. This Russell Bernard certainly had a way with you Jewish girls!"

"What do you mean, us Jewish girls?"

"Well, you and Sandy."

"Sandy Grayson is Jewish?!" Lauren was astounded.

"You bet," said Michael.

"But she's such a snob! She acts like she's the Archbishop of Canterbury."

"Whereas, in fact, she's just a Jewish girl from New Jersey who went away to prep school. My mother once met her mother at an Exeter parents' day, and Mrs. Grayson was a dead giveaway. My mother says she felt like she was talking to a delicatessen." Michael was, as usual, delighted by his mother's wit.

Lauren was less delighted, but she was pleased to learn that Sandy was not the great aristocrat she pretended to be. "I don't like Sandy Grayson," said Lauren. "I hope she's our killer. I think a woman could have done it. The murder happened right next to the river, so that even a fairly weak woman could have pushed the body into the water. And I don't think Sandy Grayson is weak in any way."

Michael had an idea. "Maybe Russell had discovered that Sandy was Jewish, and he was threatening to tell everyone at Harvard. How's that for a motive?"

"Then she should have murdered you," said Lauren. "You're a much more notorious gossip than Russell."

"Maybe she was in love with me," said Michael. "And she thought that you and I were more than just friends, so she murdered Russell to get back at you for having me. How's that for another motive?"

Michael was getting carried away, so Lauren turned to the next suspect. She found the picture of Tracy Nicolson in the Register and showed it to Michael. "Aha!" said Michael, "the famous much-divorced freshman! Does she look this

jaded in real life?" How did Tracy manage to have bloodshot
eyes in her high school graduation picture?"

"In real life she doesn't look quite so extreme, but the
voice makes up for the difference. She sounds like she's spent
the last four years of her life in a motel bar instead of in high
school getting straight A's."

"Do you think she learned how to kill a man somewhere
along the way?"

"Could be," said Lauren. "What I have to find out is
what happened between her and Russell. But, you know, she
seems so unsentimental that I have trouble believing she
would murder him for love. I mean, some of us are still high
school seniors in spirit, even those of us who aren't virgins.
We have crushes, go on dates, get kissed goodnight, that sort
of thing. But Tracy gives the impression of being way beyond
that stage: Tracy probably gets named in adultery suits."

"Maybe," said Michael. "Depends on whether you really
believe in her image. And whether *she* really believes in it.
It's possible that it's all for show, and when she's alone she
writes sonnets to Cupid. Think what it would be like then to
go to bed with Russell Bernard, fall in love with him, but
have him thinking of you as the woman whose high school
graduation picture looks like it was snapped outside the
divorce court. What do you do then when you start to lose
the man to someone supposedly more fresh-faced?"

Lauren attempted a Shirley Temple smile. "I see what
you mean. We'll keep her on the list. And I suppose we
should bear in mind that she could have killed him for love,
but she could also have killed him for some more hard-nosed
reason which we don't know about."

"Like what?"

"I always think of her as a Chicago gangster type. Maybe
it was something to do with bootlegging." Even Lauren could
not keep from joking now. She knew that it was the extreme
seriousness of the project that compelled her and Michael to
take refuge in humor, however inappropriate. But Lauren
was stunned by what Michael said next.

"How about Madam Professor?"

Lauren had not even considered Professor Baranova,
who seemed too exalted, in manner as well as in station, to
be involved in what Lauren had been looking at as a freshman tangle. Yet Professor Baranova had also heard the Rasputin
presentation, and there was no telling what she had felt about

Russell Bernard. Clearly she had liked him. Russell had never received any of the cool treatment that Lauren, for instance, sometimes felt coming her way from Professor Baranova. But then again Russell, unlike Lauren, had always done all the assigned reading and had interesting comments to offer. Was Tatiana Baranova's fondness for him more than academic? Russell Bernard certainly looked good next to Max Kohler. One thing was certain: it would be difficult to investigate Professor Baranova. The freshman class was full of indiscreet interconnections which would help Lauren and Michael pursue their detective research. But the faculty was a world unto itself.

Then there was Katherine Butler. On the one hand, she was married, so she was perhaps less likely to be involved in freshman romantic tangles. On the other hand, the marriage of a Harvard freshman to a black South African guerrilla leader was sufficiently unconventional to make the complications surrounding a murder seem ordinary by comparison. Who could say what Katherine Butler had thought of Russell Bernard? And, as Michael pointed out, if she was married to a guerrilla leader and had spent a summer working with him in South Africa, then Katherine Butler was the one member of the seminar who was certain to have some firsthand experience of violent death.

Finally, there was Melissa Wu. Lauren thought it was inconceivable that Melissa Wu would cross Harvard Square against the light, let alone murder someone alongside the river. But what if, Michael wondered, Melissa thought that Russell deserved to die, that for some reason Girl Scout honor required his death? How much, after all, did Lauren and Michael really know about Russell Bernard? That too they would have to explore. Melissa or anyone else might have been convinced that Russell was a scoundrel or a sinner, that his murder would be an act of civic responsibility. It was Melissa who had provided the whole Rasputin motif. For all her manifest goodness, she was at the very center of the murder mystery.

"The more I think about it," said Lauren, "the more the Rasputin pattern fits. It would be such an improbable sort of murder otherwise, with all those weapons. Only a person who had been in the seminar that afternoon would have felt compelled to murder someone that way."

"You've just about convinced me," said Michael. "But I'm your best friend. If we want to convince anyone else we'll have to find out lots more."

"Thank you for understanding," said Lauren, and she kissed him on the cheek. "You know, Rasputin fits in another way too. Rasputin was dangerous because of his charismatic power over the Tsarina. Russell had that kind of power too. People couldn't help being drawn to him. He seemed so strong and so brilliant and so. . . . What is there to say? It was magic. But that kind of power can make a man dangerous. I wonder if Russell was dangerous. I wonder if he was a threat to somebody in particular. I wonder if that's why he was murdered. What is it, Michael? What are you thinking about?"

Michael was dreaming with his eyes wide open. There was a smile on his face.

"I was just thinking about Rasputin's murderers. Do you know anything about them?"

"Weren't they young aristocrats?"

"Yes," said Michael. "Actually I was thinking about one of them in particular, their leader. His name was Prince Yusupov. He was one of the most fabulously wealthy young princes in the Russian Empire. He was married, I think, but he preferred to sleep with boys. Prince Yusupov was wild and extravagant and terribly decadent. And I once saw a picture of him."

"What did he look like?"

"Oh Lauren," said Michael soulfully, "he was unbearably beautiful."

4. The boy from Richmond

Lauren's detective career really began on her second Saturday night date with Scott Duchaine. She had called earlier to tell him that she didn't think she felt up to seeing *Psycho*. Perhaps they could do something else? He had agreed without asking any questions, agreed so readily that Lauren wondered if Scott was also relieved not to have to see *Psycho*. And she wondered why he would feel relieved. They agreed to go instead to the Harvard-Radcliffe orchestra concert in Sanders Theatre.

As Lauren waited for him in her room, she became more and more nervous. At first she thought she was just unsettled by the detective investigation that she was about to undertake. She tried to steel herself and only gradually realized that she was frightened of something quite different. Lauren was terrified that Scott would not show up. She remembered vividly what it had felt like to wait for Russell on Thursday night and she became more and more certain that Scott too would stand her up, that he too would turn out to be dead, murdered. It was no good trying to remind herself that Scott was actually one of the suspects, one of the most promising suspects—not a likely victim. The only thing that would really convince Lauren that Scott was alive would be his arrival, and fortunately Scott arrived exactly on time. Scott would not have been capable of keeping a lady waiting.

Scott in person seemed equally unlikely as victim or murderer. He was wearing a white shirt and a corduroy jacket the same color as his short, neatly combed chestnut hair. He was undeniably handsome, and Lauren was pleased to have dressed nicely so that they would make a good couple. Now she pretended to be not quite ready to go, partially for the sake of flirtation and partially to gain a few moments to compose herself. She left Scott in the living room with the life-size blowup of Baby Doll, while she took a last look at herself in the mirror in her bedroom. "Good luck," she said to herself. "Be brave."

The concert was to begin with a Mozart symphony. Lauren hoped that the student orchestra would not be too obviously amateurish and that she would be able to relax. Still, she reminded herself, this was not a pleasure outing. If it turned out that she was not in the mood for Mozart, she could always think about strategy. Somehow she was going to have to lead Scott onto some touchy subjects.

Lauren loved Sanders Theatre, though not enough to be willing to join the eight hundred students in the introductory economics course which met there three times a week. Lauren and Scott sat in the balcony on the old-fashioned wooden benches, and Scott talked about the course, which he was taking but not enjoying. Despite a few strong lectures from John Kenneth Galbraith, Scott was finding the subject dull. He envied Lauren her good sense in avoiding the course, no small accomplishment since half of the students in the freshman class wound up taking the course if only because they felt they really ought to know something about the subject.

Lauren was aware that she and Scott were making polite freshman conversation about courses and professors. They were not, however, discussing Professor Baranova and the freshman seminar and the murder of Russell Bernard. Lauren had the feeling that Scott was shying away from the subject, that he too was conscious of what was not being discussed. Just as the lights were going down, Lauren glanced at her program where the members of the orchestra were listed. She could barely catch her breath when she saw Russell Bernard's name among the violins. The orchestra had not had time to change the printed program.

Russell's name on the program had an uncanny effect on Lauren. It was as though he were back from the dead, supernaturally surviving the murder when even Rasputin had ultimately succumbed. The symphony began and Lauren could not keep from scanning the orchestra. Everyone in the string section was white or oriental. There was not even an empty chair. Why should there be? Lauren listened to the

Mozart and realized that Russell must have rehearsed this music over and over, ready to play in the Saturday night concert. Lauren found herself oddly saddened at the thought of Russell rehearsing the piece he would never perform. It was, of course, only the tiniest fragment of the tragedy of Russell's death at the age of eighteen, but Lauren found the larger tragedy almost too overwhelming to think about. It was easier to be moved by the smaller details.

Lauren wondered: if Russell had not been murdered, would she have come to the concert with Scott and stared at Russell playing in the orchestra? No, of course not: if Russell had not been murdered, she and Scott would be watching *Psycho* at this very moment in the Dunster House dining hall. Lauren glanced at Scott out of the corner of her eye. He too was watching the orchestra. The performance of the Mozart was unexpectedly nice. Lauren wondered if Scott had noticed Russell's name on the program. She also wondered if the southern boy sitting next to her could possibly have murdered Russell Bernard.

After the concert Lauren suggested that they go out for a drink. She hoped that a few drinks would relax her and help her to pursue her investigation. She also hoped that even the most well-bred southern gentleman could be put a little off his guard with the assistance of liquor. They went to the bar at the Sheraton-Commander Hotel on Garden Street, along the outer edge of the Cambridge Common. The Common, like the river a dangerous place at night, seemed particularly forbidding. From Garden Street it was impossible to discern what might be lurking in the dark center. Lauren had chosen the Sheraton-Commander because it would have none of the raucousness of a less stuffy Cambridge bar. It would also have hardly any students, and Lauren preferred not to run into people she knew. This conversation would be between her and Scott.

The plan turned out to be a good one. After his first bourbon and water Scott began to unwind. He sat a little less straight in his seat, and his drawl became even more marked. His usual style of polite conversation began to give way, sometimes to genuine liveliness, sometimes to a mood which was almost melancholy. Scott Duchaine began to talk about himself. Soon he was telling Lauren the story of his life.

He had grown up in Richmond, in a grand house that had no street address, only a name—Elms' Glory. Lauren found this terribly exotic. She was reminded of *Gone with the Wind*, the book she always claimed was her absolute favorite when she was in the company of more pretentious Harvard students devoted to Proust or Joyce. Scott made a wry face. Naturally his own background did not seem particularly exotic to him, and he had been brought up to regard *Gone with the Wind* as trashy.

The men in Scott's family traditionally became lawyers or politicians or both. On his mother's side he was descended from several governors of Virginia. Both of his older brothers were already in law school, and Scott was expected to follow suit. He was breaking with family tradition by attending Harvard instead of Princeton; no further deviation would be peacefully tolerated. Scott confessed to Lauren that he did not want to study law, that he found politics unappealing. Lauren, who could barely conceive of leading one's life according to other people's unpleasant expectations, asked Scott, "What *do* you want to do then? What do you like to do best?" And Scott, who seemed to have never quite come up against those questions before, could only say that he guessed he didn't know.

Then he offered hesitantly, "I do kind of like studying European history. I really do like that seminar on the Russian Revolution." For a moment Lauren thought that they were approaching the crucial subject, but Scott had something else on his mind. He wanted to tell Lauren about his European history teacher in high school.

Scott had attended an Episcopalian boys' prep school, St. Christopher's; all Richmond boys of Scott's social class went to St. Christopher's. Scott had been a day student, living at home at Elms' Glory. Lauren had hated her own public high school in New Jersey, and she was always a little put off by Michael's rhapsodies about Exeter. Scott's attitude toward St. Christopher's lay somewhere between the two extremes. On the one hand he remembered being happy there; on the other hand he looked back on the school critically. "The boys weren't very interesting," said Scott. "I don't think you would have especially liked them."

"I like you," said Lauren.

"Do you really?" Scott seemed dubious. "I don't think

I'm all that interesting. Or at least I always think that what people see of me is pretty dull."

Lauren wondered if he was hinting at the existence of some sort of secret life. Or was she seeing the secret inner life now? Or did the secret life involve murdering black men by the river at night? That would be a rather interesting extracurricular activity. Surely not everyone at St. Christopher's did that. "I don't think you're at all dull," said Lauren, uncertain as to whether she was being entirely honest with him or even with herself.

"I wonder whether you really think I'm interesting or whether you just find me exotic, as you say, because I remind you of *Gone with the Wind*." This was so close to the mark that Lauren could think of nothing to say in response. Fortunately Scott continued. "You would have liked this European history teacher I had junior year."

"Why would I have liked him?"

"Because he was so good-looking." Scott grinned. He was teasing Lauren. She had never heard him venture such a flirtatious remark.

Scott's European history teacher had only taught at St. Christopher's for one year. He had not worked out at St. Christopher's; he had not been the right sort. The mistake of hiring him in the first place had been rectified after a year by letting him go. He was a young man, just out of college. He had taught European history with great enthusiasm, which made him on the whole less respected by his students, who had been brought up to be wary of enthusiasms. He had occasionally been reprimanded by the headmaster for his slightly eccentric dress; once he had been so bold as to wear blue jeans with the required jacket and tie. Some parents had even complained that he had not presented a sufficiently unsympathetic picture of European socialism.

Scott Duchaine never wore blue jeans and he considered himself a political conservative. Yet he had been one of the very few students at St. Christopher's who had genuinely liked the European history teacher. The teacher, not unaware of this, had befriended Scott to the limited extent that this was possible at the school; he and Scott sometimes talked about European history for five minutes after class. He had also urged Scott to apply to Harvard (his own alma mater) and thus concretely influenced Scott's life. Scott had regretted the teacher's leaving, and still remembered him fondly.

The teacher had not been the right sort for St. Christopher's, because he was an irredeemable Yankee and, worse, a Jew. (Scott brought out the word Jew only very hesitantly in front of Lauren.) Scott's parents had not been pleased to hear Scott dissent from the general disapproval, and they later blamed the teacher (rightly) for Scott's going to Harvard instead of Princeton. However, when Scott insisted on Harvard, his parents gave way. Before he left for Cambridge in September, his father had warned him that at Harvard he would encounter blacks and Jews. (Actually, Scott's father had used instead of "blacks" a different word which Scott would not repeat in front of Lauren. Lauren gathered that Mr. Duchaine considered "Jews" an adequately derogatory term in itself.) Mr. Duchaine had advised his son to avoid both categories, and, with an air of don't-say-I-didn't-warn-you, insisted that both minorities would have been more appropriately underrepresented at Princeton.

"And look at you now," said Lauren. "Two months at Harvard and you're already dating a Jew. Your father would have a fit. Who knows, after a few more months you may be going out with—"

But Scott didn't let her finish. He called for two more bourbons, and sat up a little straighter. Perhaps he was afraid of the direction of the conversation, though he himself had started it. Lauren hadn't pried, though heaven knows she would have been willing to. Instead, she had merely listened sympathetically. She thought it was a point in Scott's favor that he was able to tell her so frankly about the family prejudices that were expected of him. She was not, however, naive enough to assume that Scott's frankness implied that he himself was free of those same prejudices. For one delicious moment, sitting in the bar surrounded by anonymous well-dressed adults, Lauren was able to forget that she was in Cambridge, Massachusetts, in the twentieth century and to feel that she and Scott were a scandalous pair: gentleman and Jewess. She almost giggled aloud.

Scott drank deeply, and in a moment half of his bourbon was gone. He looked at Lauren and smiled. "I like you," he said. "I liked that European history teacher. I guess I like Jews. My father wouldn't think very well of that."

"Do you like blacks?" asked Lauren, trying to keep the tone conversational.

Scott looked at her oddly. "No," he said. "I mean I guess I don't know any." He thought for a moment. "We have black servants at Elms' Glory and I like them. But I don't think that's really what you mean, is it?"

"No," said Lauren.

"What *do* you mean?"

"I guess I was wondering how much of a subversive you are, whether you go all the way or draw the line after Jews."

"Would that be such a terrible place to draw the line?" said Scott. "I guess I'm not much of a subversive." He was clearly disturbed by the conversation.

Lauren pushed on. "Are you a racist?"

"Maybe I am," said Scott. "I know that to you that sounds like a terrible thing to admit. In my family we take for granted that a black man isn't going to be as good as a white man. Even if I could convince myself that that was entirely false, I'd have to be pretty unnatural not to go on believing in it deep down. My background is, after all, what I am, isn't it?"

After a relaxed beginning the atmosphere between them was now so tense that Lauren could hardly believe that the conversation was entirely theoretical. Scott clearly had something on his mind which he was trying to talk his way around, trying to justify. Lauren decided to take the plunge and leave the realm of generalities behind. What would happen to this theoretical conversation if Lauren injected into it some names, one name in particular? She took a deep breath and said, "Did you know Russell Bernard?"

Scott's eyes told her that the question had hit a mark. But what sort of mark? Had she found Russell's murderer? "No," said Scott confusedly. "I didn't know him. Why should I know him?"

"Well," said Lauren, "you and Russell were in the same freshman seminar. I know. I was there too. So you must have known him a little bit."

"Only because he was in the seminar," said Scott. "I wouldn't call that knowing a person. I guess I know what he looked like, and what his voice sounded like, and maybe I could make some sort of judgment about whether he was smart or stupid. But I couldn't say that I knew him."

"Smart or stupid?" asked Lauren.

"Smart," Scott admitted a little grudgingly.

"I think so too," said Lauren. She pushed on. "Did you like him?"

"No," said Scott almost angrily. "I've told you I didn't

know him so how could I like him? Why are you asking me about this?"

Lauren wondered whether he had guessed why she was asking. She wasn't managing to be very subtle, but that was partly because he was reacting so strongly. "I think it's possible to like someone you don't know. I also think it's possible to dislike someone you don't know." Scott was looking at his glass. "For instance, I like your European history teacher." Scott smiled at his glass. Lauren continued hesitantly, "And I don't like your father."

Scott nodded without looking up. "I think I agree with you."

"I didn't know Russell very well either," said Lauren. "But I liked him a lot."

"Did you really?"

"Yes. A lot. I was supposed to go out with him Thursday night. I waited for him at Pamplona for an hour and I thought he was standing me up. But, of course, he had been murdered the night before."

"I suppose that excuses the gentleman." Scott had regained his ironic drawl. It was impossible to tell whether or not he was surprised to hear about Lauren's date with Russell.

"Yes. I suppose it does. I think he was an extraordinary person. I talked with him in the Yard Wednesday after the seminar, probably a few hours before he was murdered. He told me a little about Dora Carpenter—you know, that girl who died from the contaminated cocaine—and I asked if he was in love with her."

"What did he say?" Scott was moved now, not ironic.

"He said he didn't know."

"Oh."

"I remember that after talking to him I went to dinner, and then to the library for a few hours. It's so strange to think that while I was studying he was being murdered. Can you remember what you were doing that night?" Lauren wondered whether her object was completely transparent. Surely there had to be a more graceful way to elicit alibis from suspects.

Scott didn't even have to think about his answer. "I was in my room. Reading."

"That's even more frightening, to have been alone in your room while someone was being murdered by the river. Or was your roommate there?"

"No."

In other words, it was going to be virtually impossible to ascertain Scott's whereabouts on Wednesday night. Lauren decided to give up on that line and try to pursue something else. "Who do you think murdered him?" she asked. "Why would anyone have wanted to kill him?"

Scott was sad now. "It sounds to me like you care a lot about that boy."

Lauren resisted the knee-jerk impulse to say "don't call him boy." Instead she said, "Maybe I do. Does that surprise you?"

"No." Scott maintained a perfectly blank face.

"Oh, did you know?" That was a little too eager, Lauren thought.

"No," said Scott. Was he lying? "It's just that I'm not entirely surprised. Would you prefer that I were shocked?" He paused, and then he mouthed two words so softly that afterwards Lauren wasn't sure he had actually spoken them. "Or jealous?"

Now Scott looked Lauren straight in the eye, and he spoke with fierce conviction. "You want to know why anyone would have wanted to kill that boy? Maybe I can tell you. You think you liked him, but I don't think you knew him any better than I did." That, Lauren reflected, was probably true. "So when it comes to deciding what kind of person he was, it's really just your gut reaction against mine, or maybe your upbringing against mine. Well, I didn't know him, but I didn't like him. I know he was smart and successful and good-looking, and I still didn't like him. Maybe he was so smart and so successful and so good-looking that he thought he could do anything at all. Where I come from they'd call a boy like that a—" He caught himself. "Maybe I won't tell you what they'd call him. If I did, you would just think I was a racist, and you wouldn't even listen to what I'm saying. I'll put it in nice Harvard language. You know how the hero in ancient Greek drama is defeated by his own tragic flaw? And you know what that flaw is: it's hubris." How odd, Lauren thought, to hear the word drawled. "Well maybe that boy had too much hubris. Maybe that's why somebody wanted to kill him. And maybe he had it coming to him."

Lauren did not know what to make of Scott's frankness. He admitted that he had disliked Russell, but did that make him a more or less likely murder suspect? Listening to Scott's speech about hubris, Lauren could almost have believed him capable of killing Russell. But that he was capable of the murder did not mean that he had committed it. Lauren liked him less but found him more interesting. She was already drawing some conclusions about detective work: murder is not a dull crime, and therefore the suspects become more intriguing as they become more suspect. When Scott invited Lauren to come back to his room with him to continue the conversation, she readily accepted.

She accepted despite her suspicions that Scott was a murderer, and despite the likelihood that Scott had divined her suspicions. He lived, after all, in Matthews Hall with a hundred other students. If worse came to worst, Lauren could always scream. But the possibility of murder was only in the back of Lauren's mind. Of more immediate importance to her were the other implications of returning to Scott's room with him. Lauren knew that accompanying a young man back to his room was a significant gesture, but living in an age when the rules of the game were in flux, Lauren was not entirely sure what the gesture signified. She had no idea how Scott would interpret it. After all, everything they had said that evening only went to prove how alien his culture was to hers. He was exotic and therefore unpredictable. True, he had been quite timid on their last date, but that was no reason to assume that he was going to be Ashley Wilkes through and through.

"And what about you, Scarlett?" she asked herself. "What are you looking for? Are you setting yourself up for a big seduction scene?" How could she know Scott's mind when she didn't even know her own? She had no idea how far she wanted things to go and so she decided to wait and see, aware that this was a cowardly, evasive decision, which could only lead her into trouble.

They reached Scott's dorm after midnight, and his roommate was out. Scott's own little room was neat but the walls were bare. Lauren knew that this was often a problem in boys' dormitory rooms. Boys seemed to be unaware that a room should be decorated, that it should be made into an appealing place. Michael, with his Beardsley prints and china tea set, was a delightful exception. True, Scott lacked a decorative sense, but at least he did not suffer from that most common of male vices: he was not a pig. The room was orderly, and Lauren was grateful for that. She wondered what Russell's room would have looked like.

Lauren perched herself on the bare top of Scott's desk. Harvard desks were sturdy and large and wooden. Scott remained standing rather than sit on the bed. Perhaps he was afraid of making Lauren uncomfortable. Now, after the intensity of their discussion at the Sheraton-Commander, it was hard to rediscover a relaxed level of trivial conversation. For a while, Scott even talked about the weather, Cambridge cold and rain, Richmond sun. Lauren thought to herself, "What would he think if he knew that I wasn't a virgin?" And then she wondered with even greater interest, "Is he a virgin?" This question suddenly seemed so important that she had to guard herself lest, under the influence of bourbon, she should carelessly ask him by mistake.

Scott gazed into Lauren's eyes. Fortunately, he could not read her mind, but, alas, neither could she read his. She reminded herself that there was a faint theoretical possibility that Scott would try to kill her. However, she thought it much more likely that he would kiss her, and that is in fact what he did. "I like you a lot," he said, moving to stand next to the desk and bending his head to meet hers. It was, Lauren thought, an exceptionally gentle kiss, and she liked that. She was not fond of boys whose idea of a romantic embrace involved leaning over and sticking a tongue into her throat. Scott was certainly not a pig. She could smell his cologne and judge for herself that he had shaved right before going out to meet her. And yet, as the kiss was prolonged, Lauren began to feel that he might be too gentle. She could almost suspect that his heart was not in his kiss.

She put a hand behind his head, in his smooth short hair, and pressed, trying to bring a little more passion into the embrace. Feeling herself in control, Lauren became bolder and timidly Scott responded. When they had been kissing for ten minutes, Lauren began to feel that all Scott really needed was a little bit of encouragement. He was shy, but naturally romantic. Lauren lowered her hands from his face, and undid two of the buttons of his white shirt. Gently she placed one of her hands on his chest, which was smooth and hairless and oddly cold, even trembling. Lauren looked up and saw panic in Scott's eyes. He stepped back. "Excuse me," he said, and he hastily left the room.

Lauren was completely taken aback and no little bit offended. She supposed that he had gone to the bathroom, but still it was very odd, his breaking away like that so abruptly. He was an odd boy, Scott Duchaine. Had her gesture somehow seemed too sexually aggressive? Was he that much of a gentleman? Was he a virgin? Was he in love with Lauren? Was the romantic interlude over? Lauren decided that it was, regardless of Scott's intentions. She decided that when he returned to the room, she would make her excuses and go home.

Lauren was alone, waiting for Scott's return. She looked at the bookshelves where Scott kept not only the books for his Harvard courses but also his books from St. Christopher's. There were Latin texts and English poetry, and Lauren also noticed a number of books on European history. That, Lauren knew, was one of the differences between preppies and public school types like herself. During her four years in high school, Lauren had been issued in each course a textbook which belonged to the school. In the front were the signatures of the students who had used the book for the last five years, and Lauren had added her signature to the list. One of the most exciting things about Harvard was buying her own books for each course, writing her name on the crisp, new flaps, and putting the books on her shelf. But preppies like Michael and Scott had already been doing this for years.

Lauren passed over these not very exciting clues to Scott's high school career and reached for a book she could have found just as easily on her own shelf: the Harvard Freshman Register, also known as the Facebook. It was a red hard-cover album and on each page were sixteen black-and-white pictures labeled with names, addresses, high schools, and anticipated majors. Together the pages covered the entire freshman class, and every freshman owned a copy. Lauren herself was obsessed with the book, and she and Michael spent endless hours turning its pages, discussing the people they knew and speculating about those they didn't.

Scott's Register seemed rather less worn than Lauren's. Clearly he did not share her voyeuristic obsession. She turned immediately to her own picture, which appeared on the very first page: Lauren Adler. Since it was Scott's book, she tried to imagine how Scott saw her picture when, if ever, he thumbed through the Register. Lauren was pleased by her photo. It was not only flattering but also the right mood. Before sending in the snapshot she had wavered between a very artistic photograph of herself gazing into the distance, and a friendlier, less aloof picture. She had finally chosen the latter and never regretted it, since she could now laugh at those who had sent in pretentious, artistic photographs.

Lauren decided that it would be best not to be staring at her own picture when Scott returned to the room, so she began turning the pages. She only had to turn a few pages to reach the B's, and instinctively she sought the page with Russell Bernard's picture. She had turned to that page many many times. She found it now and was instantly terrified. There was a neat rectangular hole in the page. Russell Bernard's picture had been carefully razored out of the book.

5. Preppies

Sunday morning Michael and Lauren went to brunch together to discuss the progress of their investigation. They were both aware that it would be unwise to talk about such things where other Harvard students might possibly overhear. Either they would have to speak quietly with the utmost care and discretion (a habit which neither of them had ever cultivated) or else they would have to rule out all the Harvard dining halls. With great enthusiasm they adopted the latter course.

At Sunday brunch, after all, the Harvard Food Service generally lived up to its dreadful reputation. Michael hated most the "eggs Benedict," served on stale muffins in a hollandaise sauce with the consistency of Vaseline. Lauren, however, awarded top honors to the hash browned potatoes, which were soaked in oil, momentarily singed, and then served greasy and raw. Some Harvard students felt uncomfortable about spending money for meals out when they (or their parents) had already paid for all the bad food they could eat. Michael and Lauren were among those who had quickly learned to eat out without guilt.

Now they decided to go to Hemispheres, where it was possible to get a table on the roof and order all sorts of sweet crepes. But neither Lauren nor Michael was hardy enough for the November air, and so they selected an indoor table. Lauren ordered a blueberry crepe, while Michael's was to be chocolate and rum. They got down to business.

"Why didn't you ask Scott why Russell's picture was cut out of the Facebook?"

"Because I'm stupid," said Lauren, "and because I was

scared out of my mind. I mean, you can't imagine what a creepy thing that was to come across. I just slammed the book shut, and then Scott came back in so I had no time to think. I just said something about how late it was and I practically ran out the door. He probably thought I was crazy."

"Unless he's as crazy as we're starting to suspect. Your behavior might have seemed perfectly normal—to a mad murderer."

"Thanks a lot. I was scared to show him the place where the picture was missing. I was afraid he would suddenly begin to go insane around the eyes and scream 'Aha, so you found me out' and then ... I think I had a nightmare about that last night."

"Why do you think he cut out the picture?"

"I have to confess," said Lauren, "my first reaction seems incredibly silly. While I was running home to my dorm I kept thinking that it must have something to do with some kind of voodoo black magic. You know, the kind of magic where you need a picture of the victim and you stick pins in it or put spells on it. I know that's a stupid thing to think. And I know that in a way it was connected to Russell's being black: that's what made me think of voodoo. It was the first thing that came into my mind. And then I thought about how Russell's murder was almost ritualistic, a sort of execution with all those weapons. And it seemed to fit together. Maybe I'm the lunatic."

"Well," said Michael hesitantly, "it does seem like the missing picture ought to be connected to the murder somehow. But it wouldn't have to be voodoo. And it wouldn't even have to be Scott. What if somebody had hired a professional killer to murder Russell Bernard? The killer would have to be provided with a picture to identify the victim. That's the first thing I thought of when you told me about the missing picture. And couldn't anyone have cut that picture out of Scott's book, anyone who visited him or his roommate, or even anyone who wandered in when the door was unlocked? It's possible that someone wanted to implicate Scott."

"It's a good idea," Lauren conceded, "but I don't really like it. If Russell was killed by a professional, by someone who didn't know him, then what happens to my Rasputin inspiration? I still think that whoever murdered Russell is in that freshman seminar."

"You think Scott killed him?" Michael asked. There was a silence between them as Lauren swallowed a mouthful of blueberry crepe and washed it down with coffee.

"Yes," she said. "I guess I think so." They were silent again, trying to imagine Scott Duchaine down by the river putting a knife into Russell Bernard. Lauren continued. "There were things that Scott said at the Sheraton-Commander that made me think he could have killed Russell. He so clearly didn't like Russell, and it was more than just your average everyday dislike. And besides, Scott definitely had the murder on his mind. He didn't want to talk about it with me, but at the same time he couldn't stop talking about it. He couldn't bring himself to end the conversation. I mean, I couldn't have forced him to talk about Russell if he'd really been set against it. And then he tells me, 'Maybe he had it coming to him.' Can you imagine saying that about someone who was murdered three days ago? And I don't even feel that Scott is a particularly self-righteous person. He's very straight, but he isn't preachy. It's such a strange thing for him to have said."

"Strange perhaps, but probably not the sort of thing you'd say if you were the murderer. Why point a finger at yourself that way?"

"Maybe he's just too straightforward, too honest. You know, George Washington and the cherry tree. Maybe Scott could stick a knife in someone but still not be able to tell a lie afterward."

Michael began to giggle. "I like that very much. Imagine if instead of chopping down that cherry tree with the axe, George Washington had chopped down his little sister. And then confessed, because of course he couldn't tell a lie. Wouldn't that be a marvelous patriotic legend?"

"Marvelous," said Lauren, "and George Washington and Scott Duchaine are both Virginians, both honest types. But the thing that really makes me believe that Scott's the murderer is the missing picture. I just can't quite fit the facts together yet. But it was such a weird thing, that empty space in the book, and I can't imagine any circumstances strange enough to explain it. I can't believe that the mystery of the picture isn't somehow connected to the mystery of the murder. That's why I think Scott's the murderer. Don't you feel it too?"

"I do," Michael admitted, "especially when I think of

you alone in Scott's room with the mutilated Facebook. But you haven't convinced me that Scott's the one, and I'll tell you why. I was doing some investigation of my own last night, and I uncovered a few juicy tidbits. Scott may have disliked Russell enough to murder him, but on the night of the murder Russell was down by the river with somebody else."

Saturday night, while Lauren and Scott were listening to the orchestra concert at Sanders Theatre, Michael had gone to visit his old schoolmate Parker Hamilton Kendall IV. They had not been particularly close friends at Exeter, but the school tie was enough to justify the impromptu visit. Parker lived in a five-person suite in Weld Hall, but when Michael knocked at the door Parker himself came to answer. Michael was not surprised to find Parker dateless on a Saturday night. Parker was a serious young man, and anyhow Exeter students were not a dating crowd. Michael, it is true, might have been able to rustle up some sort of Saturday night adventure, but now, his imagination captured, he was caught up in the detective game.

("Now Michael," said Lauren, "don't you go ruining your love life just to help me solve the mystery."

"Sacrifices, sacrifices," said Michael petulantly. "I'm new at the game. After I warm up a bit I'm sure I'll acquire your knack for mixing dating and detection."

"Good," said Lauren. "Next time *you* can go out with Scott.")

When Parker answered the door he was wearing his sweat pants and nothing else. He had just come back from his nightly run along the river and he was about to get into the shower. He was pleased to see Michael and promised to take just a quick shower. First he mixed Michael a scotch and soda, while Michael admired the beautifully conditioned muscles of Parker's chest, his perfectly flat, smooth abdomen. It was enough to make Michael dally for a moment with the notion of taking up running, or even, perhaps, taking up Parker. Parker went off to his shower, and Michael sipped the scotch, thinking that Parker was becoming an extremely attractive man. And Parker was ever so much *younger* than Robert Redford!

("Hmmph," said Lauren, "so while I'm out dating frivolously you're working yourself to death on the investigation. I can see that your mind never once strayed from the case. Such singleness of purpose!")

So Michael's mind wandered from one thing to another—it did not occur to him to take advantage of Parker's absence to examine his Freshman Register—and soon Parker emerged from the shower. He had put on corduroys and a sweater, so he and Michael were dressed similarly. The two Exonians settled down to talk about the topic dearest to both their hearts, Exeter. The conversation began on a note of accord since both Parker and Michael were able to agree that Exeter was, by far, a more sophisticated place than Harvard.

("Do I have to hear all about that again?" said Lauren in mock exasperation.

"No, darling, I'll spare you. But it's absolutely true.")

Parker was planning to study classics at Harvard. He was working very hard because he really liked Greek and Latin, and because he did not know of any other way to work. In fact, he had been planning to spend Saturday night with Plato. Parker confided that he missed his Greek teacher at Exeter, whom he sometimes called up to check on a translation when he distrusted his Harvard professor. Parker was perfectly happy to be distracted by Michael, but left to himself he would probably not have gone in search of social activity. Michael, of course, was something of a professional at distracting people from their work, and he played his role with pleasure—especially when the victims were as handsome and well-bred as Parker.

("Don't tell me again," said Lauren. "I already know. His family isn't quite as good as yours. Is that why he's such a grind and you're such a butterfly?"

"It's not exactly that he's a grind. It's just that he's an unliberated Protestant. He hasn't yet realized that it's possible to do anything besides work hard at whatever he's supposed to be working at. I think he's actually quite happy.")

Parker and Michael discussed the quality of academics at Harvard and Exeter and agreed that Exeter provided by far the more rigorous program of study. Next they compared Harvard students and Exeter students and agreed that the latter were more interesting and more intelligent. It was in the course of this conversation that Parker said, "Aren't you friends with one of the girls in my freshman seminar, Lauren Adler?"

"Yes," said Michael. "She's wonderful. I simply adore her."

"Oh," said Parker.

"Oh what?" said Michael. "Don't you like her?" Parker's feelings about Lauren could after all be very important for the mystery. Could he be in love with her?

"Oh yes," said Parker quickly. "I do like her. But..."

"But what?"

"Well, I don't think Sandy Grayson likes her very much."

("That bitch!" Lauren shrieked. "Saying nasty things about me to Parker Hamilton Kendall IV. I hope you told him I was more wonderful than any woman who ever went to Exeter."

"I said you were wonderful."

"Say it now."

"Say what?"

"Say 'Lauren Adler is more wonderful than any woman who ever went to Exeter.'"

"Oh, come on."

"Say it!" Lauren insisted.

"Oh, have it your own way, darling: Lauren Adler is more wonderful than any woman who ever went to Exeter. There, I said it.")

Michael asked Parker why Sandy didn't like Lauren, but Parker looked nervous and said he really didn't know. So Michael changed his slant a little and asked how Parker and Sandy were getting along. Were they still just as good friends as they had been at Exeter? Oh yes, Parker insisted that they were. "You've never been lovers, have you?" said Michael, trying to sound casual but knowing that it was not the kind of question that Parker could deal with.

Sure enough, Parker turned very red, and he finally managed to say "No." But was he lying?

Casually again Michael inquired whether Sandy Grayson had a boyfriend at Harvard, and Parker said no she hadn't. Michael asked if there were any young men Sandy especially liked, and Parker, even redder than before, said that he didn't know. For a moment, Russell Bernard seemed to be present in the room. "How about you, Parker?" Michael went on. "Have you fallen in love since coming to Harvard?"

Oddly enough, Parker seemed almost relieved to be no longer discussing Sandy. His coloring became milder, a simple pink blush. At the same time, a faint smile began to appear. "Yes," Parker said. "I believe I have." But no matter how much Michael teased him, Parker refused to say with whom he had fallen in love.

("Do you think he's in love with me?" asked Lauren,

pleasantly astounded. "Do you think he could have killed Russell for love of me?"

"Perhaps. But perhaps that was just Parker's way of saying that he had finally fallen in love with Sandy after all these years. He might have killed Russell for love of her."

"Or it could be someone else entirely."

"Or even no one at all. Parker could have been teasing me, taking revenge for all those personal questions."

Lauren thought for a moment, swept back her hair dramatically with her hand, and said, "I hope it's me.")

Michael then eased up before moving in for the kill. He asked about Parker's courses, and Parker was clearly grateful to be discussing academics and not people. Then Michael asked about Tatiana Baranova's freshman seminar. Parker thought it was a fine seminar. There were, he thought, some intelligent students, and Professor Baranova was especially skillful at eliciting and guiding a good discussion. "How about that young man who was killed?" said Michael. "Russell Bernard. What did you think of him?"

("Lauren, it was just like the way you described Scott's reaction to the name. It was like I'd exploded a bomb. Parker looked like he wanted to run away."

"My God," said Lauren, "but Parker and Scott can't both have murdered Russell. Maybe everybody at Harvard is shocked at the mention of Russell's name. Maybe the murder had some enormous impact on the university that we are only beginning to suspect. And we, the detectives, are the only cool and callous ones."

"Wait," said Michael. "Let me finish. Then you won't think that Parker Hamilton Kendall IV is just reacting as Mr. Average Harvard Student. Listen.")

Watching the distraught expression on Parker's face, Michael had a sudden inspiration. "You were running down by the river the night that Russell Bernard was murdered, weren't you?" Parker's face showed that the guess was on target. Michael should have guessed sooner. Parker went running at night by the river, and Parker was the sort of disciplined person who would be unlikely to miss an evening. Even now, three days after the murder, Parker still went for his run. Michael knew that he had stumbled on something very important, but he also knew that the most difficult part was yet to come. Somehow he would now have to try to find out just what Parker had seen—or had done.

"How did you know?" said Parker, thus admitting the truth of what Michael had suggested. Parker was clearly unnerved.

Michael was on the point of saying that it really wasn't a very difficult syllogism: Parker went running by the river every night, and so therefore he must have been running by the river Wednesday night. Perhaps Parker could not see himself as such a predictable animal. At any rate, Michael realized that to admit to a lucky guess might bring the conversation to a dead end. Parker would then be free to lie however he pleased about what had happened Wednesday night. Michael had a better idea: if Parker was going to lie, he could at least be forced to lie much more cautiously. "I saw you there," said Michael. "I was walking by the river myself on Wednesday night. I was on the other side of the highway, away from the river, but I saw you across the road."

Michael was proud of inventing this fiction on the spot. Now Parker could not be sure of just how much Michael had seen. But, as he spoke the words, Michael was also aware that he was taking a dangerous risk. The murderer, whoever he or she might be, would also wonder what Michael had seen, and the murderer might not be willing to take any chances. Michael might be putting himself in danger.

Parker said, "I went running Wednesday night just like every other night. After the freshman seminar I went to dinner, and then I read Plato in my room for an hour. I usually go out running as a break from studying. There was nothing special about Wednesday night. I didn't find out until the next night that Russell Bernard had been murdered. Although Wednesday night actually seemed a little scarier than usual. Isn't that odd? Generally I don't worry about running by the river. Nobody's ever given me any trouble, and I always figure that if anyone does, I can always outrun him. But Wednesday night I was frightened for no good reason. You see, we had just been talking about Rasputin in the freshman seminar, and a girl, Melissa Wu, had described his murder. You know, the story ends with Rasputin's body in the river Neva. And the way she told the story really affected me. It was genuinely frightening."

("You see, you see," said Lauren excitedly. "The Rasputin thing wasn't just in my imagination. It was in everyone's imagination. Someone in the seminar killed Russell."

"You may be right," said Michael. "Parker, after all, does not seem to have particularly sensitive sensibilities. If the Rasputin story got to him, then it probably got to everyone, and to one other person in particular. Listen to what comes next.")

"So I was running Wednesday night," Parker continued, "and I was thinking about Rasputin. I ran on the riverbank for about a mile in the direction of M.I.T. and then I turned around and ran back to Harvard." He stopped talking, thinking about what to say next.

Michael helped him along with another inspired guess: "And you saw someone you knew."

"Yes," Parker admitted quickly. He was embarrassed and evidently wondering just how much Michael had seen. "She was walking up the bank from the water's edge and she was walking alone. So of course I stopped running to walk with her."

"Yes, she shouldn't have been down by the river alone," said Michael, pretending to know exactly who 'she' was. "What on earth was she doing there?"

"I don't know," said Parker, probably lying. He was fidgeting with the sleeve of his sweater. A piece of navy blue wool had come loose, and Parker was tugging at it nervously. And then he thought of something. Was it something he remembered, or something he had just invented? Parker said, "When she and I were walking back to Harvard Yard from the river that night, we heard something that sounded like a shot. I remember it, because, as I told you, I was a little frightened to begin with and so the shot really startled me."

(Michael and Lauren could both see how devious this might be. The shot, if there actually was a shot, would surely have been the one that was fired into Russell Bernard's heart. If Parker and his mysterious female companion could both claim to have heard that shot while walking back from the river, then they would both have alibis for the time of the murder. Had they honestly heard the shot, or did they concoct the alibi together? Or had Parker invented it on the spur of the moment? As Lauren pointed out, there was still another possibility. The night is full of noises, and some of them could resemble the explosion of a gun. For instance, there were sure to have been irregular highway noises from Memorial Drive, which followed the river. If two people were walking together, one of them could easily say, "Wasn't that a shot?" And the other person, especially if he was in a suggestible mood, would later remember that they had both heard a shot. So one person, the murderer, could have created an alibi for two. Oh yes, it might be very devious indeed.)

Parker continued, maybe too hastily. "Of course we didn't know that someone was murdered that night. We didn't hear about that until the next evening, Thursday evening. That's when the rumors began to spread."

"What did you think then?" Michael asked. "When you heard that there had been a murder?"

"Well, I was very disturbed. I called her up immediately, and we went out for a cup of coffee."

("Aha!" Lauren exclaimed. "So the unidentified female is indeed the delightful Sandy Grayson. And that's what she and Parker were talking about when I saw them at the Cafe Pamplona Thursday night."

"Bingo," said Michael.)

Michael asked another question. "Why did you want to have coffee with her then?"

Parker was flustered again. "I just thought that she and I should talk about it. I thought maybe she might have seen something when she was down by the river."

"And had she seen anything?"

"No. Nothing at all."

Parker's phone rang, and he answered it. He cupped his hand over the receiver and said to Michael, "Excuse me, it's my father. Why don't you pour yourself another scotch and wait. My father and I don't usually talk very long."

But Michael said, "No thank you, I have to go meet someone. Nice visiting with you. See you soon." Michael left the suite of rooms, waving goodbye casually, but as soon as he was outside the door, he raced down the stairs and out into the Yard as fast as he could.

Michael preferred to do no physical exercise whatsoever, but now he ran across Harvard Yard with surprising speed. There was something he had to do, and he had to do it fast. He had to get to Sandy Grayson, and he had to get to her before Parker finished talking to his father, before Parker and Sandy had time to compare notes. Michael doubted that

Parker and his father would have a great deal to say to each other, and he knew that as soon as Parker hung up on his father he would call Sandy. He would tell Sandy about Michael's visit. He would tell Sandy just how much he had told Michael and just how much he had concealed. They would reconfirm their story and decide together what Michael could be allowed to know. It was even possible that Sandy would see more sharply than Parker, would see through the lie of Michael's presence at the river on Wednesday night. Then there would be no hope of eliciting anything further from Parker or Sandy.

Michael paused for a moment to catch his breath outside Sandy's door. She lived in Hollis Hall, one of the oldest Harvard dormitories. Michael noted with satisfaction that Sandy did not live in the Hollis room that had once belonged to T. S. Eliot. He knocked and Sandy appeared. Her roommate was out. Michael was in luck.

It was a large, pretty room with wood paneling, a one-room double for two women. There were two beds, two desks, two closets, and two tastes in decoration. On one side of the room Sandy's absent roommate kept the usual Van Gogh self-portrait, Cézanne fruit, and Gauguin Polynesians. On her desk was the picture of a young man, presumably her so-called H.T.H., Hometown Honey. Sandy's side of the room indicated an interest in New England architecture. There was a Norman Rockwell reproduction and several watercolors of houses on Cape Cod. Michael immediately recognized the interchangeable works of the interchangeable Provincetown artists. The New England motifs were, he thought, entirely typical of the Jewish girl from New Jersey who had gone to prep school and hoped to expunge her ethnic background. Michael did not really like Sandy.

On Sandy's desk were no photographs, only a text of mathematical logic opened to the place where she had been studying. She, too, wore an impeccable sweater and corduroys. Staying in and studying alone on Saturday night did not mean giving in to informality. Sandy Grayson did not lie around her room in a bathrobe. She greeted Michael coolly and invited him to sit down.

Michael could afford to waste no time. "I've just come from having a chat with Parker," he said. "I thought I'd stop by and say hello to you too. You know, there's something I'm kind of curious about."

"Oh, what?" said Sandy without great interest.

Michael hesitated for a moment, and then plunged into the boldest guess of all. "I'm curious about what you were doing with Russell Bernard down by the river the night he was murdered."

Sandy's eyes remained stone cold. For a moment she didn't move. Finally she crossed one leg over the other and said with apparent composure, "Did Parker tell you that?"

"Let's just say I guessed." That was true enough. Michael had guessed—with a few facial hints from Parker. Still Michael delivered the line ironically, in such a fashion as to convince Sandy that he was not merely guessing.

"It's none of your business," said Sandy, cool and collected, surrounded by visions of New England architecture.

"Someone was murdered," said Michael.

"I didn't murder him. It's no affair of mine. Or of yours."

"You were with him the night he was killed in the place he was killed. Why?"

"He invited me to go for a walk with him. We walked down to the river."

Michael took a deep breath before putting the next question, the question which seemed to have only one possible answer. "If you went down to the river with Russell, why were you coming back from the riverbank alone?" The picture was inescapable: Russell lying dead in the water, Sandy walking back up to the highway alone and bumping into Parker.

The phone rang, and Sandy picked it up. It was Parker. Michael's time was up. Sandy put a hand over the receiver and hissed at Michael, "Get out." She glared for a second and then added, "Tell your friend Lauren to watch her step."

"Is that a death threat?" Lauren wondered aloud, swallowing the last bite of crepe.

"Either that or an orthopedic referral," said Michael. "That girl is really quite terrifying when you're alone in her room with her and she starts to hiss."

"You were very brave," said Lauren. "And absolutely brilliant. I can't get over how smart that was to run over to Sandy's while Parker was on the phone. I wouldn't have even thought of that, never mind run fast enough."

Michael only regretted that he had not had a few minutes more with Sandy. He had not had time to ask her one of the most important questions: did she remember hearing a shot on Wednesday night? Now Parker and Sandy would have conferred, and it would be impossible to tell whether Parker had invented the story of the shot.

Still, Lauren and Michael had plenty of new information to work with. Assuming that Parker's story was roughly true, they were confronted by one giant question: why did Sandy go down to the river with Russell and return alone? One possible answer was that she had left Russell's corpse in the river. So Sandy was perhaps the murderer after all. Scott Duchaine's mutilated Facebook was spooky, but Sandy Grayson had actually been on the spot. Surely nothing could be more incriminating than that.

There was also, Michael noted, the possibility that Parker was lying about the accidental encounter with Sandy on Wednesday night. Sandy and Parker could have gone down to the river together that night and murdered Russell together, Sandy with a knife, Parker with a gun, or vice versa. But why? And there was still another mystery. Parker, in a rare moment of self-revelation, had implied that he was in love with someone. With whom? Could it be Lauren? Could it be Sandy? Perhaps Parker had been running along the river, had come upon Russell and Sandy compromisingly entwined, and had murdered his rival. It did not seem likely, but suddenly nothing seemed impossible. It was certainly no less likely than the possibility of voodoo black magic.

"Michael," said Lauren, "this is an awfully serious game we're playing, isn't it? Someone has been killed. Now Sandy Grayson is threatening me. You've lied to imply that you practically witnessed the murder, so you can't expect to sleep too securely either. This is terrifying. Should we keep on going or should we give up on the murder and start studying for our courses?"

"We can't give up now," said Michael. "Now we have to find the murderer. Our own lives may depend on it." His serious expression lifted. "Besides, I don't want to study for my courses."

"To the end then?"

"To the end."

"We'll find Russell's murderer."

"Lauren?"

"Yes?"

"Do you still think you're in love with Russell Bernard?"

"In love with him? I don't know. The more I find out about people's odd reactions to him, the more intriguing I find him— even though I know I can never really know him now. I almost feel like finding his murderer will make up a little for never getting to know Russell. Does that mean I'm in love with him? Is it possible to be in love with a dead boy you hardly knew?"

"Of course," said Michael. "I'm madly in love with Lord Alfred Douglas. It's called a necrophiliac crush. I have a mild one on Prince Yusupov too, Rasputin's murderer, and on lots of other dead people."

"I suppose it's just as well they're dead. I'm sure Lord Alfred Douglas would only get you into trouble. And I don't think Prince Yusupov would be a safe friend for you either."

They laughed together. Michael said, "Lauren."

"Yes, Michael."

"Lauren, this is going to sound silly, but sometimes when I see how much you care about Russell and about finding his murderer, I become a tiny bit jealous. I sometimes think that if he were alive and you were involved with him, you'd be going out with him for crepes at Hemispheres on Sunday morning. Isn't it terrible of me to be jealous of a dead heterosexual?"

"Oh, Michael," said Lauren, "there couldn't possibly be anyone on earth I'd rather go out for crepes with than you. You know, I think you might be the best friend I ever had. Nobody's more fun than you are." She reached across the table and they squeezed hands.

Now Michael was smiling. "And you're more wonderful than any woman who ever went to Exeter."

"The highest tribute to which a woman can aspire," said Lauren. "I feel like Miss America and the Nobel Prize all rolled into one. We're in this together, Michael. You're the only person with whom I'd ever go sleuthing."

"Well then," said Michael, "let's seal that by splitting another crepe."

6. Black and white

Monday's lunch was ravioli. Lauren gestured to the small rabbitlike cafeteria lady, indicating that she would like only a very tiny quantity of that Italian treat, so unappetizing in its Harvard dining hall incarnation. The cafeteria lady nodded cheerfully but without comprehension, and piled Lauren's plate with a big heaping portion. Lauren watched helplessly. She would have to throw away most of it. Lauren took a cup of coffee (dreadful, but she was used to it) and left the cafeteria for the dining hall.

Her first stop was the condiments table. There Lauren made herself a salad of lettuce, cucumber, and extremely unfresh tomato. As she put it together, she thought about whom she should eat with. Lauren had just come from her Nietzsche course and she had walked over to the Freshman Union alone. There were no freshmen in the class she particularly cared for. (There was a very handsome junior from Leverett House whom she would have loved to eat with, but he usually walked back to Leverett with friends for lunch, whereas freshmen ate together in the Freshman Union.) Andrew Stein was in the Nietzsche class, but he was certainly not a pleasant dining companion. Lauren did not like her meals to be psychotically morbid. A month ago she had walked from Nietzsche to lunch with Andrew, and he had spent the entire meal talking about why he deserved to die. Since then Lauren had avoided him after the morning lectures and talked to him only after the Thursday afternoon discussion sections, which were not immediately followed by a meal. Lauren found Carol's or Michael's conversational styles much more suitable to the good digestion of bad food.

She knew that they would be somewhere out there in the huge dining hall. She could set out with her tray to find one of them and keep an eye open for other possible lunchmates at the same time. In the Harvard Freshman Union it was possible to sit down with someone you didn't know all that well, perhaps someone who was in a large lecture course with you, and you could make a new friend. And your new friend would probably be sitting with his or her friends, and so you could make quite a few new acquaintances. The Union was a giant social kaleidoscope that was always turning up new patterns and combinations. Lauren enjoyed the diverse possibilities and made the most of them.

Just as she was putting the finishing touches on her salad (oil, vinegar, uncrispy croutons) and preparing to venture forth with her tray, she caught a word from a conversation taking place at a table behind her back. The word was a name and the name was Russell. She froze, listened hard, and added a few croutons so as not to seem to be loitering. She heard the name Russell again from a different voice. The second voice, like the first one, provided an unmistakable ethnic identification, and when Lauren glanced over her shoulder at the table in question, she was not surprised to see that everyone there was black.

It had not been all that difficult for Harvard to join in the civil rights movement of the 1960s and admit into entering freshman classes an increasing percentage of blacks. Harvard, after all, was the most prestigious and the richest university in America. It could, in theory, attract the brightest black students and provide enough financial aid so that those accepted could attend regardless of economic background. The racial composition of Harvard's freshman class was brought much closer to that of American society. Another kind of integration was, however, much harder to achieve. Integrated admission statistics were one thing, but an actually integrated university community was something quite different—something which money and prestige could not necessarily provide.

The Freshman Union, the center of freshman social life, illustrated the problem most vividly. Why should there be tables where a dozen black men and women ate their lunch together, while at adjoining tables everyone was white? Yet there were black tables at the Harvard Freshman Union, and unofficial segregation reigned. True, there were exceptions to the rule. There were blacks who ate comfortably at tables where everyone else was white. Russell, for instance, had been a strong enough personality to ignore all the intangible barriers. And there were whites (Katherine Butler came to mind for obvious reasons) who were content (even pleased?) to sit at one of the black tables. Most whites, however, felt that they were not wanted and avoided the black tables as a matter of course. Harvard blacks, on the other hand, insisted that they sat together because they did not feel fully accepted by the rest of the Harvard community, though some had been known to say that they actively preferred black company for reasons of racial solidarity. On the whole, blacks and whites blamed each other, and the segregation persisted. The university as an institution preferred to be content with the admissions breakdown and to deny that any apparent social discomfort was more than a sociological wrinkle which would be ironed out in time.

Lauren made her resolution before turning around, and then, gathering together all the social poise that she possessed, carried her tray over to the black table and sat down in an empty seat. The conversation stopped suddenly, and a dozen black faces, male and female, were staring at Lauren. "Hello," she said. "I overheard you talking about Russell Bernard. I was a friend of his." They stared and remained silent. Lauren decided to call upon more than frankness and friendliness. Just for a moment she put her hand on the shoulder of the man sitting next to her, wearing a football jersey, and said with the subtlest hint of flirtation she could possibly manage, "Would you pass me the salt?" He smiled at her and handed her the shaker, and, as Lauren salted the pile of unappetizing ravioli, she knew that she had found one ally.

But Lauren had also made an enemy, the woman on the other side of the man in the football jersey. Had she noticed the flirtatious play in Lauren's tones? Now she spoke to Lauren in the sarcastically false black English of someone who had scored 700 on the Verbal SAT. "Russell ain't here," she said with malevolent sweetness. "He done got murdered, so he ain't comin' to dinner. You gotta see him tonight or anybody else'll do just as good?" All eyes were on her, and they only returned to Lauren when she rose with her tray.

"Excuse me," said Lauren, trembling but holding on to her dignity, "I'll go eat someplace else." But even as she stood, she could see the man in the football jersey rising alongside her.

Now his hand was on her shoulder. "You stay," he said to her. "Please." Then he turned to the woman who had spoken and said, "You shut up, Suzanne." From around the table came murmured assents. Suzanne had clearly gone too far with her rudeness and obscene insinuation. She had been insulting to Russell as well as to the white stranger, and the whole table was reacting against her. Suzanne had made it possible for Lauren to be accepted, and now Lauren and the man in the jersey both sat down again while Suzanne could only scowl.

Lauren nibbled nervously at one of the ravioli on the end of her fork. There was a minute's silence while everyone took stock of the situation, tried to decide what should happen next. Finally someone said to Lauren in a friendly though not entirely natural tone, "How did you know Russell?"

"I was in a class with him," said Lauren, "the freshman seminar on the Russian Revolution." She had earlier thought that it would be desirable to imply that she and Russell had been very close. After Suzanne's remarks, however, Lauren realized sharply that suggestions of interracial intimacy would not pave the way to a comfortable lunchtime conversation. She decided to try a slightly different tone, one which was in fact closer to the truth. She would be Russell's platonic admirer. She said with a genuinely felt sense of loss, "Russell was the smartest person in the seminar."

It was the right thing to say. After a moment's silence, there were expressions of agreement. Yes, Lauren was right, Russell was smart, the smartest, they all agreed. Now Lauren said nothing. She drank a little coffee to wet her throat and she listened. They were all talking at once, about Russell, about how sad it was that he had been killed. Lauren could only catch fragments of what they were saying, but she understood the general intent. They were mourning.

At first they spoke softly, and their conversation was pierced by the noisy lunchtime exchanges at nearby tables, almost overwhelmed by the roar of the crowded dining hall. And then, as Lauren listened, fascinated, the black men and women at her table (no, she was at their table) began to speak louder. Their tones changed. They were no longer mourning in gentle and admiring sadness. They were mourning bitterly and angrily. They were not accepting Russell's murder as an isolated, lunatic act. To them Russell's murder, for all its eccentricity, was a part of the general racial callousness which they had all experienced in one form or another. Regardless of the unknown identity and motives of Russell's murderer, as far as they were concerned Russell was killed because he was black.

And Lauren also understood the direction of their collective blame. This too, she thought, was irrational and yet somehow on target. They did not accuse American society with its long history of racial injustice. Neither did they point a finger at any individual suspect. Avoiding both the most general and the most specific solutions, they chose to blame Harvard, the university, for Russell's murder. And this, Lauren reflected, was not so very far from her own detective suspicions.

Goddamn Harvard, she heard from one side of the table. Lauren could feel their resentment against all of the other freshmen who chattered obliviously around them, flirting with each other and joking about the dreadful ravioli. On any other day Lauren would be sitting at one of those tables, equally oblivious to the black tables tucked away here and there. Today Lauren had a different perspective. Tomorrow she would probably eat with Carol or Michael, and today's lunch would seem a little unreal.

Goddamn Harvard. But weren't they being ungrateful? Russell Bernard had been chosen by Harvard, chosen from a background of relative poverty, chosen and paid for. He was to have received from Harvard as a gift the ten thousand dollars a year which Lauren's parents paid to Harvard for tuition, room and board, books, and expenses. Other students at that table were probably receiving the same gift. Harvard had chosen them too. This was Harvard's way of trying to redress the imbalance of American history. A Harvard diploma would, in theory, provide an avenue to money or power or anything at all.

Yes, they were ungrateful, but Lauren could not blame them. These students were aware of what Harvard could only ignore: that there was more to equality and integration than a set of properly proportional admissions statistics, that the existence of black tables—whoever was responsible—meant something was very wrong at Harvard, and that it was not easy to be black regardless of one's economic prospects. The world remained a hostile place, and Harvard, for the time being, was their world as it was Lauren's. Right now the fact of being young and bright and promising seemed particularly hollow, since perhaps the brightest and most promising of all of them had been brutally murdered. Somehow Harvard, which had brought him here, which had brought all of them here, was responsible.

Lauren was trying to follow three conversations at once and remember all potentially useful details. They were talking about Russell, but they were not talking about Russell alone. They were also talking about Dora, Dora Carpenter, Russell and Dora. She too had been young and bright and promising, and she too was dead.

Dora Carpenter had been three years older than these students. They had not known her as they had known Russell, their exact peer. They might have met Dora once somewhere, in passing—at a party—but her death had made her the property of all of them. Like all of them, she had felt alienated at Harvard, so much so that she had dropped out of school. She died from using contaminated cocaine, and still they blamed Harvard for her death. She and Russell were symbols of what could happen to promising young black men and women at Harvard, even at Harvard.

Russell Bernard had been poor, but he had not been a child of the slums. He had been born in Atlanta nineteen years ago, and very soon after his birth his father had disappeared, no one knew why or to where. In fact, it was not absolutely clear that his parents were ever married. At any rate, his mother never remarried, and Russell remained an only child. Russell's mother supported him and herself by working as a day maid for a wealthy white family in Atlanta. It was thus that his mother, and through her Russell himself, derived their strong appreciation of, if not reverence for, the fine points of rich respectability.

Dora Carpenter's story was altogether different. She had never been poor—quite the contrary. Her father had risen from poverty to become a prominent Manhattan lawyer. Her mother, a former nightclub singer, was already one step beyond mere respectability. Dora's mother was a wealthy bohemian. The Carpenter family had black servants of their own.

It was the disappearance of Russell's father which, ironically, made it possible for Russell to rise in the world. The absence of his father made it much easier for his mother to raise the child in her own religion: Roman Catholicism. Lauren was very surprised to learn about this. She had never dreamed that Russell was Catholic, not that she thought very much about religion one way or another. She had, she supposed, taken for granted that Russell would be Baptist if anything. That was the religion she associated with blacks. In fact, the other blacks at the table also talked about Russell's

Catholic background with some bewilderment. To them, too, it set him apart. Russell's great-great-grandmother had been born a slave to a Catholic family in Louisiana.

Russell's mother then was a Catholic, and the white Atlanta family she worked for was Baptist. They were good-natured but vulgar—trash who had made it big in business. It is debatable whether Russell's mother knew enough to appreciate the tastelessness of their furniture, but it is certain that despite their wealth she maintained an invincible condescension toward their Protestantism. Here certainly were the seeds of Russell's own healthy arrogance, arrogance mixed with Catholic humility. The other gift of Russell's religious background was somewhat more tangible. For eight years he was educated by the Jesuits, who had immediately recognized his intellectual brilliance. They had given him, in the tradition of their order, the finest education available in the world.

Lauren listened patiently, and eventually the question that was bothering her was answered in the course of the conversation. What had become of Russell's Catholicism? Everyone knew. At Harvard he had gone to mass every Sunday. Russell had remained a devout Catholic through the years. That, Lauren thought, was the strangest thing of all. Lauren knew very few people who were genuinely religious. Yet Russell, during those weeks she had known him, had gone to church every Sunday, had eaten the wafer and drunk the wine, the flesh and blood of Christ, the Son of God. Catholicism, Lauren thought, was an odd religion, but the most awesome of all religions. She wondered how much Russell's magical personality owed to his religious inspiration. She wondered if there was any connection between religion and the murder. Rasputin, she recalled, had also been profoundly and mystically devout—Russian Orthodox of course, not Roman Catholic.

Like Lauren, Dora Carpenter had been brought up without religion. She had gone to a classy private high school in Manhattan and moved on to Harvard as if it were the obvious next step. Haunted by the self-questionings common to most wealthy adolescents of that time, she found her own answers in a rediscovered blackness, in political activism, and in interesting drugs.

Russell's Jesuit education had ended when he was fourteen. The school did not have enough students to remain open, and so he went on to one of Atlanta's inferior public high schools. Most of what was taught in grades nine through twelve had been already covered by the Jesuits in elementary school. Russell did not become cynical. He remained close to some of the Jesuit fathers, and they guided him through a course of self-education. He had been their most promising student, and surely they still hoped that he would decide to enter the priesthood.

In fact, Russell's Jesuit training sent him in a different direction—into politics. The Society of Jesus from its inception in the sixteenth century had recognized the importance of secular politics and influence, and the early European Jesuits had flourished thanks to their genius for political machinations. Russell managed to take in some of this enthusiasm and perhaps some of the genius as well. When the National Black Students' Lobby was organized, Russell, though only a high school student, quickly became an important figure within the organization.

Dora too, already at Harvard, had found an outlet for her own skills and frustrations in the Lobby. The Lobby itself was conceived of not only as another force for civil rights in America, but also as a self-conscious attempt to initiate and train the black leaders of the next generation. And now two of the most talented of those leaders were dead. Their deaths both occurred within a span of weeks, and it was impossible not to link their names.

Were there other reasons to link them? No one was certain. Dora and Russell had first met in Washington a year ago when the leaders of the Lobby had made their debut in the national forum. They were friends again when Russell arrived at Harvard, just as Dora was dropping out. She wanted to devote more time to the Lobby, she did not like Harvard as a community, and she was not above taking pleasure in upsetting her parents. Dora lived in Cambridge, and she remained Russell's friend until she died.

But was there more? Some of the students at the table said Russell was in love with Dora. Others said no. Most seemed to agree that although she liked him a lot, she probably thought he was too young to be a serious romantic possibility. Had they ever been lovers? Nobody knew. What everyone knew was that the Lobby had been an enormous bond between Dora and Russell.

So far Lauren had contributed nothing to the discussion.

She sat quietly and listened sympathetically. And she was learning a great deal. An hour passed. Lauren had finished her coffee and most of her salad. The pile of ravioli remained virtually untouched, and so it would remain until she dumped it in the garbage on the way out. But now Lauren felt comfortable enough to speak up, and she made her first comment since praising Russell half an hour ago as the smartest person in the seminar. Lauren said, "The last time I saw him—Wednesday evening, the night he was killed—he was on his way to a dinner meeting of the Lobby."

It was an innocent remark, contributed in the reigning spirit of reminiscence, but Lauren immediately regretted it. No sooner did she speak than the whole table fell silent. Obviously, Lauren was not at all a part of the group if one word from her could put an end to a half hour's discussion. She was embarrassed and sad and even angry at them all for condemning her so relentlessly to be an outsider. Only gradually did it begin to dawn on her that it was not the simple fact that she had spoken but rather her specific words that had shocked them.

"He was on his way to a Lobby meeting?" someone said. "How do you know that?"

"Because he told me," said Lauren defensively and more embarrassed than ever. "It was right after the freshman seminar, which goes from four to six." She did not mention that she had found out about the meeting by suggesting that he have dinner with her. "He said he was going right to the meeting. What's the matter? Don't you believe me?"

The man in the football jersey spoke up, saying what they obviously all knew. "Russell didn't show up at the meeting that night. The meeting was here at the Union in the back room during dinner, and Russell didn't show up. I know because I was there."

"And I was too," someone said.

"And me too," said someone else. "But Russell wasn't."

"Oh my God," Lauren whispered. Now they were all thinking the same thing. At six o'clock Russell had said he was on his way to the meeting. But he never arrived. In the five minutes that it would take to cross Harvard Yard something had happened, something which perhaps ultimately drew Russell down to the river that night, drew him to his death. What had happened? Lauren immediately remembered the stories of Parker and Sandy. If they were speaking the truth about Russell and the gunshot, or if they were lying and one of them had actually murdered Russell, then the murder would have occurred between nine and ten. There were three crucial hours unaccounted for.

And then there was another possibility. Perhaps Russell had not been distracted on his way to the meeting. He could have been lying to Lauren for whatever reason, perhaps just as a graceful way to turn down her suggestion of dinner. He might never have intended to go to the meeting at all. But then why did everyone seem to have expected him at the meeting? Where did Russell go when he left Lauren Wednesday evening? These were Lauren's thoughts; the black students were probably not thinking along precisely the same lines. They did not suspect a murder mystery. They believed in the random riverside criminal. No doubt they suspected he was white and racist, but surely they did not guess, as Lauren did, that he or she was a Harvard freshman. They blamed Harvard only symbolically. But all of them, including Lauren, were wondering the same thing: why did Russell go down to the river Wednesday night?

Suzanne, Lauren's enemy, was the first to answer the question aloud. "He probably went down to the river with one of those white girls who were always chasing after him." She did not even glance at Lauren as she spoke. She didn't have to. Her insulting intention was perfectly clear. This time, however, Lauren did not move to go. She felt that she had earned her place in the group. She looked coolly around her, unfazed, even a little amused to think that Suzanne, in her attempt to be vicious, had actually hit upon the approximate truth: Sandy Grayson had indeed been down by the river with Russell. Suzanne, seeing that her comment had failed to rouse a response, tried another direction. She turned to a tiny girl at the far end of the table and said, "Maybe he was down by the river with your roommate, that crazy white lady with the gun."

Lauren was immediately alert: this was important, the crazy white lady with the gun. Suzanne seemed to know exactly what she was talking about. Could she know that Russell had gone to the river with Sandy Grayson on Wednesday night? Did Sandy Grayson have a gun? Lauren could easily imagine it. Sandy, after all, was ice cold. And at the same time that Lauren shuddered at the thought of Sandy calmly pulling the trigger, something deep inside her giggled at the picture of snobby Sandy Grayson living with a black roommate. For a moment Lauren considered the possibility that someone in the Harvard Housing Office had a sense of humor.

The tiny black woman was explaining in a high-pitched voice that yes, her roommate really did have a gun, a little one which she kept in her desk. Her father had given it to her when she left home in case she ever needed it to protect herself. There was general laughter, and Suzanne suggested crudely that certain men could probably make better use of the gun to protect themselves from her. Clearly no one at the table except Lauren was connecting the gun with Russell's murder. Only Lauren suspected Sandy of worse than unrequited lust, and so only Lauren realized that the gun was a vital clue.

Someone was asking what the crazy white woman with the gun looked like. Without thinking Lauren spoke up to answer the question and began to describe Sandy Grayson: neat, short dark hair, tortoiseshell glasses, preppie clothes— the snobbiest expressions at Harvard. They all listened to her for a moment, and then Suzanne began to laugh out loud and a few others joined in. Lauren wondered what was so funny.

The laughter subsided, and the tiny girl at the end of the table said, "That's not my roommate. She doesn't look anything like that. And she's not stuck-up either. She's real friendly in a crazy kind of way."

"What?" Lauren was puzzled. "What does she look like then? Who is she?"

"My roommate's the one from Chicago that people always say looks like she's going through her third divorce. And she really does look like that. She sure went through Russell fast, anyway. He stayed in our suite some nights last month—I don't care, I have the private room—and then they were through with each other. I don't know who put an end to it, but that girl's sex life really moves quick. Now she's mixed up with a blond from California who's got a convertible and a surfboard. He should last a few weeks. But you want to know something that's really crazy about her? Last night she came in late and she was stoned, and do you know what she told me? She said she knew who murdered Russell Bernard. So I said 'Who?' but she just laughed, she was so stoned, and she kept saying, 'Poor guy, poor guy.' And this morning she couldn't even remember saying anything at all about Russell. She's crazy."

7. Reactionary and frivolous

Tracy Nicolson and Russell Bernard had been lovers. And Tracy had a gun. Those were the two thoughts that occupied Lauren as she left the Freshman Union after lunch at the black table. It had already crossed her mind, of course, that there might have been something between Russell and Tracy, but it was nevertheless shocking to have her suspicions explicitly confirmed. And—Lauren could not keep from admitting to herself—the shock was reinforced by jealousy.

Aware of the perversity of this initial reaction, Lauren tried to concentrate on what was surely the more important new piece of information, the completely unsuspected discovery: Tracy Nicolson had a gun. It was a surprise, but it also fit perfectly with Lauren's picture of Tracy as a Chicago gangster. And it was a frighteningly concrete sort of clue to the murder mystery.

Suddenly Lauren had a suspect with a weapon. And it was the crucial weapon, since, after all, any student could have come up with a blunt object. In a pinch, the unabridged works of William Shakespeare would probably have done well enough. And a knife would also be easy to purchase. It was really the gun that made Lauren despair of her freshman suspects. It was not that she didn't know that there were lots of ways, legally and illegally, to acquire a gun. It was just that Lauren herself wouldn't have begun to know how to go about getting a gun, and she couldn't really imagine that any other freshman would know better than she did. Guns seemed to be for adults, not for college students. And sure enough, Tracy's gun had come from her father. Lauren reflected:

somebody had fired a bullet into Russell's heart—and Tracy had a gun.

But did it make sense? Was there a motive? Suppose Tracy had accidentally run into Russell and Sandy down by the river on Wednesday night. Why would Tracy have been carrying her gun then? Well, if she had a gun, Lauren thought, she might as well have carried it to walk by the river at night. So then: she bumped into Russell and Sandy.

No, it would be too coincidental. Lauren reconsidered. Suppose Tracy had actually *followed* Russell and Sandy down to the river on Wednesday night. And Tracy had seen something happen between the two of them, something that had infuriated her. It was easy to imagine what that might have been, although Lauren shuddered with distaste (and jealousy again) at the thought of a tender interlude between Russell and Sandy. Then Sandy had gone away (but why?), and Russell had been left alone by the river. And Tracy had murdered him.

The motive would have been jealousy. At first Lauren had thought this inconsistent with Tracy's tough disposition, but now she was beginning to feel that Tracy's hard-bitten personality could even make her a more likely suspect. Tracy, once enraged, would surely be able to follow through. And, especially since she actually had been Russell's lover, Tracy might well have been passionately jealous. In fact she would probably have had more of a motive than Sandy, whose own romantic involvement with Russell, Lauren sincerely hoped, had not progressed as far.

Tracy was now the suspect most on Lauren's mind. Leaving the Union, she had caught a glimpse of Tracy eating lunch at a table of friends, all white. Tracy had been laughing raucously and obviously enjoying herself. Bert Rosen had been sitting at the table too. How did he fit in? Surely he was Tracy's new lover. Lauren wondered: was there something Tracy didn't want Russell, her old lover, to tell Bert, her new lover? Could she have killed Russell to silence him, to close forever that chapter in her life? Or perhaps it was Bert who had wanted to close that chapter of Tracy's life. Could he have murdered Russell out of jealousy?

Lauren set out for the library. She had lots of Nietzsche to cover. But she knew she would read with even more difficulty than usual, because her mind was already fully occupied with compelling images of Tracy Nicolson laughing over lunch, Tracy Nicolson taking out her gun, Tracy Nicolson committing murder by the side of the river. Those were Lauren's thoughts as she walked from the Union to the library, and she was startled when a woman stepped up from behind her to say hello. It was Katherine Butler.

In fact, Lauren had had Katherine Butler in the back of her mind during lunch. Katherine was the only white student Lauren knew who sometimes ate her meals at tables where everyone else was black. Lauren had often noticed Katherine surrounded by black men and women in the Union. Katherine would be talking energetically—head high, long brown hair falling straight down behind her, no mere reticent observer as Lauren had been. Lauren did not know for certain, but she suspected that in such circumstances Katherine was usually talking about South Africa. Lauren wondered how Katherine was treated by someone like Suzanne, who was so particularly hostile toward white women interested in black men.

Lauren had never had much to do with Katherine outside class. They had always exchanged friendly greetings when they passed but had never settled down to a talk. Lauren was a little intimidated by Katherine's very serious political involvement, while Katherine, Lauren suspected, had probably correctly assessed Lauren's essential frivolousness. They were not compatible. So Katherine's apparent eagerness to join her now was a bit out of the ordinary, and Lauren immediately wondered whether Katherine had noticed her at lunch. Perhaps Katherine had decided that Lauren was worthy of greater interest. This would certainly be convenient, since Lauren, in the course of investigating the members of the freshman seminar, was going to have to have a talk with Katherine sooner or later. Lauren reminded herself that if Tracy was the suspect who definitely possessed a gun, Katherine was the suspect who almost certainly knew how to use one.

Katherine asked after Lauren's classes, but since Lauren was very rarely interested in talking about her classes (wasn't it enough that she was taking them?), Katherine was soon talking about her own. Katherine was taking the same enormous introductory economics course that Scott Duchaine was in, the course Lauren was always congratulating herself on having avoided. Katherine, of course, was genuinely interested in economics: the South African revolution would have to have an economic program. In fact, Katherine already knew a great deal about economics. While still in high school in South Africa she had participated in a clandestine Marxist study group. It was there that she had met her future husband.

Katherine felt that she already knew introductory economics and she resented being required to take the large Harvard lecture course. As far as she was concerned, she was ready to take advanced seminars on industrial development in the Third World ("ready to learn something really useful"), but Harvard, with all the arrogance that comes from being the most famous university in America, insisted that only Harvard's own introductory course could provide a real background in economics. Certainly a South African Marxist study group would not be accepted as a substitute prerequisite for advanced seminars.

Katherine not only knew all the material in the introductory economics course, but she also found the presentation politically offensive. "Most of the Harvard economics professors are completely reactionary," she informed Lauren, who nodded and tried to look distressed. Lauren was thinking about changing the subject. She asked whether Katherine was liking the freshman seminar on the Russian Revolution.

Katherine was not entirely displeased with the seminar. Of course, she could not but disapprove of Professor Baranova, whose almost aesthetic distaste for the Russian Revolution came across with every ironic gesture. On the other hand, Katherine was finding the reading extremely interesting. In fact, she had finished Trotsky's *History of the Russian Revolution* and was reading it through again. "It's a brilliant piece of class analysis!" she said, in the same rapt tone that Lauren or Michael would have used to admire an attractive man. "Don't you think so?"

Lauren wondered if this last question, so nearly rhetorical, was not intended sarcastically. Lauren, of course, had read only the tiniest fraction of last week's assignment in Trotsky, and this week she had been too preoccupied to even look at the book. She would have to do a fair bit of skimming tonight or tomorrow, since it was now Monday and the seminar would meet again on Wednesday afternoon. The seminar would meet, and Russell would not be there. Lauren wondered how that would feel.

Lauren nodded to indicate that she too thought Trotsky's

History of the Russian Revolution was a brilliant piece of class analysis. Then she asked quickly, "Do you like the people in the class?"

"They don't know anything about politics," said Katherine promptly. "They're frivolous." She spoke with so complete an air of objectivity that she seemed to ignore the fact that she was addressing her comment to Lauren, one of the frivolous.

Frivolous and proud of it, Lauren thought to herself. And if you think *I'm* bad, you should meet my friend Michael. But Lauren said instead, "I think it's an interesting group of people. I like most of them a lot. I especially liked Russell Bernard. In fact, I was just talking about him at lunch with some of his friends." Lauren carefully watched Katherine's face and decided, with some satisfaction, that Katherine was extremely interested. Then she *had* noticed Lauren in the Union. And Katherine's curiosity had been sufficiently aroused to prod her into striking up a conversation. Good, Lauren thought to herself, this is what I want to talk about too. I'm not particularly interested in whether or not you are too advanced to take freshman economics.

Katherine and Lauren had walked right past the library. Now they stopped walking and faced each other. They stood in Harvard Yard, in front of University Hall, at the foot of the statue of the seventeenth-century founder, John Harvard. By stopping, they both seemed to admit that they were not merely chatting on the way to somewhere. They were having a conversation of more than incidental interest to them both.

"Oh," said Katherine, "I think I saw you at lunch." Her uncertainty was patently false.

"Oh did you?"

"Yes, I think I did." Katherine sounded more certain now. She was searching for a way to prolong the discussion and, after a few moments, inquired lamely, "Was it a good lunch?"

Lauren coyly pretended to misunderstand. "A good lunch? The ravioli was disgusting."

"No. I mean I know it was disgusting. I mean was it an interesting lunch?"

"Yes," said Lauren. "Extremely." She enjoyed teasing Katherine.

"Did you like those people you were eating with?"

"Yes." Lauren realized that this was very true, that with the exception of Suzanne she had liked them a lot. She wondered if it would be possible to remain friends with any of them. She wondered if any of them were friends of Katherine's. "Do you know them?" Lauren asked.

"Yes," said Katherine.

"And do you like them?"

"No." Katherine was quite emphatic.

Lauren was taken aback and even a little indignant. Why shouldn't Katherine like them? Why on earth didn't she? Lauren had taken for granted that because they were black, Katherine would surely know them, and because Katherine was devoted to a black cause, she would surely like them. Lauren had not thought Katherine would have it in her to dislike a member of an oppressed race or class, but apparently Katherine's political correctness didn't work quite that way. Lauren had liked those people she'd had lunch with, and she wanted to know what was wrong with them in Katherine's eyes. "Why don't you like them?"

"They're reactionaries."

Lauren was surprised once again. And yet it made sense: if Katherine disliked those people, that would be why. Either they had to be reactionaries or they had to be frivolous. Perhaps they were both. Lauren was on the point of snapping that they couldn't possibly be reactionary, but she decided to try a more noncommittal line. "I didn't know," she said with what she thought was a rather sweet air of concerned naiveté.

"They know nothing about politics. They know nothing about Marxism or Leninism or Maoism. They're completely indifferent to the kinds of revolutions that have to take place all over the world during the next fifty years, the kinds of revolutions that will take place inevitably. And they are American Negroes. They should be able to appreciate better than anyone the meaning of social and economic oppression. Instead they come to Harvard, bourgeois, elitist Harvard, and they try to become part of the bourgeois elite of the United States of America, one of the most reactionary countries in the world. They talk about ethnic solidarity, but all they really mean by it is some kind of cocktail party social connection between a handful of black Americans who will eventually be doctors, lawyers, and businessmen. They think of Africa as a cultural heritage, not as the scene of a great revolutionary struggle. They pretend to be concerned about racial injustice, but they only mean that they wish they could get ahead faster. They're disgraceful."

This was spoken fiercely, and Lauren was only barely maintaining her equanimity under the weight of such an extended denunciation of the people she had innocently claimed to like. Lauren didn't care whether or not her friends were revolutionaries. In fact, she rather preferred that they not be. If they were revolutionaries, they would always be making long speeches at her like the one Katherine had just delivered. Lauren was willing to hear the speech once as a curiosity and also as a part of her investigation, but she did not want to hear it again, and she had a feeling that it might be one of Katherine's favorite conversation pieces.

It had not occurred to Lauren that Katherine believed in good blacks and bad blacks, and that Lauren had ended up sitting with the bad ones. "You know," she said to Katherine, "they're really not as completely unconcerned about politics as you think. Some of those people I was eating with are part of the National Black Students' Lobby."

Katherine smiled. It was not a nice smile. It was the mean, smug, condescending smile with which one prepares to respond to an incredibly stupid remark. Lauren had to glance up for a moment to make sure that the statue of John Harvard was not also smiling contemptuously at her. The statue remained expressionless. Lauren wondered what on earth she had said to deserve that smile, and in a moment she found out. Katherine was icily amused that Lauren could even begin to consider membership in the National Black Students' Lobby a mark of political involvement. "I'd like to say that the whole organization is just junk," said Katherine, "but it's really a little more than that. It's reactionary junk, harmful junk."

Lauren listened with amazement while Katherine explained just why the National Black Students' Lobby was a reactionary organization. Katherine provided historical background. The black American civil rights movement of the 1960s was an essentially conservative phenomenon. It was led by Baptist ministers who never appreciated Marxism, Leninism, or Maoism. The movement was concerned with bourgeois civil liberties without any understanding of the determining substructure of social and economic oppression. Only a social and economic revolution could give real and lasting meaning to civil rights in America. And furthermore, the civil rights movement was shamelessly preoccupied with the plight of American Negroes who, in fact, could never be truly emancipated until a world revolution put an end to racial and economic oppression in Africa and Asia. On the whole, the civil rights movement of the 1960s was to be scorned for its shallowness, shortsightedness, and religious scruples.

The movement had not been, however, entirely without merit. Civil disobedience had been a positive sign that not all black leaders were entirely content to remain within the framework of the American legal status quo. Civil disobedience was the first shaky step toward revolution; what was needed next was a will to violence. The late 1960s had showed some promise for the advent of true revolutionary violence. The civil rights movement had had a few praiseworthy heirs, organizations that had been willing to take the next step along the path of political radicalization. And the social situation had been conducive to this development. Katherine reminisced nostalgically for a minute about the Newark riots. That was the sort of material out of which a revolution could be made. What was lacking was Marxist class consciousness, Leninist political organization, and Maoist international solidarity.

But the social ferment passed, and other less worthy aspects of the civil rights movement came to predominate among black Americans: there were new organizations which had discarded even civil disobedience in their eagerness to live up to the good intentions of white liberal lawyers. The National Black Students' Lobby was one such organization. Its educational emphasis revealed all too clearly its insidious aim of fully integrating young black Americans, racially, socially, and economically, into white bourgeois imperialist America. Katherine did not speak of the Lobby only with contempt; she spoke with real hatred.

The National Black Students' Lobby dared to have its own South African policy. That was what Katherine Butler could never forgive. The Lobby was, in fact, one of a number of black American groups that were attempting to pressure the American government to pressure the South African government about apartheid. While this might seem admirable and reasonable to Lauren, to Katherine it represented the basest effort to undermine the South African revolution. The Lobby favored negotiations with the vile South African government, which Katherine and her comrades were determined to destroy. As she saw it, the Lobby, with its saccharine liberal good intentions, provided a means of justifying and whitewashing continued American contacts with South

Africa—contacts which, in fact, helped to prop up the racist regime. As far as Katherine was concerned, the members of the Lobby might just as well be agents of Johannesburg.

Lauren, of course, heard this entire diatribe as a personal attack on Russell. She wondered to what extent Katherine had Russell in mind. It was time to find out. Lauren said, "You can't really think that Russell Bernard was an agent of the South African government?"

Katherine just smiled. "Can't I?" Russell Bernard was one of the people who was most responsible for the Lobby's South Africa policy. He had believed that the Lobby shouldn't limit itself to educational issues, that it should spread its reactionary poison to all areas of American policy. Russell Bernard had given a speech in Washington about how American pressure for South African reform would help to diminish the influence of Marxist revolutionaries in South Africa. "It was a beautiful Boy Scout speech all about God and Democracy." Katherine seemed to hate Russell particularly. "Did you know that Russell Bernard went to church every Sunday? Talk about Uncle Tom."

Lauren was a little sick of Katherine by now, but she was also thinking of her investigation. Lauren spoke with seeming carelessness, "It sounds like you're not sorry he's dead."

Katherine smiled again. "I'm a terrorist and a revolutionary," she said. "I can't afford to be sentimental about the death of an individual reactionary." Katherine was still smiling. "And Russell Bernard's death may do some good. On a national level it will probably have only a tiny effect. American policy isn't really influenced by those Uncle Tom organizations anyway, and Russell was just one among many. But Russell was an important figure here at Harvard, a big black man on campus." Katherine was sneering. "His death will help me and my friends. We are always trying to explain to undergraduates, especially black undergraduates, about the inevitability of revolution in South Africa, in the Third World, and one day in America. A lot of corrupted black students were attracted to the Lobby with its liberal clichés. Russell's death may make it easier for us to win people over to our side." She paused thoughtfully. "You know, it really is very convenient. If I were going to kill one person at Harvard, I think I'd have killed Russell Bernard."

Lauren shivered and asked, "Have you ever killed anyone, Katherine?"

"Yes." Katherine's answer was flat. Then she turned sarcastic. "Have you?"

"No," said Lauren, returning Katherine's gaze, "but sometimes I think I might like to."

"Good, then there's hope for you. All you need now is a revolutionary ideology."

"I take it you've got one for me."

"I could teach you a few things," said Katherine, "but I have a feeling you might rather have learned from Russell Bernard." She paused for that to sink in, and then continued with intentional unkindness. "It really was convenient his being murdered like that, a real blow to the Lobby. And Dora Carpenter's death is sort of an extra bonus. Shooting herself up with cocaine, isn't that a laugh? She was a rich bitch. She was about as black as you are."

"Or as you are," said Lauren coolly. "As black as you and me."

Lauren was lying in bed in her nightgown. It was not yet midnight, and she was far from sleepy. She was in her nightgown and under her covers in order to reassure herself. It had been a frighteningly interesting day, and she would not have wanted to go to sleep anyway before Carol returned from the *Crimson*. It was not a night to be alone, and, in fact, Lauren was not alone. Michael sat perched on her desk. He was wearing pajamas—warm ski pajamas; the lavender silk smoking jacket was for decoration, not for extra warmth. Lauren was not sure what the rest of the dormitory thought of all the time she and Michael spent in each other's rooms in pajamas. It was certainly suggestive, though in fact nothing could have been more innocent.

Lauren was describing her day to Michael: luncheon at the black table followed by chit-chat with Katherine Butler. They talked about Tracy Nicolson's gun and about Katherine Butler's terrorist connections. It was Lauren's opinion that Katherine could easily have murdered Russell. Clearly Katherine had hated Russell, and she herself had named the motive: fierce political competition. Could political murder somehow account for the fact that Russell had not shown up at that last Lobby meeting?

It was Michael who pointed out that Katherine need not have committed the murder personally. Presumably there were others who followed her line, perhaps even other members of Katherine's South African organization. Any one of them, Harvard student or not, could have been assigned to eliminate Russell if he was seen as a significant threat. It was even possible that Katherine herself was not in on the murder. She might merely have spoken of Russell to more sinister figures who had decided to take action. Lauren agreed that this was possible, but as a solution it did not please her. Katherine had to have some connection to the murder, or there would be no place for the Rasputin motif. And one of the things Lauren especially liked about the political explanation was that it fit in beautifully with the Rasputin murder. Rasputin too had been murdered in order to destroy his political influence.

But how great was Russell's political influence? Katherine thought he was dangerous, but was it possible that Katherine's perspective was exaggerated, even hysterical? And what was the actual political significance of Katherine's own circle of comrades? Katherine might conceivably be part of a powerful movement in South Africa, but in an American context she might be only on the fringe of the fringe. Michael and Lauren said in unison, "The lunatic fringe."

Michael thought Katherine's politics were just amusing. "I mean honestly, what on earth can it possibly mean to be a Marxist-Leninist-Maoist Harvard freshman. It's completely silly. The girl is ridiculous."

"Yes, of course," said Lauren. "I think she's ridiculous too, but that's not the big question. The big question is whether or not she's sane. Does she take her politics seriously to the point of insanity? Would she murder Russell Bernard? I think she would."

The question of sanity was important. Murder among Harvard freshmen was not likely to be a sane crime, and especially not this murder with its ritualistic alternation of weapons. Katherine's political extremism suggested a possibly warped mental perspective. What about the other suspects? What about Scott Duchaine? Lauren had had inklings Saturday night that all was not well beneath Scott's courteous exterior, and then of course the missing Facebook picture led one to suspect something completely weird.

Scott's motive would be the opposite of Katherine's. Scott would have killed Russell because he was black; Katherine would have killed him for not being black enough. Who could say which was more likely or which was more crazy? Michael pointed out that they could at least safely conclude that Katherine and Scott were not in it together.

Michael also had news about Brian O'Donnell, the other racist suspect. Michael had inquired through his mother's Irish cleaning lady and managed to learn a little about Brian's father, the police chief. The news was ominous. Brian's father was notoriously racist, had indeed once been reprimanded for his flagrant unfairness to blacks in handling Boston's tense racial situation. There had even been talk of an investigation of alleged acts of police brutality. Brian had obviously been brought up to make the sort of remark he had made to Lauren a week ago after the seminar on the night of Russell Bernard's murder. But was Brian's racism psychopathological? Could it lead to murder? That was harder to decide.

And what about Tracy Nicolson with her gun? And Sandy Grayson with her New England watercolors? Were they sane? One of the things that interested Lauren about her prime female suspects was that all three of them—Katherine, Tracy, and Sandy—were women whom one could imagine committing murder. In fact, they were more credible murderers than the likes of Scott Duchaine or Parker Hamilton Kendall IV. "Radcliffe women," sighed Michael. "One more terrifying than the next." Lauren took this as a compliment, as it was intended.

A key turned in the door, and Michael and Lauren both looked up with a frightened start. They were on edge. But of course it was only Carol at the door, home from the *Crimson*, with Brian O'Donnell standing behind her in the hall. He declined Carol's invitation to come in, though he called out, "Hi, Laurie, hi, Mikey." Lauren and Michael exchanged glances.

Carol came in gurgling over how sweet Brian was to walk her home. "Don't you think he's cute?" she asked dreamily. Michael and Lauren exchanged more glances. It was a little scary to think of Carol getting involved with Brian while Lauren still had him on her list of suspects.

"What about Baby Doll in Los Angeles?" said Lauren.

"Oh, he's cute too," said Carol. "They can both be cute, can't they?" Then she became dreamy again. "But Brian is so big," she cooed.

Carol began to get ready for bed. Michael watched as Lauren picked up the phone and dialed. It was around midnight. Michael listened to Lauren's end of the conversation. "Hi, Tracy? This is Lauren Adler. How are you?" Pause. "I'm okay." Pause. "No, I haven't started reading Trotsky either." Giggles. "I called to see if you wanted to go out for a, um, for a drink tomorrow afternoon. There was something I wanted to talk to you about." Pause. "You might be busy? Oh, I'm sorry. I really did want to talk to you. I wanted to talk to you about Russell Bernard." Pause. "Oh, you think you might be able to get free? Good. Shall we meet at Thirty-three Dunster Street? Around four? Great. I'll see you then." Lauren hung up.

"You're a brave girl," said Michael.

"I go to Radcliffe too."

"But you don't have a gun."

The phone rang, and Michael and Lauren nearly jumped. They stared at the phone, wondering whether it could be Tracy calling back. Neither of them wanted to answer the late night call. They watched the ringing phone.

"Well, aren't you going to answer it," said Carol, scampering over to the phone. Her bathrobe was decorated with a design of giant strawberries. She picked up the receiver, said hello, and immediately shrieked with delight. "Baby Doll!" she squealed. "I love you so much, Baby Doll!"

8. Girl talk

Lauren ordered a gin and tonic, and Tracy ordered scotch on the rocks. They sat on tall bar stools facing each other across a high, round, wooden table for two. Tracy wore a fur coat over a silk shirt and tight jeans. She lit a cigarette and looked more divorced than ever. "So how are things going?" asked Lauren brightly.

Tracy did not respond brightly. She looked Lauren in the eye and said coolly, "What do you have to say to me about Russell Bernard?" Tracy was obviously going to be uncompromisingly direct.

For a moment Lauren thought of being equally direct ("Did you kill him?"), but she decided that it would be better to be evasive and vague. With luck, Tracy could thus be induced to speak her mind. Tracy had made time for this meeting because Lauren had mentioned Russell's name on the phone. Now Lauren wanted to know why that name had power. She said, "I just wanted to talk about Russell with someone. I've been thinking about him a lot ever since he was killed."

"What have you been thinking about him? And why do you want to talk about him with me?" Lauren fumbled for the best answer, and Tracy, after a moment, proceeded to answer her own questions. "Do you want me to tell you what you've been thinking about him? You've been thinking about how sexy he was. And you've been wondering whether or not you could possibly be in love with him and whether you have to be out of your mind to be in love with someone who's dead. And, most of all, you've been remembering in detail how fantastic he seemed to be and feeling miserable at the thought that now he's absolutely out of the picture. No possibilities whatsoever. No flirtation. No long talks. No sexy nights. No college romance. No scandalous wedding. And no beautiful mulatto children. The whole fantasy is completely out the window. And you keep thinking about what might have been."

Lauren had all sorts of reactions to this. First of all, she was genuinely impressed by Tracy's penetration. Everything was right on the mark. Tracy seemed to have guessed exactly how Lauren was feeling about Russell, guessed the entire fantasy, every detail, right down to the exquisitely beautiful mulatto children. And Tracy had nothing to go on but intuition—unless, of course, Michael was even more indiscreet than Lauren supposed. For a moment Lauren considered the possibility, but she quickly discarded it: the Exeter circles in which Michael might conceivably have spoken too much would surely not have brought the tale back to Tracy Nicolson.

So there sat Tracy—all-knowing, inspired by divine intuition, wrapped up in an extremely uncollegiate fur coat, emptying her scotch, looking like a million-and-one trips to Las Vegas. She was certainly impressive. Sitting across from her, Lauren felt like a silly, naive, and utterly transparent little girl. But Lauren didn't just feel unsophisticated: she felt humiliated. She knew that her little fantasies about Russell were embarrassing to say the least, but there was no harm in that as long as they remained private fantasies. To have her cherished sentimental obsessions thrown in her face out loud was almost more than Lauren could bear with dignity. And, in fact, it would have been too much were it not for one other thing which gave her consolation and even a tiny sense of triumph: Tracy's crystal ball was damn good, but it wasn't perfect.

Tracy had managed to describe Lauren's odd infatuation with Russell Bernard, but, in a sense, she had failed to note the most important element. Lauren was, above all, preoccupied with finding Russell's murderer, and Tracy did not seem to be aware of that. Lauren had invited Tracy out for the purpose of pursuing the investigation. Lauren had hoped to induce Tracy to talk about Russell, and Tracy was indeed talking. So Lauren, despite her humiliation, felt also that she could salvage some sort of victory.

Lauren's emotional state was extremely complicated. Tracy had not only guessed at Lauren's secret love for Russell, but she had described precisely the sense of loss, the oppressive obsession with what might have been. Tracy's description suddenly made Lauren even more intensely wistful and melancholy. Lauren, however, had intuition of her own. She looked up at Tracy and said meaningfully, "Maybe that *is* how I feel about Russell. Have you had those fantasies too? I wonder."

"Go on wondering," said Tracy. "You're a smart girl. You'll figure it out. Which brings me to the next point: why are you coming to me of all people to talk about Russell Bernard? I like you fine, but you and I aren't such good friends. Why do you want to bare your heart to me, or, as it turns out, have me bare it for you? You know, I'm really not the type for cozy confidences." Lauren began to mumble, but Tracy cut her off. "Don't bother trying to explain. I already know. You're under the impression that I might know something special about Russell, that there might have been something between him and me, that we might have been lovers. And that possibility makes you jealous and excited and extremely curious about me, and you find yourself strangely drawn to me. You want to talk about Russell to someone who actually knew him, if possible in the biblical sense. I think that deep down you really want to ask me what he was like in bed."

This, Lauren thought, was once again alarmingly accurate. She herself had been unaware of the question forming in the back of her mind, but once Tracy had spoken the words there could be no denying that Lauren was indeed itching to ask. "I'm embarrassed to have to admit that you're right," said Lauren. Flatter, flatter, flatter, she thought. Tracy still seemed unaware that Lauren was investigating the murder.

"Yes," said Tracy, obviously gratified, "I sort of thought I might be. If I were Russell's lover—and I'm not saying I was and I'm not saying I wasn't—then it stands to reason that you would find me intriguing, if only to wonder what it was he saw in me."

"I think I could guess at that," said Lauren. "You're amazing." Flatter, flatter, flatter. But, Lauren thought, it was also true. Tracy was amazing.

"Thank you," said Tracy. "I like you too. Perhaps you and I will be friends."

"I'd like that."

"Okay, let's talk about Russell," said Tracy, "to sort of

clear things between us. That way I won't have to be constantly in the role of the woman who might or might not have been Russell's lover. And you won't have to do the part of the girl who almost went out on a date with the man of her dreams except that he was murdered first."

Lauren laughed in a friendly fashion. "By the way," she said without apparent slyness, "how did you know about my date with Russell? Surely *that* wasn't just brilliant intuition."

"Oh no," said Tracy, also laughing, "I'm not that good. I knew about your date because Russell told me."

"Oh."

"Oh nothing, it wasn't a big deal. I just ran into him in Harvard Yard before dinner, the night of the seminar, probably right after he'd talked to you."

"The night he was murdered," said Lauren helpfully.

"Yes, the night he was murdered. He told me he had a date with you, and then I forgot about it completely until you called last night and said you wanted to talk about Russell."

Lauren thought to herself, you're lying, Tracy Nicolson, you didn't just forget about the date. I ran into you at lunch Thursday afternoon, when nobody knew yet that Russell was dead, and you warned me to be careful about that date. You said that a guy like Russell could be a real killer. What did you mean by that? But Lauren just said, "Where was Russell going that night when you ran into him?"

"To dinner," said Tracy. "He was going to a dinner meeting of that dreary Black Students' Lobby. I don't think he was particularly looking forward to it, he seemed to have other things on his mind, but he was very dutiful about things like that. I don't think he ever missed a meeting."

You're wrong, thought Lauren, he missed that one. I wonder where he went instead. Apparently, wherever he was going, he wasn't about to confide in you.

"Let me tell you about Russell," said Tracy. "I guess I can tell you as much as anyone. He and I were pretty good friends. And we were lovers too, in case you were still wondering." Tracy lit another cigarette, ordered another scotch, and then put her next question in the routine and dispassionate tone of a Gallup questionnaire. "Have you ever had a black lover?"

Lauren would have dearly liked to say yes. But, alas, it

would not have been true. Tracy seemed to feel that a black lover was a normal part of a healthy American adolescence. For a moment Lauren considered lying, but in the end she decided to tell the truth. After all, if by confessing her innocence she gave Tracy cause to feel superior, this might at least put Tracy off guard about more important things. "No," Lauren muttered, but inwardly, for the thousandth time, she cursed her well-intentioned parents for bringing her up in the suburbs. How the hell was she supposed to find a black lover in the New Jersey suburbs? In Lauren's horrible high school there had been exactly one black, female, and the senior class had voted her "most unforgettable."

"I thought maybe not," said Tracy with infinite condescension. "But you will eventually—if you want to, and I think you probably do. But let me tell you something about black men. They have problems. They're lots of trouble. Russell Bernard wasn't the first black man I ever slept with, but he's gonna be the last."

Promises, promises, thought Lauren, but she said, "Why? What was wrong with Russell?"

But Tracy was going off on another tack. "Let me tell you about this boyfriend I had in high school. You know, I grew up in Chicago, which is a pretty tough place. I guess you wouldn't know about that sort of thing. You kind of look like you were finished in the suburbs. But the city is really different. My father is a hotshot politician in Chicago who also dabbles a little in big business and organized crime. He's sweet though—especially to me—and he's sexy in a crude sort of way, which is really the best way if you ask me." Lauren listened to Tracy's almost lewdly hoarse tones, watched the movement of her rough features, generously adorned with green eye shadow, framed with artificially blond hair—and had to admit that crudity was not without effect.

"My father tried to be very protective of me," Tracy continued, "but somehow it all backfired. I guess I just didn't want to be protected. You know, he's proud of me, but he never dreamed I would go to Radcliffe. He would have wanted me to do something pinker and more ladylike. He doesn't understand at all when I tell him I'm going to go to Harvard Business School and make more money than he does. Anyway, what I'm trying to say is that I didn't really end up being as protected and dainty as he would have liked." No kidding, thought Lauren, you seem pretty dainty to me. I like the dainty green nail polish.

"When I was in high school in Chicago, I was carrying on for years, on and off, with this black guy who was ten years older than me and sold a lot of drugs and stuff."

"Did you take him to the senior prom?" asked Lauren with genuine interest.

"No," said Tracy. "I wasn't really into proms."

"Neither was I, but if I'd had a black lover who was ten years older than me and sold drugs, I would definitely have been into proms."

"We did other stuff," said Tracy. "Mostly sex and drugs. It's really nice having a boyfriend who's a dealer. You really get spoiled. But, you see, there was a bad side to it also. I mean, this guy could be a real bastard. When he was stoned sometimes he used to beat me around and scream things at me. He felt inferior because he was black and lower class and uneducated, and he used to take it out on me. And he used to sleep with all these other women and then tell me about it. I was incredibly jealous. I wanted to kill him." She seemed to catch herself. "I don't get quite that jealous anymore. Maybe I sort of got used to it."

"So what happened with him?" asked Lauren.

"This past summer he suddenly disappeared. He didn't even say he was leaving. That's what kind of a bastard he was. I think he went to L.A. He was actually born and raised in L.A., so that's probably where he'd disappear to. But, you know, a dealer can work anywhere." It was all a little much, Lauren thought. She had to keep reminding herself that Tracy was only eighteen years old, at most nineteen, that Tracy had actually never been divorced even once, that Tracy was, in fact, a teenager with a really professional act. Tracy's confessions of weakness (her not extremely wonderful affair with the black dealer) were presented with the same hoarse, worldly tone, and Lauren was beginning to be aware of the incongruities in Tracy's image. The heavy makeup was covering up not wrinkles but perhaps a little bit of acne.

"I figured it was best to just forget about this guy," said Tracy, "even though I was still hung up on him, I don't know why. And so I just didn't think about him. Then I came to Harvard in September and went to the first meeting of the freshman seminar, and there was Russell Bernard. That's the thing: Russell Bernard looked exactly like this other guy. It's really strange. Same beard, same eyes, same build. And, you see, the resemblance was purely physical. As far as personality goes, Russell was the complete opposite. He was gentle, he was educated, he was cultured, he was comfortable with whites. And he didn't touch drugs—he was religious, you know. No dope. I thought that was a real minus. He actually disapproved of things like that, I think. But that was only a small flaw. Otherwise he seemed to be pretty perfect, and physically he was an exact copy of this other guy I was still hung up on."

"And then?" said Lauren, perhaps a bit too eagerly.

"Well I'm not going to describe for you what Russell was like in bed. But I'll just tell you that he was good. I can really appreciate that right now. You probably know I'm carrying on with Bert Rosen, the blond in the seminar. He's got his strong points. For instance, he always has lots of dope, and that's a nice change. But Bert—don't tell him I told you this—is the world's worst lover. I know, he looks like he'd be a lot of fun, California beach boy and all that, but actually he's incredibly boring in bed. He just pumps, that's all. It's really dull. Russell wasn't like that." Lauren made a mental note of this. It was a precious piece of gossip: Bert pumps.

Tracy and Lauren were both giggling about Bert, and Lauren was finding that she liked Tracy more and more. Tracy wasn't just tough; she was also funny. And yet Lauren was wary, because, as she watched Tracy perform, she was conscious of the level of tension which sustained the performance. It was a strain on Tracy to keep up the show without intermission, and Lauren could see that the scotch and the cigarettes were not just stage props. They were vital. It was the combination of toughness and tension that made Lauren believe that Tracy had it in her, under the right circumstances, to pick up her gun and plug someone. Lauren enjoyed being friendly with Tracy, but not for a moment did she cease to think about the mystery of Russell's murder.

"So tell me about *your* love life at Harvard," Tracy was saying. And Lauren didn't mind the question at all, even though she knew that Tracy was once again flaunting her own superior worldliness.

"Nothing much to tell, unfortunately," said Lauren. "I have been dating someone though, you know, Saturday night dates, a good-night kiss, that sort of thing, nothing very sexy. I know that sounds extremely old-fashioned, but he's pretty old-fashioned, this young man." Talking to Tracy, Lauren was deeply grateful that at least she was not a virgin. She wondered if she should find a way to tell Tracy, but decided that it was probably being taken for granted. If Tracy thought Lauren was a virgin, she would probably have enjoyed making a point of it.

"Who's the old-fashioned young man?" inquired Tracy.

"Someone you know."

"Oh really?"

"Scott Duchaine."

For a split second Lauren saw in Tracy's eyes something which she never expected to see there: simple shock. And then the shock vanished, and once again Tracy was in her utterly unshockable persona, the woman who'd seen everything, maybe twice. It all happened so fast that Lauren didn't even have time to ask what was the matter. But that brief look on Tracy's painted face was enough to alert Lauren, and she wondered why Tracy Nicolson should be shocked at Lauren's dates with Scott Duchaine. What could have passed between Tracy and Scott?

"What do you think of him?" said Tracy cautiously.

"I like him. He's sweet. Why, what do you think of him?"

"Oh, I guess he's sweet," said Tracy. "Do you think all this wild dating will lead to something?"

"Who knows? What do you suggest?"

"I suggest not, but my advice isn't so important since I don't think the whole thing is likely to get off the ground one way or another."

Lauren thought of Scott's odd behavior on Saturday. She thought of Scott's Facebook. Surely Tracy couldn't know about that. "Thanks for the show of confidence," said Lauren. "What's wrong with Scott?"

"Oh there's something wrong with every man." Tracy was being evasive.

Lauren decided to press another point. "What was wrong with Russell?"

"What do you mean?" Tracy was ever so slightly taken aback.

"You said before that Russell was going to be your last black lover. What was wrong with him?"

"Oh that," said Tracy, apparently relieved, and Lauren

wondered what had been going through her mind. "Things just didn't work out between us."

"Were you still lovers when Russell was murdered?" asked Lauren.

"No," Tracy answered promptly. "That was all over. I was already involved with Bert. I mean, what did you think? My lover gets murdered, and immediately I begin carrying on with someone else? I don't work *that* fast." Lauren wondered about this. It wasn't a question of how fast Tracy actually worked, though that in itself was not an uninteresting question. It was more a matter of whether the timing of Tracy's affairs somehow fitted in with the murder. Lauren remembered that the first time she had been aware of Bert and Tracy as a couple had been last Wednesday at the seminar when their thighs might or might not have been pressed together under the seminar table. And that was the day Russell had been murdered. Furthermore, the very first time Lauren had seen Tracy and Bert behaving like lovers in public had been the next day at lunch. And Russell was already dead then, but no one knew about it yet—except the murderer. How did this all fit together? Could Tracy or Bert have murdered Russell? Lauren was sure of one thing: Tracy was no longer speaking frankly. Lauren knew that she would have to weigh carefully anything that Tracy now said.

Tracy lit another cigarette. "The reason things didn't work out between me and Russell was because he was involved with someone else, someone I couldn't compete with, and that really bothered me." Dora Carpenter, Lauren thought, it was Dora Carpenter. How could Tracy hope to compete with Dora? No wonder Tracy didn't think well of the Black Students' Lobby. Everything Lauren had heard implied that Russell had been in love with Dora. But just how much would that have bothered Tracy? Was Dora's death really an accidental tragedy? "But Russell's dead now," said Tracy, "so all this really doesn't matter, does it?"

"I had lunch with your roommate yesterday," said Lauren, changing the subject.

"Who, Squeaky?" said Tracy, rather surprised. It was true, Lauren thought, that the two roommates would indeed sing very funny duets, Squeaky and Hoarsey.

"Yes," said Lauren. "She told me that you had said you knew who killed Russell Bernard."

"Did she?" Tracy's face was expressionless.

"Yes, she did." Lauren paused. "Do you know?"

"What do you think?"

"I think you might."

"Maybe I do," said Tracy, still expressionless.

"Who was it then?"

"Ah, that's the million-dollar question. But I really shouldn't say. Because I can't prove it. If I could prove it, I would have told the police right away. But it's just my intuition, which is usually on target, isn't it?" Lauren had to admit that it was.

"Is the murderer someone I know?" Lauren asked.

"Yes," said Tracy, "as a matter of fact."

"Is it someone in our freshman seminar?" Lauren asked, aware that she was trembling slightly.

"Yes," said Tracy. "Very good."

"Why did it happen?" Lauren asked.

"Twisted love," Tracy replied. "Why else does someone murder someone else?" She spoke as if she were extremely knowledgeable on the subject.

"How is it possible that you should know who killed him?"

"Because I know some things that nobody else knows."

Lauren decided to lead Tracy on. "He didn't go down to the river alone that night, did he?" In fact, Lauren had every reason to suppose that Russell had gone down to the river with Sandy Grayson.

"No, I don't think he did," said Tracy.

"And someone else was following?" Lauren suggested.

"Yes, perhaps," said Tracy noncommittally. Was it Tracy who followed Russell and Sandy? Or was it Sandy who followed Russell and Tracy? And how did Dora Carpenter fit in?

"You know because you were there," said Lauren. It was an accusation, not a question.

"No," said Tracy, smiling, well aware of Lauren's implications. "I wasn't there. I'm just guessing. I was with Bert that night." Tracy had prepared an alibi, the obvious alibi. Lauren didn't doubt for a moment that Bert would confirm it. Bert and Tracy would cover each other. Parker and Sandy would cover each other. Lauren would never manage to pin the murder on one of them.

"Then who killed Russell?" she asked, almost in despair.

"Someone you know," said Tracy, teasing.

"Yes?"

"Someone in the seminar."

"Yes?"

"Russell's lover," said Tracy, "his other lover, the one I couldn't compete with."

Lauren was shocked. "You mean Sandy Grayson," she said. "Sandy's in the seminar. You think Sandy killed Russell? You mean Sandy's the lover you couldn't compete with? I thought you were talking about Dora Carpenter."

"Dora Carpenter? Sandy Grayson?" Tracy was laughing. She was drunk. "Are you kidding? Russell was murdered by Scott Duchaine."

"Russell and Scott were lovers," Tracy explained with complete assurance. "That's what I know that nobody else knows. That's how I can know that Scott murdered Russell."

"I don't believe you," said Lauren. "I think you're lying." Why was Tracy telling her this? Lauren did not want it to be true. She did not want to have to think of Scott and Russell as lovers. She could accept homosexuality in general, she could cherish it in Michael, but she was disturbed at coming upon it unawares. It particularly disturbed her in connection with Scott and Russell, the one her supposed suitor, and the other the constant subject of her fantasies. It was a wildly improbable story, and yet not without a certain weird southern plausibility. "You're lying," she said again.

"Now why would I lie to you?" said Tracy.

"I don't know. You tell me."

"I can't imagine. There now, don't be so shocked. It's only homosexuality." Tracy was playing her favorite role again.

"I'm not shocked," said Lauren indignantly, even though she actually was, a little. "I'm just surprised. It really doesn't seem very likely to me." At the same time she was remembering Scott's strange reactions to Russell's name, remembering how timidly Scott had kissed her that night, how he had suddenly left the room. She was also remembering Russell's short story about the two best friends, black and white, in love with the same woman. "Tell me why you think so," Lauren challenged.

"Well, I haven't actually watched them going at it," said Tracy, "though I'm not saying I wouldn't have liked to." Lauren found this remark in extremely bad taste but, she thought, she might have liked to also. Tracy continued. "And I don't have any photographs of the two of them all over each other, nothing hard core like that. But I did hear the story from someone well-informed on the situation. I heard about it from Russell." Naturally, thought Lauren, a dead source which I cannot possibly check.

"Russell didn't just confess to me to purify his soul. In a way I guessed. One night I dropped in to see Russell in his room unannounced, and Scott was there. Oh, everything was perfectly decent really. They were both sitting on Russell's bed. They were fully dressed, all four feet were on the floor. When I got there Scott began to make excuses about how he had to leave, and I was watching the two of them say goodbye to each other, and I could see they were really uncomfortable, and I suddenly had this inspiration. So as soon as Scott had left, I began asking Russell some questions. He didn't say anything, but I kept coming back to the subject all evening. And finally, around three in the morning, after he'd proved his masculinity a couple of times, he confessed to me that he and Scott had been to bed together." Was Tracy lying to Lauren? Was Russell lying to Tracy? Was the story plausible?

"I don't know how involved they were," Tracy continued. "I don't know how many times they actually went to bed together, but I know it was more than once. I asked. It couldn't have been that many times, since they only knew each other for two months, and they were incredibly secretive about it." Tracy spoke with the air of one who had never been secretive about such things. "I think I'm the only one who knows, and now you do. I do know that it was more than just kicks for both of them. They were sort of emotionally caught up in each other in a sort of sick way. That's why Russell always had Scott on his mind. That's why I couldn't compete with Scott. Not because Russell was so gay, but for the opposite reason, because he'd had more experience with women. He could take me in stride, just as I could take him. But Scott was something different, and I could tell that Russell was thinking about him a lot, maybe all the time, and that was what really started to bother me. I didn't mind Russell's not being serious about me, until I saw him begin to become serious about someone else. That was when I knew it wouldn't work between me and Russell. I don't put up with being that kind of second fiddle. Did you know Russell played the violin?"

"Yes," said Lauren, "I knew. But wait a minute. Are you trying to tell me that it was Scott who murdered Russell out of jealousy? It sounds to me like you were the jealous one."

"And so maybe I killed Russell, huh? But I didn't. I wasn't that jealous. And I don't think Scott actually murdered Russell out of jealousy. Not that he wasn't jealous—he certainly was, especially since when Russell was seeing women, Scott felt even more homosexual by comparison. You see, Scott hates being homosexual, Russell told me that. Russell himself had mixed feelings about sleeping with men—he had all sorts of Catholic doubts about sex in general, which is part of what made him such an interesting lover—but Scott really hated himself. So, of course, he hated Russell too. And the more he found himself falling in love with Russell, the more he must have hated him. That's why Scott killed him." Suddenly Lauren had a new perspective on the missing picture of Russell in Scott's Freshman Register. Had Scott destroyed the picture because he couldn't bear to look at it? Or did he sleep with it under his pillow?

"You see," Tracy continued, "being gay must be something really horrible for someone from Scott's background. I'm sure his family expects him to be super straight, especially in that department. And, of course, blacks are just supposed to be slaves down South. I'm sure it was all that southern stuff in his background that attracted Scott to Russell in the first place. And made him hate Russell at the same time. It's really sick, but, to put it bluntly, I think Scott killed Russell to get free of him." Lauren could almost believe it herself, but still she had the feeling that Tracy might be lying, creating an extravagant and fascinating fiction to divert Lauren. But to divert her from what?

"Does Scott know that you know?" Lauren asked.

"I don't think so. I never said anything about all this to him. Why should I? The only thing I really know for sure is that Scott went to bed with Russell. And it was never any of my business to discuss that with Scott. As for the murder, that's just my guess, my woman's intuition. And I'm damn sure it's true, but I can't prove it. If I could prove it, I'd tell the police, not Scott."

Lauren made a suggestion. "The other reason not to tell Scott is that you'd be in danger then—I mean, if he really is the murderer..." Lauren knew that she herself would not dare to confront Scott with the story. It might possibly be true.

"I can take care of myself," said Tracy.

"Have you told anyone else besides your roommate that you think you know who killed Russell?"

"I don't think so, but I might have, maybe when I was stoned. I don't think it's likely to get back to Scott."

"Perhaps you should be careful," said Lauren with devious intent. "Maybe you should have a gun or something to protect yourself."

Tracy paused only for a moment before answering, but Lauren was watching intently and noticed the hesitation. Tracy said, "Don't worry about it, I can take care of myself." She said nothing about the gun which Lauren knew she possessed. Why was Tracy unwilling to tell Lauren about the gun? There was a moment of uncomfortable silence between them, and then Tracy took out her wallet to pay for the drinks. "I've got to run," she said. "I'm meeting Bert for dinner. You know, I'm getting tired of him already. On paper he seems like fun: sports car, money, dope, that sort of thing. But really he's pretty dull. I don't think he's going to last very long."

They rose to leave, and Tracy said, "Hey, have you done any of the reading for the seminar tomorrow, that Trotsky book?"

"No," confessed Lauren, giggling, "not a word."

"Me neither, and do you want to know the worst? I'm giving the presentation tomorrow." They were both laughing. "Honestly, I have to talk about Kerensky. Do you remember which one he was?"

"I think he was in the pre-Bolshevik provisional government," offered Lauren helpfully, "but he might have been on *Rocky and Bullwinkle*."

"Great, thanks a lot, I feel like I've started my research. I'll get to the Encyclopaedia Britannica after dinner, and then I'll thumb through the card catalog and make up a good bibliography. Thank God for the Encyclopaedia Britannica."

9. The Kerensky discussion

November is generally a chilly month in Cambridge, Massachusetts. But every November there are a few days when the sun shines brightly, and the digital thermometer high up over Harvard Square manages to register a temperature in the fifties. On such days it is impossible to believe that the long, slushy Cambridge winter is just around the corner along with the usual Harvard winter sports: final exams and research papers. Wednesday was one of those sunny November days, and Michael and Lauren easily convinced themselves that it was ice cream weather. Michael walked Lauren over to the meeting of her freshman seminar, both of them licking chocolate ice cream cones.

They had spent the whole afternoon talking about Scott and Russell and Tracy. Lauren was a little surprised and not entirely pleased by Michael's reactions. Lauren had described her conversation with Tracy in great detail, and Michael thought Tracy sounded absolutely marvelous. He was properly impressed by her showy intuitions, and he was utterly captivated by Lauren's rendering of Tracy's act. "When are you going to buy me a fur coat?" he asked Lauren with mock impatience. "The weather is going to turn really cold any day now."

"Just as soon as you start gathering nuts for winter," said Lauren. "Why don't you go start in the Math Department?"

Michael decided not only that he adored Tracy, but also that he was quite certain she had committed the murder. "It sounds to me like she was just leading you around in circles, telling you stories, maybe true, maybe not, to distract you. She'd be a grand murderess. For the sake of theatrical effect,

103

I certainly hope she was wearing her fur coat when she murdered him. When are you going to buy me a fur coat?"

"Just as soon as I buy you your one-way ticket to Jellystone Park, Exeter-under-the-Stars."

Michael made Lauren promise to introduce him to Tracy, promise that the three of them would go out together some evening soon. "But we have to do it soon," Michael insisted, "before some notorious underworld figure bumps her off in the night. I'm sure she's up to her fur collar in international heroin smuggling."

Lauren, who thought that Michael's adoration of Tracy was just a little bit overdone, was even less pleased by his reaction to the revelations about Scott and Russell. It wasn't so much that Michael believed the story was true (in fact, he emphasized that he believed Tracy capable of the most splendid lies), but rather that he enthusiastically hoped so. Michael had repeated over and over that it was the most marvelous story he had ever heard until Lauren had at last interrupted irritably to say that she didn't really see what was so marvelous about it.

Michael was always gleeful to discover that somebody appealing and apparently straight was actually gay, though he was not above trying to imply that he had expected it all along. Lauren herself was also usually delighted to learn that one Harvard professor or another indulged in what Michael referred to as "decadent practices," but she saw it not so much as a personal triumph for her, but rather as a blow against stuffiness in general. In this particular case she was not delighted. The story impinged upon her fantasies about Russell, and she resented that. And as for Scott, well, it was not particularly pleasing to learn that one's supposed admirer might be less than wildly passionate about women. And it was, of course, still less pleasing to think that he might be homicidally psychotic. It did occur to Lauren to wonder if Michael's glee stemmed partially from some sort of mild jealousy of Lauren's feelings about Russell and of her Saturday night dates with Scott.

"I simply don't believe the story is true," said Lauren, fully intending to dump some cold water on Michael's enthusiasm.

"Maybe not, maybe not," said Michael, "but I do hope it is. I do understand that the whole idea is extravagantly dramatic for a Harvard freshman saga, but, you know, once

you start working on the assumption that someone in your
seminar murdered Russell, you're already conceding a certain
element of melodrama. I mean, the romance of Russell and
Scott is no more improbable and twisted than the murder
mystery we started out with. But it's more than that, Lauren.
The story about Russell and Scott is so plausible, so aesthetically satisfying."

"I don't know what you're talking about," Lauren insisted,
but she was not being quite honest.

"Well, first of all," said Michael, "they make a handsome
couple. Don't they? Admit it."

"No, I don't want to admit it," Lauren pouted. "Russell
and I made a handsome couple. Scott and I make a handsome
couple. But Russell and Scott make a weird couple." This last
judgment was made only half seriously. Lauren was making
fun of herself. She was beginning to concede Michael's point.

Michael was aware of this, and he too spoke in humorous
tones. "There, there," he said with mock reproach. "You're
being just the teenciest bit narrow-minded. I seem to recall
that less than a week ago you were fantasizing about having
simultaneous affairs with Scott and Russell. Don't you think
you might have been unconsciously aware of some kind of
sexual current between them?"

"No," said Lauren grumpily. "And it's not nice to quote
people's fantasies against them. Do I ever remind you of the
time you spent the whole night describing to me in exhaus-
tive detail what—"

But Michael interrupted her. "And of course you were
absolutely right. What Russell and Scott have in common is
the South. Their romance is practically American history."

"Not very romantic. To me American history is what you
endure in order to graduate from high school in New Jersey.
Interracial homosexuality never figured very prominently in
my American history class. I'm sure I would have noticed."

"Actually American history at Exeter was concerned with
precisely those themes." Michael's reverence for Exeter led
him to cherish the rather remarkable belief that the faculty,
administration, and trustees encouraged the more attractive
boys to be aware of each other in all sorts of postpubescent
ways. To hear Michael talk you would think that Exeter
teachers taught nothing but homosexuality in their classes,
from physical education to Greek. Lauren suspected that

Michael's memory exaggerated (not to say entirely invented) this unorthodox educational emphasis.

"Speaking of Exeter, the intellectual pinnacle of America, you said you were going to call up that guy you knew from school, the one who had read Trotsky in Russian and could tell me what the book is about."

"Oh no!" said Michael. "I forgot. I'm so sorry. Last night I fell asleep early in the evening. I was trying to read the assigned portions of Wordsworth's *Prelude* while lying in bed, and the combination was fatal. I slept very soundly all night long. I'm so sorry I forgot to call and find out about that Trotsky book for you. What will you do?"

"Well, either I have to read the book in the next two minutes, or else I'll have to fake it again. I can barely remember what it feels like to come to this class after doing the reading. Don't worry about it, Michael. I'll be fine."

As Michael and Lauren approached the building in which the seminar met, they noticed two other couples walking along different paths through Harvard Yard toward the same destination. Parker and Sandy were walking along one path, looking very preppie and proper. Lauren caught a word of their conversation across the Yard, and was horrified to realize that they were actually talking about Trotsky. Parker nodded hello in the direction of Michael and Lauren, and they nodded back. Sandy did not look up.

On another converging path another couple provided a wonderfully comic contrast to the preppie pair. Brian O'Donnell was wearing a green sweat shirt lettered with the slogan "Kiss Me I'm Irish." And walking alongside him, dressed all in pink, was someone who could really appreciate a sweat shirt with a cute slogan: Carol. "Your roommate is really outdoing herself," said Michael. "Does she go to Paris especially to buy her pink acrylic sweaters? And who is that extremely fashionable European escort?"

Lauren was not at all pleased to see Carol promenading so contentedly with big Beef. Lauren had not yet forgiven Brian for his remark about Russell, and neither had she forgotten about Brian's racist father. Brian was a moron, but perhaps a vicious one—even a dangerous one. Lauren had tried to talk to Carol about Brian and to suggest subtly that he was disgracefully stupid, but Carol seemed, on the whole, unconcerned. Now she was listening with an expression of delighted and rapt interest, while Brian grunted about heaven knows what, probably football. "It's something about her Los Angeles soul," said Lauren to Michael. "Whenever the sun comes out she immediately begins to flirt with whatever is crouching in the nearest cave." But Brian's attendance on Carol made Lauren uneasy. She couldn't say exactly why.

Michael and Lauren and Sandy and Parker and Carol and Brian arrived at the door of the same building at the same time. They were all a little embarrassed, but Parker most of all. Not only did he have to accept Sandy's very ungracious refusal to take notice of anyone, but he furthermore had to submit to the indignity of Brian's greeting: "Hey, Parkie!"

Carol and Brian stopped outside of the building to take leave of each other; Carol was going down to the pool to swim some laps. Michael decided to walk down to the pool with Carol, maybe to swim, maybe just to watch the swimmers. But first he wanted to take a peek at the divine Tracy. However, when Lauren checked the seminar room, she had to report back to Michael that Tracy had not yet arrived. Michael decided that there would be other opportunities to meet Tracy, so he and Carol went off together. Lauren returned to the seminar room, trying not to think about the extremely fresh-looking copy of Trotsky's *History of the Russian Revolution* which she held in her hand.

It was easy not to think about Trotsky with Scott Duchaine so near. Lauren sat down next to Scott, smiled at him, and said hello with all the false casualness she could muster. He smiled in return, and it was clear that he too was not as relaxed as he might have hoped to appear. He was probably uncomfortable about the odd interlude that had taken place between them Saturday night when their embraces had come to such an abrupt and still unexplained end. But for Lauren that was the most minor cause of discomfort. She was thinking about the mutilated Freshman Register and about Tracy's story.

The students chatted quietly, awaiting the arrival of Professor Baranova. Lauren and Scott made very lame conversation about the unexpectedly sunny weather, while Lauren looked him over with enormous fascination. Much as she wanted Tracy's story to be a lie, she had to admit that she had never before found Scott so compellingly interesting. What was going on inside his head? Also, more than ever before, she found herself tensely conscious of Scott as a sexual being,

not merely a cardboard cutout from *Gone with the Wind*.
She followed the line where his neatly combed hair met his
forehead, and she felt an urge to reach out her hand and
touch him. She observed his mouth as he spoke, and was for
the first time aware of the lips and teeth and tongue which
produced the seductive southern accent. She caught a hint of
the same cologne that he had worn when they had kissed
Saturday night. The tiny triangle of throat revealed above the
top button of his shirt made her remember how cold his chest
had been.

She watched his hands on the seminar table, and decided that they were somehow sensual and cruel. They were not
the polite, chivalrous hands which Lauren would have liked
to attribute to a southern gentleman. She thought again about
Gone with the Wind and remembered the scene in which
Rhett Butler realizes Scarlett's desperate situation by observing her scarred hands. For a moment Lauren could imagine
that Scott's were the hands of Russell's murderer. But how
much was it really possible to tell from a pair of hands?

Had Russell and Scott gone to bed with each other? Was
it conceivable that they had even kissed each other? And did
Scott then murder Russell by the river? Strike him, stab him,
shoot him, and dump his corpse in the water? Scott was
talking now. He was asking whether Lauren was doing anything Saturday night. *Gone with the Wind* was showing at the
Harvard Square Theatre, and he wondered if she'd like to go
see it with him. Lauren then heard herself say yes, she'd like
that very much.

Waiting for the seminar to begin, Lauren remembered
how she had appraised the small group the week before, how
she had evaluated everyone's attractiveness instead of following the class discussion. Now, after Russell's murder and a
week's worth of detecting, Lauren examined this group with
a new intensity and a sense of genuine urgency. Last week's
beauty contest seemed frivolous and shallow; now Lauren had
to know what was happening deep inside of these Harvard
students. She had to reconstruct their passions and their
lives. One of them, she sincerely believed, was a murderer.

Not everyone was present. Most emphatically absent, of
course, was Russell himself. Lauren had not imagined what
an enormous difference his absence would make in this

group. It would be even more noticeable when the discussion was under way, since Russell had always been an avid and well-prepared participant. Professor Baranova had obviously thought well of Russell, had valued his contributions. She had permitted, perhaps even encouraged him to become, after herself, the dominant figure in the class.

In fact, Lauren now began to fear that with Russell out of the way Sandy Grayson would make herself the center of the class discussion. Not that Professor Baranova particularly cared for Sandy, just that Sandy was always so disgustingly well prepared (something which Lauren had managed to forgive in Russell). Sandy had dull and pretentious opinions about all the class material. When Professor Baranova asked a difficult question which no one else could answer, Sandy always had something uninteresting to offer. Lauren looked across the seminar table at Sandy busy reviewing her reading notes and began to fear she could come to dislike the freshman seminar.

Now Sandy would have no real competition. Katherine Butler always did all the reading and was frequently ready to begin some sort of political polemic which would, in the end, turn out to be not about the Russian Revolution but about South Africa. Professor Baranova, however, did not like Katherine's speeches—once she had actually coolly interrupted Katherine, urging upon the young revolutionary greater conciseness and scholarly perspective—so Katherine often lapsed into dejected silence. From her expressions at such moments it was clear that she was reflecting scornfully on other people's reactionary natures, living for the day when the oppressors would be cast down from their palaces and she could make speeches all the time.

Scott and Parker were also always prepared for class, but they were too well brought up to be talkative. Andrew Stein, of course, could not bring himself to utter a word for fear of cracking up on the spot. Melissa Wu was diligent but timid; she usually preferred not to speak up unless somebody posed a question that could be answered directly from her extensive reading notes, those specimens of perfect penmanship. Bert and Tracy were not very serious students, perhaps less serious than Lauren herself, and as for Brian O'Donnell, his rare remarks were merely a cause for snickering. The question of whether or not he did the reading had to be subordinated to the question of whether or not poor Beef could actually read.

It was remarkable, Lauren thought, how the loss of one crucial student could make a lively seminar suddenly seem so unpromising. There was no doubt about it: Sandy would be the star pupil from now on. Surely Sandy could not have murdered Russell just so that she would be able to talk more in class?

If Sandy were to replace Russell as the dominant figure, the whole spirit of the seminar would change. The new tone would be set by Sandy, the preppie Jew working hard to be WASP. Lauren could imagine nothing stuffier. Russell's absence would also make the seminar ethnically monotonous, extremely white in spite of Melissa Wu, who was somehow too tiny and too well behaved to provide any color.

Russell would never return to the seminar, but there were others with less forceful excuses for being absent. Tracy and Bert had not yet arrived and Lauren took for granted that they were together. Her first reaction was that they were perhaps in bed in one of their rooms. Even now Bert might be pumping away while Tracy, rather bored, tried to remind him that they were late for the seminar. Lauren grinned to herself maliciously. But then she remembered that Tracy was giving the presentation on Kerensky that day, and Lauren could deduce from her own research habits just where Tracy might be: in Lamont Library, copying furiously out of the "K" volume of the Encyclopaedia Britannica. And Bert was standing by to render assistance; maybe he was putting together the fake bibliography from the card catalog.

That would certainly be an obliging sort of boyfriend, thought Lauren, even if he is a pumper. Scott Duchaine was probably too honorable to compile dishonest bibliographies, even for the woman he loved. Lauren caught herself; she should not be thinking of Scott as boyfriend material. She peeked at him out of the corner of her eye. He was sitting with those ominous hands flush on the table. Who could say how obliging Scott might be, or what precisely was taboo according to his code of honor?

The other person still missing was Professor Baranova, and as long as Bert and Tracy arrived before she did, they would be fine. The seminar would not begin without the professor, but she had given everyone to understand at the first meeting that she would look very poorly on tardiness. Lauren hoped that Tracy and Bert would make it on time, but at the same time she thought it would be interesting to see how rough, tough Tracy Nicolson faced up to Tatiana Baranova's disapproving glare.

Now, before Professor Baranova arrived to transform this group of students into a Harvard seminar, Lauren was able to watch them and think about the murder mystery. How could she fit together what she knew about these diverse Harvard freshmen to make some sense out of Russell's murder?

Lauren looked across the table at Sandy Grayson, who did not look up to return Lauren's gaze. Sandy was still reviewing her reading notes, occasionally making a few notes on her notes. Sandy had been, very probably, down by the river with Russell the night he was murdered, exactly one week ago. She had virtually admitted this to Michael. What then could be easier to suppose than that Sandy had committed the murder? And yet the evidence was by no means conclusive. Sandy could easily have separated peacefully from Russell down by the river that night and returned to Harvard Yard with Parker. That would have left Russell alone, easy prey for anyone hiding in the dark.

Lauren could imagine the scene: a dark form lying flat on the riverbank, unseen, watching Sandy and Russell enact some little soap opera episode... watching them separate unpleasantly, watching Russell alone for a moment, and then leaping. It would not have been a random riverbank killer, since the murderer could have just as easily chosen the unaccompanied Sandy, a weaker victim. The killer was after Russell.

On the one hand, Lauren would have liked for it to be Sandy who had murdered Russell. Lauren disliked Sandy more than ever, and could imagine with some satisfaction the prospect of a cement-block prison cell decorated with New England watercolors, not to mention the tantalizing possibility of Chemise Lacoste prison stripes. And yet, somewhere deep inside, Lauren would have been sorry to discover that Sandy was the murderer. Sandy was such a tedious little prig. Everything she touched became dull. As a solution to the murder mystery, she would be disappointingly undramatic. Russell deserved a worthier nemesis.

And so Lauren willingly considered the other suspects. Suppose Sandy had indeed left Russell still alive down by the river that night. Who then was the figure crouching in the dark?

There was one other person who had admitted to being

at the river. He was sitting next to Sandy now, not quite at his ease. While Sandy diligently prepared to take over the class discussion Parker chatted politely with Melissa Wu, who maintained her side of the conversation with more than equal politeness. Lauren had trouble believing in Parker as the murderer but, she suddenly realized, he was superficially no more unlikely than Scott Duchaine, who was now up at the top of the list of suspects. There were important similarities between the two boys, the Virginia gentleman and his New England counterpart. Both were serious, polite, and nicely dressed. Both possessed by birth that sense of social superiority that Sandy Grayson studiously aspired to master. If Scott could have a steamy secret life, then surely Parker could have one too. Who was Parker in love with? Scott?

At the end of the table Katherine Butler was sitting between Brian O'Donnell and Andrew Stein. Lauren noticed with amusement that Katherine was talking to the boys about a planned demonstration against apartheid to be held in Boston the following week. Andrew was clearly not listening. He seemed to have eaten almost an entire eraser in nervous anticipation of the commencement of class discussion. Brian, meanwhile, was listening with an utterly vacant expression. If he had indeed realized that he was listening to Marxist propaganda, he would surely have stopped his ears, but Lauren suspected that poor Brian hadn't the faintest idea what Katherine was or what on earth she was talking about.

Katherine had a cold-blooded, hardheaded reason for killing Russell. She hated the political organization that he led, believed that Russell and the whole Lobby were evil and reactionary. She would not have murdered from sexual jealousy. Her motive could be seen as politically pragmatic. But, of course, the common sense of Katherine's motive could not be credited too seriously, since it had to be placed in the general context of Katherine's personality, which was, Lauren thought, at least mildly unbalanced. But didn't that make her an even more likely murderer? Hadn't Katherine actually said that if she were going to kill one person at Harvard, she thought she'd kill Russell Bernard? But could his murderer really have had the nerve to say that after committing the crime? Perhaps—if she really were unbalanced. Could it have been Katherine who silently watched Russell and Sandy separate on the riverbank?

And what about Scott Duchaine and Tracy Nicolson?

Tracy had believed that Scott was the murderer. She believed this because she claimed to know that Scott and Russell had been lovers. It was indeed a shocking piece of information, but, assuming it was true, did it really prove conclusively that Scott had murdered Russell? No, in fact, it didn't. And yet, if that piece of information was false, if Russell and Scott were not lovers, if Tracy was lying to Lauren, then didn't that prove conclusively that Tracy was trying to distract Lauren from something of enormous significance? And what could that be? What else if not Tracy's own involvement? Lauren was eager to take a fresh look at Tracy today, Tracy without a glass of scotch, but Tracy had not yet appeared.

And now Professor Baranova entered. She was always a few minutes late, and today she was even a bit later than usual. She seemed to prefer to arrive after her students were already present and seated. That way she could immediately begin the seminar without any uncomfortable undefined period of waiting on her part. In addition, Lauren realized, Professor Baranova's lateness allowed her to make a grander entrance. The students waited for her with a sense of anticipation, and she always proved herself worthy of the dramatic tension.

Today, as always, she was stunning. In addition to her usual wonderful woolen garments of silver and beige, she was wearing a long scarf that was profoundly maroon. Her diamond earrings flashed. She took her place at the head of the seminar table and put before her a beautifully bound old copy of Trotsky. Lauren looked at the spine and realized with a small thrill that Professor Baranova's Trotsky was not in English, nor even in Russian, but in French. The details of her life always seemed to be gorgeous, and Lauren longed to see the inside of her home.

When Professor Baranova spoke, the class was absolutely silent. She said, "As you all know, there has been a tragedy. One of the students in this class was killed. He was a very intelligent and interesting young man. I myself am deeply regretful."

Tatiana Baranova was immediately aware of the absent students and she did not hesitate to remark on the fact that "Miss Nicolson" (the "Miss" was affixed with appropriate irony, and the irony enhanced by the Russian accent), Miss

Nicolson who was supposed to open the seminar with a little talk about Kerensky, was evidently indisposed. "Well, we can talk about Kerensky without Miss Nicolson, but we must be careful, since our little presentations tend to be so extremely diverting—like yours last week, Melissa—that we never have enough time to discuss the assigned reading. Though sometimes it's just as well to leave the assigned reading alone and let the discussion move more freely." Lauren could hardly have agreed more, and she even managed an earnest little nod of assent. Professor Baranova, who might or might not have seen Lauren's nod, then qualified her earlier opinion. "As long as you are all doing the assigned reading on your own."

"What shall we say about Kerensky?" she continued. "I myself would prefer not to speak at first, since I am biased. Mr. Kerensky was a close friend of my father. Someone tell me, why is Kerensky important?"

Melissa Wu raised her hand (Melissa never spoke without raising her hand and waiting to be called on) and informed the class very seriously that Kerensky was important in the provisional government that ruled Russia between February and October 1917. Melissa was quite reliable about dates.

"Yes, thank you, Melissa," said Professor Baranova with transparently false gratitude. "I wonder if we could go any deeper. Last week, when you gave your very compelling presentation about Rasputin, we discussed the statement that without Rasputin there would have been no Lenin. In fact, it was Kerensky who said it, I believe. Similar statements have often been made about Kerensky himself. He is seen as one of the major causes of the Bolshevik revolution, a more immediate cause than Rasputin. Why might one argue that without Kerensky there would have been no Bolshevik triumph?"

Sandy spoke without raising her hand. "Kerensky was weak and indecisive. The political turmoil of 1917 was too much for him. His inability to govern paved the way for someone more forceful—Lenin." This was not, Lauren thought, the most tactful way to formulate your opinion after the professor had announced that Kerensky was a close friend of her father.

But Professor Baranova showed no sign of being offended. "Yes," she said, "I think that may be true, though I don't

think it's entirely to Kerensky's discredit. The situation may
have called for certain expedients which were not in his
nature."

"He didn't smash the Bolsheviks when he could have,"
said Brian. "He didn't kill Lenin the way Lenin would have
killed him." The whole seminar was a little surprised. Every
now and then something stuck in Brian's brain, something
that interested him for one primitive reason or another, and
now everyone was slightly shocked to hear Brian utter two
sentences which were ridiculous only in tone and delivery,
but not in content.

"Yes, that also may be true, Brian. Very good." Everybody patronized Brian, and Professor Baranova patronized
everybody—except for Russell, Lauren thought—she hadn't
patronized Russell. "What do you think of that, Brian? Should
Kerensky have tried to arrange for the execution of the
Bolsheviks?"

"Yes" was Brian's red-blooded, all-American response.
He was not interested in ethical subtleties.

There was an embarrassing silence. Where would the
discussion go from there? Scott Duchaine courteously shifted
the topic by pointing out that Kerensky had failed to withdraw Russia from World War One, and Lenin was able to
appeal to the people's desire for peace. Sandy Grayson was
about to follow up on this when Katherine Butler interrupted
vehemently.

"That's what was wrong with Kerensky," she insisted.
"He was completely out of touch with the masses. The
Russian masses were revolutionary in 1917—that's clear from
reading Trotsky—and Kerensky was a bourgeois liberal. The
masses wanted Lenin." Katherine took these things very seriously, Lauren thought. The rest of the group was equally
ill at ease with Katherine's convictions.

But Professor Baranova merely pointed out what even
Katherine should have considered. "Trotsky perhaps does not
paint an entirely accurate picture, vivid though it may be, of
the mood of the Russian people. He was not without political
bias."

"The Russian people were very religious," said Sandy, as
if she were the expert. "Even in 1917 the Orthodox Church
was much more important than the Revolution to the vast
majority of Russian peasants. I did some additional reading
this week since the Trotsky was so patently unobjective. . . ."

Sandy continued, and Lauren stopped listening. Sandy was unbearable. Now she was doing additional reading. Lauren was thinking about those religious Russian peasants. She was thinking of Russell, who had been a devout Catholic. He had gone to church every Sunday. But what was religion to the average Harvard student? To the suspects in the seminar? Last week Lauren had evaluated everyone's appearance; this week she decided to survey religion.

Start with Sandy. Sandy was Jewish. Presumably, she did not like being Jewish. She was certainly not religious, but she would probably prefer to be a lapsed Episcopalian rather than a lapsed Jew. Religion might be important to Sandy—as something to conceal. Lauren made a silent resolution that every day she would tell one new person that Sandy Grayson was Jewish.

Now Parker was probably genuinely Episcopalian. And Scott certainly was—hadn't he said that St. Christopher's was an Episcopalian prep school? That was another link between the two young aristocrats. Did they go to church? It was not impossible—if only for the sake of good form and family tradition. Parker, of course, seemed to be devoted to his pagan Greek philosophers. But what about Scott? Did he go to church on Sunday mornings after his Saturday night dates with Lauren? If she ever stayed the night she might find out, but that was beginning to seem less and less likely.

"I don't really like reading this book," Scott was saying at Lauren's side. He was holding his copy of Trotsky in his hand, and Lauren noted that it did genuinely look read. "I mean obviously I'm not a Russian, and I'm not a Communist, and I don't believe that the Russian Revolution was the most glorious event in the history of mankind. And Trotsky does believe that, and he goes on about it for hundreds of pages. So naturally it starts to irritate me after a while. But you know—" Scott paused to choose his words. "Sometimes I find that it gets to me, just the way it's written, the emotional enthusiasm. I completely forget what the book is about, and I start rooting for the Russian Revolution as if it were a baseball team."

Some people laughed appreciatively, including Professor Baranova. Katherine Butler looked scornful, and Brian O'Donnell perked up at the mention of baseball.

"I know what you mean," said Parker, agreeing with Scott. "That's what I kept thinking while I was reading.

Trotsky really can write. I guess in the end he wasn't a very successful politician, but he was a good writer. Of course I've only read it in the English translation." Parker sounded apologetic. "But I wish I could read it in Russian." He was such a scholarly young man, Parker Hamilton Kendall IV. Naturally he wouldn't want to make any final judgments until he'd read the original. Lauren thought about Parker's Greek and Latin with vague respect but entirely without envy.

Professor Baranova picked up her own beautifully bound French Trotsky and said, "I didn't do the reading in Russian this week, and I haven't actually read Trotsky in Russian for many years. But I do remember that he wrote powerful prose."

Katherine Butler almost snorted at this tribute to Trotsky's prose. Surely there could be no discussion of Trotsky more frivolous than this one. Lauren returned to her survey of religion. Katherine Butler was the daughter of liberal missionaries—Methodist perhaps? Katherine had apparently rejected her parents' religion emphatically. Lauren did not doubt that Katherine's atheism was a proud banner available for public display. Surely Katherine, deep down, had extremely strong, perhaps Freudian, feelings about religion. Giggling to herself, Lauren then decided to put Katherine and Melissa in the same category: missionary Christianity. Melissa went to church; Lauren was quite certain of that.

Brian O'Donnell seemed to be the only other Catholic besides Russell. (Russell, however, was very unexpectedly Catholic, and Lauren was prepared for the possibility that someone else might still surprise her on that count.) Lauren wondered if Russell and Brian had gone to the same Catholic church in Cambridge. Did Brian know that Russell was Catholic? Could that have mattered?

Lauren noticed that Brian had begun to doze after Scott's allusion to baseball had failed to initiate a discussion about sports. Lauren sympathized with Brian, since Sandy Grayson was holding the floor. She had done so much extra reading and had so much to say about Trotsky's personal role in the Revolution. And Sandy was such a bore. Even Professor Baranova looked bored, and Lauren resolved to come to the rescue.

Lauren waited for Sandy to pause for breath and then interrupted her quite gracefully. "Excuse me, Sandy." Lauren's tone was almost too polite, calculated to irritate Sandy all the more. "Isn't it interesting that the losers are so much more sympathetic than the winners. I mean, Kerensky is more appealing than Lenin. And Trotsky beats Stalin easy." A remark such as this really didn't depend on doing the reading, so Lauren didn't think she had anything to lose.

Professor Baranova looked pleased at Lauren's interruption, and immediately responded herself before Sandy could. "I told you that my father and Kerensky were friends. It might interest you to know that my father also claimed to find Lenin personally likable, despite their political differences. On the other hand, my father always insisted that Trotsky was obnoxious and irritating in person. My father knew Stalin only very slightly, not well enough to have formed any sort of personal impression."

What were Tatiana Baranova's religious sentiments? Lauren imagined that the professor was elegantly skeptical, but she surely had had at least one devout Russian Orthodox grandparent. Perhaps that was a possible connection to Rasputin, but it was hard to see what to make of it. Professor Baranova seemed to have more direct connections to various other characters in Russian history.

Lauren had found the likes and dislikes of the Menshevik Baranov rather diverting. Now, however, Sandy Grayson was talking again, and Lauren turned her attention to Andrew Stein. Andrew was Jewish, and he was also the freshman Dr. Strangelove. Freud may have seen religion as a mass neurosis, but Andrew Stein was the emblem of a new age in which neurosis became a personal religion with its own little rituals. Jews, Lauren thought, were supposed to enjoy their neuroses and cultivate them, not become crippled by them. And Lauren should know; wasn't she Jewish too?

Lauren was not particularly interested in her own religion, but neither was she ashamed of it. One thing that it was possible to learn in the suburbs was that, on the whole, those who tried to hide their origins, like Sandy, ended up seeming sillier than even the most vulgarly ethnic. Lauren's parents had been anxious for her to be aware of what they called her cultural heritage, and for some years she was pressured to attend an afternoon Hebrew School connected to the local New Jersey Jewish Center. New Jersey Judaism was not an appetizing concoction, and Lauren eventually managed to get herself expelled from Hebrew School at the age of ten for extreme misbehavior.

Lauren turned her attention to the absent seminar members, Bert and Tracy. What excuse would they offer for their misbehavior? And what about religion? Tracy's religion seemed hardly relevant; surely she was raised in some sort of nondescript Protestantism which she had discarded long since. And Bert was, like Sandy, an extremely assimilated Jew. Though Bert relied upon natural attributes—blond hair, blue eyes, California cool—where Sandy depended on studious, conscious effort. Bert was a wonder.

And, in fact, there he was. Bert had opened the door of the seminar room and taken a step inside. He stood there solemn but radiant, a visitor from the alien planet of California. Where was Tracy?

"You're quite late," said Professor Baranova. "And Miss Nicolson, I gather, will be even later, if she chooses to appear at all."

Bert met the professor's gaze fairly and spoke only one sentence in response. "Tracy has been murdered," he said. For a moment the room was icily still, and then the silence was pierced by Andrew Stein with a strange, repressed sound that might have been a scream and might have been a laugh.

10. Spoiled children

Professor Baranova announced that the class was over. She did not want to continue the discussion—not that it really would have been possible to do so. The nine students would have sat silently and stared at each other; it was not the time to discuss the Russian Revolution. Of the eleven students who had been at last week's meeting, two were now dead. It seemed impossible not to reflect on that fact with shock and also with some fear.

Lauren thought it only natural that Andrew Stein, who was genuinely mentally disturbed, should react badly to news of this nature. His muffled shriek, however, intensified the sense of terror for everyone in the room. After all, no one, not even the most stable and well-adjusted, could be expected to take such things in stride. For a moment all eyes turned from Bert to Andrew. Andrew—looking desperately feverish—grabbed his book and left the room, passing Bert, who still stood at the door where he had entered a moment before. It was then that Professor Baranova announced that the class was over.

At first no one else moved. They sat and stared with various ghostly expressions. And their unwillingness, their inability to move, was more than just stunned inertia. Outside it was already dark, and no one was ready to face the darkness. They sat together in the lighted room, surrounded by the portraits of distinguished Harvard alumni of past centuries. This room was an island of safety, and no one wanted to face the world outside. Harvard was suddenly not a reassuring place to live. For a moment Lauren sincerely wished she were in New Jersey with her parents.

It was left to Professor Baranova to make the first move and she did so. She rose at her place and took her beautiful French edition of Trotsky in hand. "Good evening," she said. "I'll see you all here next week." This was said with complete poise, but it was perhaps not precisely the right thing to say. Considering the circumstances, no one could help reflecting on the possibility that Professor Baranova might *not* see all of them next week. Two had already been murdered. Superstition demanded a third.

Scott Duchaine also rose to his feet, a few seconds after Professor Baranova. His manner conveyed the impression of one who could never sit while a lady was standing. But Scott's intention was more specific than mere southern courtesy. Scott was aware that it was dark outside and that someone had been murdered. He said, "Professor Baranova, may I walk you home?" It was breathtakingly gallant to have remained cool enough to think of offering himself as an escort. It was also, despite the frightening circumstances, a little bold. Professor Baranova was so much above them all. Could one really just offer to walk her home?

Apparently one could. Professor Baranova turned to Scott and said, "Yes, thank you. I would be very grateful." Was she frightened also? If so, it was not in her voice. There was not even the hint of a tremor.

Surely both she and Scott were aware that the attention of every student was focused on them. Their exchange could not but have the effect of a staged scene. Now she walked to his place, and he stood back to let her pass so that he could leave the room behind her as a gentleman should. Lauren couldn't help thinking that they made a handsome couple. In a moment they were gone.

Sandy was next to move. She put her briefcase on the seminar table in front of her, placed her books and notes inside, and rose to leave. On her face was an expression of businesslike self-absorption. She did not look at the other students who were staring at her. And then Brian O'Donnell got to his feet and stood towering over the class. He said, "Sandy, can I walk you?" It was clearly well meant, but the gesture came off as a sort of parody of Scott's gallantry. Brian was an awkward substitute for Scott, and Sandy was well aware of the potentially comic aspects of the situation. In fact, by feeling foolish, she really made the situation foolish. If Sandy had been a more gracious person, Lauren thought, there might have been a dignified way to accept Brian or reject him. But Sandy just looked angry and snapped, "I can manage perfectly well by myself."

Brian's mental capabilities did not include that of judging what was too obvious to require saying. And so he said, "It might be dangerous outside."

Sandy gave him a withering look of hatred and declined even more abruptly than the first time. When she left the room, everyone felt a little bit better. Sandy's sort of unpleasantness did not fit in well with the general mood of sad shock.

Brian remained standing, unsure of what had just happened. He perhaps felt that he had been somehow rejected, and in an attempt to recover his balance he turned in precisely the wrong direction. He looked down at Katherine Butler, who had been sitting next to him, and said, "Can I walk *you*?" But Katherine didn't want Brian's company either right then. Perhaps she wasn't even frightened. She, after all, had presumably been in more genuinely dangerous situations. She declined without being rude, and then rose and left the room herself.

So Brian was still standing, twice rejected, but now the remaining students began to move. There was a shuffling of papers and a reaching for coats. Without speaking they left the room together and made their way out of the building. Outside it was darker than Lauren would have imagined. It must have been almost six. The sunny November day had given way to a cold, windy night. The students shivered, and not only because they were cold. No one wanted to walk out any further into the night, and so instead they huddled against the building and found reassurance in numbers.

There were five of them. Bert was unquestionably the center of the group. He had been the bearer of the news and he alone among them might know more of what had happened. Melissa was there. She was a good soul, if ever there was a good soul, and wherever condolences were to be extended surely she would be there. Her obvious emotion over Tracy's death was all the more touching, considering that she and Tracy were such very different types. Brian was there too, wearing an expression of beefish puzzlement which surely reflected not only the tragedy but also the fact that no one seemed to want him as an escort. And Parker had also stayed. Why? Lauren allowed herself to wonder if Parker might not be waiting to offer to accompany Lauren herself across Harvard

Yard. The five of them had not spoken a word, but now Parker broke the silence. He said to Bert, "What happened? Tell us what happened."

The night before, Bert and Tracy had had dinner together in the Freshman Union. They had eaten with some of Tracy's friends, and Tracy had been in high spirits. She had told one raucous story after another and was so boisterously lively that Bert had thought she might be drunk. (Damn right she was drunk, thought Lauren. Tracy drank half a gallon of scotch that afternoon. I know. I was there. But Lauren just said, "Was there anything particular on her mind?" Bert said no, he didn't think so. And then he recalled that Tracy had talked about this guy she'd been seeing when she was in high school. "A black guy. She had told me about him before, but not very much. I wonder if he was on her mind last night? Maybe.")

Tracy and Bert had left the Freshman Union together after dinner, and walked across the street to Lamont Library. They both had work to do and agreed to meet at the entrance when the library closed at midnight. They could then go out for a drink perhaps and decide whether to spend the night in his room or in hers.

Tracy settled down in the reference room to start on Kerensky with the Encyclopaedia Britannica. Bert meanwhile took one of the comfortable chairs in a corner of the main reading room, put his feet up on a wooden stool, and tried to read Trotsky. He intended to summarize it for Tracy later. Unfortunately, he fell asleep almost immediately.

He awoke at eleven, found Trotsky lying on the floor beside him, and shamefacedly went off to tell Tracy what had happened. But Tracy was not in the reference room, and the reference librarian could not remember seeing where or when she had gone. And so Bert figured that she had moved to some other corner of the library. The "K" volume of the encyclopedia was lying open on one of the reference desks. Perhaps she meant to return to it, but perhaps she had simply neglected to put it back on the shelf. Tracy was not especially careful about things like that. ("Weren't you worried?" asked Melissa Wu. "No," said Bert, "there really didn't seem to be any reason to worry." "What did you do then?"

asked Lauren. "I went back to my comfortable chair," said Bert with a sheepish expression, "and I fell asleep again.")

At quarter to twelve Bert was blasted awake by the long and hideous Lamont warning signal. The library was about to close for the night. Bert checked the reference room again on his way out, but Tracy was not there. ("What about the encyclopedia?" asked Lauren. Bert thought for a moment and then said, "It wasn't open on the desk anymore. Somebody must have put it back on the shelf.")

Bert left the library and waited for Tracy in the dark out front. He waited as all the late studiers trooped out of the library. They were not a happy-looking lot. Bert found their weary faces depressing; they were not, after all, as well rested as he was, after his four-hour nap. Bert could hardly imagine discovering Tracy among these sadly studious cases. And, indeed, she did not appear. ("Recognize anyone in particular coming out of the library?" asked Lauren. "No, not really," said Bert, "but my friends don't usually study late." Then he remembered someone. "You know who was there? That guy in our seminar, the really nervous one, the one who ran out of the room just before. What's his name?" "Andrew," said Parker. "Andrew Stein," said Melissa. "Yeah," said Bert, "he was coming out of the library last night. He had a pile of books, and he looked even worse than everyone else.")

By a quarter past twelve the library staff had all gone, and the building was dark. Bert still waited. He didn't worry. He was not the worrying type. He was from Los Angeles. He had his car nearby, and he had been thinking that he and Tracy could even drive into Boston for a late drink. He still assumed she would show up. She must have left the library early, maybe gone to her room or to visit a friend. She would remember the appointment and return to the library.

(Lauren was trembling as Bert spoke. The psychological circumstances were so terrifyingly similar to her own situation the week before. Just as Lauren had waited at Pamplona when Russell had already been murdered, so Bert waited in front of the library for Tracy and waited in vain. Anyone could imagine how Bert must have felt as he waited for Tracy, but perhaps only Lauren could understand how Bert felt when he looked back on his failed appointment with the horrible knowledge of just why he had been stood up.)

Bert waited for a half hour and then set off to see whether Tracy was in her room. But only Tracy's tiny black roommate was at home, and she hadn't seen Tracy all evening. Tracy was apparently not to be found, and Bert walked back to his own room for the night, a little puzzled.

It still did not occur to Bert to be concerned about Tracy's safety. What did occur to him was the likelihood that Tracy was spending the night with someone else. He was jealous, particularly since Tracy had stood him up like that without even a message. If she was going to be unfaithful, she didn't have to rub it in his face. Bert was jealous, but he was not shocked. Tracy had never struck him as a "one-man woman," and their affair, which had begun quite recently, was a casual one, no big commitments, no promises of fidelity. Bert was jealous, but, in the end, California won out. ("I guess I just wanted to get even," said Bert, looking ashamed of himself. "You called up another girl?" Lauren guessed. "Oh Lauren, don't say that," said Melissa. "Well, as a matter of fact . . ." said Bert, looking more embarrassed than ever, "you see, I do have this little black book . . ." "You really have a little black book?" exclaimed Lauren. "I didn't know people really had little black books." "In Los Angeles we do, I guess," said Bert.)

So when Bert couldn't find Tracy, he took out his little black book and called up a cute girl in his economics class to see if she wanted to go out for a drink later in the week. She was perfectly eager. Bert then went to bed and fell asleep for the third and final time that evening, and he slept without anxiety. It takes a lot of sound sleep to stay cool and blond three thousand miles from Malibu Beach.

(Melissa Wu was shocked that Bert could take Tracy's disappearance so lightly. In his place, Melissa would certainly have called the police. Reading between the lines, Lauren could see that Melissa would not have simply taken for granted that this was a minor episode in a promiscuous career. Lauren, however, sympathized entirely with Bert's position. It would have been all too likely that Tracy had gone off to bed with someone else, especially considering— and Bert would presumably not have known to take this into account—that Bert was a boring lover.

A student who stayed out all night was not a cause for alarm, but merely an item for speculative gossip. People were forever turning up mornings in other people's rooms. In fact, Lauren and Carol had an explicit agreement that if one of them failed to come home at night, the other would not worry. The police were to be notified only if two days passed without any message.)

The next morning Bert was not permitted to sleep through his economics lecture. He was awakened by a visit from the police. Tracy Nicolson had been found murdered, and the police were investigating. Tracy's roommate had suggested Bert as someone who might know about where Tracy had been the night before. The police had wanted to question Bert and he had told them the whole story, just as he was retelling it now. From the nature of their questions, however, it was clear to Bert that the police did not regard him simply as a source of information. Bert was a suspect. Wasn't the dead woman's lover always the first suspect?

(But Lauren knew rather more than the police. She had penetrated much deeper into the mystery. And now, for the first time since hearing the news of Tracy's death, Lauren's mind returned fully to her own detective investigation. She now had two murders to think about, and she did not doubt for a moment that they were intimately connected.

While Lauren did not rule out the possibility that Tracy could have been murdered by a jealous lover—and she was aware that simply because Bert was the most publicly acknowledged did not mean that he was the only one—Lauren could also imagine an even more compelling motive for Tracy's murder. Tracy had thought she knew who had murdered Russell, and that would have been a powerful reason to try to silence her forever. It was fortunate for Lauren that she had spoken to Tracy the day before; a day later would have been too late. And yet that very talk might well have been fatally unfortunate for Tracy, if the murderer had somehow found out that Tracy had been confiding her secret. In that case the circumstances might prove ominous for Lauren as well.

Tracy had claimed to know who killed Russell Bernard. She had said the murderer was Scott Duchaine. Lauren had doubted this. In fact, Lauren had gone so far as to suspect Tracy herself. And now Tracy was dead, murdered. What stronger proof could there be that Tracy had known just what she was talking about, known too well? Was Scott Duchaine Russell's lover and murderer? Had he come to realize that Tracy knew? And did he finally murder her to protect the secret?

It was almost impossible to believe of Scott. Lauren was remembering Scott's gallant gesture in the seminar when he

had offered to escort Professor Baranova. Suddenly, Lauren
felt dizzy. Was it possible that Professor Baranova's escort was
the murderer himself? Lauren was struck by the irresistible
certainty that Tatiana Baranova was being murdered at that
very moment. But it was too absurd. Lauren forced the
thought out of her head.)

Bert learned from the police that Tracy had been shot in
the middle of the Cambridge Common, probably between
ten and eleven at night. The Cambridge Common was an
expanse of grass and trees and ball fields. It was virtually
across the street from Harvard Square and Harvard Yard. By
day it was a pleasant place, full of young Cambridge parents
with their children, crafts people selling handmade beaded
jewelry displayed on blankets, and students passing back and
forth between Harvard Yard and the Radcliffe Quad. At night,
however, the Common belonged to disreputable and dangerous riffraff. Students were advised not to walk through the
Common alone at night.

Tracy's body had been found at dawn, lying facedown in
the grass, a short distance from one of the footpaths. There
were always a number of homeless bums who slept in the
Common at night, but they awoke and disappeared when it
became light, so as not to attract the attention of the police.
That morning a policeman had noticed that there was somebody still sleeping in the middle of the Common. For a
moment he had the impression that it was some sort of large
animal, but then he realized it was a person in a fur coat. The
cop walked toward the corpse, yelling, "Hey, get up, get out
of there!" When she didn't respond he turned her over
roughly, and finally realized she was dead, not loitering.
("She was wearing the fur coat when she was murdered?"
said Lauren aloud. Michael would be overwhelmed. "Yeah,"
said Bert, "she always wore that coat. She really liked it. It
was a birthday present from her father. I think it was worth a
lot of money.")

Tracy's pocketbook was gone, and the police thought the
murder might be connected to the theft. True, nobody had
taken the fur coat, but the bulky coat would have been much
harder to sneak away with. There was also the possibility of
some sort of attempted sexual assault. There were any number of strays who might have tried to grab a girl or her
handbag in the Common at night. And, in this case, an
attempted robbery or rape might easily have turned into

murder: Tracy was killed with her own gun. She must have been carrying it with her through Cambridge at night for protection. She must have taken it out to ward off her assailant. But the policy of carrying a weapon for self-defense is not without dangers of its own. Your weapon can be wrestled away and turned against you.

Melissa was crying quietly as Bert finished his story. Lauren put an arm around Melissa to comfort her. Melissa was shivering, and Lauren was relieved when Parker finally spoke up and offered to take poor Melissa home. Melissa, Lauren thought, was really not someone who ought to be involved in these things. Melissa was too quintessentially sweet. And yet it was Melissa, with her little talk on Rasputin, who had given the murder mystery its characteristic mark.

Melissa and Parker disappeared into the darkness, and Lauren was left with Bert and Brian. There were a few small clusters of other students walking through Harvard Yard. They would be returning from dinner. Lauren would have to go out for something to eat later. Or if she were too frightened to leave her room, she could miss dinner tonight; she would feel all the more virtuous tomorrow. Or perhaps she could prevail upon Michael to go out and bring back Pepperidge Farm cookies.

For now, she didn't want to move. She wanted to see what Bert would say next. And, besides, she felt genuinely secure between Bert and Brian. Brian was so large, and Bert was not unathletic. After all, she thought half jokingly, if one of them turns out to be the killer, at least the other one can protect me.

With Brian it was always hard to tell whether he was not listening or merely not understanding. Now he had the oblivious air of a large cow. He stared way down at his sneakers while fiddling absently with the zipper of his king-size high school varsity jacket. He stood just a tiny bit apart from Bert and Lauren, and indeed he was not really involved in their conversation. But he did not move to go.

Bert also wore a high school varsity jacket (his letter was for swimming), and Lauren, standing between the two jackets, felt that she really ought to be carrying pom-poms. Bert's face showed real pain though, or at any rate the pained perplexity of a golden boy who had never before encountered tragedy. Lauren was touched, and she wondered just how much Bert had cared about Tracy. Bert was perhaps thinking the same thing, since now he said aloud, "I can't believe she's dead. The police got through with me around lunchtime, and then I went back to my room and lay down on my bed, and I just kept thinking about Tracy being dead, and it was completely unreal. When I finally looked at my watch it was four-thirty, and I realized that I was supposed to be at the seminar, and that none of you would know about Tracy. And so I thought I should come tell you all. And now I guess I'll go back to my room and think about her some more. She was so tough. I'd have thought she'd be indestructible." He paused, and then added as an afterthought, without particular emphasis, "Like Rasputin."

Lauren held her breath for a moment at the mention of the name. But it was only one more reason to shudder on a night when there was already reason enough. Lauren knew that everyone in the class must have been affected by the telling of the murder of Rasputin, and still it was shocking to hear her conviction so frankly confirmed. Lauren believed more than ever that someone in the seminar had murdered Russell. And surely the same person had murdered Tracy.

"We were sort of an odd pair," said Bert. "She was so tough and formidable, and I'm not really tough at all." No, Lauren thought, you really aren't exactly tough, are you? But there's something indestructible about you too, something triumphantly easygoing, the certainty that the surf will always rise again for you. Even now, when you're in the middle of this tragedy, I can look at you without any fear that this is going to somehow leave a terrible mark on your life. I can look at you with the certainty that there will be other girl friends soon enough—because you're such a nice guy, and you're so pleasingly handsome, and you're so obviously one of those rare college freshmen who have already had a bit of experience with women. So why am I not interested in you? Is it just that I suspect your type of being shallow?

Bert was talking about himself, trying to explain why he was different from Tracy. "I grew up in Beverly Hills," he said, as if that in itself conveyed everything. "But Tracy's father was rich too." Actually, Bert's father had had financial ups and downs, but regardless of the fluctuations in annual income the Rosens had always spoiled their son lavishly. They had wanted absolutely the best for him, and he had, in turn, provided them with the son of their dreams. He was the all-American boy beyond even the wildest imaginings. He had been socially successful from the earliest inklings of adolescence, and his academic record consisted of an array of perfect grades starting in first grade and culminating inevitably at Harvard.

"And the strange thing is," Bert continued, "Tracy's background was actually pretty similar. She also had a father who did everything to give her the best, and she paid him back with straight A's. And she still turned out so different from me. I don't think I have any of her guts. Why should that be? She was just as much a spoiled child as I was."

"What was her religion?" said Lauren, not entirely irrelevantly.

Bert thought for a moment. "I don't know," he said finally, surprised at his own ignorance. "I'm sure she wasn't Jewish. And I don't think she was Catholic. She never talked about religion. I don't think she was very religious one way or another. I'm not."

Bert looked very sad. Lauren watched him looking sad, and wanted to comfort him. But what was there to say? Bert himself finally brought out a rhetorical question in a soft, reflective voice. "Why was Tracy walking through the Cambridge Common last night?"

Lauren couldn't help him with that. She pointed out to Bert that to answer his question they would have to know what happened to Tracy in the library while Bert was napping. Whom did she talk to? What was she thinking about? When did she leave? The missing hours would have to be filled in. But it was a large library, and every night there were hundreds of students studying there, walking in and out. No one was likely to have been keeping an eye on Tracy—except perhaps for one person, and he or she would not step forward now.

"It's the same story with Russell Bernard," said Lauren, speaking of what was actually, despite the more recent tragedy, still uppermost in her mind. "Nobody knows what Russell was doing the night that he was murdered. There was a political meeting he was supposed to go to that evening at dinnertime, but he didn't show up. I don't know what he did instead, but whatever it was might be connected to the murder."

"Oh," said Bert, "have you been thinking about Russell's murder, trying to figure out how it happened?"

"No, not really," said Lauren quickly, realizing that she had perhaps spoken too much. There was no point in giving Bert a glimpse of her investigations. After all, Bert was in the seminar; he himself might be the murderer she was looking for. And even if he wasn't the murderer, there was nothing that he could contribute to the solution of the mystery.

But Lauren was wrong about that. Because the next thing Bert said, and he said it with his usual casualness, was this: "I know where Russell Bernard was at dinnertime that night." Bert spoke indifferently, as if everyone at Harvard could be expected to know where Russell had been that night.

"You do?" Lauren could not control her surprise, and she was aware of the enormous contrast between his ease and her palpitations.

"Yeah, sure, he was going to see Professor Baranova that night at her house. He told me himself, right before the seminar started. I talked to him for a minute when we were both coming in. I remember thinking it was a little odd." Bert was clearly someone who took odd things in his stride.

"He told you *that*?" Lauren was incredulous. "How could he have told you that? He told me right after the seminar that he was going to this meeting. And he told Tracy the same thing. You can ask—" Lauren caught herself: it would not be possible to ask Tracy anything.

Bert thought for a moment. "Maybe he did say something about a meeting. Maybe he hadn't decided whether to go to the meeting or to go to Professor Baranova's."

Lauren was baffled for a moment, until she realized just why Russell might have told Bert one story, and then told Tracy and herself a different one. The realization was staggering. Whatever the relationship was between Russell Bernard and Tatiana Baranova, it was not purely professorial. Russell might have been shy about mentioning his date to Lauren and Tracy. Bert, on the other hand, could not conceivably be jealous. He might, in fact, have been impressed. Was Russell boasting? If so, he had been wasting his time, because Bert was too confident of himself on that score to pay much attention to other people's triumphs.

"Why was he going to see Professor Baranova?" asked Lauren, trying to suppress a quaver.

"I don't know," said Bert. "I didn't ask."

In Lauren's mind she was screaming at him. What do you mean you didn't ask? How could you not ask? There isn't anyone in the world who wouldn't have asked! If I had been there I would have asked till I was blue! Don't you cool Californians even have any normal human curiosity about other people's business?

But Lauren said nothing. It was too late now. Bert was staring off into the darkness. He was already thinking of other things, and Lauren could imagine what those things might be. "Were you in love with her?" asked Lauren sympathetically.

"Yes," he answered. And Lauren remembered how she had felt when she heard about Russell's murder. And she remembered how Russell had felt about Dora Carpenter even after her death. It was a bizarre pattern: all these Harvard students in love with other dead Harvard students.

Suddenly Lauren was aware of Brian, who had seemed like such an insignificant presence. He had been only a few feet away the whole time. Had he been listening? Now he was staring at Lauren so strangely that she was terrified all over again. She did not expect such intensity from Brian. She said, "I should be getting back to my room."

And Brian said, "I'll walk you."

Lauren looked up at Brian's hulking form, and then turned to Bert. "Will you walk with us too?" she said, and there might have been a note of pleading in her voice.

Bert was glad to walk with them, and so all three found their way across Harvard Yard to Thayer Hall. There Lauren said goodnight to both young men, ran up the stairs, and locked herself in her room.

Lauren sat on her bed without moving. She was thinking about Tatiana Baranova and Scott Duchaine, remembering their grand exit from the seminar room. Was the elegant professor somehow involved in Russell's death? Had she really received a visit from Russell the night he was murdered? And why? What was going on? Tatiana Baranova was more mysterious than ever before, and Lauren was wondering what had become of her after she walked off into the night with Scott Duchaine.

Lauren called the Cambridge directory assistance and then dialed again. On the other end the phone began to ring. At the fourth ring, the phone was answered. The voice at the other end said hello in an unmistakable Russian accent. Feeling immensely relieved, Lauren hung up the phone. Tatiana Baranova was alive.

11. Good Resolutions

Lauren was dreaming about *Gone with the Wind*. In her dream she was reading the book, turning the pages—or was she watching the movie? And, of course, at the same time, she was in the book herself even as she was reading it. It was a kind of dream that she had had before: one in which she dreamed herself into a very familiar book or film. And even within the dream, Lauren could recognize the pattern and say to herself on some untraceable level of consciousness, "This is a kind of dream that I have. I know I am dreaming."

Lauren was walking along a very stately street in antebellum Atlanta. The street was deserted because someone had been killed. Was it Rasputin? Lauren passed one beautiful white mansion after another, and she kept thinking, "I would like to live in one of those mansions." But then she reconsidered, because it seemed possible that those houses might all be in her hometown in New Jersey. Finally she came to her own home (it was New Jersey!) but her parents were not there. Where could they be?

There was an enormous flight of stairs which Lauren easily identified as being in the house which Rhett Butler built for Scarlett O'Hara after their marriage. Someone said that Rhett Butler was coming, but for a moment Lauren thought the name was Russell Bernard. Rhett Bernard, Russell Butler. She turned around sharply, but the man was not Russell. He took her in his arms and carried her up the grand staircase—or were these the stairs of Thayer Hall? Because now he carried her into her own Harvard room, and he locked the door behind them. He carried her to the bed, and, lying on the bed, Lauren gazed up into his eyes and realized with almost unbearable terror just who he was.

And then she awoke with only one thought in her mind, something she had not allowed herself to look at squarely the night before. Now there was no avoiding it. Scott Duchaine was the murderer.

Of course Scott Duchaine was the murderer. Tracy had said that he was, and now Tracy had been killed. The obvious reason for Tracy's death—Lauren had foreseen it when Tracy had confided in her—was that Tracy's talking was dangerous for the murderer, for Scott. He had killed her so that she would shut up, and surely he would not have been driven to that extreme unless her accusation was true. Scott must have killed Russell as well. In the windy and frightening air of the previous evening, in the seminar and then surrounded by Melissa and Parker and Brian and Bert, Lauren had allowed herself to avoid this obvious truth. But now, in the light of day, after a night's sleep, she could not but see clearly. Her dream merely told her what unconsciously she had known since the day before.

Lauren got out of bed and pulled up the shades to let the sun into her little box of a room. She stood at the window in her Laura Ashley flannel nightgown with the delicate lavender floral pattern, and she looked out on another beautiful November day. Carol was whistling off key in the next room. What did it mean, this solution to the murder mystery? What was Lauren to do now? That was difficult to say; Lauren thought vaguely that she would have to consult with Michael. But despite the unresolved loose ends and the dangerous decisions still before her, Lauren felt very peaceful and satisfied with herself. She had solved the mystery. For a week her level of mental tension had been extremely high, perhaps higher than she had realized, and now she could relax from the rigorous intellectual demands of detective investigation.

Michael could help her to decide whether to confront Scott or whether to go straight to the police and put the problem in their hands. One way or another the whole business was nearly over. It was with a wonderful sensation of relief and liberation that Lauren began to think about what her own life would be like with the murder mystery behind her. The discovery of the identity of the murderer had the effect of eliminating definitively her number one romantic possibility. Now Lauren would not even allow herself to picture Scott's face; that dream had been too vivid. And how does one go about facing the fact that one's Saturday night date is a vicious killer? Lauren consoled herself with the thought that there were lots of other men at Harvard, and she did not doubt that some of the choicer ones would fall her way sooner or later.

Now was a time for fresh starts. Lauren looked around her little room and decided that the first thing to be done was a general straightening up. She began to take pairs of jeans off of her desk chair (when had she last sat down at that desk?) and put them on hangers in the closet. When the chair was clean, she turned her attention to the array of perfumes and cosmetics that covered the top of the sturdy wooden dresser Harvard had given her. Harvard furniture was so masculine—men had lived in these rooms for three centuries— and Lauren loved covering the surfaces with her Chanel bottles and Elizabeth Arden jars. But they would have to be arranged more neatly.

Lauren looked up at her beloved spider plant which hung by the window and she felt instantly remorseful. In her preoccupation with murder, Lauren had forgotten to water the poor thing all week. Now Lauren went off to the communal hall bathroom to bring back some water. She passed through Carol's room, calling out, "Good morning, roommate." Carol looked up from her letter to Baby Doll and returned the salutation. Carol was looking cheerful, but then Carol always looked cheerful. Now Lauren would take the time to find out what was really going on with Brian O'Donnell. And now, after all, it was certain that Brian was not the murderer. He was still an oafish beef, but he was not a killer, and if Carol really yearned for him . . . well, Lauren would not be unpleasant about it.

"It's a wonderful day," said Carol, sustaining at great length the first syllable of "wonderful." And then she remembered about Tracy Nicolson's murder which was on the front page of the *Crimson* spread out on her desk. "What terrible news though!" she exclaimed, switching from joy to distress without missing a beat. "You knew her, didn't you? She was in your seminar, just like Russell Bernard."

"Yes," said Lauren.

"Gosh," said Carol, "it's not a very lucky seminar, is it? And everyone thought you were so lucky to get chosen for it." And then she had an idea. "Maybe I could sit in on the next meeting and write an article for the *Crimson* about how depressing it is, now that two of the students are dead. I really need a good story to convince the editors to take me onto the paper. They weren't so thrilled by my interviews with the women who serve the food at the Freshman Union."

"I don't think the professor would let you sit in," said Lauren discouragingly, thinking that it would be safest to keep Carol far away from that unlucky seminar.

"Oh well," said Carol, cheerfully resigned and returning to her original sentiment, "it is a wonderful day. I'm going to finish my letter to my Baby Doll, and then I have to go meet Brian before the economics lecture." Lauren was impressed by the way Carol sent off her daily avowals of true love to California but still seemed ready to play the field in Massachusetts without any intrusive emotional complications.

"What's with Brian?" Lauren inquired generally. "Does Baby Doll have something to worry about?"

"Oh, you're awful!" Carol squealed, evading the question. And then she added with patently false propriety, "Brian's just going to help me with my economics."

Now Lauren was genuinely stunned. She didn't even bother to watch her words. "He's a dinosaur," she shrieked. "How can he help you with your economics? You're at least ten thousand times as smart as he is."

Carol's expression clouded just a bit, and she spoke in what was for her a pensive manner. "It's true. He really doesn't understand a bit of it." Her expression brightened. "But it makes him feel so good to explain it to me. I sort of sit and admire his muscles. They're enormous."

Lauren was amused now. "Carol darling," she said, "you are the eighth wonder of the world."

Carol then asked with seeming irrelevance whether Lauren wanted to go with her to the football game next Saturday. Lauren promised to think about it. It might be fun to go with Carol to watch Brian get knocked down by other Neanderthals. Perhaps Michael would even come along and provide a running homosexual commentary.

After watering the spider plant, Lauren went off to the bathroom again and took a hot shower. Then she got dressed— old jeans and a loose cotton top covered with bright ethnic embroidery. She admired herself in the full-length mirror that hung on the back of the door. Some Harvard freshmen, upon arriving in Cambridge, went right out to buy file cabinets or pocket calculators. Lauren's first purchase had been the full-length mirror. Three centuries of men had left Harvard rooms only inadequately mirrored.

Now Lauren realized with concern that while preoccupied with her detective investigation, she had managed to put on a pound or two. Something would have to be done about that. And while she was making resolutions, she might as well think about studying. Reluctantly she turned away from the mirror and seated herself on the newly cleared desk chair. She collected the loose papers on her desk in a pile, and discovered underneath not only Professor Moorhead's book *China and the West* and Nietzsche's *Genealogy of Morals* but also *Fear of Flying*. Lauren realized that her investigations had caused her to neglect not only her school work but even her novel. That was really taking things too far.

Now Lauren resolved to be virtuous. Thinking about how nice it would be to go to Professor Moorhead's office hour and tell him how much she liked his book, Lauren opened *China and the West* to page one. The murder investigation was over, and Scott was the murderer. Lauren began to read about China with a clear mind.

And then Carol knocked. She had finished her letter and was going out to mail it. She wanted to know if she could mail anything for Lauren. "No," said Lauren, thinking that she should perhaps write to her parents soon or they would call her up and complain that she never wrote to them. "But thanks for offering." She remained seated at her desk with the book open in front of her. She felt very virtuously studious and wonderfully free of the obsession which had taken up the last week.

"By the way," said Carol, still standing in the doorway, "are you going out with Scott Duchaine this weekend again?"

"No," said Lauren, thinking that she was going to have to break her *Gone with the Wind* date with Scott. He was, after all, the murderer.

"He's cute," said Carol.

Cuter than you think, Lauren thought, but she said, "I don't think he's for me."

"Oh," said Carol. "I just brought it up because I saw him the other night at a party. I forgot to tell you about it. He and I had a little talk, and he was very polite. I think he likes you. But if he's not your type..."

"He went to a party last night?" said Lauren, thinking that there was something horrible about Scott murdering Tracy on Tuesday night and then going to a party on Wednesday night. Escorting Professor Baranova home for the sake of safety and then going off to a freshman party to talk politely with Carol: it was a bit too brazen.

"No, it wasn't last night," said Carol, "it was the night before."

Lauren froze. "Tuesday night?"

"Yeah, Tuesday," said Carol. "This girl I know up at Radcliffe was giving the party, and she must have known Scott from somewhere. It wasn't a big deal, the party, about twenty-five people. It was fun."

"Tuesday night?" Lauren repeated.

"Sure, Tuesday."

"What time?"

"From about eight-thirty till midnight. That's how long I was there. I would have taken you along, but you weren't around." Carol obviously wondered if Lauren was somehow offended not to have been asked. Why else should Lauren be reacting so oddly?

"Was Scott there the whole time?" Lauren asked, almost trembling.

"I think so."

"He didn't slip out for a half hour?"

"I don't think so, but it's possible. It was a small group though, so I probably would have noticed. I was sort of watching him, you know, seeing as you were going out with him and all. He is cute."

"He stayed till midnight?"

"Sure, a group of us walked back to the Yard together from Radcliffe, including him." Carol looked at her watch. "I've got to run now. I'm late for my economics lesson." She giggled and disappeared.

Lauren stared at page one of *China and the West,* but the words made no sense. She closed the book. The police said Tracy had been killed between ten and eleven. Scott was at a party with twenty-five other people between eight-thirty and midnight. He could conceivably have slipped out, raced to the Common, bumped into Tracy by prearrangement, murdered her, and raced back to the party at Radcliffe. It hardly seemed likely. And Carol thought Scott had been at the party all evening. There was no reason why Carol should be mistaken.

Which meant that Scott probably did *not* kill Tracy Nicolson, even if she *had* been telling people that he was a homosexual and a murderer. And if Scott didn't kill Tracy, was there really any reason to believe that he had killed Russell? The murder investigation was on again. The mystery had not been solved after all.

At lunch that day, Lauren was surprised and pleased to see approaching her the boy who had sat next to her at the black table on Monday. He had been wearing a football jersey then and he was wearing one now. He wanted to tell Lauren that that very afternoon there was to be a memorial service for Russell Bernard at Memorial Church in Harvard Yard. There had been very few notices, and this young man wanted to be sure that Lauren knew about it, since she had been a friend of Russell's. In fact, Lauren had not seen any notices, and she was grateful for the message. She knew that the personal invitation was intended as a special sort of inclusion.

Realizing with a touch of relief that she would have to skip her Nietzsche discussion section, she headed back to her room to change into something more appropriate. The jeans and embroidered top were thrown over the desk chair, and Lauren decided on a gray wool skirt with a matching sweater. She put her wavy hair up with several bobby pins and, after more than a passing glance in the full-length mirror, decided that she looked suitably severe. Walking the very short distance from Thayer Hall to Memorial Church, Lauren passed Katherine Butler, dressed in an old Mao jacket, walking in the opposite direction. Katherine would certainly not be going to Russell's memorial service.

Memorial Church faces Widener Library across the innermost of those quadrangles which make up Harvard Yard. Both buildings are brick, and both have imposing white classical columns. Some say that Widener predominates on account of its grand flight of stone steps. Others, however, feel that the church is more impressive, thanks to its high steeple and the clamorous bell that was always intruding on Lauren's sleep.

The church is a very large version of a New England small-town church. Harvard is no longer either a Puritan or an Anglican bastion, and Memorial Church serves as an ecumenical institution. (In fact, once a year, a portable ark of the covenant is provided so that the church can house Yom Kippur services.) As its name suggests, Memorial Church is dedicated to the memory of those sons of Harvard who died for their country. The chapels are covered with the names of those fallen in battle. It was the right place for a memorial service.

Lauren entered the church and was immediately struck by how many people were gathered there. It seemed as if every black student at Harvard was present, though surely Katherine Butler had a circle of comrades who were staying away. Lauren, guessing from the personal nature of her own invitation, had supposed that it would be a small group of close friends who might occupy the first three rows of the big church. Instead Lauren could barely find a place at a pew. Apparently, the announcement of the service had passed by word of mouth through all the black circles at Harvard, and they regarded the service as an occasion of solidarity.

Lauren looked over the crowd. They were dressed formally and soberly, dark colors, no blue jeans. Lauren looked for people from the freshman seminar, but recognized no one until she finally discerned Melissa Wu. Melissa was so small that Lauren could barely see her on the other side of a very large black man. Why Melissa of all people? What was she doing there? And how had she found out about it?

The service began with a hymn which Lauren didn't know—but everyone else seemed to. The ecumenical elasticity of Memorial Church was once again being tested; the New England church was now black Baptist. The incongruity of church and congregation would have been dissonant enough in itself. But, Lauren reminded herself, there was yet another oddity to consider. Russell himself was a Catholic, and the tone of this memorial service must have been very far from his own religious rituals.

When the hymn ended, one of the students—a young man whom Lauren did not recognize—got up to deliver a eulogy, which was to be the heart of the memorial service. Like most eulogies, this one was too admiring to be interesting. Lauren found herself not quite able to pay attention, and she scanned the faces of the audience, wondering if they were actually listening more intently than she was. Lauren did gather from the speaker that two weeks earlier there had been an identical service for Dora Carpenter with pretty much the same faces.

One of the reasons that the eulogy was so dull was that it was, quite frankly, a political plea. The speaker, Lauren gathered, was prominent in the Black Students' Lobby, had known Russell from the Lobby, and was concerned about the Lobby above all other things. The story of Russell's life was told solely in terms of his efforts on behalf of that organization. Lauren wondered whether everyone present was already a great fan of the Lobby, or whether perhaps Russell's death was being used to propagandize and recruit. Lauren had not forgotten her conversation with Katherine Butler. Apparently, there were blacks at Harvard who sneered at the Lobby, who attacked its nonrevolutionary outlook and aims. Lauren was not surprised when the eulogy ended with an impassioned call to take up the work which Russell Bernard and Dora Carpenter would carry on no longer.

Yes, it was a dull speech. Lauren was glad when it was over and the students sang another hymn. The hymn concluded the service, and slowly people began to file out of the pews and into the aisles, moving in small groups and talking softly to each other. Lauren, walking alone, caught a few phrases of conversation about midterms and hourlies. The academic routine was already reasserting itself. Only Lauren, who guessed that Russell's murderer was another Harvard freshman, continued to be preoccupied. She was thinking about Russell, not about midterms.

Scott Duchaine was perhaps not the murderer at all. He had an alibi for the time of Tracy's death. The question was: what should Lauren do next? How should she pursue her investigation? She was puzzling over this as she walked slowly up the center aisle of Memorial Church, surrounded by black students. At the pew on her right, at the very back of the church, Lauren saw a woman wearing a black veil. The woman was elegantly dressed in black; she even wore a pair of black gloves. She was obviously waiting for a place to open up in the stream of students moving down the aisle. Lauren courteously paused before the pew and gestured to the woman to enter the aisle. As she took the place that Lauren had made for her, the woman spoke from behind her veil. She said, "Thank you, Lauren." The dignified Russian accent was unmistakable.

They were moving outside onto the steps of the church

now and Lauren moved alongside of Professor Baranova, who finally lifted her black veil to reveal the magnificent cheekbones and diamond earrings. Lauren couldn't help wondering whether the veil was intended solely as an accessory of mourning, or whether it was also meant as a sort of incognito. It was quite odd to find Professor Baranova here—fascinating, and particularly fascinating in the light of what Lauren had learned from Bert Rosen the night before. Russell had been at Tatiana Baranova's house the evening that he was murdered. Lauren tried to think of what to say, and rejected "Fancy running into you here" as a bit too flip.

"How are you, Lauren?" said the professor politely.

"Fine," said Lauren, still flustered. "And how are you?"

"I'm quite well."

"It's terrible, isn't it?" said Lauren finally, referring vaguely to Russell and Tracy. Lauren wanted to talk, but she wasn't sure how to go about it.

"Yes, terrible."

Lauren decided that the thing to do was to formally ask Professor Baranova if they could talk, perhaps even make an appointment if right now would be inconvenient. Then Lauren could somehow find out if Russell had indeed visited her on the night of the murder, and why. But before Lauren was able to get out a word to this effect, Professor Baranova said, "Please excuse me, I have to get a taxi and go right home. I'm expecting a phone call from my husband in Washington. I'll see you at the seminar next Wednesday."

In a moment she was walking off; the veil was pulled back from her face and waved lightly in the wind. She carried herself beautifully, though she moved less slowly than Lauren would have expected. Lauren herself was left gaping, empty-handed, without even an appointment. She stood staring at the receding form in black, wondering what exactly had brought this even more than usually aloof Harvard professor to a memorial service for one of her students. When Professor Baranova had disappeared from sight, Lauren turned around to take another look at Memorial Church. Most of the people had left, but standing on the steps of the church, twenty feet away, watching Lauren, was Melissa Wu.

Melissa stood at the foot of a tall white column which made her seem all the more petite. She was dressed severely in a navy blue skirt and white blouse, with tiny black shoes on modestly low heels. The ensemble had the air of a parochial school uniform. Melissa always wore skirts and blouses, but usually she displayed a taste for girlishly light colors and cute decorative patterns. How long had she been standing under the column watching Lauren? Had she recognized Professor Baranova?

Now Melissa descended the remaining steps and approached Lauren. They exchanged greetings very solemnly, in tones appropriate to the memorial service from which they had just come. Lauren thought that Melissa was not looking well. Lauren remembered how upset Melissa had seemed the night before when she had listened to Bert's story, how relieved she herself had been when Parker had finally taken Melissa home. And now here she was, turning up so unexpectedly at the memorial service. On the one hand, Lauren couldn't help thinking that if the whole freshman class were murdered, Melissa would still finish her reading assignment. But on the other hand, there was no denying that something was bothering her now. Had these murders actually succeeded in destroying Melissa's cheerful, industrious equilibrium?

"It's terrible," said Lauren, just as she had said to Professor Baranova a minute before. There was really no other way to begin a conversation under the circumstances. Melissa nodded earnestly and agreed.

"Were you and Russell particularly good friends?" asked Lauren, who hardly thought it was likely. Still, there had to be some explanation for Melissa's presence at the memorial service. Lauren tried not to make the question sound suggestive, though she suspected that Melissa probably wouldn't notice even intentional insinuations.

"No, not really," said Melissa, "but I liked him, and I felt very bad when he was killed. It was a tragedy, wasn't it?"

"Sure," said Lauren encouragingly. "I felt bad too." And then she asked, "How did you know about the service?"

"There's a little notice on the board in the lobby of the church, and I saw it when I came Sunday morning." Well, that explained that: no wonder that Lauren hadn't seen the notice, no wonder Melissa had. But it didn't explain how Professor Baranova had known about the service. Surely *she* didn't attend Memorial Church every Sunday. It seemed unlikely that she went to church much at all, unless there was some secret but terribly elegant Russian basilica in Cambridge. Lauren did not want to bring up the subject with Melissa. If Melissa had seen Professor Baranova, she was certainly keeping quiet about it—for surely even Melissa would have considered the professorial presence remarkable. And if Melissa had not seen, well then it was perhaps better not to go into it. It did not seem likely that Melissa would be able to offer much insight into Tatiana Baranova's relations with Russell Bernard.

Instead Lauren asked politely, "Oh, what is your religion?"

"Christian," Melissa assured her. Lauren wondered about Melissa's categories: Christian versus heathen perhaps? It was, Lauren thought, a real missionary mentality. Lauren was about to press further when her thoughts, already occupied with Asia, were further distracted by the small notebook which peeked out of Melissa's leather bag. The cover of the notebook was marked with the Harvard insignia, and along the top, in Melissa's perfect block printing, was the name "Professor Moorhead." Obviously, these were Melissa's notes for the Chinese civilization course. The hourly exam was approaching, and Lauren had skipped the last two lectures on account of her detective preoccupations. She now felt a sudden uncontrollable eagerness at the thought of copying Melissa's no doubt impeccably thorough and exquisitely neat lecture notes.

Lauren made her request very timidly, and Melissa agreed after a moment's hesitation. She was apparently unused to the notion of people copying other people's notes. But Melissa offered to let Lauren keep the notebook overnight, and Lauren gratefully invited Melissa up to her room for a cup of coffee. They were, after all, standing virtually at the entrance to Thayer Hall. But Melissa, of course, didn't drink coffee. So Lauren suggested cocoa, and after another moment's hesitation (what was the big moral dilemma now?) Melissa accepted.

Lauren was now very glad to have straightened her room that morning. She had a feeling that Melissa might be genuinely scandalized by a messy room. Lauren boiled water in her hot pot, and then made two mugs of cocoa. She did not yet have a set of elaborate china cups like Michael's, but she was planning to buy some soon. For the time being she was using Carol's mugs, which were decorated with a design of pink elephants. Lauren was about to make a joke about the silly mugs, when Melissa said, "These are really cute." Sure enough, she was admiring the pink elephants.

"Yes, aren't they?" said Lauren. "You know, when Jackie Kennedy was First Lady, she ordered a set of two hundred for cocoa at the White House."

"I thought that elephants stood for the Republican party," said Melissa, perplexed.

"Well yes, they do," said Lauren. And then, "Actually I was joking about Jackie Kennedy."

"Oh," said Melissa, and now she laughed appreciatively.

Lauren decided to stop making jokes. She tried to think of some Girl Scout conversation. Finally she said, "I think making cocoa is a nice way to get to know people." It was lame, but it was better than nothing.

Melissa gave this remark rather more thoughtful consideration than Lauren thought it deserved. "I guess that's true," she said at last. And then, shyly, "Can I ask you for some advice about something?"

"Sure," said Lauren, "anything." Could Melissa know something about the murders?

"Well, it's very embarrassing." She paused and then spoke while looking at her cup of cocoa. "There's this boy I like. And I'd really like to get to know him better." She looked up at Lauren pleadingly. "What shall I do?"

Lauren was completely disarmed. She had not been expecting anything so Dear Abby. She thought to herself in the accents of Mae West, Honey, you've come to the right place. But she said very reassuringly, "We'll think of something." And then, "Who is he?"

Melissa looked back down at her cup of cocoa and declined to answer. And no matter how Lauren pressed, Melissa wouldn't say. So Lauren, eternally grateful for the Chinese civilization notes, agreed to help work out an approach to Mr. X. "You have to flirt with him," said Lauren, but the blank look in Melissa's eyes made clear what Lauren should anyhow have guessed: Melissa was not a natural flirt.

"For instance," said Lauren, "you can flirt by paying him a compliment. You can tell him how smart he is—something silly like that—but you have to do it so that he'll know you're teasing him."

"He *is* very smart," said Melissa informatively.

"Yes, but that's not the point," said Lauren, thinking that it might be very difficult to teach Melissa to flirt. Lauren could try to work on "You're *so* smart" or perhaps even "You're *so* good," though the latter might be a bit suggestive for Melissa. Or perhaps, Lauren thought, Melissa could put her tiny little foot next to that of Mr. X and say coyly, "You have *such* a big foot." Perhaps that was also too suggestive.

Lauren heard Carol walking into the other room, and immediately Lauren was inspired. She had remembered Carol's approach to Brian. "Listen," Lauren said to Melissa, "is this boy in any of your classes?" Melissa nodded. "Well then, you have to ask him for help with the classwork. That way you have a perfect academic excuse to get together regularly, and he'll feel very good about helping you, and in no time at all he'll be asking you out on dates, if he doesn't just grab you first."

Melissa looked shocked at the possibility of being grabbed. "Oh, he's very polite," she assured Lauren, and for a split second the thought of Scott Duchaine passed through Lauren's mind. "But you see," said Melissa, "I don't really need any help with my classwork."

"Yes, I know that," said Lauren, "but..." She floundered. Obviously, there was no point in trying to make Melissa understand the tactic of feigning ignorance. Melissa was too honest, too much the good girl. "Listen," said Lauren, "you say he's smart?"

"Oh yes," said Melissa, "very smart."

"Well then, wouldn't you find it educationally valuable to discuss the course material with him?"

"Yes," said Melissa thoughtfully. "I guess I would."

"Okay. And wouldn't that help you understand the subject even better than you do now?"

"Yes," said Melissa hesitantly, suspecting that she was being illicitly tempted.

"Well then, couldn't you tell him he was helping you?"

"Yes," said Melissa. A smile broke across her face. She had overcome her qualms. She was on her way. "I'll ask him to help me. We'll have a discussion."

"Good girl," said Lauren enthusiastically. "Now, won't you tell me who he is? I'm dying to know."

"Do you promise not to tell?" said Melissa, in a tone that contained both giggles and extreme solemnity.

"Cross my heart," said Lauren.

Melissa was clearly dying to tell, and tell she did. "It's Parker Hamilton Kendall IV." She recited all three names very proudly and gave a particularly delighted emphasis to the numeral.

12. The Whore of Babylon

Melissa left, and Lauren stretched out on the bed to think about what she had just learned. Melissa had a crush on Parker. But how did Parker feel about Melissa? Was it possible that she was the secret love Parker had mentioned to Michael? If Parker was actually mooning over Melissa instead of over Sandy or even Lauren, that would take him a little further away from the complications of the murder mystery. Lauren could see that Parker and Melissa would make a cute couple, and they would win all sorts of prizes for unworldliness. Lauren resolved to do what she could to bring the two of them together.

Lauren Adler Detective Agency and Dating Service, she thought to herself sleepily. She had slept badly the night before, after hearing of Tracy's murder, and she had been awakened early this morning by her own nightmare. Now she began to doze, and the next thing she knew, Carol was rousing her from a very restless sleep. "Didn't you see the notice?" Carol was saying.

And Lauren mumbled, "No, of course not. The notice was put up inside Memorial Church. I don't go to church on Sunday." In the middle of this, Lauren became aware that Carol couldn't possibly have been talking about the notice of Russell's memorial service.

"What notice?" Lauren asked, now fully awake.

"The notice about the dorm meeting," said Carol. "We're having a dorm meeting downstairs in fifteen minutes. We're going to discuss security. It's because of the murders. And the notice was on the bulletin board downstairs, not in Memorial Church. What were you saying about the church?"

147

"Oh nothing," said Lauren quickly. "It must have been some dream I was having." Lauren looked at the clock. "I've missed dinner. What was it?"

"There were french fries and ice cream," said Carol contentedly. Sweet and crunchy, thought Lauren. There had presumably also been some dreadful main course which Carol had eaten but failed to notice since it had been neither sweet nor crunchy.

"I'll go out for something to eat later," said Lauren without a trace of disappointment. "Now when is this meeting?"

"It's in fifteen minutes," Carol squealed. "That's what I've been trying to tell you."

"Oh my God!" cried Lauren. "We'd better get ready."

An assembly of the dormitory was always a treat for Lauren and Carol. The other girls of Thayer Hall were surprisingly unworldly and rather shy about sex. Lauren and Carol, of course, were happy to talk with the utmost frankness at the slightest provocation, and they managed, not entirely unintentionally, to give the impression that they were rather more sexually experienced than was honestly the case. And so, despite the fact that neither one of them had actually gone to bed with anyone during these first two months of freshman year, they had succeeded in becoming a little disreputable. When Tina Black's high school boyfriend wanted to come visit her from Kentucky, she asked Lauren and Carol if he could sleep on their floor since they didn't have to worry about their reputations. Lauren and Carol were deeply disappointed when he canceled his visit.

Whenever the girls of Thayer gathered for cocoa either Lauren or Carol was sure to be relating some obscene little vignette. Such gatherings were, of course, twice as much fun when the boys of Thayer, who lived upstairs, were present. The boys included several Harvard athletes, several studious nonentities, and the unique Michael Hunt. Lauren suspected them all of being roughly equally inexperienced with women, though the athletes could be relied on to boast manfully, especially when they were working on a six-pack.

Twenty-five minutes later (Lauren believed in being flirtatiously late even to dormitory security meetings) the two roommates were dressed for their parts and ready to go. Lauren was wearing her very tightest jeans and a button-down shirt, unbuttoned low enough so that anyone could see she wasn't wearing a bra. She had put on lots of makeup, purples and blues, and looking in the mirror she could scarcely believe she was the same person who had stood in front of that same mirror that same day dressed for a memorial service.

Carol had actually gone so far as to put on hot pants, which, as far as Lauren knew, were out of fashion everywhere in America except the inside of Carol's head. Then there were gold lamé, high-heeled sandals, and an orange tube top that really "hugged the boobs," as Carol put it with quaint Los Angeles expressiveness. All in all, she was not dressed for November—but then she wasn't planning to step outside for even a moment.

"You look like the high school slut," said Carol to Lauren admiringly as they went out the door.

"Thank you, roommate. You look like the Whore of Babylon."

"Babylon?" Carol was puzzled. "Where's Babylon?"

Everyone was already assembled when they arrived, and the grand entrance was everything they could have wished for. The other girls, grouped together on one side of the room, giggled timidly, but the football players cheered and Michael cried out, "Oo-la-la!" Lauren and Carol remained momentarily posed in the doorway for effect, and then pointedly chose not to sit with the other girls. Carol sat down in the midst of the football players, while Lauren made her way to the corner where Michael was enjoying the spectacle.

"You look wonderful!" Michael whispered. "And Carol looks like the Whore of Babylon."

"Be sure to tell her that later," said Lauren, knowing that Michael would be amused at Carol's response.

The two dormitory proctors were responsible for running the meeting. These were Dina Salten, a graduate student in psychology, and Curt James, who was in the law school. Every freshman dorm had its proctors—older students, who were supposed to help smooth out the uncertainties of freshman year. Curt had a suite of rooms upstairs on the boys' floor, though on the whole he was a somewhat retiring proctor. He was small and dapper and undeniably cute. He had been a Harvard undergraduate, then a Rhodes Scholar, and was now a Harvard law student. He had short hair, conservative manners, and a certain air of being left over from the Harvard of the 1950s. In fact, he was much younger than that, and, though you would think it unlikely to look at him, he had had the opportunity at least to observe the turmoil of the late sixties as an undergraduate.

Curt was very out of place among the football players, though they all liked him well enough. He was friendlier with Michael, while maintaining a reserve which, Lauren suspected, derived from some understanding that Michael's interest was more than just friendly. Curt occasionally gave evidence of heterosexuality by bringing home someone from a nearby women's college to the boisterous amusement of the football players. On such occasions Michael made witty remarks that were, Lauren thought, perhaps just a bit too witty.

If Curt was a somewhat uninvolved proctor, Dina was just the opposite. In fact right now they were meeting in Dina's room, and she was seated in the center, about to open the meeting, while Curt was off in the corner near Michael and Lauren. He was always happy to defer to Dina. If Curt seemed untouched by the sixties, Dina was the opposite: a living memorial. She had worked for Eugene McCarthy in 1968 and George McGovern in 1972, and in between she had devoted herself to student radicalism at Harvard. Her walls were still covered with antiwar posters, though the war was over, and caricatures of Richard Nixon, though he was no longer president. Dina's dissertation in progress was on the psychology of student protest. She was a willing and active freshman proctor, always eager to help. The girls on the floor, however, were a bit wary of her. They were already conscious of a generation gap. Ironically, Curt, who didn't care much at all about the students, had an easier rapport with his boys.

Now Dina did all the talking. She explained that the night before all the Harvard proctors had met with the Harvard police and the Cambridge police. There had been two murders within a single week. It was frightening, and everyone on the Harvard campus should be taking exceptional precautions.

The police were inclined to believe that the murders of Russell Bernard and Tracy Nicolson were separate crimes, committed by different men. It was of course also possible that the two freshmen could have been killed by the same person. The police, however, did not feel that the sort of man who would assault a woman at night would necessarily also be the sort to attack a lone black man. Thus, there were probably two deranged and dangerous men at large in Cambridge, and they were not just ordinary purse-snatchers. Harvard women were especially urged to be extremely careful.

("I object," whispered Michael to Lauren. "Russell Bernard wasn't a woman, and I gather he was a lot tougher than I am."

"Carol and I will take care of you," whispered Lauren, aware that Dina was looking in their direction reproachfully as if to imply that whisperers who didn't pay attention were that much more likely to end up as victims.)

Dina was reciting a list of sensible precautions. Stay away from the river and the Common at night. No one should go out alone after dark. The girls in the dorm, if they had to go out at night, should ask one of the boys to accompany them. (The boys gave a rousing cheer at this point, and Curt drowsily nodded his acceptance on their behalf, his sole contribution to the meeting.) The girls should also feel free to call the Harvard police to escort them anywhere at night. If a mugger demanded money, they should hand it over immediately with no resistance. And finally, they should report anything suspicious to the police, who were working full-time to track down these criminals.

Lauren noticed that some of the other girls were actually taking notes on Dina's little talk, actually listing the various extremely obvious safety precautions. This was really the height of ridiculous earnestness, and Lauren gleefully pointed it out to Michael who was equally delighted. He took out a pen and scrap of paper, and immediately composed for Lauren a little poem:

> Don't talk to strangers!
> Don't talk to strays!
> For once you've been murdered,
> You can't get straight A's!

Lauren gave him a discreet kiss on the cheek, and Michael pointed out that at least Carol wasn't taking notes. Carol was tickling one of the football players behind the ears.

The meeting was over. Lauren, having slept through dinner, was hungry. She would have liked to go out with Michael. She had many things to tell him, and they had not had a real chance to talk since Tracy's murder. Lauren wanted to tell him what she had been thinking about Scott Duchaine, about the possibility of Tatiana Baranova's connection to

Russell, even about Melissa Wu's crush. However, Lauren could see that what Michael really wanted just then was to engage Curt James in a flirtatious conversation. She would leave Michael to Curt; after all, Michael would do the same for her. Lauren decided that she would talk to Michael later in the evening, and for now she would go out into Cambridge alone to get something to eat.

Lauren knew that she really ought to change her clothes before going out to dinner. After all, purple eye shadow was perfect for dorm meetings, but it was really not something to wear in the streets unless you wanted to attract a not very well-mannered sort of attention. But Lauren was hungry, and so she buttoned up her shirt, threw a jacket on over the ensemble, and headed for Grendel's Den.

As she entered the big room, with its high wooden ceiling and old-Anglo-Saxon-new-bohemian ambience, Lauren was aware that her appearance was a bit extreme. She did not really care, however, until a few seconds later when she caught sight of Sandy Grayson and Parker Hamilton Kendall IV dining in the corner and looking rather more old Anglo-Saxon than new bohemian. While Lauren was delighted to appear as the class slut for the benefit of her dormitory, she was not eager to be reviewed in that role by Parker and Sandy. Lauren suddenly wished very strongly that she was wearing somewhat less in the way of purple eye shadow.

Lauren's immediate reaction to the sight of Parker and Sandy was an overwhelming and terrible sense of déjà vu. She was remembering that night, exactly one week before, when she had walked into the Cafe Pamplona and seen the two of them together. And Lauren had sat alone and waited for Russell, who never appeared. Now Lauren thought of retreating in search of another restaurant, but instead she gathered courage; there was no turning back now. After all, it was possible that they had already seen her, and she would certainly not want to seem to be afraid of Sandy. But it would be unpleasant to have them watching her eat alone. In a moment Lauren had made her decision, and in another moment she was at their table. "May I join you?" she was asking cheerfully, but even as she spoke she was already taking a seat and thus rendering the question superfluous.

"Yes, yes, please," Parker was saying awkwardly, striving

to remain polite in the face of what even he must have recognized as a potentially explosive situation.

Was that an ugly little smile Lauren saw on Sandy's face? Was Sandy amused by Lauren's purple eye shadow? Lauren knew that it was better to be the class slut than to seem to be ashamed of herself. She rose to the occasion. "Sandy darling," she exclaimed in her very best imitation of Michael's imitation of Tallulah Bankhead, "Sandy darling, I adore your sweater. Brown is my favorite color." Take that, you little bitch, Lauren was thinking.

Sandy said nothing, but at least that hint of a grin had been driven from her face. Her features now resolved themselves into an expression of simple, cold hatred which Lauren found altogether more tolerable. She couldn't help wondering just why Sandy should hate her so much. Was it that Sandy saw her as a rival for the affections of Russell Bernard? And was this sense of rivalry really to continue past Russell's death? Was it possible that Russell had said something to Sandy about Lauren? Naturally, Lauren would have liked to know, but it would probably be easier and more rewarding to cross-examine Russell's corpse than to pry the information out of Sandy.

It was also possible that Sandy resented Lauren more generally for reasons of tangled self-hatred. That is to say, Lauren was the Jewish girl from New Jersey without the prep school finish. She was someone capable of putting on purple makeup for fun, capable of allowing herself to be a little vulgar. Lauren didn't kill herself studying either (God knows!) —she was actually enjoying college. Would it be so surprising if Sandy, beneath her fierce snobbery, suffered from some elusive shadow of a doubt about the path she had chosen? And wasn't it somehow an affront to Sandy's values that Lauren, without ever leaving New Jersey, was equally capable of getting into Harvard? Lauren herself was pretty sure that given the choice between being a princess and a preppie, she would go for the princess every time.

While the two girls were thinking evil thoughts about each other, Parker was being polite. He was asking Lauren how she was doing.

Lauren was doing fine. She told them about the dorm meeting, since she was eager to bring up the subject of the murders. Parker and Sandy had also just come from meetings in their respective dorms; the meetings were obviously dictated by a university-wide memorandum. Sandy expressed the opinion that the meetings were a waste of time, since the suggested safety precautions were all no more than common sense. Lauren hastened to agree. Watching the two of them closely, she said, "Yeah, like telling us not to go walking by the river at night. Girls don't go walking alone by the river anyway." Parker and Sandy both winced. Walking by the river was obviously not a comfortable topic of conversation.

For just that reason Lauren decided to push it a little further. She turned to Sandy and said, girl to girl, "*I* certainly wouldn't go walking by the river alone. And if I went down there with someone you can be sure that I'd stick to him like glue."

"I'm sure you would," said Sandy, but her delivery was weak.

It was, Lauren thought, great fun to bait Sandy, even if baiting was not the best way to elicit useful information. Still, she thought, I can't always be thinking about my investigation. Sometimes I have to have some fun. Now she prepared to put a little bit of New Jersey into her voice just to remind Sandy of the heritage they shared. Lauren said, "You know, there was a memorial service for Russell Bernard this afternoon in Memorial Church. I went there instead of going to my Nietzsche discussion section."

"A memorial service. I didn't know about that," said Parker.

"Oh," said Lauren conversationally, "it was really just for Russell's friends. You didn't know him that well, did you?" Lauren turned to Sandy. "But you were a sort of friend of Russell's, weren't you, Sandy? I'm surprised you weren't invited. You really should have been there."

Lauren intended for this to be offensive, but it was more successful than she had dared hope. Sandy announced that she had a lot of studying to do, put ten dollars on the table, and walked out of the restaurant. Parker watched her go, obviously uncertain whether courtesy demanded that he go with Sandy or stay with Lauren. The most correct WASP upbringing did not prescribe an etiquette for situations in which Jewish girls attempted to claw at each other. The decision was made for him, however, because in a moment Sandy was gone and Parker was left with Lauren. It was now that Lauren's fettuccine Alfredo arrived, and she began to eat contentedly.

Parker very nearly apologized for Sandy's rudeness. He said that she didn't seem to be quite herself, and he was obviously extremely uncomfortable about her abrupt exit. Lauren gloated inwardly over the triumph of having induced Sandy, despite her well-mannered affectations, to behave in a fashion that Parker, the Boston Brahmin, would have to regard as dubious, if not downright vulgar. It must have been tormenting Sandy at that very moment, to have acted so extremely unaristocratically in front of Parker. On the other hand, Parker seemed to have missed completely the little digs that Lauren had used to provoke Sandy. Otherwise he would hardly be apologizing to Lauren now.

Lauren looked him over carefully as she nibbled at her fettuccine. He was sweet. And he did look vaguely like the young Robert Redford. And he would be perfect for Melissa. Lauren herself found him a little too tame—but he could hardly be too tame for Melissa. Which woman would Parker prefer, Melissa or Lauren? Or Sandy?

Lauren had something more important to wonder about, and the fact that she was not interested in Parker as a romantic possibility did not for a moment inhibit her from applying her charms to investigative purposes. She reached a hand across the table and touched his hand ever so gently to get his attention. Her eyes were full of emotional preoccupation mixed with just a hint of sexual availability as she said, "Parker, there's something I have to ask you about."

"Yes?" Lauren sensed a stirring of response in his voice.

"What happened between Russell and Sandy down by the river the night that Russell was murdered?"

The flicker of interest which she had seen in his eyes a moment before now vanished. His answer was almost mechanical. "I'd rather not talk about that," he said. "I wouldn't feel right talking about that." The voice was almost too mechanical, without any true emotional indignation. Lauren wondered if he might not, in fact, be very anxious to talk about that very subject. Perhaps there was something he wanted to get off his mind. But how was Lauren to go about prying it loose?

Lauren was forming a plan. "I'm sorry," she said. "I didn't mean to offend you. . . ."

"Oh, you didn't offend me," Parker hastened to assure her. Now he was apologizing. Good.

"Look," said Lauren, plotting furiously, "let's change the

subject." She paused as if to think of a new subject at random. "You know," she said, "I had a long talk with someone today, and we talked about you."

"About me?" Parker blushed. He had obviously given little thought to the possibility that people might talk about him.

"Yes, about you. It was interesting. And now that I'm talking to you, I keep thinking of that other conversation." Surely even Parker would have to respond to bait like that. And he did.

"Who were you talking to?" he asked.

"Melissa Wu."

Lauren watched him carefully and saw plenty. Before, when she had touched his hand, he had definitely responded. But now, at the mere mention of Melissa's name, he responded with rather more intensity. He was excited. He was nervous. It was all in the eyes. "You talked with Melissa Wu about me?" he said. He was stammering.

"Yes," said Lauren, delighted at the reaction she had provoked. Parker was hooked. Now Lauren could afford to string him along. "I really like Melissa," said Lauren with mock sincerity. "Don't you?"

"Yes," said Parker. "But what—"

Lauren didn't let him finish. "She's such a sweet girl. And I think she's very pretty. Have you ever noticed what small feet she has?"

"No, not really," said Parker who obviously missed out on freshman class jokes. "But what—"

"Melissa and I have become good friends," said Lauren, well aware that she was lying. It would do no harm to have Parker believe that she was a person who could influence Melissa. Now she would allow Parker to ask his question.

"But what did you and Melissa say about me?" he asked, barely concealing his rather unaristocratic extreme impatience to know.

Lauren looked him straight in the eye. She still spoke with extravagant sweetness, but now the sweetness was patently false. It was possible to glimpse the hardness of the scheme which lay behind. Lauren quoted Parker's own words back to him. "I'd rather not talk about that. I wouldn't feel right talking about that."

Lauren watched intently as Parker slowly began to appreciate what was going on. She would reveal her piece of confidential information if he would reveal his. Melissa was the prize that Lauren would use to tempt Parker into indiscretion. Lauren thought with some amusement about how horrified Melissa would be to know that her name was being made use of so shamelessly.

"Sandy's my friend," Parker pleaded. "I know she wouldn't want me to talk about her with you."

Now Lauren knew that she had Parker where she wanted him. If he was not going to denounce and reject immediately Lauren's wicked proposal for the exchange of information, then ultimately he would accept her terms. Temptation, once contemplated, would be irresistible. Lauren knew that she could just sit tight, finish her fettuccine, and wait for him to come around. However, she decided to try to make it easier for Parker to concede.

"You know," she said, "if the police find out that Sandy was down by the river with Russell that night, they're going to be very suspicious." That last sentence could be interpreted as a veiled threat. But now Lauren put aside threats. "If you and I can establish just what really did happen down by the river that night, then perhaps we can clear Sandy. That's why I want to know." Would Parker really believe in Lauren's good intentions toward Sandy? Surely he would only fall for this if he very much wanted to fall for it. And he did.

"I'd like to be able to prove that she had nothing to do with the murder," said Parker hesitantly. "But—I don't know if you'll believe me—but I really don't know what happened between Russell and Sandy that night. I ran into Sandy when she was walking up from the riverbank—Michael Hunt probably told you—but I don't know what happened before."

Lauren was dubious. "Sandy wouldn't tell you?" Was Parker telling the truth? He certainly had every justification for lying.

"I haven't asked," said Parker.

"You haven't asked?" Lauren was stunned. This was even more incredible than Bert's not asking Russell about his appointment with Professor Baranova. "But aren't you curious? Don't you want to know?"

"No," said Parker. And from his tone it was suddenly clear to Lauren what he must be thinking. He didn't want to know, because he was afraid of what he might find out. Was he afraid to discover that Russell and Sandy had been lovers? Was he jealous? Or was he afraid of something more serious? Did Parker perhaps allow himself to consider the possibility that Sandy had actually murdered Russell? That would explain why he was afraid to know the truth. If Parker himself was capable of suspecting Sandy, then Lauren would have to be that much more suspicious.

"So you don't know anything?" said Lauren.

"I do know one thing," said Parker. "Sandy was in love with Russell Bernard, or infatuated with him or obsessed with him or something. I know, because she used to talk about him all the time. Every Wednesday, after the seminar, she used to insist that she and I go over every word that Russell had spoken in class. It wasn't that she admitted to being in love with him or anything. It was just that she talked about him all the time, as if he were the only natural topic of conversation. And then Russell was murdered. And since then she's never spoken about him again except for that night at the Cafe Pamplona, the night after the murder—remember, you were there. Sandy and I had just heard about the murder from someone on the *Crimson*. At Pamplona Sandy told me that she didn't want the police to know she'd been with Russell the night before because she didn't want to get mixed up in the whole thing. She said it would distract her from her studying."

Parker was obviously uncomfortable about all this. In Sandy's place he would have dutifully gone to the police to offer his information. He was willing to keep the secret for her, but he couldn't help thinking that she was not behaving quite rightly, nor even help contemplating the possibility that... It was clearly a relief for Parker to tell all this to Lauren.

Lauren stuck to her side of the bargain. She told him more or less what Melissa had said that afternoon, though she did not include an account of Melissa's hopelessly unsuccessful lessons in flirtation. It would be better, Lauren thought, if Parker and Melissa did not come to see each other as comic figures. Lauren would preserve that perspective for herself. Still, even Lauren could not help being a bit jealous when she saw Parker's face light up at the news that he was indeed loved. That he reciprocated was quite evident. They would make a good couple, Lauren thought, and a very handsome one. And, if it worked out, Lauren would always be amused at her own role in bringing them together.

Parker's expression of jubilation gave way to one of perplexity. Lauren could guess what was the matter. Parker

had no more idea than Melissa of what to do next. Lauren
took him in hand.

"Follow me," said Lauren, and she led him over to
Grendel's public telephone. She called Harvard Information
and was given Melissa's phone number. Then Lauren gave
Parker a dime. "Be brave," she said. "Call Melissa. Ask her if
she'd like to go see *Gone With the Wind* on Saturday night at
the Harvard Square Theater. I promise you she'll say yes."
And Parker, nervous but resolute, did just as he was told.

Parker had to meet a friend from Exeter at Kirkland
House that night. He had stayed too long at the restaurant,
and now he was late for his appointment. He offered to walk
Lauren back to Harvard Yard, but she assured him that she
would be fine by herself. It seemed silly to make him go so
far out of his way. Besides, Lauren had had enough of Parker
for one evening. He was not all that interesting, and Lauren
preferred not to spend another fifteen minutes talking about
Melissa Wu. And so it was that only a few hours after the
special dormitory meeting on safety precautions, Lauren set
out into the Cambridge night alone.

It was only a short walk, and Lauren had done it many
times before. Tonight, however, it seemed more frightening
than usual. Lauren kept feeling that someone was following
her, but she refused to allow herself to turn around. She did
not want to surrender to irrational fears. It was only a block
to Harvard Square where there were a handful of people
moving in the cold. Lauren pulled her jacket tight around
her. A drunk appeared from nowhere and called out obscenely.
Lauren hurried on. What happened, she wondered, between
Russell and Sandy that night by the river?

Inside Harvard Yard there was almost no one. The lights
were on in all the hundreds of dormitory rooms, but the Yard
itself was empty. It did not seem like such a safe place,
Harvard Yard. It was full of buildings and trees that might
easily conceal anyone at all. Lauren was very glad to finally
reach the entrance of Thayer Hall and lock the dormitory
door soundly behind her.

And then, when Lauren put the key in the lock to enter
her room, she heard a scream. The scream came from inside
the room. And then the scream came again, and Lauren
knew that it was Carol. She was screaming, "Stop, stop."

Bravely Lauren turned the doorknob and threw open the door. She heard Carol shriek again, and she saw the outline of a man in the room. Now Lauren screamed for help at the top of her lungs, and she reached for the light switch.

The light went on. The man was Brian O'Donnell. Carol was on the bed still screaming, but her shrieks were degenerating into hysterical giggles. Her orange tube top was disarranged. She had not been screaming out of fear for her life, but only to try to stop Lauren from walking in on her in the middle of her carrying on. Lauren too began to giggle, from sheer emotional relief. The situation was, after all, pretty funny. Brian was obviously desperately embarrassed, and would have liked nothing better than to hide. But he was too large to hide, and so he had to content himself with buttoning up his shirt. Meanwhile Carol and Lauren were laughing. And now the other girls on the floor all began to gather in the hallway to see what was the matter.

13. Duets with Professor Baranova

Tatiana Baranova lived almost a mile from Harvard Yard, way out beyond Radcliffe. Lauren was glad to have Michael along on the walk, and not only because Michael was such delightful company. It was Friday night, around eight-thirty—dark and cold. And there was no way to avoid passing the Cambridge Common where Tracy Nicolson had been murdered three nights before. Michael and Lauren did not dare walk right through the middle of the unlucky Common; they were not that brazen. Instead they walked timidly along the edge, peering into the darkness at the center, where it was possible to imagine sinister figures doing sinister things.

Lauren had called Professor Baranova that afternoon. It seemed the obvious next step to try to find out whether Russell had visited Professor Baranova on the night of his death, and what had passed between them. Surely the encounter, if it really had taken place, could not be without significance. Perhaps Tatiana Baranova would be more forthcoming than Sandy Grayson about her own share in Russell Bernard's last hours.

Lauren was a little nervous about taking her investigation up among the faculty. Investigating her fellow students was one thing; Lauren's amateurishness hardly seemed to matter. But the Harvard faculty was such a lofty institution. The unapproachability of the faculty was indeed one of the great subjects of conversation on the Harvard campus. True, most of the discussion took place in whining tones among people who would have had little to say to their professors anyway. But all this complaining contributed to the myth of the Harvard Professor whom one did not dare disturb from concentration on the next Pulitzer or Nobel Prize. And this was what made it all the more remarkable that Russell and Professor Baranova should have been on visiting terms. Lauren would probably have been hesitant about calling on one of her professors to discuss an academic issue. For the much less appropriate motive of pursuing her investigation, however, she was prepared to confront the colossus.

Lauren then turned to the great instrument of her craft: the telephone. At first she was relieved when no one answered Professor Baranova's office number, but then she accepted that it would be cowardly to leave the task for Monday. If the professor had gone home for the weekend, Lauren would call her at home, an act so bold as to astound almost any Harvard freshman. Lauren got the number again from Information, reflecting as she dialed that this was probably no more difficult for her than calling Melissa Wu had been for Parker. Parker had been very brave and had been rewarded with a Saturday night date.

Lauren did almost as well: a Friday night date. When Professor Baranova answered the phone, the sound of her voice had immediately reminded Lauren of the occasion two nights before when she had called to check that the professor was still alive. Now again Lauren was tempted to simply hang up, but she gathered her courage and identified herself. When Lauren said that she wanted to talk, Professor Baranova at first suggested that they wait for Monday, but upon hearing that it was urgent she invited Lauren to come over to her house that very night at nine.

Michael and Lauren were both very impressed at their first sight of the house. It was enormous and elaborate. There were turrets and balconies and many tiny eccentric windows of which several were lit. The whole effect was pleasing—an antique mansion—and it stood twenty yards back from the narrow Cambridge street behind a profusion of bushes and several imposing trees. The house was beautiful at night but also intimidating. In fact, the whole adventure was intimidating; rather than walk briskly up the path to the door, Lauren preferred to dally in the street with Michael for a while. They chatted while she nerved herself.

"So this is my big Friday night date," said Lauren.

"Yes, darling, and I'd love to chaperone you and have a

peek inside this *palazzo*, not to mention a peek at the famous professor, but I think you're old enough to do it by yourself."

"Maybe I'm not old enough. I'm scared. Maybe I'll turn around and walk back to Harvard Square with you." Lauren was joking, and Michael knew that she only wanted to be prodded a little.

"Naturally I'd be grateful for your protection," said Michael, "but unfortunately I can't invite you along for the evening. I'm going to go to an extremely gay party at Adams House where everyone is going to be male and almost everyone will be from Exeter."

"Oh pretty please can I come?"

"You know you wouldn't like it. It will be extremely silly. Everyone will be trying to be very British, and they'll talk about the Theater, and someone might even try to talk about Contemporary Fiction, in which case I would have to go home immediately."

Lauren laughed and felt a little braver. "Now don't you start carrying on with any of those little Exeter prigs. You know I have my heart set on your falling in love with someone impossibly vulgar, perhaps a Greek immigrant who works in a pizzeria."

Michael made a face. "Maybe if he's a Praxiteles. And you don't have to worry about me and the boys at the party. Those Exeter boys never actually sleep with anyone. By the way, I invited Curt James to go to the party with me." Michael blushed. "Curt said no, but he smiled very flirtatiously while he was saying it."

"Sorry," said Lauren, "but Curt isn't vulgar enough. And besides, he's not gay."

"Hmmmph. Did I ever tell you about the professional hockey player—"

Lauren didn't let him finish. "You tell me every day." There was a silence, and Michael could see that Lauren was still not ready to approach the house.

"Just think," said Michael, "tomorrow will be *your* big date."

"Oh no!" Lauren giggled. "Don't remind me." That afternoon Scott Duchaine had called and left a message with Carol that he would come by Saturday at seven-thirty to pick Lauren up for *Gone with the Wind*. "Should I go?" she asked.

"Of course you should go," said Michael. "If Carol was

gaping at Scott at a party all night Tuesday, then he couldn't have murdered Tracy. And besides, you know you're dying to see *Gone with the Wind* for the two-hundredth time."

"It's true," said Lauren. "I find it reassuring to think about Tara. But I don't find it reassuring to think about Scott. Why am I still scared of him? Do you think he *was* Russell's lover?" Suddenly Lauren had an idea. "Michael, why don't you come with us?"

"I don't think Scott would like it too much. I think in Richmond they don't have that old New England Ivy League tradition of bringing along a gay chaperone on a Saturday night date."

"Surely it happens somewhere in a Tennessee Williams play?"

"Tennessee Williams is *not* from Richmond. Tennessee Williams wouldn't even be able to get his shoes shined in Richmond."

"Don't you get snobby with me about Tennessee Williams," said Lauren, full of mock indignation. "I happen to like Tennessee Williams. Scott and I are going to go see *Gone with the Wind*, and you can go get your shoes shined in Richmond, Mr. Robert E. Lee."

They both laughed happily. "Listen," said Michael, "I'll try to round up some of the boys at the party to go see *Gone with the Wind* tomorrow, and we'll sit a few rows behind you. That way I can keep an eye on the two of you."

Ridiculously enough, Lauren found this reassuring. She was ready to call on Tatiana Baranova now. Lauren and Michael kissed each other goodbye on both cheeks, and Michael said, "Ciao, bella." Lauren started up the long path to the front door, waving to Michael over her shoulder.

Lauren rang the bell. A few seconds later a light went out in one of the upper windows, and then Lauren waited. It was some time before Professor Baranova finally opened the door and invited Lauren to come in.

Professor Baranova's appearance at the door was a new confirmation of her beauty. In fact, she was even more impressive here—in her natural setting—than in the seminar. Or was this odd New England mansion really her natural setting? Was it perhaps necessary, in order to fully appreciate the presence of this woman, to see her at the Paris Opera, or walking along the Neva in prerevolutionary Saint Petersburg? Her hair was pulled back as always, this time with a cream-colored silk scarf. Now there was no black veil to hide the diamond earrings and exquisite bone structure.

The Russian accent was very distinctive: scholarly, but with an almost musical intonation. Lauren was again reminded of the night when she had telephoned and then hung up reassured. Only now did Lauren realize that it might have been frightening to receive that call, to hear the phone click while standing in this peculiar palace and wondering who might have been at the other end.

But Professor Baranova did not appear to be afraid of her large, strange house. She carried herself with complete assurance; she was absolutely at home here. Lauren followed her down a long hall whose walls were covered from one end to another with books. It was a gallery, a small library in itself, and although Lauren had no time to do more than glimpse some of the titles, she could see that organization and thought and even a sense of aesthetics had gone into the ordering. The books were beautiful and old, with hard backs and perceptibly foreign bindings. The titles were also in foreign languages—Russian, German, French, Italian. Lauren did not doubt that somewhere on these shelves belonged the beautiful volume of Trotsky that Professor Baranova had brought to class on Wednesday. Gazing at the books as she passed, Lauren thought to herself, So this is the life of a professor. And it was not without appeal.

Professor Baranova suggested coffee and then went off to the kitchen to prepare it. Lauren was left alone in the huge living room. There was a large and obviously precious Persian rug which Lauren immediately coveted. There was an aging grand piano in the corner, and on the other side of the room was the foot of an equally grand staircase whose banister ascended into the unknown upper regions of the house. A page of handwritten music was framed and hanging over the piano.

And inevitably there were more books. Here Lauren saw the classics of world literature, which meant perhaps that the books in the hallway were the histories. Here in the living room was a beautiful old set of Proust, in French of course, and on another shelf the plays of Schiller in German. There were English books too: Jane Austen, D. H. Lawrence, Virginia Woolf, lots of things that Lauren had read and loved.

And one whole wall was covered with shelves of records. Professor Baranova's specialty was the history of Russian music, and so the records were no surprise. The collection was almost exclusively classical.

It was a beautiful house, perfectly suited to the beautiful professor. In fact, it was so perfectly suited that Lauren could not even imagine the presence of the absent husband, the famous Professor Max Kohler. Lauren knew that he looked like a toad, and she could hardly picture him crouched on top of the grand piano. Perhaps it was aesthetically for the best that he was off in Washington advising foreign policy.

And yet, it was frightening to think of Professor Baranova living here alone. Surely she too was frightened, especially now that two students, two of her own students, had been murdered. She reentered the room carrying a lacquered wooden tray on which rode two elegant china cups of coffee. They settled into the gorgeous and probably antique sofa. Lauren, by way of making conversation, inquired, "The page of music framed on the wall, it's original?"

"Yes," said the older woman, smiling, pleased to be asked—"it's just a scrap, but it is in the original hand of the composer."

"Oh, who?" asked Lauren.

"Tchaikovsky."

"What then was the very important thing that you wanted to discuss with me?" Her tone was kind, interested.

Lauren cleared her throat several times, crossed, uncrossed, and recrossed her legs, and finally spoke up timidly. "I wanted to talk to you about Russell Bernard."

"Oh?" The face betrayed nothing. The tone was still interested, but no more apparently interested than before.

"Yes, Russell," said Lauren, shuffling some more, searching for the least awkward lines. "I've been thinking about him a lot since he died—was killed. And then I saw you at the memorial service, and since then I've been thinking about talking to you about him. I mean, I've been wanting to talk about him with somebody, but I haven't really had anyone to talk about him with. So when I saw you at the memorial service, I thought that perhaps you, uh, appreciated him." Lauren chose the last words carefully and tried to speak them in a tone that was not improperly suggestive. She did not want to give offence. Her mission would seem peculiar enough as it was.

But Professor Baranova did not seem to find it strange to want to talk about Russell Bernard. In fact, she seemed to want to talk about him herself. No further prodding was required to start her reflecting aloud on the character of the dead boy.

Tatiana Baranova had also thought that Russell was remarkable. He was bright, genuinely bright. It had been intellectually exciting to have him as a student in her class. Some people, usually outside of Harvard but occasionally even from within, contended that all Harvard students were bright, even brilliant. That was ridiculous. Harvard was full of stupid people and dull people, professors as well as students. (Lauren happened to agree. And now it occurred to her to wonder nervously whether Professor Baranova considered her to be one of the bright ones. Lauren did not doubt her own brightness, but she was also aware that in the freshman seminar she had not given a particularly impressive academic display.)

Professor Baranova continued—softly, thoughtfully—looking not at Lauren but across the room, perhaps at the framed piece of Tchaikovsky on the wall. Russell was not only bright. He was also talented, perhaps very much so—it was difficult to tell. Did Lauren know that he played the violin? Was she aware of how good he was? Oh yes, he was quite extraordinary. Especially considering that he regarded the violin as merely a hobby, and that he had received a rather unimpressive training—or at any rate he had never studied with anyone of note. Actually he had taken lessons from a Jesuit priest in Atlanta. The whole arrangement sounded like some sort of grotesque little comic novella, but the fact was that Russell had been genuinely good. Ah well, the Jesuits were workers of miracles, always had been—a little bit terrifying, but miracle workers nonetheless—especially in matters of education.

And Russell had loved playing, loved music, and yet he had never cared about it as a professional. He never thought about being a musician. Professor Baranova had once wanted to be a pianist, a professional pianist. She had received the finest conservatory training in Paris, and she had worked at her music furiously, more than she had ever worked on anything else before or since. But, unfortunately, she was not

quite sufficiently talented . . . and finally she had admitted
defeat, given up music, and decided to do something else.

Decided to do something else! Lauren was a little awed
by this self-deprecating explanation of Professor Baranova's
career as a Harvard professor of history. Sort of a fallback, an
acceptable second choice. And, of course, Professor Baranova's
whole monologue was very strange. She was not a woman
from whom one expected to hear either stories of her own
frustrated ambitions or dreamy reflections on the personali-
ties of her students. In her manner were mingled her cus-
tomary aloofness and an unexpected tenderness. Professor
Baranova had obviously needed to talk about Russell Bernard,
and Lauren's opening had struck the right chord. The two of
them sat sadly on the sofa, and the myth of the unapproach-
able Harvard professor had never before seemed so extremely mythical.

Professor Baranova continued. Russell had been interested in politics, more passionately interested in politics than
in music, and that was something that she could not understand. Of course, she had very mixed feelings about politics
and political people. Her father had been an important
Russian socialist, a Menshevik, and politics had meant everything to him. And her husband—at last she mentioned the
absent husband—well, he was up to his neck in American
foreign policy. At this her features formed a rather charming
expression of cultured distaste. Of course her father and her
husband were the most important men in her life, but she
had always found their political obsessions—no lesser word
would do—more than a little alien. Politics were fascinating,
but ugly. Why did men find them so appealing? How could
Russell have cared more for the National Black Students'
Lobby than for the violin?

Lauren was thinking about Tracy Nicolson. Tracy's father
was a corrupt Chicago politician. Tracy herself would have
made a fierce politician, and no one would ever have sighed
over the musical sensibilities she was neglecting. It was odd,
perhaps terrible, Lauren thought, how little Tracy seemed to
have to do with the tragedy. Tracy too had been murdered
and, in fact, more recently than Russell. And yet for Professor Baranova and also for Lauren herself, the real tragedy was
the death of Russell. There had been a second murder, and
yet Lauren knew in her heart that she was still searching for
the murderer of Russell Bernard. Her whole investigation

was a product of, a tribute to, her obsession with him. And she was not unique. Professor Baranova also could not get Russell out of her mind.

"I suppose it's a terrible tragedy," Tatiana Baranova was saying. "One feels that the world has lost something: a musician, a civil rights leader, maybe just a personality. And yet, of course, one never knows. Perhaps there was no more than great potential, and perhaps not even that. I suppose that he might have ended up going to law school and becoming quite tedious and distasteful."

Now, Lauren thought, now is the time to try an even trickier subject. She swallowed hard and then said, "Russell was here the night he was killed, wasn't he?" She spoke sadly and without emphasis, as if this remark were a natural part of their mutual reminiscences. But what would Professor Baranova say now?

She did not seem to be shocked, or at any rate she gave nothing away. She put one hand thoughtfully on the side of her face and said quite calmly, perhaps with a hint of perplexity, "Yes, he was here that evening, but how do you know?" And then, without leaving time for the question to be answered, she added, "I thought that the only ones who knew about that were myself and the police."

"The police?" said Lauren, very much surprised. It was uncanny how Professor Baranova had turned the tables, shocking Lauren while remaining unshockable herself.

"Yes, the police. Naturally when I found out he had been murdered, I went straight to the police to tell them Russell had been here that evening. I believe that's the sort of thing that the police are supposed to be interested in, reconstructing the last hours of the victim. I imagine it could be of some use in apprehending the murderer. But, in fact, the police weren't very interested in what I had to say, and I can hardly blame them, since I didn't have anything particularly interesting to tell them. But it was quite interesting for me, or comic at any rate. The American police have such red faces and barbarous manners. And they barely speak English. They are quite remarkable to observe up close."

Why was it that Lauren had taken so completely for granted that if there had actually been a meeting between Russell and Professor Baranova that fateful night, then she would have kept it secret from the police? Was it possible that the meeting was in no way clandestine or sinister, that she had nothing to hide? Sandy Grayson was keeping her encounter with Russell secret from the police, but that did not mean that anyone else would necessarily do likewise. There was something awe-inspiring in Professor Baranova's command of any situation.

"But how did you know he was here?" she was inquiring for the second time.

Lauren did not tell the truth. She did not fully trust the professor, and for that reason she hesitated to bring Bert Rosen's name into the conversation. "Russell told me," she said. "He mentioned to me after the seminar that he might be going to visit you later in the evening."

"Russell told you?" There was something strange and disturbing in her tone. Was it that she did not believe Lauren, saw through the lie? Or was it perhaps that she was annoyed? For Russell to talk to Lauren about Professor Baranova was perhaps an indiscretion on his part. Was it perhaps something that he should not have mentioned to anyone, a violation of trust? It might be regarded as mildly unprofessional for a professor to have singled out one of her students for a special friendship, even if the friendship was perfectly innocent, as this one seemed to be. Lauren regretted casting unjust aspersions on Russell, little though they could hurt him now. But were the aspersions actually unjust? True, Russell had not confided in Lauren. But he had confided in Bert. And wasn't that equally indiscreet? What sort of a person was Russell Bernard really?

Lauren looked up suddenly. Was it possible that there was someone outside the big window, looking into the living room? Or was it just her own guilty conscience, troubled by the questions she had to ask and the lies she had to tell? Lauren felt very lost in the incredible complications and twists of the mystery she was uncovering. It was hard to believe that she would ever see her way clear to a true solution, that she would ever be able to identify the murderer. But this was no time to give up the fight. Lauren took a deep breath and plunged onward. "What sort of things were on Russell's mind that night?" she asked.

Once again Professor Baranova accepted the question as not entirely inappropriate. Once again she seemed quite ready to discuss Russell. They had talked about music that night, she and Russell. She liked to talk about music with Russell. And they played duets together, she at the piano while he played his violin. The duets were the reason for their meeting. They had similar taste, and they played well together; it was a pleasure for them both. On that particular night they had played Beethoven.

But they had not played duets for long, because Russell had had other things on his mind. He had been thinking about politics, about his Lobby, and he had talked about that. Professor Baranova had listened very patiently, as she listened to her father and to her husband. Now she could not really remember just what Russell had been talking about that night, except that it had something to do with a rival organization on campus, an organization rather more to the left—quite extreme. Professor Baranova pronounced these last two words with that charming little grimace.

She also knew (as Lauren had already guessed) that Russell had been speaking of the group to which Katherine Butler belonged. Professor Baranova remembered his having mentioned Katherine that night, such a strange girl Katherine Butler, but not stupid. Anyway Russell had been talking about the Lobby and whether it would be able to maintain itself against this challenge from the left. And he had been afraid that without Dora Carpenter the Lobby would be much weaker. Of course, without Russell himself the Lobby would be that much weaker still. "You know," she concluded, "I think he was in love with Dora Carpenter. Very terrible that she should die, and then he should be murdered. It has the air of some sort of tragic Russian ballet."

And Lauren nodded her assent, thinking that in fact the drama was even more extraordinary, since Tracy might have been in love with Russell and she was the next to die. Was it some sort of terrible chain? Lauren could not help recalling that Bert had been in love with Tracy. It was frightening just to think about it. But the fear that it inspired was nothing compared to the terror that Lauren felt at the very next moment, when she looked up and saw a man standing at the foot of the stairs.

"I'd like you to meet my husband," said Professor Baranova, all grace and good manners. The man approached, and Lauren's initial terror subsided as she recognized the features of Max Kohler. They were now famous features; they had appeared often enough in the newspapers during the last six months when he had been working in the State Department. The *Harvard Crimson* devoted particular attention to the career of this Harvard professor of diplomatic history, and Lauren knew that Carol would have killed for an opportunity to interview Max Kohler. Lauren had not expected to see him tonight, here in the living room of his own home. The appearance of the stranger had been startling, and it was a great relief to discover that the stranger's face was at least a familiar one.

"My husband is back from Washington for the weekend."

His face was ugly, but powerfully ugly. It was clear that he was a man of some consequence. In the newspaper photographs he looked like a toad, but in person he seemed more like one of those grotesque types of lizard, perhaps an iguana. His body was small and slightly humped. His shoulders barely existed. As he crossed the room toward his wife and her guest, it was impossible for the guest not to be reminded of Beauty and the Beast.

He stayed only a minute, said hello to his wife and to Lauren, and then turned and reascended the stairs. The few words he had spoken did not convey the impression of a nice man, a sympathetic man, but again one could believe that behind his ugliness was a powerful personality. And, in fact, behind the powerful personality there was now real power. Lauren wondered why she had suddenly thought of Bert Rosen. And then she realized: Max Kohler was a caricature of a German-Jewish intellectual, while Bert Rosen was a caricature of a new generation of American Jews, blond, blue-eyed, relaxed, and fun. She imagined Bert Rosen and Max Kohler side by side. Surely the comparison ought to yield some sort of insight about Jews in the twentieth century? But Lauren had other things to think about now.

Max Kohler ascended the stairs, and Lauren watched him go uneasily. Earlier she had supposed herself to be alone in the house with Professor Baranova, but now it was clear that this had not been the case. It was unnerving to review the last hour's conversation and realize that any part of it could have been overheard. And at the same time it was reassuring to think that there was a man in the house. Or at least it would have been reassuring if the man himself were not of such disturbing aspect. He gives me the creeps, Lauren thought.

"I'd like to talk about you for a moment," said Professor

Baranova, when they were alone together again. Lauren nodded, wondering what was going to come next. "I want to talk to you about your work in the freshman seminar."

"Oh." Lauren was aware that her expression was instantly one of guilt.

"I'm not entirely pleased with your work in the seminar. Your contributions to the class discussion are few and not particularly choice. I am aware that this is because you're not doing the reading." Lauren silently pleaded guilty. "I mentioned before that, contrary to popular opinion, not everyone at Harvard is bright. I chose you for this seminar because I thought that you were one of the bright ones. I still think so. But you are not putting any of your intelligence into the seminar. I am disappointed." Lauren looked more ashamed than ever. "I am disappointed not because I am strict and old-fashioned and European, though I am all of those things, but because a teacher's work is rewarding only when the students respond."

Lauren was genuinely touched by this appeal, and her regard for her professor reached a new height. Lauren knew that she could not give a reasonable defense of her own academic irresponsibility. If Lauren was bored with her Harvard classes, surely that was at least partially her own fault. Lauren wondered: had she just sunk into a temporarily unmotivated period, or was she really fundamentally frivolous? "I'm sorry," she said finally. "I know you're right. I've been distracted lately."

"I know this is a rather big question, but have you thought about what you want to do with your life?"

"I've thought, but I haven't thought of anything. That's part of the problem. I don't know what I want to do. I don't know what I want to study. Up until now my whole education consisted of reading novels in my lap during school, and now I feel like I can't quite adapt to Harvard academics. I find lots of things interesting, for a while, and then my mind begins to wander." For a moment, right then, Lauren allowed herself to wonder whether it was perhaps her destiny to become a detective. It was true that she had persevered in her investigation. Her interest and her efforts had not lagged.

"Will you try a little harder for me?" asked Professor Baranova.

"Yes, I will try, I promise," said Lauren. And she meant it.

Lauren and Professor Baranova exchanged smiles. It was clear that their talk was over. It was quite late. Lauren was ready to walk home, but Professor Baranova insisted on calling a taxi, as a safety precaution. Lauren was secretly relieved. The darkness outside was ominous, and she was not entirely sure of the way back to Harvard Square.

While waiting for the taxi, Lauren asked, "By the way, how did you find out about the memorial service for Russell?"

"It was quite an odd coincidence actually. Thursday morning—yesterday morning—I was working in my office in the stacks of Widener, and Katherine Butler came to return to me a book she had borrowed about Trotsky's organization of the Red Army. But before she knocked on my door she stopped in the corridor to finish an argument she was having with someone. And I could not help overhearing the gist of their argument from within my office. Her companion—judging from the voice—was a young black man, and they were talking about the memorial service to be held that afternoon. Katherine was trying to convince him not to go."

14. Gone with the Wind

It was Saturday night, and the Harvard Square Theater was full. *Gone with the Wind* was always very popular among Harvard students, who were, after all, as romantic as any other collection of young Americans and highly susceptible to Vivien Leigh and Clark Gable. There was also additional interest in the fact that Ashley Wilkes was a Harvard man. To be sure of a good seat for the movie it would have been better to come a little early, but Lauren, as a matter of principle, had not been quite ready to go out when Scott arrived. Scott had had to wait for fifteen minutes in Carol's room, while Lauren fiddled with her mascara and admired herself in the mirror.

She did not find it easy to face Scott after all that she had suspected during the past week. She was nervous walking alone with him across Harvard Yard to the Square, and she did not feel any better when the two of them entered the theater, which was already full. The huge anonymous crowd of Harvard students made Lauren feel that much more alone with Scott, so she looked around for familiar faces.

Her search was quickly rewarded. Sitting toward the back were Carol and Brian. They too had a Saturday night date to see *Gone with the Wind*. Carol was chattering flirtatiously with a chocolate bar in one hand and popcorn in the other, sweet and crunchy. Lauren automatically noted to herself that Carol would have to diet tomorrow. When Lauren called out hello, Carol turned her head, squealed something happy, and waved her chocolate bar. Lauren found the exchange of greetings reassuring.

On the other side of the theater Lauren saw Parker and

Melissa. Lauren knew that she deserved full credit for that particular date and she was feeling quite proud of herself. Successful matchmaking was really remarkably satisfying. (There, she thought, is another possible profession for me. I should have mentioned it to Professor Baranova last night when we were discussing my academic interests.) Parker and Melissa were looking a bit stiff; in fact, they didn't seem to be talking at all. Oh well, it hardly mattered. The movie would begin in five minutes, and then they could be as quiet as they liked and think of things to say to each other after the film. Lauren waved to Parker and Melissa and they waved back rather too enthusiastically, obviously relieved by any distraction whatsoever from the embarrassment of their mutual shyness. Lauren, with all this waving as she walked down the aisle, was beginning to feel like Queen Elizabeth greeting the people of England.

And then at last she caught sight of Michael and his friends. There were five of them including Michael, all looking very prep and extremely effete. Michael had promised to come to the movie to watch over Lauren—to protect her from Scott—and now she began to worry about finding two seats near Michael and the boys. Perhaps she should not have spent so much time with her mascara. But Michael had thought of everything. He had thrown his coat and somebody else's over the two seats directly in front of him, so that they were, in effect, reserved. Lauren did not doubt that those two places were intended for her and Scott. With a cry of innocent delight, she called Scott's attention to the empty seats.

Lauren then said hello to Michael with much mock surprise, and he exclaimed upon the coincidence with perhaps a bit too much Stanislavskian intensity. Scott seemed vaguely aware that something was going on, and he looked suddenly uncomfortable. When he and Lauren were finally seated, and the noise of three hundred conversations gave them a relative degree of privacy, Scott whispered to Lauren, "Is he a friend of yours?" Scott, with a slight movement of his head, confirmed that he was asking about Michael, who was sitting behind them quite absorbed in his own chattering.

"Yes," said Lauren, "my very best friend at Harvard. He's wonderful and he lives right upstairs from me."

"Ah," said Scott, and he became ironically old-fashioned, "a rival for your affections?" His irony did not seem quite so relaxed as usual.

"Oh no!" said Lauren, whispering with as much cheerful emphasis as she could manage. She prepared to drop what she hoped would be a small bombshell. "Michael's gay."

"What?"

"Gay, homosexual, likes boys—you know. So I don't really think I'm entitled to count him as a beau. What do you think?"

Scott looked more uncomfortable than ever, and if he was preparing some response, Lauren never found out, because right then the lights in the theater went out. The movie was about to begin. Lauren would not be able to press the discussion right now but at least she had given him something to think about during the film. "Enjoy the movie," she whispered to him, full of false teenage enthusiasm.

Lauren had read *Gone with the Wind* several times and seen the movie on perhaps a dozen different occasions. Scarlett O'Hara was very emphatically Lauren's kind of heroine, a woman who knew how to conquer a man's world by exercising those charms which men, poor things, found so completely irresistible. For Lauren the beginning of the movie never failed to thrill... the image of Scarlett herself, utterly radiant, with the Tarleton twins in adoring attendance. They were so dashingly presentable—the Tarleton twins—even if they were dumb, and Lauren had often thought that it would be worth the trouble to find their contemporary equivalents. There had been some, extremely shrewd flatterers perhaps, who had remarked on Lauren's resemblance to Vivien Leigh. Lauren would have dearly liked to acquire a southern accent (after all, if Vivien Leigh could have one!), but one had to beware the possibility of seeming merely ridiculous. Now if Lauren were to marry Scott Duchaine and go to live in Richmond... but really she shouldn't be allowing herself such fantasies right now. Scott was too complicated a problem.

And then Mammy appeared, and Lauren began to feel a bit less rhapsodic. Lauren had always known that *Gone with the Wind* was considered offensive to blacks on account of its caricatures of the slaves. Lauren preferred to overlook this criticism of her favorite film, and, to tell the truth, she herself had always enjoyed the antics of Mammy and Prissy and Pork. Now, however, after her intensive preoccupation with Russell Bernard, she was not entirely at ease. She could not keep from imagining what it would be like to see this film with Russell instead of with Scott. And Scott, to make matters worse, was indulging in a not quite silent and certainly racist guffaw while Mammy was lacing Scarlett into her gown. Meanwhile, from the gay boys behind them came a series of titters, and Lauren could not help disapproving.

Lauren was happy to submerge such anxieties in one grand swoon when Clark Gable finally appeared at the Wilkes's barbecue. Lauren believed devoutly that there never was and never would be another man as overwhelmingly sexually attractive as Clark Gable, and Rhett Butler was his most devastating incarnation. As she gasped for the thousandth time, she heard Michael gasping behind her. Out of the corner of her eye she stole a look at Scott, but he was remaining impassive.

When the Civil War broke out and Scarlett was sent to Atlanta, Lauren had the opportunity to reflect on Russell Bernard's city. Hollywood's version of nineteenth-century Atlanta was thoroughly romantic, and Lauren had to remind herself that Russell's Atlanta had surely been very different. She allowed herself to pick up an already well-worn fantasy of visiting Atlanta with Russell, but now she tried to imagine the visit taking place just before the Civil War. (After all, Russell was dead; the fantasy was equally improbable in either century.) Scarlett O'Hara had been scandalous enough, but her scandals would sink into insignificance alongside Lauren's advent with Russell.

As the movie went on, Lauren was aware that she was becoming increasingly nervous, and she knew that Scott was the cause. But how and why? At last she realized. She was dreading the relentless approach of that magnificent scene among scenes in which Rhett Butler carries Scarlett O'Hara up the grand staircase and into her bedroom against her will. That was the scene that Lauren had dreamed so vividly Wednesday night, and the face of Rhett Butler had turned out to be the face of Scott Duchaine. Now, as the scene drew near, Lauren could feel the terror of the nightmare returning to her. And she would have to relive the dream with Scott Duchaine actually sitting right beside her.

Finally it was time. Shivering with excitement and fear, Lauren watched Clark Gable and Vivien Leigh enact the scene. And just then, as Rhett carried Scarlett off, Lauren felt a hand on her hand and she almost screamed. Looking down, away from the screen, she saw that Scott Duchaine had put his hand on hers. It was no more than the classic movie move, and it had happened to Lauren a hundred times. It would have been nothing if it had not occurred at that precise moment, and if it had not been Scott.

Her first reaction was an impulse to withdraw her hand, but she knew that Scott would be quite right in interpreting this as a gesture of rejection. She did not want to reject him, especially not before she had a chance to talk to him after the movie. And he, after all, could hardly have known about her dream. It could only have been a terrible coincidence, his choosing that particular moment to take her hand. Lauren remembered how Scott's hands had seemed so cruel when she had seen them resting on the seminar table Wednesday afternoon. But now, in the dark, she liked the feel of his hand. It was very cool and smooth, whereas most of the hands that had reached for hers in dark movie theaters had been sweaty and nervous. Instead of withdrawing her hand, Lauren turned it slightly around and clasped his. Now they were holding hands properly, and Lauren was pleased.

She gave a moment's thought to the other couples in the theater. Parker and Melissa were, no doubt, sitting rigidly in their seats, being careful not to touch each other. Oh well— Lauren could always take Parker aside and give him a few easy lessons on how to take a girl's hand, and then Lauren could teach Melissa how to respond, and with luck the two of them would manage to connect. A truly electric passion, Lauren thought.

As for Carol and Brian, Lauren did not doubt that they had moved beyond holding hands. Carol admitted to being addicted to making out at the movies, and Lauren supposed that they would simply become more and more obscene until someone sitting nearby asked them to please cut it out.

Lauren was content to hold Scott's hand and enjoy the rest of the movie. At last came the famous ending with Clark Gable walking off into the fog, not giving a damn, and Vivien Leigh resolving to wait until tomorrow. For Lauren it was a happy ending because she did not doubt for a moment that Scarlett, if she wanted to, would get Rhett back in the end. That was why Scarlett was Lauren's heroine.

The lights went on. The movie was over. Scott and Lauren let go of each other's hands. He smiled at her and said, "So what do you think of the South now?"

"Is it really exactly like that?" asked Lauren, teasing him.

"Yes, exactly," he said, teasing her.

"Well, I must go and visit sometime."

"You really must. And southern hospitality is famous." Lauren wondered if that was an invitation. Scott continued to banter. "And what do you think of southern gentlemen after seeing a movie like that?"

Lauren smiled sweetly. "I think they're clearly no match for southern ladies."

Scott suggested that they go out for a drink, but Lauren had been forming a more manageable plan. Lauren was in the mood for ice cream (as usual), and Bailey's was right around the corner. The walk would not entail wandering through deserted parts of Cambridge alone with Scott. They would not even go near either the river or the Common. So Lauren suggested Bailey's, and she did it loudly so that Michael would hear. As she and Scott walked up the aisle, she heard with relief that Michael was suggesting Bailey's to his friends. Michael's presence would be reassuring.

Outside the theater Lauren caught sight of Brian and Carol heading for the Yard, his arm around her. Lauren was nervous about the two of them, but she knew her fears lacked a reasonable foundation. Then she saw Melissa and Parker standing in front of the theater, obviously uncertain about what they were to do next. Motioning to Scott to follow her, Lauren went up to the two of them.

"Hi," she said. "Great movie, huh? Talk about romantic." Parker and Melissa nodded and looked embarrassed. "So where are you two going now? Cappuccino at the Cafe Pamplona?"

"Oh," said Melissa, "is that the little place near Baskin-Robbins?"

"What, you've never been to the Cafe Pamplona?" said Lauren. "Oh, but you've got to go. Parker, you've been there, haven't you?" And in a moment Lauren had the two of them on their way to Pamplona.

Scott had watched Lauren handling Parker and Melissa, and now he remarked, not unappreciatively, in his ironic southern drawl, "I see that you like to take an interest in other people's lives."

* * *

Bailey's is an important part of the Harvard experience. The ice cream is good enough, but in itself it is not an irresistible draw. You go to Bailey's for the hot fudge. Bailey's hot fudge is virtually unique: magnificently thick, not in the least syrupy. The boy behind the counter takes an old-fashioned metal ice cream dish on a metal saucer, and puts in a scoop of vanilla ice cream (or perhaps chocolate chip). He covers the ice cream with hot fudge, which slides slowly over the side of the dish and onto the saucer (from where you will later indelicately rescue it with an importunate finger). Finally there is marshmallow topping (sloppier still) or whipped cream (somewhat neater) and an option on nuts.

These sundaes were an essential part of freshman year, and many students found themselves exchanging their deepest confidences (confessions of love, repetitions of scandal) over Bailey's hot fudge sundaes. Lauren and Michael, for instance, went to Bailey's constantly, and there was something about the richness of the hot fudge which enabled them to discuss their lives and the lives of others in a completely uninhibited, not to say shameless, fashion.

Lauren and Scott ordered two sundaes and two cups of coffee, and they found a table among the crowd of people, many of whom had also just come from the movie. Lauren knew that there were important and difficult things which she would have to try to talk about with Scott, but for the moment she was too cowardly. She preferred to stick with the movie. "The South does seem very romantic," she said.

"I don't know," said Scott. "When you live there it seems like a place just like any other place. What does it mean when you say that someplace is romantic?" He was being playful, only pretending to be disillusioned. "Don't you think that romance is in the eye of the beholder? Maybe it's not the South that's romantic. Maybe it's you." This came off as a rather charming compliment, and Lauren was not displeased.

"Still," Lauren argued, "there are certain people and places and things that inspire a romantic response pretty consistently. Whereas people never ever seem to respond romantically to, say, Detroit. Or Richard Nixon. So it's only fair to say that part of the romantic magic belongs to the thing itself. Otherwise people wouldn't be able to agree among themselves, even roughly, on what is or is not romantic." Lauren, of course, was thinking of Russell Bernard. Surely it was no coincidence that in such a small freshman seminar, so many people had harbored romantic thoughts about him. There were Tracy Nicolson and Sandy Grayson and Lauren herself. And perhaps others, like Scott for instance. Lauren was toying with the possibility of suggesting aloud the case of Russell Bernard as romanticized object, but suddenly she saw Scott's face clouding over, and she asked, "What's the matter?"

"Nothing," said Scott. "Just that your friend is here."

Lauren turned around and rallied some more mock surprise to greet Michael and his friends. They took a nearby table, and Lauren turned back to Scott. "Are you sure nothing's the matter?"

"Nothing," said Scott.

"Is it Michael?" asked Lauren. "Does *he* make you uncomfortable?"

"No," said Scott. He paused. "Well, maybe a little."

"Tell me why," Lauren insisted.

"Well," he paused nervously, "because he's what you said."

Lauren realized immediately what Scott was referring to, but she preferred to deliberately misunderstand him. "That he's my best friend? I told you you shouldn't be jealous. He really is gay."

"Yeah," said Scott. "Maybe that's what makes me uncomfortable."

Lauren played dumb. "I don't follow you."

"Because he's queer," said Scott finally, and he expressed himself with considerable repressed hostility.

Lauren looked shocked. "But lots of people are gay," she objected. "Lots and lots of them. More than you'd think." She was baiting him.

"Not in Richmond," he insisted. "People don't stand for that sort of thing in Richmond. We don't like queers. And that's why your friend makes me uncomfortable. I can't help it. It's just the way I am, the way I was brought up. I can't help it any more than I can help being racist, like I explained to you last week. I always seem to be confessing my illiberal prejudices to you, don't I? Would you like to know what my father says about queers?"

"No, thank you," said Lauren. Against such resolute bigotry she continued to press her attack. "I'm sure there are plenty of homosexuals in Richmond," she said.

"I don't know any."

"I bet you do. Probably there are people you think you

know quite well who are actually gay. I sometimes think that everyone's gay to some extent or another."

"Everyone?"

"Sure, everyone."

"Not me."

"Maybe even you."

"No."

"Are you so sure?"

"Hey, what are you trying to say?" He was looking at her hard, perhaps trying to figure out just what she thought she knew.

"Nothing really," said Lauren. "Just that perhaps not even you are immune."

"What makes you think that?"

"Just a guess. I just thought that perhaps you might have had some homosexual experiences. Maybe even recently." She paused and then said it all. "Maybe with Russell Bernard."

Around them the air was full of chatter from the dozens of tables. Michael's table was gossiping intently. Between Lauren and Scott there was silence. She knew that her suggestion was inexcusable and outrageous, regardless of whether it was true or false. She looked at Scott in his brown corduroy blazer and gray sweater. She regarded his short hair and regular features. She thought about his background and his general comportment. He seemed so straight, so square. How could her accusation possibly be on the mark?

"That's not true," said Scott. "It's ridiculous. It's insane." He was cool, not flustered. It was impossible to tell whether or not he was on the edge of desperation.

"Ridiculous and insane perhaps," said Lauren, pressing her bluff. "But are you sure it's not true?"

"You said it was just a guess," said Scott warily. "Well, you guessed wrong."

"What if it's more than a guess? What if someone told me?"

"You tell me who told you, and I'll kill the lying bastard."

"What if Russell's the one who said it. Are you going to kill him?"

"Russell told you that?"

"No. He didn't tell me. He told Tracy Nicolson. Are you going to kill her?" Lauren paused, but Scott said nothing. She continued. "Tracy told me the same day that she was murdered. And she told me something else as well. She told me that you murdered Russell. She said that you hated Russell for what he had forced you to see about yourself. You couldn't accept yourself as someone who wanted to sleep with men, who did sleep with men, with a black man. So you hated Russell, and you murdered him to liberate yourself."

The conversation all around them did not lag, and Lauren took courage from the presence of all those other people, including Michael. She was safe for the moment. She could interrogate Scott without fear, and so she had made her point as strongly as possible. Now she stared at him, alert for any sign or expression that would betray him, and she saw something that she never expected to see, something she would not have even been able to imagine a moment before. She saw tears in Scott's eyes. He said without vehemence, "I did hate him. But I didn't kill him. I may have wanted to, but I would never have been able to bring myself to do it." And then Scott began to talk about what had passed between him and Russell Bernard.

Scott and Russell had both been intelligent enough to be aware that they were enacting one of the great clichés of the American South: black and white meeting in a relationship of hatred and attraction, perversely intertwined. It made sense only against a background of two hundred years of plantation slavery followed by a hundred years of uneasy emancipation. It was a part of the history, the mythology, the literature of the South, and Scott and Russell had both recognized that. Which didn't make its force any less powerful, any less irresistible.

Scott had noticed Russell at the very first meeting of the freshman seminar. To say that he had noticed Russell would perhaps be stating the case too weakly, but it was the most that Scott would have been willing to admit to himself at the time. In fact, as a boy in Richmond he had often noticed men, especially black men, in that very same way. He had been so peculiarly aware of them. Scott had preferred to call this awareness "racism," and he had tried to believe that it derived from a sense of distaste and condescension. Scott had always been ready to confess to being a racist, because he had wanted to be one. Racism served as a mask for other feelings. Racism, unacceptable though it might be at Harvard, was far more acceptable to Scott than those other feelings. And of course it would have been more acceptable to his friends, to his family, and most particularly to his father. So Scott had continued to notice Russell at the weekly seminar meetings while feigning aloof indifference and hoping that Russell was not aware of being noticed.

Then one evening Scott had been walking across Harvard Yard, and Russell had been sitting on the steps of one of the dormitories. Scott had had to walk past him, and though very nervous and excited, he had been determined not to recognize Russell. Russell, however—perhaps in revenge for Scott's aloofness—had called out to him and beckoned him over to the steps. Scott had obeyed the summons, and as he listened to Russell making conversation, he was already too dizzy to be aware of anything except for a certainty that Russell knew. Russell knew that Scott had been noticing him, and Russell was willing to interpret that attention in the way that Scott had never dared. Scott knew that he stood at the edge of the abyss, but he did not have it in him to decline when Russell suggested that they go upstairs to his room. Again Scott followed obediently. Inside the room Russell locked the door, and the two boys stood face to face. Then, at the same moment, each reached out for the other.

(Once again, as so often before in the course of her investigation, Lauren was jealous. She was never going to be able to make love to Russell Bernard. She had never even been invited to see his room. What did it look like, Russell's room? She wanted Scott to describe it to her.)

There was a crucifix on the wall over the bed. That was the thing that Scott remembered most vividly: the wooden crucifix. The room was otherwise not lavishly decorated; it was, in fact, virtually austere. Austere and neat: it did not suggest a sloppy life. There was a bulletin board over the desk on which were tacked notices of activities and meetings of the Black Students' Lobby. Russell never talked about the Lobby with Scott.

On the wall above the dresser were several small pictures and photographs. There was a postcard of a medieval rendering of the Virgin Mary. And there were three photographs: one of Russell's mother, one of a priest (no doubt a Jesuit mentor), and one of a sad, delicate teenager, a white teenager. Scott had asked Russell about this boy, but Russell had refused to discuss the subject. Scott, who had soon felt himself driven to look for Russell's story in *The New Yorker*, imagined that the photograph fit the description of the fictional white best friend. Scott also supposed that there had been something more intense, perhaps traumatic, between the two friends. Although Scott and Russell never explicitly discussed this point, Scott could guess that Russell might have had some previous experiences with men. Whereas Scott had none.

(Lauren could guess further that Scott was also quite inexperienced with women. She did not press him on this point now, as she was much too interested in the discussion of homosexuality. How, for instance, had Russell regarded the subject? Had he been as anguished as Scott?)

Scott knew that Russell felt guilty about all sex, with men and with women—a specifically religious guilt. Russell was a Catholic and he was afraid of hell. And yet Russell was not chaste. However, since Catholicism considers sinful all sex out of wedlock, heterosexual and homosexual, Russell did not feel the latter to be so much more wicked than the former. And he succumbed to both temptations with an equally troubled conscience. Catholicism thus acted to confuse the distinction between "sin" and "perversion." For Scott, a not particularly devout Episcopalian, the dilemma was far more excruciating. He was not afraid of hell; he feared instead the unimaginably powerful contempt and disgust which his secret would surely inspire in his father, his family, and the entire Richmond society to which he belonged. It was impossible that he, the self-proclaimed product of his own upbringing, should not feel for himself some of that same disgust and hatred. His father (unlike Russell's Father) would have accepted, possibly applauded, a Harvard-Radcliffe collegiate fling. Scott's world, however, would unhesitatingly despise him for sleeping with a man. And for sleeping with a black man—Scott could not even imagine what would happen if anyone ever found out.

(Lynching? Lauren wondered to herself. Tar and feathers? Ritual castration? Did that sort of thing go on down South?)

So Scott hated himself and he hated Russell. He had wanted to kill Russell and he had even thought of killing himself. But something prevented him from following either course, something beyond mere cowardice or even biblical morality. Deep down inside him, on a level he could barely bring himself to see, he wanted to live now and he wanted Russell to live too.

("You were in love with him," said Lauren. "No, I wasn't," said Scott. "Don't say that. I hated him.")

After that first time, Scott resolved never to see Russell again, but there was no way not to see him at the freshman seminar on Wednesday. When their eyes met guiltily across the seminar table it was clear that they both hated each other, and it was equally clear that the scene in Russell's room would surely recur. And it did. ("You became lovers," said Lauren. "No," said Scott, "it just kept happening.") Very secretly and full of guilt they continued to sleep together, though they never managed to become friends.

"You wanted to kill him. But you didn't. I almost believe you." In fact, Lauren wanted very much to believe him. She found his story moving and almost convincing. But did she dare believe it completely?

"Believe me," he said imploringly.

"My roommate Carol saw you at a party Tuesday evening, so I can believe that you didn't murder Tracy Nicolson. But last week, when I asked you if you remembered what you were doing the night Russell was murdered, you said you'd been sitting home alone in your room. At least if your roommate had been there, he could vouch for you, and I would know that you were telling the truth."

"But my roommate wasn't there. He'd gone to spend the night with his girlfriend. And the reason I was home alone was because I was expecting someone."

"Who?"

"Can't you guess?"

Lauren guessed. Just as she had waited for Russell Thursday night at Pamplona, Scott had waited alone in his room all the night before. And Russell, of course, had not come.

"When Russell didn't show up I was confused," said Scott. "And I was angry. I thought that he was trying to stop the whole thing—you know, without even telling me—I knew we didn't owe each other much in the way of common courtesies. We were barely polite to each other. I told you, we weren't friends. And then I began to hope that he wouldn't show up, that he really was ending it. Because I had given up believing that I was strong enough to do it—you know, to stop it myself—no matter how much I wanted to. So by the next evening when I finally learned that he was dead, I was able to be almost glad—at least relieved. I was so happy to be really free of him. I know that sounds horrible, rejoicing over his death. It wasn't all rejoicing. I guess it hurt me too. But, you know, in a way I preferred that he should be dead than that he should have decided to drop me." Lauren knew all too well. "But the important thing was that one way or another, I was free of him. I even hoped that maybe no one would ever know what had happened between us. I thought I could keep it secret. I thought that if no one knew about it, then it would be like nothing had ever happened, and I wouldn't despise myself quite so much."

"Well, did you find that you despised yourself any less?"

"No."

"That's because it really happened, and there's no use trying to pretend that it didn't."

"I know."

"And because you really are gay, and there's no use trying to pretend that you're not."

"Don't say that."

"And you'll go on despising yourself until you accept that you're gay and accept that it isn't such a terrible thing to be."

"I won't ever accept that."

"Then you'll always be miserable."

"I'd rather be miserable. You can't imagine what the people I grew up with would think of me. People in Richmond would think it was somewhat questionable of me to be going out for ice cream with you. You're not their sort. They thought it was peculiar that I was on friendly terms with a Jewish history teacher. Imagine what they'd think if they knew that..." He couldn't finish.

Lauren said, "Tell me about the history teacher."

"There's nothing to tell," said Scott defensively. "Now you won't believe me, but there's really nothing to tell." He was quiet for a moment. "I don't know if he was, um, like that."

"Gay."

"Yeah. He might have been. But, you know, he had enough problems in Richmond without *that*. He was friendly to me but no more than friendly. Maybe I wanted more. I don't know what I wanted."

"You had a crush on him," said Lauren helpfully. "A schoolboy crush. I think it's sweet."

Scott winced, but he couldn't help saying, "I wonder if he knew."

"Probably he knew. I think it's the sort of thing people tend to know—when other people have crushes on them, I mean. One day maybe you'll run into him and you can ask."

Scott looked pretty horrified at that, but Lauren guessed that he was secretly intrigued by the suggestion. The only thing Scott said was "Christ, Richmond."

"You know, Scott, you're not living in Richmond anymore. And you don't have to live in Richmond ever again if you don't want to."

"No?" It was as if this idea, the possibility of not spending his life in Richmond, had never occurred to Scott. Now he was turning it over in his mind, cautiously—it was a revolutionary notion.

"You'll be much happier if you learn to like yourself the way you are," Lauren prodded.

Scott very nearly smiled. "I'll think about it," he said.

"Good," said Lauren, "think about it." She hesitated for a moment and then spoke again. "Scott," she said, "there's something else I want to ask you."

"Shoot. Why not? It looks like I don't have any secrets from you."

"Scott, what happened to the picture of Russell Bernard that was razored out of your Freshman Register?"

"Christ, you really do know everything. How do you know about that?"

"Well, last Saturday night when you left me alone in your room I was flipping through your Facebook. I wasn't snooping. I mean, I'm always flipping through somebody's copy of the Facebook. It's my winter sport..."

Scott had taken out his wallet and put it on the table next to the empty ice cream dishes and coffee cups. They both looked at the wallet for a moment, and then Scott opened it. Lauren leaned over the table and saw a photograph inside clear plastic. It was a black and white photograph which showed a very handsome man and woman standing beside each other. "My parents," said Scott. "And that's Elms' Glory." He put his finger on the big white house in the background. Then Scott slipped his finger inside the plastic envelope, behind the photograph of his parents. Another photograph fell out onto the table, which Lauren recognized immediately. She had seen it a thousand times in the Freshman Register. It was, of course, Russell Bernard.

Lauren was ready to go home and fall asleep. Ice cream at Bailey's had been even more fascinating than usual, but it had been emotionally exhausting. It was much easier to convince Parker to ask Melissa out on a date than to convince Scott to accept being gay. Lauren enjoyed meddling in other people's lives, and she derived satisfaction from the knowledge that she was doing good, but now she needed some rest to restore her energies.

She was prepared to trust Scott to walk her from Bailey's back to her dorm. It would be a short walk across Harvard Square and then across Harvard Yard. She silently motioned to Michael at the other table not to bother following; she did not need an escort. Michael winked at her, and Lauren thought that she would have plenty to discuss with him later.

Lauren and Scott walked through Harvard Yard without saying a word. She had a feeling that they were being followed, but when she turned around she saw nothing. It was very dark. Lauren, almost without thinking, took Scott's arm. It felt reassuring. She looked up at Scott, and he smiled. Despite all his psychological anguish he would obviously always be a natural gentleman. They walked past Matthews Hall and Massachusetts Hall and Johnston Gate. They walked past Hollis Hall where Sandy Grayson lived. They turned the corner of Harvard Yard, and Lauren looked out across the deserted space. The Yard seemed larger than usual and perhaps a little bit eerie. Lauren found herself thinking about ghosts.

Finally she said, "You know, Scott, somebody murdered Russell and somebody murdered Tracy, maybe the same person. But the police haven't picked up anyone at all. Who could have murdered them?"

Suddenly Lauren was certain that someone was back there in the darkness, but before she could even turn around she heard the voice coming from behind them. And the voice said, "I murdered them."

15. The Dostoyevsky analysis

"I murdered them," said Andrew Stein, and he began to laugh hysterically. He seemed to have appeared from nowhere, and there was no telling how long he had been following. Despite the darkness, Andrew's face managed to suggest an oddly greenish coloring. His nose seemed pointier, his eyes more feverish than usual. His profusion of thick, dark hair was blowing insanely in the wind. He wore a wool overcoat down to his knees, and around his neck was a long flapping scarf. His laughter subsided into an odd chuckle. Lauren and Scott stood alone in Harvard Yard with the Dr. Strangelove of the freshman class.

"That's not funny," said Scott, a little harshly. Scott had been shaken by Andrew's sudden appearance and frightening exclamation. Now Scott was reacting with an attempt to reassert his own dignity, already somewhat battered during the course of the evening. The whole effect was unfortunately awkward. "That's nothing to joke about," he admonished.

Lauren privately agreed that calling out such things in the middle of the night was not funny. But she knew better than to try to reprimand someone as obviously unbalanced as Andrew. In fact, she was fascinated by Andrew's extraordinary claim. What truth could there possibly be in it? What had made him think of accusing himself in such a dramatic fashion?

Andrew, perhaps sensing that Lauren would be more sympathetic than Scott, now turned to her. "I'm sorry," he said. "I'm sorry I frightened you." There was something devious about his apology, and something even more devious about the profession of ignorance that followed. "I don't know

191

why I said it. I really haven't any idea why." He was addressing himself to Lauren exclusively, ignoring Scott. Scott's expression conveyed fierce disapproval. Was Andrew simply reacting to that or did he have some other reason to dislike Scott?

"Maybe you just wanted attention," suggested Scott, but his irony fell flat. Andrew was not susceptible to irony with a southern accent.

"Maybe," said Andrew slyly, still without looking at Scott. "I'll have to discuss that with my psychiatrist." He was being just faintly ironical himself, at Scott's expense. Andrew continued to address himself to Lauren. "I've just come from the movies," he said.

"Oh, so have we," said Lauren, trying for a friendly tone. "We went to see *Gone with the Wind* at the Harvard Square Theater. Were you there too?"

Andrew laughed in a manner that would have been rude if it had not been so patently eccentric. "No, no," he said. "I went to see *M* at the Brattle. Maybe that's why I was thinking of murderers. I was watching the movie and I liked Peter Lorre so much. He was so sympathetic. I could understand exactly why... I could identify with him." He looked to Lauren for support. "Do you know what I mean?"

Lauren nodded earnestly. Scott said contemptuously, "*I* don't know what you mean," but Andrew ignored him.

Andrew continued. "Watching the movie, I could almost imagine that I was Peter Lorre, that I was the murderer. The next thing I knew, I'd forgotten who I really was. And then I heard you saying something about the murderer and I thought you were talking about me. I'll have to talk about this with my psychiatrist."

He's absolutely bonkers, thought Lauren. Scott's judgment was even less charitable. "You've had your fun," said Scott to Andrew. "Now why don't you run along home and leave us alone."

Andrew simply ignored him and looked at Lauren with sly piteousness. "I don't want to go home alone now," he said. "I'm frightened. Will you walk along with me? Will you walk back to my dorm with me?" Scott was apparently to be excluded from this pathetic invitation, but Lauren had no intention of going off alone with Andrew Stein. He was much too creepy. On the other hand, she was not heartless enough to leave him alone in the dark if he claimed to be frightened. And furthermore, she would not be sorry to have a little bit of time to hear what Andrew might have to say in connection with the murders of Russell Bernard and Tracy Nicolson. So Lauren turned to Scott and suggested that they walk Andrew home. Scott was clearly exasperated, but he could hardly decline. He might be rude to Andrew, but he would not be rude to Lauren. And Andrew himself appeared resigned to having Scott along as well. Perhaps he was even secretly pleased to have the opportunity to irritate Scott further. The three of them set out together for Andrew's dorm: Andrew strangely cheerful, Scott silently enraged, and Lauren extremely curious.

It was not a short walk, since Andrew did not live in Harvard Yard like most freshmen. He had been assigned to Hurlbut Hall, one of the so-called "Union" dorms. It was located just behind the Freshman Union. The Union dorms were considered somewhat less desirable dormitory assignments, since they were geographically, and therefore spiritually, a little bit out of the mainstream of Harvard freshman life. Andrew Stein, who did not need additional geographical reasons to feel set apart, felt keenly the stigma of living in Hurlbut Hall.

He detested Hurlbut. He despised the other people who lived there. The building was hideous and falling apart. The other students were less than human, and they were in league together to drive Andrew mad. Such were Andrew's repeated confidences as he and Lauren and Scott made their way to Hurlbut Hall. By the time they arrived, Lauren hardly knew what to expect. But Hurlbut Hall did not seem particularly horrible; it was quite an ordinary building. From inside came the noises of rowdy—no doubt athletic—healthy, normal, red-blooded American boys, drinking beer and insulting each other obscenely in a rather good-natured fashion. The same ritual took place every Saturday night among the football players upstairs in Lauren's own dorm. Lauren could well imagine how badly Andrew Stein fitted into the spirit of such gatherings. Lauren would have supposed that the others simply left him alone, but Andrew claimed to be conscious of special persecution. Their revelries drove him from the dorm. Thanks to their clamor, he was failing all his courses. He had discussed this with his psychiatrist many times.

Lauren was not surprised when Andrew invited her up

to his room to visit. Lauren accepted the invitation on behalf of herself and Scott. Poor Scott, he was not enjoying Andrew's diatribes. Yet Lauren thought it might actually be healthy for Scott to spend some time observing a genuine loony. It might help him to appreciate his own relative normality, in spite of what Richmond might think.

Any visitor to Andrew Stein's room in Hurlbut Hall would surely have noticed immediately the central ornament, Andrew's special contribution to the art of interior decoration. Hanging from the ceiling in the center of the room was a rope noose. Lauren was by no means certain that a Hurlbut ceiling would support a hanging body, but nevertheless the intended message was excruciatingly clear, perhaps even ridiculously so. Once again Lauren hoped that Scott was learning something about putting his own suicidal impulses in perspective. She doubted that Scott would want to take Andrew Stein as his role model.

Lauren considered the various possible conversational reactions to the hanging noose: "Isn't *that* a charming touch?" or "I *do* like cowboys!" or even "Somebody's stolen your fern!" She and Michael could later spend happy hours inventing new variations, but for now Lauren thought it best to say nothing and let Andrew initiate conversation. Lauren would be very casual—as if every Harvard dormitory room had a noose hanging from the ceiling. Still she did wonder: did Andrew collect suicide implements? He had a noose. Did he also have a gun?

The noose was hanging alone in midair, while the rest of the room down below formed one large, unified mess. How wise Harvard had been to give one of its rare freshman single rooms to Andrew Stein. It was impossible to imagine anyone living with him. At first Lauren thought that the room's disorder was utterly random. But by concentrating her attention she was almost able to perceive a sense of purpose behind it all. The mess itself consisted of thousands of loose pieces of paper and hundreds of open books lying faceup or facedown. The clusters of papers and books covered the unmade bed, carpeted the wooden floor, and peeked out from the open dresser drawers. Yet all seemed somehow to converge on the immense heap which covered Andrew's desk, and on the summit of that heap was one book alone. The book was open, and the exposed pages were covered with red underlinings and dense marginal notes. This volume seemed to be the focus of the rest of the chaos.

Lauren and Scott stood without moving. In fact, it was virtually impossible to move without treading on one of the little piles of papers. Andrew, lacking the social grace to clear away a place for them to sit, also remained standing. Finally he said, as if to explain the condition of his room, "I'm in the middle of writing a paper for my Dostoyevsky course. I'm writing about *The Brothers Karamazov*." He gestured unmistakably toward the book that sat enthroned on the pile on the desk. So this was how Andrew went about writing a paper.

Now Andrew began to talk more freely. "I'm writing about Ivan Karamazov. I've made some notes," he said, gesturing at the thousands of sheets of paper lying all over the room, "and I've made a few starts on the paper, but I'm not happy with it yet. I want it to be perfect, the paper. It has to be perfect, because I failed the first hourly. I didn't write anything at all on the hourly because all my thoughts were too complicated. I might not write anything on the midterm either. Class exams make me very nervous." He began to fidget as if to illustrate his point. "So the paper has to be perfect. I'll be up all night working on it."

"Oh, is it due tomorrow?" Lauren inquired politely.

"No, it's due next Friday, but I may not sleep at all between now and then. I'm writing about Ivan and how he feels about the murder. You know, he feels guilty. He feels as if he'd actually committed the murder, because he knows that he hated his father and wanted him to die. Don't you think that's interesting?"

"Yes," said Lauren, hoping he'd continue.

And he did. "It's like me telling you before that I was the murderer."

"Yes, I see," said Lauren. "Did you want Russell and Tracy to die?"

Andrew paused to think. "I'm not sure," he said. "You know, Dostoyevsky thinks he knows who committed the murder in *The Brothers Karamazov*, but I think Dostoyevsky is wrong."

"What do you mean he's wrong?" said Scott, extremely irritated. "Dostoyevsky wrote the book, didn't he?"

"Maybe," said Andrew.

"Who is the murderer?" asked Lauren, not sure whether

she was referring to *The Brothers Karamazov* or her own investigation.

"Ah," said Andrew, grinning, "I won't say." Then he seemed to relent. "Maybe I'll tell in my paper." He changed the subject. "I have to finish this paper so I can begin working on my Nietzsche paper. Have you started working on yours?"

"No," said Lauren, oh so truthfully.

"I've made some notes," said Andrew, gesturing modestly at the mess around him. "I love Nietzsche. I talk about Nietzsche all the time with my psychiatrist. I'm going to write about *The Genealogy of Morals*, about how the Jews, the priest people, subvert the natural moral order. Nietzsche thinks that it was the deviousness of the ancient Jewish priests that made it possible for the meek to dominate the strong by appealing to so-called morality. I think that's very interesting. I think that we Jews are a little insidious, don't you think so?"

"I don't know," said Lauren. Scott had fallen out of the conversation. He seemed to have given up listening. He was standing still, holding on to his temper, not even looking around.

"Do you think so?" said Andrew to Scott.

"I don't know either," Scott mumbled.

"I think Nietzsche was an anti-Semite," said Andrew. "So I suppose he wouldn't have liked me. But I like him. I like him because he despises conventional morality. So do I. Morality is so simple. Nietzsche idealized force instead, but I think that's too simple also." Andrew looked around himself carefully and then leaned over and whispered in Lauren's ear, "The world is not a sane place."

"What did he say?" said Scott. It was true that Andrew had given the impression of whispering so that Scott would not hear.

"Relax, Scott," said Lauren, "don't worry about it."

"Yes, Scott, relax," said Andrew, obviously delighted at Scott's irritation. Andrew continued. "Morality is so simple. But amorality and violence are very complicated, and Nietzsche didn't understand that. Nietzsche couldn't understand because he lived in a less violent age. He was too naïve, too romantic about amorality. But I'm not romantic about it. I understand it. I grew up in an American city in the twentieth century. Do you know that people are murdered all the time in big cities? Isn't that interesting?"

"I don't know," said Lauren evasively. "I'm from the suburbs." And then conversationally, "Where are you from?"

"Chicago. Chicago is extremely violent and very complicated."

Something clicked in Lauren's head. "Chicago. Tracy Nicolson was from Chicago. Did you know her there before coming to Harvard?"

Andrew hesitated before answering. "No," he said, "not really."

"Well," said Lauren, "it must be funny to run up against someone from your hometown at Harvard a thousand miles away. Were you and Tracy friends?"

"I don't know," said Andrew.

"It was very sad, her being killed." Lauren was pressing the subject. "Don't you think so?"

"Sad? I don't know. I think it was extraordinary."

What on earth did he mean? "Didn't you like her?"

"Oh yes, I liked Tracy," said Andrew. "And I also like Bert Rosen." Lauren was fascinated by how automatically Andrew linked the two names. "I like Bert even if he is one of the insidious priest people." Andrew giggled. "A healthy blond blue-eyed priest person. Nietzsche would not have believed in Bert Rosen. I like Bert because he helps me with my papers."

"What?"

Andrew looked positively evil. "Bert helps me with my papers." Andrew reached under a pile of papers on the bed and felt around for something. When he had found it, he popped it in his mouth.

"What was that?" Lauren asked. Even Scott was interested.

"Speed," said Andrew gleefully. "Bert sells it to me. That way I can stay up all night to work on my paper. I don't talk about that with my psychiatrist. He wouldn't approve." So Bert was doing a little business on the side. Andrew continued. "Sometimes I take speed before my classes, so I'll be able to stay awake."

"I know that problem," said Lauren, "but tell me, when do you sleep?"

"That's my secret." Andrew seemed well pleased with his own mysteriousness. "I don't sleep during my classes, even though I don't like them. I wish I didn't have to go to my classes. I wish I could stay here in my room all the time and work on my papers."

"You don't like Professor Baranova's freshman seminar on the Russian Revolution?"

"No. I hate it. Because of the professor. She's always trying to humiliate me. I think she hates me. I think she's an anti-Semite." Lauren did not bother to point out that Professor Baranova's famous husband was undeniably Jewish. Surely Andrew had already accounted for this in his own special way. "And I hate Sandy Grayson," Andrew continued. "She never looks at me. She never says hello to me. I think she's also an anti-Semite."

Lauren couldn't resist. "She may be an anti-Semite, but she's as Jewish as you and me."

"Really?"

"Really." Lauren was truly gratified by Andrew's apparent delight in this item of information.

"I don't suppose she wants people to know that she's Jewish," said Andrew thoughtfully. There were moments when he was relatively lucid. Now he was obviously plotting something. "Listen," he said, looking up with a mean smile. "The next time I pass her and she's getting ready not to say hello to me, I'll just say shalom. A nice peaceful greeting from Jew to Jew. She'll hate that, won't she?"

"Yes," Lauren assured him encouragingly. "She certainly will." Lauren was already wondering if other Harvard students could be induced to give Sandy a traditional Hebrew greeting. If everyone at Harvard was always saying "shalom" to Sandy Grayson, she would soon go as crazy as Andrew. What a blow to her Episcopalian fantasies! Andrew's looniness was clearly not without redeeming moments of inspiration.

"Do you know who else I hate?" said Andrew.

"Who?"

"Who, Wu," said Andrew. "I hate Melissa Wu."

"How can you possibly hate Melissa Wu," objected Lauren. "She's the sweetest little girl who ever lived. I hardly think she's an anti-Semite. She probably doesn't even know what Jews are, unless she had to do a book report about them in fourth grade."

"That's what I used to think," said Andrew. "But now I know better. Now I know that she's evil."

"What on earth makes you think so?"

"I'll tell you. Do you remember two weeks ago she gave

a presentation on Rasputin? That's when I realized what she was really like."

"And what is she really like?"

"She's evil. The way she talked about Rasputin was evil. The way she described his murder was very frightening. I was frightened afterward for a whole week. I kept thinking about the way they had murdered Rasputin, the way they had killed him over and over again to be sure that he was dead. It wasn't enough just to poison him. You know, I'm very afraid of being poisoned. I talk about that with my psychiatrist all the time."

"Did you talk about Rasputin with your psychiatrist?" asked Lauren gently.

"No, of course not. He would have thought I was crazy."

"But you've been thinking about Rasputin."

"Oh, yes. I wonder if I've been behaving strangely because of that." Lauren also wondered, though she was uncertain as to what would constitute strange behavior for the likes of Andrew Stein.

"Do you know whom I do like in that freshman seminar?"

"Who?" asked Lauren patiently. She would have to leave soon. Scott was fidgeting almost as much as Andrew. Scott would soon be unwilling to stay any longer, and Lauren did not want to remain behind without him.

"I like Katherine Butler."

"You do?"

"Yes. She's very friendly to me. A few weeks ago she invited me to a meeting with her friends. I was very pleased to be invited."

"Did you go?"

"Oh, yes. Naturally."

"And did you have a good time?"

"Oh, yes. Almost everyone there was black except for me and Katherine. I didn't say anything, but Katherine talked a lot. I just watched. Do you think that Katherine Butler is beautiful?"

"Yes, I do," said Lauren diplomatically. "What did she talk about that evening?"

"She was talking about violence. That's what everyone there was talking about. That's why I enjoyed it so much. Afterward Katherine suggested that I join the group. She said that I could be a useful member." Andrew looked dubious for a moment, but then his face brightened. "Who knows?

Perhaps I'll become a revolutionary. We read *The Possessed* in my Dostoyevsky class. I liked that. I like *Crime and Punishment* better. Do you like *Crime and Punishment*?"

"I prefer crime," Lauren joked, trying to keep things light.

"Oh, I do too," Andrew replied very seriously. Then he contemplated for a moment and added a reservation. "But I also like punishment."

"I was joking," said Lauren, "but I do like the novel."

"Raskolnikov is like Nietzsche. He also believes that amorality is something simple, that murder is a simple straight-forward act. And that's one reason why he can't bear up afterward. It all turns out to be much more complicated than he was expecting."

"Yes, I see."

"And there's another thing. Raskolnikov believed that he was a grand Promethean figure, and then he went and killed an old lady to prove it. That was petty. He lacked conviction. That's another reason why he couldn't make it afterward. He should have murdered someone worthy of the act, someone whose life meant something."

"What do you think of the murder of Russell Bernard?" asked Lauren. She had been waiting to ask that question.

But Andrew said only, "Ah, Russell Bernard, he should have been in a Dostoyevsky novel." And Andrew refused to say anything more.

Lauren glanced at Scott. He was completely miserable and glaringly hostile. It would be better to go. Andrew was also starting to seem less communicative. Perhaps she should not have bothered coming here in the first place. She had thought that perhaps Andrew knew something about the murder, but she had not been able to get anything coherent out of him. For all intents and purposes, he had been merely babbling for the last hour. "We have to go," said Lauren.

"I'm sorry," said Andrew. "But I suppose I had better start working on my paper." And as his guests turned toward the door, he added, "Be careful. There's a murderer out there."

16. Popcorn

Lauren was relieved to be free of Andrew Stein, so relieved that she did not even give a second thought to walking across Harvard Yard with Scott Duchaine at two in the morning. Her only thought about Scott was an awareness that he was even more relieved than she was at their escape from Andrew. It had become so oppressive, being cooped up in that little pen of a room with Dr. Strangelove, his ravings, his noose, and his notes on Dostoyevsky. Lauren was happy to push all this out of her mind, but even as she did so she was aware that there had been something more profoundly disturbing about that conversation. She couldn't quite put her finger on what it was, and she couldn't bring herself to think back on the whole scene. For the moment she did not want to think about Andrew Stein.

Lauren and Scott walked quickly and in silence. She took his arm again to reassure him. She liked Scott now more than ever. In fact, thanks to their conversation at Bailey's, for the first time she found him truly interesting. There was something very sexy about his spiritual struggles between inappropriate passion and ingrained propriety. She wondered what he was thinking about, but he said nothing until they reached Lauren's dorm. Then they stopped, and Lauren looked up at him, still holding his arm. "He's really mixed up," said Scott.

"He sure is," said Lauren. "You know, you aren't in such bad shape. You know that, don't you?"

"I don't know."

"I'm sorry if it sounded like I was lecturing you before in Bailey's, telling you how to live your life, telling you how you'd be happiest. I must have sounded pretty presumptuous, urging you to accept yourself and all that stuff."

"It's okay. You were probably right about everything."

"I hope you don't hate me for knowing about you and Russell." And Lauren thought, almost automatically, I hope you don't kill me for knowing about you and Russell.

"No, I don't hate you," said Scott. "Before, I wanted more than anything in the world for nobody to know ever. But now that I've told you, I almost feel good about it, glad to have told somebody." He added shyly, "And if it had to be somebody, I'm glad it was you." Then even more shyly, he asked, "Are we friends?"

"Yes," said Lauren warmly, "we're friends." And she leaned over and kissed him on the cheek. "Would you like to come upstairs for a few minutes for a cup of cocoa?"

Lauren was not quite sure of her own intentions. Was it just a friendly invitation to show him that she liked him and trusted him? Or did she actually find his newly revealed secrets so appealing that she would consider encouraging him to seduce her and so to prove himself? The latter course would be entirely unprincipled, since, after all, she had been encouraging him to accept that he was gay. It would not be quite nice to tempt him now to prove that he really wasn't. Lauren knew all that, but she also knew that she was weak about principles. She never had the opportunity, however, to find out what her intentions really were. When she opened the door to her room and invited Scott in, they found Carol and Michael seated happily on the floor with Carol's popcorn popper.

There was a big bowl of popcorn from which they were munching, and the popper was rapidly producing more. Michael and Carol were obviously in the midst of a cozy chat, and Lauren immediately began to be concerned with how Scott would fit into the general coziness. She was even less comfortable when she saw Carol's and Michael's expressions of titilated curiosity at the sight of Scott. Just the other day Lauren had told Carol that she was not particularly interested in Scott, and now here she was bringing him home at two in the morning. And Michael, who had thought Lauren was out sleuthing—who had, at her request, followed her to the movies and to Bailey's—what was he to think of her sudden disappearance into the night and then reappearance with Scott in tow? In fact, Michael had probably been worried about Lauren. He was probably waiting up with Carol and the popper just to make sure that Lauren arrived home safely. Lauren could not keep from looking a little sheepish.

"Scott," she said hastily, "this is my roommate Carol."

"We've met!" cried Carol. Her initial surprise had passed, and she was now on what she considered her company manners. "We met at that party at Radcliffe Tuesday night. I'm *so* pleased to see you again."

Taking his cue from Carol, Scott said, "Yes, I remember. I feel fortunate to have this chance to renew our acquaintance."

But ironic inflections were lost on Carol, who simply cooed in his face, "You're *so* charming, *such* a gentleman."

"And this is my friend Michael," said Lauren.

"Enchanté," said Michael, holding out his hand as if expecting it to be kissed. Scott, who had begun to extend his own hand for a manly handshake, did not know quite what to do. He withdrew his hand nervously, and, at Lauren's insistence, sat down on the floor. Lauren too sat down, sadly aware that Scott was not at his ease.

"We were just talking about Brian O'Donnell, that most magnificent specimen of manhood," Michael explained.

"Oh, you're awful!" Carol squealed at Michael, and then she turned to the newcomers. "Brian was my date this evening. He just left a while ago. I think Michael scared him away. You know, Brian is really very shy. I wonder why big men always turn out to be so shy."

"I'm sure I don't know," said Michael. Scott nearly grimaced.

"What happened with Brian?" Lauren was asking Carol.

"Yes, Carol," Michael put in, "tell Lauren what happened with *le Boeuf*."

"Well," Carol began, but between giggling and blushing she never got any further than that.

"You didn't!" said Lauren. "Tell me that you didn't!"

"Well, I didn't really," Carol equivocated.

"What do you mean you didn't really?"

"Yes, tell her what you mean," Michael encouraged.

"Well," said Carol, "we didn't exactly do *that*."

"But you did everything else?"

"Oh yes, and Lauren, he was wonderful!"

"Yes, but tell Lauren why you didn't go all the way," urged Michael happily.

"Well . . ." Carol was blushing again, but she was eager to

explain. "Well, I'm still in love with my Baby Doll in California. I love him and I want to marry him. And so I want to be true." She gazed lovingly upward at the poster of Baby Doll in his bathing suit on the wall.

"But Carol," Lauren objected, "if you really wanted to be faithful, why were you doing everything else?"

"Well . . . because my Baby Doll is in California. And because Brian is so attractive." At this last remark Lauren and Michael could not keep from exchanging looks. They did not think Brian was in the least attractive, but Carol, after all, was special. Lauren, at the same time, could barely contain her wonder at Carol's cheerful contentment with her system for reconciling true love and an incidental football player. There was an ethic of sexual fidelity at the root of all this that Lauren found tantalizingly elusive. One could only conclude for the thousandth time that Carol was a wonder. Lauren also reflected nervously, though not without some amusement, on what Scott Duchaine was making of this sort of lighthearted chat.

"But wait," Michael was saying. "There's another reason why Brian and Carol decided to resist the ultimate temptation. Tell them Carol."

"Well . . . Brian is a Catholic. And he's protecting his virginity. So it worked out best for both of us this way."

"Isn't that just exquisite plotting!" cried Michael. "Isn't it a little jewel of a vignette!"

"It's really quite something," Lauren agreed. "Carol, you are a wonder."

"She's a wonderful, wonderful wonder," Michael affirmed. "I think I may have to ask her to marry me." Michael turned to Scott. "Don't you think I should?"

Lauren took a deep breath. Michael was teasing Scott, and she hoped Scott would be able to manage. But her fears were misplaced. Scott entered graciously into the spirit of the game. "You'd better propose immediately," he said, "before I beat you to it."

Lauren was shocked and delighted, and Michael was obviously taken aback by Scott's unexpected self-composure. Meanwhile Carol was cooing, "Oh, you boys are both so *charming!*"

Carol had been told by Lauren that Michael was gay, but Carol couldn't quite manage to believe it. Carol had been brought up to believe that all men were drawn irresistibly to

her "boobs," and so the concept of male homosexuality was
alien to her. To some extent she exempted Michael from the
category of suitors: how else could she manage to sit on the
floor with him eating popcorn and discussing her sex life at
two in the morning? On the other hand, she allowed herself
to believe that Michael was not entirely immune to her
allures, and he in turn teased her with extravagantly gallant
gestures, such as proposals of marriage. Carol knew that
these were humorously intended, but she nevertheless considered them tribute, and Scott's assent was an unadulterated
conquest.

Carol filled the bowl again with freshly popped popcorn.
The four of them had been putting away handful after hand-
ful. Then Carol turned to Scott and asked out of the blue,
"Will you be going to church tomorrow?"

Scott was understandably surprised by the question, and
he thought a moment before answering. "Perhaps I will," he
said. It was obviously something he had just decided on. "I
haven't gone to church for a while, but perhaps I'd like to go
tomorrow morning."

Lauren would have liked to follow up on this, but Carol
next turned to Michael. "And are you going to go to church
tomorrow?"

"If I don't sleep too late," he said. "I have to do my part
to help keep up the tone of the Church of England in
America. The wonderful thing about living in a country with
lots of religions is that some can be so much more dignified
than others."

"Well," said Carol, "I want you boys to tell me if you see
Brian at church tomorrow."

"Brian O'Donnell is Catholic," said Michael and Scott,
not only in unison, but with the same unmistakable air of
Episcopalian condescension.

"What?" Carol was confused.

"We don't all go to the same church," explained Michael.
"Remember Henry the Eighth and all his wives? It's very
complicated, but we won't go into it now. Tell me anyway
why you would want us to spy on Brian O'Donnell in
church."

Carol blushed, as if it were Michael and not she who had
brought up the subject. "It's sort of embarrassing," she
confessed, but she was only too eager to continue. "You see,
Brian told me that tomorrow morning he would have to go to

church to confess about what he and I did tonight. He says he has to receive absolution. It sounded a little odd to me, and I wanted to know if he was really going to go and do it."

Lauren and Michael and Scott were already laughing happily over Brian, and Carol joined in. "I'm sure he'll go and do it," said Michael. "He's just the type."

"And will the priest forgive him?" Carol wanted to know.

"Oh yes," Michael assured her.

"Well," said Carol, "with a system like that a person could do just about anything!"

But Michael just snorted, "Catholics!"

"You said it," said Scott. They were as one. But Lauren was wondering if Russell Bernard had gone to the same church as Brian O'Donnell. Had they seen each other there every Sunday? Had Russell confessed himself? And what had he confessed?

"Oh, Catholics are so attractive!" said Carol, obviously thinking about Brian.

"It's true," said Lauren, thinking of Russell.

"It's sometimes true," Michael conceded.

Scott said nothing.

"Speaking of people who aren't Episcopalian," said Michael, "I have stories to tell you about the delightful Sandy Grayson." The stories were clearly intended for Lauren, but Michael was happy to tell them to the group. Scott, after all, knew Sandy from the seminar, and Carol was content to listen to stories about anyone as long as there were boys present and plenty of popcorn.

Michael had been informed that very evening by his Exeter friends that Sandy Grayson had been speaking ill about him behind his back. She had mentioned to one boy that she hated Michael and to another that Michael was a disgrace to Exeter. He was a disgrace, in particular, because of the kinds of people he associated with. That, of course, could only be a reference to Lauren herself. "Can you imagine?" cried Michael indignantly. "*She* thinks *I* am an unworthy Exonian!"

"There, there," comforted Lauren. "How do you think I feel: pariah woman, gutter girl. I gather I wouldn't be fit to scrub the floors of the synagogue at Exeter. Oh, excuse me." Carol and Scott would not have known what to make of this exchange, but Lauren and Michael were obviously more amused than offended. All four of them laughed and ate popcorn.

"And listen to this," continued Michael, looking at Lauren more meaningfully. "Sandy has been saying all these terrible things about me and, at the same time, making people swear not to tell me what she's been saying. So naturally everyone was only too eager to tell me the story. But still, I don't think that sounds particularly courageous of Sandy Grayson. Some of my friends have even told me that she seems almost afraid that I'll find out what she's saying about me. Now why should she be afraid of me?"

"Maybe she has a crush on you," suggested Carol helpfully.

"Hmmmm," said Michael, always ready to consider that possibility.

Lauren, however, could imagine a more compelling reason, and she was sure Michael had reached the same conclusion. Michael and Lauren knew Sandy had been down by the river with Russell the night of the murder. And Sandy had not told the police. To some extent her fate was in their hands.

Michael continued. "It's strange that she should be saying these things about me if she's afraid of my finding out. It almost sounds a little bit unbalanced. And there's more evidence that Sandy's not as stable as she once was. She got a B+ on her hourly in mathematical logic. She's never gotten a B before in her life. People say she was extremely upset by it."

"Poor darling!" Lauren was not sympathetic.

"She got the graded exam booklet back on Thursday morning," said Michael, even more meaningfully, "but she took the hourly exactly one week before—last Thursday morning. Perhaps she was feeling distracted." Lauren got the message. Sandy had taken the hourly the morning after Russell had been murdered, but before anyone should have known about Russell's death. What had happened down by the river Wednesday night?

"And there's another thing Exeter people are saying about Sandy Grayson, and I don't know how this story got started," said Michael. "People are saying that she was more than a little interested in that black boy who was killed down by the river—you know, Russell Bernard."

Lauren wanted to see how Scott would react to this reference to Russell, but Carol immediately spoke up. "Lauren liked him too!" cried Carol in a spirit of mock accusation. In grade school Carol had almost certainly been one of those little girls who constantly teased other little girls about liking little boys. The great reward of such teasing was, of course, being teased back in return. "Lauren liked him. She was going to go out on a date with him, but then he was killed. I told her she shouldn't, but she wouldn't listen to me." Lauren was a little embarrassed now, and Carol cried out, "Oh look! Lauren's blushing!" Then Carol appealed to Scott, the Southerner. She was teasing him, unaware of how precisely she was hitting the target. She said, "*You* don't think she should have gone out with Russell Bernard, do you? It wouldn't have been proper. I mean, considering that he was black."

Lauren held her breath, waiting for Scott's response, but he answered with complete cool. "I don't know," he said. "I gather the young man in question was quite irresistible."

Lauren was thrilled by Scott's comeback, and even Michael, who did not know all the facts, seemed surprised. Scott was looking rather pleased with his own daring. Carol exclaimed happily, "Oh you're all very wicked!" Lauren wanted to show Scott how proud she was of him, and so, smiling, she flirtatiously leaned her head against his shoulder. He smiled and put his arm around her, while Michael raised his eyebrows in curiosity and Carol cried out, "Look at the lovebirds!"

"Yes, what have you two been up to tonight?" asked Michael.

"We've been paying a visit," said Lauren, still resting against Scott's shoulder. "We've been visiting a boy in our freshman seminar who is completely insane. We passed a dreadful hour with him." But even as Lauren summed it up this way, she knew she was missing something important. Something had happened between her and Scott and Andrew, but she couldn't put her finger on it. There had been something connected to the murders. If only she could remember.

"But before that we saw *Gone with the Wind*," said Scott. "That was much more fun."

Carol moaned dramatically. "Clark Gable is so gorgeous! I could just die!"

"He's unbearably gorgeous," said Michael wistfully.

"He *is* gorgeous," Lauren agreed.

"He sure is," said Scott.

When they had popped all the popcorn, Carol decided

that it was time for her to go to bed. Scott also thought he should be going home. Lauren was sorry to see him go but she was also anxious to start thinking about the evening they had spent together and, inevitably, to discuss him with Michael. And so at three in the morning, Lauren and Michael tucked Carol into her bed and retired to Lauren's little bedroom for further discussion.

They talked quietly so that Carol would be able to fall asleep. And they spoke with a sense of urgency, not only because their subject was deadly serious, but also because it was three in the morning and they knew they would soon be too tired to concentrate. They talked about Scott first, and Lauren kept coming back to the same point. "I don't believe he killed Russell," she said. "I like Scott. And I think that he was in love with Russell."

"Yes, but that's just the point. It's the fact that he was in love with Russell that makes him a suspect."

"I just can't believe that. He was too enchanted by Russell to be able to kill him. Besides, I don't think Scott would kill anyone. He's confused and unhappy, not vicious."

"In other words, you don't want to believe it. You don't want Scott to have murdered Russell."

"I guess that's about it—not very professional of me, is it?"

"Well," said Michael, "if we're going to pick our killer by whom we want it to be, then the solution is easy. We both know whom we would most like to see guilty."

"Sandy," said Lauren.

"Of course, Sandy."

"Well, she was down by the river. And she didn't go to the police the way Professor Baranova did. Sandy has to be hiding something."

"There's only one problem," said Michael. "What about Tracy? Why would she have killed Tracy? Unless Tracy's murder was completely unconnected to Russell's, was genuinely the work of a Cambridge thug—and neither of us believes that for a moment—then somehow the two murders have to be solved together. And Sandy Grayson just doesn't fit."

Michael and Lauren agreed that Sandy might have murdered Russell on account of unrequited passion—certainly a more reasonable motive than consummated passion as in Scott's case—but then what? Why would Sandy have murdered

Tracy? Scott, on the other hand, had a first-class motive for doing away with Tracy. Tracy had suspected Scott of killing Russell.

"Couldn't there be other reasons why Sandy hated Tracy?" suggested Lauren hopefully. "Maybe Sandy was jealous of Tracy's affair with Russell."

"Maybe." Michael was dubious. "But why would she have been jealous after Russell was already dead?"

"She hates *me* even though Russell is dead," Lauren pointed out, not unreasonably.

"That's true."

They both fell silent. Lauren was trying to remember what it was that had been said in Andrew Stein's room that was making her so uncomfortable, so certain that she had missed something extremely important. Meanwhile, Michael was thinking along different lines. Finally he spoke up. "I think I see what we have to do next."

"What's that?"

"We have to go to the police and tell them Sandy was down by the river with Russell that night."

"Do you think so?" It seemed to Lauren a very weighty step, the decision to finally share their discoveries with the police. It would be virtually an accusation.

"We have to," said Michael. "We're not going to find anything else out from Sandy. Perhaps the police will."

"What if she didn't kill Russell?"

"Then let her explain to the police what really happened."

"What if she denies being there?"

"Then we'll give the police Parker's name and let them confirm the story with him."

"What if the police manage to mess things up? You know, I went to the police when all this started, and they implied that I was crazy. They weren't very on the ball. I don't quite believe that they're capable of catching the right criminal." In fact, Lauren was feeling jealously protective of her own investigations. She had worked hard and found out a great deal, but she had not solved the mystery. She was reluctant to let the police in on her secrets.

Michael understood what was bothering her. "You've been fabulous, Lauren," he said. "You and I have figured out all sorts of things the police would never have guessed at, starting right from the beginning with your inspiration about Rasputin. The police have been working on the case for a week now, and they still don't know Sandy Grayson was down by the river that night. But I think it's time to let the police in on it. She'd never let us interrogate her."

"I suppose you're right."

"And there's another reason. If Sandy killed Russell, then she probably killed Tracy. And if she killed them both, there's no reason why she shouldn't kill someone else. And, as you are well aware, you and I are two of her least favorite people at Harvard."

"We'll go to the police tomorrow," said Lauren. "I think this may be the end of our investigation. I wish I were more certain that we'd got the right person. Just think. Somewhere out there right now is the killer."

"The killer is probably asleep and we should be too," said Michael, and just as he spoke, the telephone rang in Carol's room.

There is nothing so terrifyingly shattering as the sudden ring of the telephone at three in the morning. Lauren and Michael both froze. The phone rang again, and then they heard Carol sleepily answering, "Hello."

In a moment Carol was crooning rapturously, "Baby Doll, I love you," and Lauren and Michael were exchanging glances. It was, of course, only midnight in California, and Baby Doll was just checking in with his true love. And while Lauren and Michael might think it funny that he should call tonight after Carol's escapade with Brian, Carol herself was babbling into the receiver a string of adorable teenage nothings. She had apparently forgotten Brian. She loved her Baby Doll. "Oh, Baby Doll," she cried, "I wish I was with you in southern California. There's no place like Los Angeles."

And suddenly it clicked in Lauren's mind. She remembered what she had been trying to recall from the conversation with Scott and Andrew. It was indeed important. It was so important that in a flash Lauren knew who had murdered Russell Bernard and Tracy Nicolson. She just had to figure out the details.

17. Details

Sunday morning Lauren slept late. She awoke at noon and did not bother to try to recall any of her dreams. Instead she thought back on Saturday night and everything that had happened. She could remember it all very clearly, all the characters, all the conversations, all the revelations. She could hardly believe that these things had taken place only the night before; their clarity was not the clarity of recent memory, but that of more distant events—already organized and analyzed, a part of the vivid past. And this was very strange, because there was still so much to do today. But at last Lauren could act.

Lauren got out of bed and went to the window. She opened it, leaned out into the fresh air, and rested her hands on the rusty bars of the fire escape. The weather was changing. November had been mild: cold and windy from time to time, but there had also been sunny days. But now Lauren could feel that the air was changing. Harvard Yard seemed somehow starker than it had been the day before. Winter was definitely approaching.

Lauren dressed warmly, made a quick phone call, and went out in search of brunch. She decided to eat in the dining hall at Winthrop House, down by the river. She didn't see anyone there she knew, but she didn't mind eating alone. She did not even want a novel to read. There was so much to think about; *Fear of Flying* could wait. She would have time for that soon enough. Now she was too absorbed in her calculations and intuitions even to notice the dreadful food she was consuming. She ate steadily. The brain was excessively active; it required nutritional energy. Lauren sat surrounded by several hundred brunching students, but if any one of them had been watching her with particular attention she would not have been aware.

After brunch Lauren wanted to walk. She did not consciously decide on a particular walk, but she was not surprised to find herself crossing over Memorial Drive to the bank of the Charles River. It was a brisk, beautiful day, but once again Lauren was aware of winter lurking behind the autumn. Was it the suggestion of winter that created the faintly sinister impression? No, the things that were frightening Lauren were going on in her head, not in the atmosphere, and those things would soon be resolved.

There were few people down by the river that morning. Occasionally a jogger ran past, breathing heavily, wearing a sweat suit with the Harvard insignia. The river looked very fine—graceful and deceptively clean. It was broad daylight, so there was no real reason to be afraid. Lauren tried to imagine the murder that had taken place here almost two weeks ago. Just where had it been? Just how had it been done? She closed her eyes to help herself envision more clearly the scene in the darkness of night. Now she could hear the water moving. She could sense its presence, but, of course, she couldn't see it. That was how it must have been that night.

"Hi, Lauren," said a voice very close to Lauren's shoulder. She opened her eyes and turned around. There was Melissa Wu. She had approached quietly indeed on those two tiniest feet in the freshman class.

"Hello, Melissa."

"Hi. I saw you from across Memorial Drive."

"Oh?"

"I wanted to tell you about last night."

"Tell me."

"I had such a nice time. He's so nice."

"Is he?" Lauren knew she sounded distracted. "Come on," she said. "Let's walk up to Harvard Yard. You can tell me all about it. We shouldn't be hanging around here down by the river. It's not really safe. It'll be dark before you know it."

That evening Lauren was in her room alone. She was wearing Levi's and a pale gray lamb's wool sweater with a crew neck. Her makeup was modest, and her hair was pulled back just far enough to reveal a pair of elegant amethyst stud earrings which she usually reserved for special occasions.

They had been a gift from her parents for her sixteenth birthday. It was nine o'clock. Lauren was looking at herself in the mirror when there came a knock on the door. She lingered still a moment in front of the mirror, running her hands over her hair, and then went to greet her visitor.

Bert Rosen was leaning against the wall of the deserted dormitory hallway. He was not standing stiffly at attention in the doorway, or fidgeting nervously as some boys might do when calling on a girl in the evening. Bert was entirely at his ease, leaning against the wall, smiling good-naturedly. He wore jeans and moccasins and an old Hawaiian shirt full of faded jungle colors. The shirt was tucked in loosely, somehow emphasizing his perfect surfer's physique. His graceful neck and smooth, shaven face were mysteriously tan. His hair was blonder, his eyes bluer than Lauren remembered. Of course, the last time she had seen him had been Wednesday night in the dark, and that had been the night after Tracy's murder. Bert's sunny good looks had been, not surprisingly, not quite up to par. But now he was radiant, an angel from the paradise of California, somehow fallen into the midst of a nervous, pushy, rushed Ivy League world. The tension of that world didn't touch Bert Rosen. He smiled easily, showing beautiful white movie-star teeth, and said, "Hi, Lauren, how's it going?"

"Okay. How are you?"

"Great."

"Won't you come in?" Lauren was aware that his ease was somehow making her stiff. She resolved to resist this. She did not relish the role of the stiff one.

Bert came in and looked around Carol's room. His eyes rested for a moment on the poster of Baby Doll up on the wall. Surely Bert and Baby Doll had seen each other on the beach at some time or another. Baby Doll was also a surfer. "My roommate's boyfriend," Lauren explained. "He's also from Los Angeles."

"Fantastic place, Los Angeles," said Bert, blue eyes sparkling.

"So I've heard." Lauren led Bert through Carol's room and into her own little room which had been straightened up that afternoon. Lauren gestured to Bert to sit down on the bed, and he did so, immediately leaning back against the wall. He was making himself at home, not in the least abashed to be sitting on Lauren's bed. He was a cool character, Bert Rosen. Lauren seated herself on the desk top, resting her feet on the desk chair. It gave her some satisfaction to think that if he was the cooler of the two, she at least had the higher perch.

Lauren noticed that Bert did not bother to ask why she had called that morning and invited him over. He was apparently not cursed with any sort of urgent curiosity. Or perhaps he was just too entirely accustomed to being invited over by girls for no particular reason. Lauren herself felt that she owed him some sort of explanation. "I called you up because, because..." Again his ease succeeded in making her more clumsy. "Well, because the last time I saw you was Wednesday night, when you were feeling so bad, after Tracy was murdered the night before. And I wanted to see how you were, to make sure you were okay." He certainly looked okay. Lauren knew her explanation sounded lame, and this bothered her. She did not want Bert to think she had invited him over because she had a crush on him. He seemed to take that sort of thing all too much for granted. And, in fact, she did not have a crush on him, and never had, though he was in his way eminently worthy of crushes. Carol would go wild for him, Lauren thought, wondering again at the remarkable tan. Carol would definitely want to share Bert's sun lamp.

But Bert's expression had changed. When Lauren mentioned Tracy's murder, his smile began to fade, and now his face was genuinely pensive. That too was becoming. "Are you thinking about Tracy?" Lauren asked.

"Yes."

"Terrible that she was murdered."

"Terrible."

Their eyes met, and they looked at each other directly. Lauren did not know what he was reading in her eyes or trying to read. She herself could deduce little from his, but enough to believe that his soul was not as cloudless as his eyes were blue. Still looking him full in the face, Lauren said, "It frightens me just thinking about Tracy." And then, "I think I'd feel better if we smoked a joint."

"I'd feel better too," said Bert, and reaching into the pocket of the Hawaiian shirt, he produced one slim, very neatly rolled joint. Either he had been expecting Lauren's request, or he simply never traveled without. The latter possibility would be just another little attribute of California cool. A lighted match now appeared so quickly that Lauren didn't quite see where it had been conjured from. Bert placed the joint very gracefully between his lips and held the match to the tip. In a moment the joint was glowing and the match was gone. Bert inhaled delicately—no huffing and puffing, no inflated squirrel cheeks full of smoke.

Lauren watched with fascination. Here Bert's casualness was raised to an almost aristocratic art. And yet the performance was flawed, and Lauren noticed the flaw. Surely Bert ought to have offered the joint to her first, then lit it for her while she held it between her lips. There was an etiquette of chivalry for smoking marijuana, and Bert should have known it. His cool was not perfect. Either there lurked behind it a secret egotism too irresistible to permit him to defer to a lady, or else Bert was not fully at ease. Perhaps his nerves needed calming; perhaps the California cool was not entirely natural this evening. Was that why he had greedily smoked first?

Conscious of his breach of etiquette, Lauren leaned over with dignity from the top of the desk to take the joint from Bert, who sat across from her on the bed. She herself inhaled with what she hoped was at least reasonably good form. Lauren knew she was no marijuana glamour model, but she fancied that freshly painted peach fingernails lent a little something extra to the act. She breathed out a wisp of smoke, and thus fortified and reassured by the friendly smell of the burning marijuana, she proceeded to her business. "This is really good," she said, and then, as if spontaneously, "I wonder if you could do me a favor?" Her manner was, she hoped, appealingly flirtatious.

"Anything," said Bert gallantly, but not without a hint of obscenity.

"I'd like to buy some grass," she said, "and this stuff is good. Would you sell me some?"

"I'm sorry," said Bert, smiling. "I'd be happy to sell you some. But I don't really have anything much to sell. I don't do that sort of thing."

"Oh." Lauren looked disappointed. And then she looked up curiously, as if she had recalled something. "I was just remembering a talk I had with Tracy," she said, "a long talk, the day that she died. She said that you always had a lot of dope around. I guess that's why I thought you might be able to sell me some."

"No, sorry. Tracy was probably exaggerating. She tended to put things a little strongly. Don't you think so?"

"Perhaps." Lauren sounded unconvinced. "There's another thing. Last night I was talking to Andrew Stein—you know, that crazy boy in our freshman seminar. And he told me that you had sold him some speed."

Lauren watched Bert hesitate. Was he going to deny the story? Tracy was dead, so there was nothing to prevent Bert from claiming she had exaggerated. Andrew Stein, on the other hand, was alive, nuts perhaps, but definitely alive. Even now he was probably working furiously on his papers with the ornamental noose dangling over his head. Andrew Stein could be called to confirm his story. Bert decided not to deny it. "Well, yes I did sell him that speed," he said sheepishly. "But that was sort of an exceptional case. A friend of mine had given me the stuff—and I never use it—so when Andrew mentioned to me that he was looking for some, I gave it to him. I guess I sold it to him. He's pretty crazy, sort of a sad case, and I really couldn't refuse him."

"No. I suppose you couldn't. I see what you mean." Lauren leaned over and passed the joint back to Bert, who took it with just a hint of suppressed eagerness and put it immediately to his lips. Bert the beachboy was nervous. And with good reason. Lauren said, "I guess you could say you were doing Andrew Stein a favor when you sold him the speed." She took a deep breath. "But you didn't do Dora Carpenter much of a favor when you sold her that cocaine." There. Lauren had said it.

Bert's face betrayed absolutely nothing. He raised the joint and inhaled again, almost mechanically. He did not pass it back to Lauren. Chivalry had now become altogether irrelevant. Lauren looked at him sitting on her bed, leaning against the wall, expressionless. But now the casualness was palpably false. Beneath the Hawaiian colors and artificial tan there was tension. Lauren was more certain than ever that she had solved the mystery.

Lauren continued to speak. She intended to share with Bert all of the deductions that she had made since late last night when she had finally remembered the important thing from her conversation with Andrew Stein. Baby Doll had called from California, and Lauren had been reminded of Bert, and of the fact that Bert had sold speed to Andrew. Then everything else had fallen into place. There were a few inessential gaps in Lauren's solution to the mystery, but she knew that Bert would be able to fill them in.

"I'm sure you didn't know there was anything wrong with the cocaine that you sold to Dora Carpenter. I'm sure you didn't mean to kill her. You were selling the stuff to make money, a little bit of extra pocket cash. Hundreds of dollars? Thousands of dollars? I don't know, and it hardly matters. Why shouldn't you be dealing? You know, free enterprise and the self-made man. And I think things have usually gone pretty easily for you. But something went very wrong this once. Somebody gave you contaminated stuff—maybe he didn't even know, maybe nobody's to blame—and you sold it to Dora Carpenter. And the stuff killed her."

Bert remained impassive, and Lauren continued. "Very bad luck for Dora Carpenter, but maybe bad luck for you too. A Harvard freshman caught selling cocaine might conceivably be given a second chance, but if the stuff he was selling had actually killed someone, well, I don't think anyone would be feeling very indulgent toward him. You'd be thrown out of Harvard for sure. Maybe you'd go to prison. One way or another, a very bright, very attractive young man would have screwed up his very promising future. But none of this had to happen. You could perfectly well have escaped scot-free. Your luck might have held. You could stop dealing and let the whole thing slip into the past. And you'd be fine—as long as nobody knew that you were the one who sold the cocaine to Dora Carpenter.

"But somebody knew. One close friend of Dora Carpenter's just happened to know. He was a devout Catholic, you know, probably had a strong sense of sin and expiation and divine retribution. And besides, he was in love with Dora. What happened? Did he confront you, tell you that he knew, tell you that he was going to turn you in? Or perhaps he hadn't decided yet what he should do, but he wanted you to know that he knew, to know that you weren't going to be able to forget Dora Carpenter and pretend that the whole thing never happened, to know that your blond, blue-eyed future, full of Harvard prestige and California sun, was about to explode in your face. Russell Bernard knew that you'd sold that cocaine to Dora Carpenter and that's why you killed him."

"Yes," said Bert matter-of-factly, "Russell came to my room one night and told me that he knew I'd sold the cocaine to Dora Carpenter. He told me I was a murderer."

"And what did you say then?" Lauren was very curious. Finally everything was being revealed to her. She could imagine the scene: Bert perhaps stretched out on his own bed as he was now stretched out on hers, Russell standing over him, accusing him. Lauren wondered if Russell had found Bert attractive.

"I denied it. I said I'd never sold anything to Dora Carpenter."

"And then what did he say?"

"He said I was a liar, and I said he was mistaken. But he seemed a little confused. I think he had been expecting some sort of hysterical scene in which I confessed and begged for mercy."

"But you just insisted that you'd had nothing to do with it. I see. So he went away wondering what would happen if he denounced you to the police and you denied the whole thing. Maybe it wouldn't have been easy for him to prove anything. And while he was trying to decide whether or not he should go to the police, you decided to do something about it. After all, sooner or later he would have said something to someone. So last Wednesday, after the freshman seminar, after the discussion of Rasputin, you followed him."

For the first time Bert's face showed surprise. "What makes you think that?" he asked. "What makes you think I was following him?"

"You told me that Russell confided in you about his appointment with Professor Baranova. That seemed strange to me at the time, because he didn't seem to have told anyone else. And I hadn't thought that you and he were such particularly good friends. Then when I talked to Professor Baranova myself it was clear to me that the two of them had been pretty careful not to publicize their friendship. So either Russell had been indiscreet in telling you, or you had been intentionally dishonest in telling me. Last night I decided that you had been lying. And yet somehow you knew about Russell's appointment with Professor Baranova. How did you know if Russell didn't tell you? Obviously you must have been following him that night.

"You must have started following him as soon as the seminar was over. You must have been watching in the darkness when I joined Russell and Sandy in the middle of the Yard, when Sandy walked away furiously, when Russell and I had our little conversation. Perhaps you weren't close enough to hear what we were saying. You would have found it interesting. We were talking about Dora Carpenter and whether or not Russell had been in love with her.

"Russell told me that he was going to a dinner meeting of the Black Students' Lobby. I went back to my room before going to dinner, leaving him alone in the Yard, alone with you. And then Russell saw someone else he knew, someone else who had just come out of the seminar. He saw Tracy, didn't he? Or did she see him? At any rate they exchanged a few words. I know Russell told her that he was going to meet me for coffee the following evening. She knew about that when I saw her at lunch the next day. Remember, you were there. Why did Russell tell Tracy about me? Was he indiscreet after all? Maybe a little. But telling her about a date with me would hardly have been an indiscretion on the same scale as talking about Professor Baranova. It might have been mentioned in a spirit of friendly rivalry. Russell says: what's new in your life? Tracy says: I'm having an affair with Bert Rosen. Russell says: I'm going out with Lauren Adler tomorrow night.

"Did Tracy tell you that she and Russell had been lovers? Perhaps you guessed? At any rate it must have been clear to you that night, while you were spying on them, that they were more than casually acquainted. But you would have been too far away to hear their conversation. You must have wondered just what they were saying to each other. Did Russell say: I hear you're going out with Bert Rosen—I think I should tell you that he's the one who's responsible for the death of Dora Carpenter. Did Russell say something like that to Tracy? Or had he already told her on some other occasion? Who knows what sort of things passed between those two? You must have been curious.

"One thing he told her was that he was on his way to a meeting of the Black Students' Lobby, the same thing he had told me. But he didn't go to that meeting. He had another appointment, and he was too discreet to talk about it with me or with Tracy. You were the only one who knew that he went to visit Professor Baranova that night, and you knew because you followed him."

Lauren looked at Bert's completely impassive face. He lifted the joint to his lips and inhaled. He blew out the smoke and still his face was expressionless. A few strands of sunny blond hair had fallen down over his brow, adding to his appeal an aspect of freshness, of uncombed boyishness. Lauren could hardly believe that anything she was saying was true. Still she went on.

"First Russell went back to his room, and you waited

outside the dorm. When he reappeared he was carrying a violin case, right? If he'd been going to an orchestra rehearsal you might have given up for the night, but he was heading for someplace else. So you followed him past the Cambridge Common, past Radcliffe, all the way to Professor Baranova's house. Why didn't you kill him along the way, I wonder? Were there still a few people on the streets at seven o'clock? Were you curious to see where he would lead you? Were you afraid he'd defend himself with the violin case? Or were you perhaps not quite ready to do the job? Were you still unsure about whether murder was going to be absolutely necessary? Were you unsure about whether it would really be worth the risk? Or had you just not quite gotten up the nerve? I don't imagine that committing murder is such an easy thing to do, even for someone who manages most things pretty easily.

"It's a strange house, Professor Baranova's, with all those odd little windows and towers. She would have answered the door, and you would probably have recognized her from the street. The way she carries herself is not very common around here. It would be easy to know her from a distance, even her silhouette in the lighted doorway. A few seconds would have been enough. And soon after, you began to hear very faintly the notes of a Beethoven duet for piano and violin.

"That living room has a big picture window surrounded by bushes which reach up to the bottom of the window and even a little bit further. The tops of the bushes are visible from inside the room. Did you give in to the temptation to creep up to the window, to hide in the bushes, to peek in at the musicians? She would have been sitting at the piano, her back to you. Perhaps you could have seen her fingers moving on the keyboard. And he would have been standing behind her, looking over her shoulder at the music on the piano stand. The framed sheet of music on the wall is Tchaikovsky, by the way.

"They stopped playing, and they talked for a while on the sofa. Perhaps she made coffee. But you, crouching outside in the bushes, would not have been able to hear what they were saying. You could tell, though, that it was a serious, confidential talk, that Russell was disturbed. You must have wondered just what Russell was confiding to Professor Baranova, and there was nothing for you to do but hope that he wasn't confiding the one thing that would have destroyed you. You were spying on them that night, weren't you? You were hiding in the bushes, looking in the window."

"And I was hiding there again the night that *you* went to visit Professor Baranova," said Bert in a tone of friendly conversation. "You were smart to call a taxi that night."

"I realized Wednesday night that you were curious about the murders," said Bert. "Remember the talk we had about Tracy that evening after the seminar? Since then I've been keeping an eye on you. That's why I followed you and your friend Friday night to Professor Baranova's house."

"There's something I don't understand," said Lauren. "The only reason I was going to visit Professor Baranova in the first place was because you told me that Russell had visited her. Why did you tell me that?"

"Why do you think?"

"To confuse me, I suppose. Did you think that if I thought there was a professor involved I would become more timid about prying? Or did you think that talking to Professor Baranova would put me on the wrong track? It almost did, you know. I asked her what Russell had talked about the night he was killed, what had been on his mind. And she told me he was worried about how Dora Carpenter's death would affect the Black Students' Lobby. And that only made me more suspicious of Katherine Butler, believe it or not, because she's involved in a rival political group and hates Russell's Lobby for being too peaceful. It didn't occur to me then that the important fact, the true clue, was that he was thinking about Dora Carpenter. That's why I wasn't able to put everything together until Andrew Stein told me that you were selling him speed."

"Good work," said Bert. No longer expressionless, now he was smiling, perhaps ironically. He was showing beautiful white teeth with perhaps a hint of gold flashing somewhere in the back of his mouth. The smile implied a certain complicity between him and Lauren. They now shared the same secrets.

"Help me finish the story," said Lauren. "You followed Russell back from Professor Baranova's house to his own room. And there was someone waiting in front of his dorm, Sandy Grayson. Right?" Bert nodded, not unimpressed. "She wanted to see him and to talk to him. A few hours earlier she had behaved very badly, walking away rudely from Russell and me. She was probably feeling uncertain about how Russell had taken that, whether he'd noticed how rude it was. She wanted to reassure herself that she hadn't lowered his opinion of her. But how did they get down to the river?"

Bert laughed and helped Lauren finish the story. "From where I was watching, it was pretty clear that the last thing the boy wanted was to have that cat up in his room with him. She looked like she was ready to jump on him. She was practically hysterical in a cool, repressed sort of way. So he dropped off the violin in his room and then agreed to go for a walk with her—agreed pretty reluctantly I'd say. And she did all the rest. She was the one who was choosing the path, and he was just following, trying to be agreeable, trying to calm her. I suppose she wasn't thinking about where she was going, but she headed straight for the river. It was almost like she wanted to go someplace dangerous. She couldn't have been more helpful if she'd actually planned it with me in advance. I wonder if in some weird, unconscious way she was trying to get him killed.

"I wasn't able to hear their conversation while I was following them, but when they stopped on the riverbank I was able to get close enough. I was lying flat on the grass behind a bench. It was pretty pathetic. She kept saying that she was desperately in love with him, and that she'd never been in love with anyone else before, and she was begging him to say he felt the same way about her. And the strange thing was that she kept saying this in that calm, serious tone she uses in the seminar when she wants to make a point about the Russian Revolution. Except that here it was pretty plain that she was cracking underneath. Meanwhile, he kept saying that he was very flattered, but he wasn't in love with anyone, and he hoped they could be friends. Though he didn't sound completely convincing on any of those counts.

"Oh, there's something else I overheard that night that will interest you. Russell and Sandy actually spoke about you that night. She said something unflattering about you—probably because, as you say, she was ashamed of that scene in the Yard earlier in the evening—and Russell came to your defense. Which made Sandy even angrier, and she said—shall I tell you what she said?"

"Please."

"She said, still in that very academic tone, that you were a vulgar little bitch of a whore. Excuse me, I'm only quoting.

Anyway, then Russell finally became angry and stopped being nice to her. In fact, he said the meanest thing he could possibly have said. He said he liked you much better than he liked her."

"So that's why she hates me so much. What did she do then?"

"She smacked him across the face and walked away, leaving him alone on the riverbank. He didn't follow her. I'm sure he was relieved."

It took time for the full import of this to sink in. For an instant Lauren was thrilled to hear of Russell's coming to her defense. And then Lauren's satisfaction gave way to the realization that in speaking up for her, Russell had made his own murder that much more certain. By offending Sandy on Lauren's behalf, Russell had found himself left alone on the riverbank, alone with Bert.

Lauren took up the story. "So Russell stood there, at the edge of the river, gazing across the water perhaps, glad to be rid of Sandy Grayson, wondering if he'd been too harsh. And you rose from behind the bench, silently. He probably never even knew it was you. The next sound would have been something crashing down on Russell's skull. What did you use?"

"A flashlight."

"Well prepared," said Lauren. "So after you knocked him out you were able to use the beam to take a quick look at the unconscious body. And I know what happened next. You put the knife in his back to finish him off. You removed the watch and the wallet to make it look like he was killed by a mugger. If you'd stopped right there you would have been fine. I'd never have figured out the mystery. I'd never even have tried. And I bet the police wouldn't have figured it out either. But you didn't stop there. You looked at the body and you began to wonder if it was really dead. You were thinking of Rasputin, weren't you?"

Was it possible that for just an instant there was real terror in Bert's blue eyes? Was he remembering? "Rasputin," he whispered, as if to confirm Lauren's suggestion.

"And so you stabbed him again, and then you took a risk. You fired the gun into his heart. That was stupid. Someone could have heard the report. In fact, at least two people did: Sandy Grayson and Parker Hamilton Kendall IV, walking back to Harvard Yard. But no one came rushing to the scene

of the crime. After all, it might have been taken for just some .
kind of traffic noise from Memorial Drive.

"After firing the gun you should have run away as fast as
you could. But you were still thinking of Rasputin, weren't
you? Just to be absolutely certain, you dragged Russell's
corpse to the water and shoved it in facedown. Just like
Rasputin in the Neva. Finally you were able to believe that
Russell was dead, that he wouldn't stand up and accuse you.
You had struck him and stabbed him and shot him and
drowned him. And that was what gave you away. As soon as I
heard the details of the murder, I knew that the murderer
was not a river bum. I knew that it was someone in our
freshman seminar. And now I know that it was you."

"I suppose it hadn't occurred to you that someone would
notice the Rasputin thing. You must have been too worried
about someone knowing about Dora Carpenter and the cocaine and figuring out that way that you were the murderer.
After you'd murdered Russell it was even more important
that nobody should ever find anything out: I mean, then you
were a real first-degree murderer, not just a careless dealer.
And there was one person in particular who might figure it
out—she was pretty sharp—and that's why there was a
second murder.

"You know, last Tuesday when I had lunch with Tracy, the
day she was killed, I practically accused *her* of killing Russell.
And she told me she couldn't have done it because she spent
the night of the murder with you. Which means that you
must have killed Russell and then gone straight to Tracy's
room so you'd have an alibi for most of the evening and all of
the night. No wonder you were afraid she suspected you. Ten
minutes after killing Russell you were in her room. You must
have imagined that it somehow showed, that she could read it
in your face, that she could smell it on your breath."

"She knew," said Bert sadly.

"After all, it's possible she didn't even have to guess from
your face. She had been Russell's lover. He might have told
her all about Dora Carpenter. And, like I said, she was damn
sharp. She could put things together."

"She knew," Bert repeated.

"How do you know she knew?" Lauren challenged him.

"I thought she knew from the beginning, but then I

knew for sure from something her roommate said. One evening I went to visit Tracy and she wasn't in, so I talked to her roommate for a few minutes. I found out everything I had to know."

Lauren remembered the tiny black roommate with the high-pitched voice. "What did she say?"

Bert replied without hesitation. "She told me that Tracy had said she knew who killed Russell Bernard."

Lauren remembered the girl had said the same thing at lunch at the black table Monday afternoon, had said that Tracy had claimed to know who had killed Russell. And everyone at the table had dismissed Tracy Nicolson as that crazy white lady with the gun.

"Killing Tracy was easy, wasn't it? You didn't really nap in the library that evening and wake up to find her gone. You left with her by appointment. You made up some excuse for going to Radcliffe, perhaps to return a book at Hilles Library. You didn't even have to use your gun, because she was carrying hers in her pocketbook: she knew there was a murderer at large. In the middle of the Cambridge Common you took her pocketbook, took out her gun, and killed her. Then you ran back to the library and reclaimed your chair. You'd only been gone fifteen minutes; you could always say you had been in the bathroom. At midnight the library closed, and you very conspicuously waited out front for Tracy. Naturally she stood you up. The whole plan was perfect except for one thing: she didn't actually know you'd killed Russell."

"She knew. Her roommate told me. She had told her roommate."

"But she didn't tell her roommate who the murderer was. When I had lunch with Tracy on Tuesday she told me who she thought it was. And she didn't think it was you. She thought it was Scott Duchaine. She was usually sharp, but this time she was wrong. Think about it. Would she have gone on sleeping with you if she had thought you were the killer? Would she have walked through the Cambridge Common with you in the middle of the night? Why haven't you let yourself think about that? Not a very nice thought, is it? She didn't know. There was no reason to kill her. You killed your own lover for nothing, you bastard."

Bert sat very still on the bed. Lauren could not tell what effect her words were having. Was he being struck with regret? With guilt? With horror? Or was he taking the news in stride, staying cool. He put the joint to his lips and saw that it was no longer lit. He leaned forward and rubbed the ashes into his jeans, just above the knee, thus adding another gray faded spot to a pair of already beautifully faded blue jeans. And then, the next thing Lauren knew, he had jumped on her. He had pulled her off the desk and now stood behind her with his hand cupped tightly over her mouth. His other hand had produced, seemingly from thin air, an open switchblade which he held an inch from Lauren's throat. Lauren was aware that he smelled very fresh and clean, no nervous sweat. She closed her eyes so as not to see the knife, and she heard him whisper in her ear, "I've got a damn good reason to kill you, though, don't I? This isn't going to be for nothing. You were real smart to figure it all out, and I'm grateful to you for telling me the whole story. But you're not going to get to tell anyone else."

Only a few seconds had passed, but to Lauren, with the knife at her throat, they seemed like decades. Now finally she heard the voice she had been waiting for. "Unhand that woman," it said, and Lauren opened her eyes to see Michael climbing in the window from the fire escape.

Bert was stunned, and he loosened his grip. Lauren wriggled free and raced across the room into Michael's arms. Bert stood facing them, holding his knife in one hand, wondering perhaps if he could kill them both. And then his face registered a new shock as he saw Carol climbing in through the window. She was wearing a bright red sweat shirt that featured Snoopy lying in his doghouse. The caption was "Happiness is a Place in the Sun." Carol was saying happily, "This is going to make such a great story for the *Crimson*. Now I know I'll make it onto the paper. With a story like this, they'll probably want to make me president of the *Crimson*."

Bert closed the switchblade and put it in his jacket. He could see that everything was up. His face did not register defeat, but he was clearly waiting for them to decide what to do with him. Lauren was still recovering from her fright and Michael was comforting her, and Carol was already imagining herself as the editor of *The New York Times*. None of them knew what to say to Bert. At that moment, however, Brian O'Donnell pushed his enormous bulk through the window and said, "Hey, somebody call the cops!"

18. Back to the river

"Take me out for a walk," said Lauren to Michael. "I need some air."

"We really should take our prisoner to the police." Michael gestured at Bert.

"Carol and Brian can do that. We'll meet them there in a half hour. Do you mind, Carol?"

Carol didn't mind at all, so Lauren put on her coat and left with Michael, who had already been wearing his coat while waiting out on the fire escape. "Where to?" asked Michael, looking around him in the darkness.

"To the river," said Lauren. Michael looked at her strangely. "Please," she said, "just for a few minutes. I want to see the river again tonight. That's where it all started."

So Lauren and Michael strolled arm in arm in the direction of the river. They did not speak, and Lauren kept thinking that finally it was all over—but she couldn't quite believe it. It was almost too fanciful, the idea that the mystery could simply be solved by naming one name, the correct name, the name of the murderer. And then there was nothing more to be done. Lauren was glad to be distracted from these thoughts when she and Michael briefly encountered Parker and Melissa. They were returning from the Kirkland House library where they had been studying together, a romantic evening. Parker and Melissa had not been walking arm in arm. Ah well, that too would eventually come to pass.

Lauren and Michael finally reached the river. Lauren had been there earlier that day to watch the water flowing in the sun. Now she could barely discern the river in the darkness, but she knew it was there. She did not go all the way down to the water's edge. It was enough to be on the riverbank. Besides, Michael was nervous. Lauren herself was irrationally unafraid. Russell's murderer was no longer at large; life in general seemed much less sinister.

"It's all over," said Lauren. The words sounded more convincing when she spoke them out loud.

"You were wonderful," said Michael.

"And what happens now? Does Harvard just go on, just as it was before—minus Russell, minus Tracy, minus Bert?"

"I guess so. Not everything's the same, of course. There are Parker and Melissa for instance. Dare I suppose that they have succumbed to Cupid's arrows? Surely for them nothing will be as before." Lauren and Michael giggled. Then Michael said hesitantly, "And perhaps you and I have changed a bit ourselves. Haven't we learned a few things about ourselves, even about life?"

"Yes," said Lauren. She was thinking that Michael was the best friend she had ever had. "And I suppose other things will change," she said. "Andrew Stein will have to find someone else to sell him speed, or else he'll have to do without. I would venture to say that the quality of his papers will not be noticeably affected. Strange, isn't it, that that loony boy really solved the whole mystery for us. Every time I see him from now on, that will be the first thing that comes to my mind.

"And what am I going to think when I see Katherine Butler? She didn't kill Russell, but I know she's glad he's dead. That's almost more horrible. I think that in her own way, with her little cadre of militant black Harvard students, she's as crazy as Andrew Stein—and more dangerous. She sees Russell's death in terms of a political advantage to an utterly meaningless little splinter college political discussion group.

"But the worst is going to be seeing Sandy Grayson every week at the freshman seminar until Christmas and then running into her every so often for the next four years. She hates me. I think she's always going to hate me, especially now, because she's probably going to have to go to the police and tell her story. And you know, she didn't kill Russell—but remember what Bert said? That it was almost as though Sandy was conspiring with him to bring about Russell's death. What am I supposed to think about that?"

"You know," said Michael, "even if Sandy hadn't led

Russell down to the river, even if she hadn't left him alone there, Bert might perfectly well have found some other opportunity to kill Russell."

"Yes, I suppose."

"And you know, don't you, that in her twisted, compulsive, repressed little way, Sandy is just as mentally unbalanced as Andrew and Katherine."

"I suppose. But I don't think I'm ever going to get used to having her glare at me. I'm always going to think of that scene between her and Russell down here by the river. I think it's always going to upset me to think about her." Lauren paused. "But you know who I am absolutely determined to get used to? Brian O'Donnell. He's part of our team, I suppose, now that he helped us take care of Bert. And besides, I have a feeling that Beef is going to be spending a lot of time around my room in the future. I want to try to forget that remark about how where he comes from they put knives into black men who touch white women. That still gives me the creeps, and I don't want to always be thinking of him as a mentally deficient racist lunk. Enough that he should be just a mentally deficient lunk."

"Hear! Hear!" said Michael. "And we mustn't ruin Carol's fun."

"I suppose I shouldn't just look on the bad side. Not everyone involved in this mess has been horrible. After all, two weeks ago I was dating Scott Duchaine and I was finding him, despite his southern accent, relatively uninteresting. A few days ago, on the other hand, I was virtually certain that he was a murderer. And now I have a feeling that he and I are going to be friends."

"I think you're going to be very good for him," said Michael.

"I think *you* might be good for him too," said Lauren suggestively. "Perhaps you two will become friends through me."

"What an idea!" exclaimed Michael, pretending to be scandalized.

"Well at least there would be no religious objections. Is it too early to start thinking about the bridesmaids' dresses?"

"Rather."

Lauren had thought of something else. "Do you know who else I feel I never appreciated before I got involved in the murder mystery? Professor Baranova. I'd always thought she was very elegant and imposing, but I had never particularly liked her—if you know what I mean. She was the professor and I was the student—the student who didn't do the assigned reading. But when I spent Friday evening with her, I found her absolutely fascinating. I couldn't take my eyes off her. And the story of her friendship with Russell makes her seem not only more fascinating than ever but also more human. Do you think she and I could be friends?"

"I think you might have to do the reading assignments to really and truly win her over."

"It's worth it. It's interesting, isn't it, that the two people I find I want to be friends with—Scott Duchaine and Tatiana Baranova—were both mixed up with Russell, one way or another."

"Tracy was too."

"Yes," said Lauren. "I would have liked to have been friends with Tracy too. You know, I somehow feel that she and Russell made a good pair, unlikely though that may seem."

"No more unlikely than Russell and Scott."

"Russell chose interesting people, didn't he—his friends and lovers: Tracy, Scott, Professor Baranova, Dora Carpenter."

"And you."

"Me?"

"He liked you too. He had good taste."

"When we talk about him now, two weeks after his death, I still feel like he's larger than life. I can hardly believe that Bert Rosen could possibly have killed him—shallow Bert, nothing but tanned surfaces."

But strangely enough Michael came to Bert's defense. "You shouldn't underestimate him, you know. Prince Yusupov was not nearly as much of a personality as Rasputin, but he killed Rasputin nevertheless. Now Prince Yusupov was extremely beautiful, but that may have been a purely incidental quality, of interest only to me and to some of his more fortunate contemporaries. The one indisputable fact about Prince Yusupov is that he was a prince. Sometimes aristocracy compensates for weakness of character. And, in the end, Prince Yusupov did manage to kill Rasputin, although the murder was no easy job. Prince Yusupov had a certain superficial nobility, even if it was the corrupt and decadent nobility of the doomed Russian aristocracy. You're wondering what I'm talking about, aren't you? Well, I guess I think that Bert Rosen and Prince Yusupov are somehow spiritually related, that Bert is some kind of California royalty—handsome, rich, corrupt, superficial. Am I making sense?"

"I don't know," said Lauren. "I'm not quite following, but it sounds like there might be something to it." She looked out into the invisible water. She was thinking about Russell. He had been only an eighteen-year-old boy. Even Professor Baranova had been willing to admit the possibility that he might have become a completely uninteresting adult. Harvard had given the world many famous men, but those constituted only a tiny percentage of all who had graduated during the last three centuries. Perhaps it was Tracy who had been destined to become president of the United States, to change the world. Who could say now? Russell had been promising, but he might never have been more than that. The most one could say for certain was that he had been a magnificent eighteen-year-old.

"How did we ever get mixed up in all this?" said Lauren aloud. "Are we crazy too?"

"Perhaps."

"Because I found him fascinating? Because I cared about him? Was I trying to find his murderer for his sake or for mine?"

"Does it matter?"

"I thought that if I found the murderer, I'd be able to forget Russell, to put him out of my mind, accounts settled. But now I see that it's going to be just the opposite. After these last two weeks I'm going to be thinking about him for as long as I live. I think I'll always be a little in love with him. He was extraordinary."

"So are you," said Michael.

"You too." They looked at each other fondly.

"Now Lauren, we've really got to get to the police station. What do you say we take the long way around, by way of Bailey's? I feel an inexplicable but all too familiar craving for vanilla ice cream and hot fudge."

ABOUT THE AUTHOR

VICTORIA SILVER graduated from Radcliffe *magna cum laude* and now lives in San Francisco where she enjoys a certain notoriety. She also enjoys chocolate, cowboys, murder, and suede, in various combinations.